Samuel Rawson Gardiner

History of England

From the accession of James I. to the disgrace of chief justice coke. 1603-1616. In two volumes.
Vol. 2

SALZWASSER
VERLAG

Samuel Rawson Gardiner

History of England

From the accession of James I. to the disgrace of chief justice coke. 1603-1616. In two volumes. Vol. 2

Reprint of the original, first published in 1863.

1st Edition 2022 | ISBN: 978-3-37500-719-5

Verlag (Publisher): Salzwasser Verlag GmbH, Zeilweg 44, 60439 Frankfurt, Deutschland
Vertretungsberechtigt (Authorized to represent): E. Roepke, Zeilweg 44, 60439 Frankfurt, Deutschland
Druck (Print): Books on Demand GmbH, In de Tarpen 42, 22848 Norderstedt, Deutschland

HISTORY OF ENGLAND.

1603—1616.

VOL. II.

HISTORY OF ENGLAND

FROM

THE ACCESSION OF JAMES I.

TO

THE DISGRACE OF CHIEF-JUSTICE COKE.

1603—1616.

BY

SAMUEL RAWSON GARDINER.

IN TWO VOLUMES.

VOL. II.

LONDON:

1863.

CONTENTS

OF

THE SECOND VOLUME.

CHAPTER X.

THE PROTESTANT ALLIANCE.

CHAPTER X.—(*continued*).

CHAPTER XI.

RESULTS OF IRRESPONSIBLE GOVERNMENT.

CHAPTER XI.—(*continued*).

CHAPTER XII.

THE PARLIAMENT OF 1614.

CHAPTER XII.—(*continued*).

CHAPTER XIII.

THE TRIAL OF THE EARL OF SOMERSET.

CHAPTER XIV.

THE DISGRACE OF CHIEF-JUSTICE COKE.

CHAPTER XIV.—(*continued*).

APPENDIX.

ERRATA.

In a few copies an error has crept in at p. 172, by which the amount of the Benevolence has been overestimated by £4,100.

Where any alteration is necessary, therefore, the reader is requested to read at

Line 16 *from bottom for*, 'In the course of two more years a last payment of £9,000 was gradually raised,' *read*, 'In the following year a last payment of less than £5,000 was raised.'

Line 13 *from bottom for*, '£46,600' *read* '£42,600.'

Line 9 *from bottom for*, '£70,000 or about,' *read* '£66,000 or rather less than.'

Page 389, *line* 2 *from top for*, 'Sir Henry Neville,' *read*, 'Sir Henry Nevill.'

HISTORY OF ENGLAND.

1603–1616.

CHAPTER X.

THE PROTESTANT ALLIANCE.

CH. X. 1610. Arabella Stuart.

THERE can be no better proof of the indistinct notions on the important subject of personal liberty which still prevailed in England, than the complete indifference with which Englishmen heard of the harsh treatment to which Arabella Stuart had been subjected by the King. At the present day such a story as hers would rouse the indignation of the whole population from one end of the kingdom to the other. Politics would be forgotten and business would be interrupted till justice had been done. In 1610, not a syllable was breathed in her favour. A few letter-writers told the news to their correspondents amidst the rest of the gossip of the day. With the exception of those who were immediately concerned in the tragedy, not a single Englishman thought it worthy of more than a passing thought.

During the first six years of his reign, James had treated his cousin with consideration. The pension which she received from Elizabeth was increased soon after he came to the throne, and she was allowed to occupy apartments in the palace, and to pass her time with the ladies who were attached to the court of the Queen.

CH. X. 1603. Her letters to the Earl and Countess of Shrewsbury.

A few letters have been preserved which she wrote in 1603 to her uncle and aunt, the Earl and Countess of Shrewsbury.* Their style is lively and agreeable, and they convey the impression of a gentle and affectionate, as well as of an accomplished woman. She could be amusing without being sarcastic, and she could find fault without bitterness. She had no ambition to figure among the great ladies by whom the Queen was surrounded, far less to aspire to the dignity of a pretender to the Crown. She had a good word for all who showed her any kindness, however small. She expressed her especial gratitude to Cecil for his declaration, at Raleigh's trial, of his assurance that she had been totally ignorant of any conspiracy against the King. In one of her letters she answered a jest of her uncle's, by assuring him with the most winning earnestness that she intended to prove that it was possible for a woman to retain her purity and innocence in the midst of the follies with which a life at court was surrounded. In another she stepped forward to act the part of a peacemaker, and conjured the earl to forgive once more that notorious termagant, his stepmother, the Dowager Countess. Altogether, it is impossible to rise from the perusal of these letters without the conviction that, if only a man who was worthy of her should be found, she would be fitted, above all the ladies of that age, to fulfil the quiet domestic duties of a wife and mother. With the life which she was forced to lead she was ill at ease; she did not care for the perpetual round of gaieties in which the Queen delighted, and she submitted with but an ill grace to take her part in the childish games by means of which the ladies of the court contrived to while away the weary hours.

1604. Offers of marriage declined.

Offers were made for her hand by various foreign potentates, but these were invariably declined.† To one of such a nature as hers was, it would have been intolerable to promise to marry a man whom she had never seen. But as the years passed on, it was evident

* Lady Shrewsbury was a sister of Arabella's mother. The letters are in Add. MS. 22, 563.

† Fowler to Shrewsbury, Oct. 3, 1604, Lodge's *Illustrations*, iii. 97.

that she was anxious to escape from the uncongenial life which she was leading. A little before Christmas, 1609, the Court was startled by hearing that she had been suddenly arrested, and summoned before the Council. All that we know of what passed on that occasion is that the King assured her that he would have no objection to her marriage with any subject of his.* It may be gathered from this that some rumour had reached him that she was engaged in negotiations to marry a foreigner, and that he was afraid lest after such a marriage she might be made use of by those who would in her name lay claim to the crown of England. However this may have been, her explanations were considered satisfactory. She was set at liberty at once, and immediately afterwards James showed that he had again received her into favour, by granting her an addition to her income.†

1609. She is brought before the Council.

A few weeks after she made her peace with the King, she had given her heart to young William Seymour. On the 2nd of February he found his way to her apartments, and obtained from her own lips the assurance of her willingness to become his wife. The promise which James had given made it difficult to believe that they would meet with any obstruction from him, and they parted with the full intention of asking his approval of their marriage. Unfortunately, however, either from an instinctive apprehension that he might refuse his consent, or from disinclination to expose their happiness so soon to the eyes of the world, they did not at once tell their own story to the King. Twice again they met clandestinely. Two days after their last meeting the King was in possession of their secret. They were both summoned before the Council and examined on the subject.

1610. Promises to marry Seymour.

* Arabella to the King. Disraeli's *Curiosities of Literature*, third ser. (1823), ii. 276. There can have been no suspicion of her having formed any intention of marrying Seymour, or James would certainly not have used this language. Perhaps the true history of her arrest at this time is to be found in a letter of Beecher's mentioning a report which had reached Paris, that Lerma was desirous of marrying her to a relation of his own.—Beecher to Salisbury, Jan. 20, 1610, *S. P. Fr.*

† Chamberlain to Winwood, *Winw.* iii. 117.

CH. X. 1610.

Reasons for James's dislike of the marriage.

William Seymour was perhaps the only man in England to whom James would have objected as a husband for Arabella.* His father, Lord Beauchamp, as the son of the Earl of Hertford and of Catharine Gray, inherited from his mother the claims of the Suffolk line. It is true that Lord Beauchamp's eldest son was still alive, but if, as actually happened, he should die without children, a plausible title to the throne might at any time be made out in behalf of his brother William. Since the accession of James, the marriage of the Earl of Hertford had been pronounced by a competent tribunal to be valid, and it might be argued that the Act under which the Suffolk family had claimed the Crown was passed by a lawful Parliament, whereas the Parliament which acknowledged the title of James was itself incompetent to change the succession, as it had not been summoned by a lawful King. Such reasoning would have been worthless in itself, but arguments are never wanting in a political crisis, and if James did not speedily come to terms with his Parliament, such a crisis might occur at any time.

That any political motive was mingled with Seymour's love for Arabella is in the highest degree improbable, and it is certain that an attempt to change the dynasty would as yet have failed to meet with the slightest response in the nation. James, however, could not divest himself of the notion that there was a settled plan to connect the title of the Seymours, with the title, such as it was, of Arabella. He did not consider himself bound by the words of a promise which he had made without foreseeing the particular circumstances in which he would be called upon to fulfil it, and he forbade the lovers to think any further of marriage. Seymour engaged that he would give up all claims to his affianced wife, and it was supposed that the whole matter was at an end.

The marriage privately celebrated.

For a little more than three months after this scene before the Council, Seymour kept his promise. At last affection prevailed over all other considerations. To-

* Beaulieu to Trumbull, Feb. 15, 1610, *Winw.* iii. 119. W. Seymour to the Council, Feb. 10, 1610. The King to the Bishop of Durham, March 13, 1611, Add. MS. 4161, foll. 24, 51.

wards the end of May,* he had made up his mind to fulfil the promise which he had given to Arabella rather than that which he had given to the King. She readily gave her consent, and they were privately married a few days afterwards at Greenwich.

Arabella and her husband committed to custody.

Early in July, James heard of what had happened. He was indignant at what he considered to be the presumption of the young couple. He determined to treat them as Seymour's grandparents had been treated by Elizabeth. He was frightened lest the marriage concealed some attempt upon his crown, and, under the influence of fear, he became regardless of the misery which he was inflicting. Arabella was committed to the custody of Sir Thomas Parry, at Lambeth; and Seymour was at once sent to the Tower.

From her place of confinement, Arabella used her utmost endeavours to move the heart of her oppressor. It was all in vain. She had eaten of the forbidden tree, he said, and she must take the consequences.† Her only consolation was derived from the letters which she contrived at intervals to despatch to her husband.‡ Even this consolation was soon to be taken from her. The correspondence was discovered, and James determined to make its continuance impossible by removing her to a distance from London. Durham was selected as the place of her banishment, where she was to reside under the care of the Bishop.

1611.

She is ordered to remove to Durham.

On the 15th of March she left Lambeth under the Bishop's charge.§ Her health had given way under her sufferings, and her weakness was such that it was only with difficulty that the party reached Highgate. There she remained for six days,‖ and it was not until the 21st that she was removed as far as Barnet. The King declared that if he was King of England, she should sooner or later go to Durham; but he gave her permission

* Rodney's Declaration, Add. MS. 4161, fol. 26.

† Lady Jane Drummond to Arabella, Disraeli, i. 278.

‡ Arabella to her husband, Disraeli, i. 273.

§ Bishop of Durham to the Council, March 16, 1611, *S. P. Dom.* lxii. 30.

‖ Bishop of Durham to Salisbury, with enclosure, March 21, 1611, *S. P. Dom.* lxii. 39.

CH. X. 1611.

to remain till the 11th of June at Barnet, in order to recruit her health. She remained accordingly for some time under the charge of Sir James Crofts, the Bishop having continued his journey to the north without her.

Her flight from Barnet.

Before the day appointed for her departure arrived, she had contrived a scheme by which she hoped to escape, together with her husband, from the tyranny of James. On the 3rd of June she disguised herself as a man, and left the house in which she had been for some weeks, accompanied by a gentleman named Markham. At a little distance they found horses waiting for them at a roadside inn. She was so pale and weak that the ostler expressed doubts of the possibility of her reaching London. About six in the evening she arrived at Blackwall, where a boat, in which were some of her attendants, was in waiting. It was not till the next morning that the party reached Leigh, where they expected to find a French vessel which had been engaged to take them on board. Not perceiving the signal which the captain of this vessel had agreed to hoist, or any ship within sight, they rowed up to another vessel which was bound for Berwick, and attempted to induce the master to change his course. He refused to do so, but pointed them to the French ship of which they were in quest. As soon as they were on board, Arabella's attendants, fearful of pursuit, persuaded the captain to set sail, in spite of the remonstrances of the lady herself, who was only anxious to wait for her husband.

Seymour succeeds in escaping to Ostend.

Meanwhile, Seymour had effected his escape without difficulty. When he arrived at Leigh, he was disappointed to find that the French vessel had already sailed. He was, however, able to persuade the master of a collier to carry him over to the Continent. The master of the vessel kept his promise, and landed him safely at Ostend.

Arabella taken near Calais.

His wife was less fortunate. With her whole heart fixed upon the safety of her husband, when the vessel in which she was was within a few miles of Calais, she caused it to linger on its course, in hopes of hearing some tidings of him for whose sake she had ventured amongst so many dangers. Here, within sight of the port of safety, the fugitives were overtaken by a vessel which had been

Ch. X.

1611.

despatched from Dover in pursuit of them. Arabella calmly resigned herself to her fate. She did not care what became of herself if she could be sure that her husband had reached the Continent in safety.*

Her imprisonment and death.

Arabella was committed to the Tower. Her reason gave way, and in this miserable state she died after an imprisonment of four years. It was not till after her death that Seymour obtained permission to return to England.†

The Countess of Shrewsbury.

A few days after Arabella's recapture, the Countess of Shrewsbury was summoned before the Council on the charge of having furnished her niece with money, and of having been an accomplice in her flight. She boldly answered that she had done nothing wrong; if the Council had any charge to bring against her, she would be ready to defend herself at a public trial.‡ She was committed to the Tower for a year, and then was brought before a Commission appointed to examine her. She refused to answer any questions, alleging that she had taken a vow to give no evidence, and that it was the privilege of the nobility to answer only when called upon before their peers. The judges declared that she was bound to answer, and the Commission reported that if she were brought into the Star Chamber the fit punishment for her contumacy would be imprisonment during pleasure, and a fine of £20,000. This threat, however, was not carried into execution, but she was sent back to the Tower, where she remained for some years, till she was released in order that she might be present at her husband's deathbed.

Approaching crisis in Germany.

To those who at this time paid the slightest attention to the affairs of the Continent, it must have been evident that a crisis was approaching in Germany which would bring that country prominently before the eyes of Europe; for it was there alone that the question which had been

* More to Winwood, June 8, 1611, *Winw.* iii. 279. Examination of John Bright, June 12, 1611, *S. P. Dom.* lxiv. 30, i. Cocket to Nottingham, June 5, 1611, Add. *MS.* 4161, fol. 73. The Bailiffs of Ipswich to Suffolk, June 8, 1611, Add. *MS.* 416, fol. 81.

† The Council to Seymour, Jan. 5, 1616, *S. P. Dom.* lxxxvi. 1, i.

‡ More to Winwood, June 18, 1611, *Winw.* iii. 28. Northampton to the King, June 9, 1611, *S. P. Dom.* lxiv. 23.

CH. X. 1611.

decided throughout the rest of the Continent was still waiting for a solution. The attempt to establish the ecclesiastical dominion of the Pope in alliance with the temporal supremacy of the House of Austria, which had succeeded in Italy and in the southern portion of the Netherlands, had failed before the consolidated nationalities of England, France, and Holland. Different as were the political and ecclesiastical principles which prevailed in the three countries, they agreed in their determination to settle their own affairs, and to resist all foreign interference, from whatever quarter it might come.

Political institutions of Germany.

It was obviously the interest as well as the duty of the three powers to obtain a general recognition of the principle of national independence upon which their own existence was based. Until this had been done, it was impossible to look upon the peace of Europe as permanently secured. Unfortunately, the political institutions of Germany were not such as to give much hope that the example which had been set in Western Europe would speedily be imitated there. If, indeed, at the time of the Reformation, the authority of the central government of the Empire had been stronger than it was, the ecclesiastical question would, in all probability, have been settled, once for all, for the whole country, and whatever that settlement might have been, an united Germany would have been strong enough to defend it against foreign powers. As it was, the only solution which could save the country from an endless intestine war, was to consider that, for the purposes of the ecclesiastical settlement, each of the States was to be regarded as having full power to determine upon its own affairs.

Difficulty of accepting the principle of non-intervention.

As might have been expected, however, this principle of non-intervention had never been frankly accepted by the Catholic party in Europe; and, in Germany, there were difficulties in the way of its recognition which had not presented themselves in other parts of the Continent. In the first place, whatever prestige was still attached to the government of the Empire was on the side of the Catholics. To break up the national government in other countries, it was necessary to act in direct violation of the laws, whereas in Germany the allies of the Pope were able to support themselves by an authority which was still regarded with reverence by the whole nation, and which possessed a legal claim to exercise at least some control over the affairs of the country. But even if this had not been the case, the extreme smallness of many of the territories in question made it difficult to regard them as entitled to the same privileges as those which were finally conceded to larger countries. It was something more than argument which had forced Spain to sign the treaties of Vervins and London, and the truce of Antwerp, and it was certain that argument alone would not induce the Emperor to respect the rights of such potentates as the Margrave of Baden or the Count of Oldenberg.

The Diet of Augsburg.

It was, therefore, not till after a struggle of nearly forty years' duration, that this principle was even partially accepted by the Catholic party at the Diet of Augsburg in 1555. But even the concessions which were made at that time were clogged with restrictions which deprived them of a great part of their value. In the first place, the constitution of the Empire stood in the way of the full recognition of the rights of the States to complete independence in matters of religion. It knew nothing of the population of the States, excepting as they were represented by the Elector or Duke who happened to govern them. It was, however, always possible that, whilst the population of a State had adopted one of the two forms of religion, the other might be favoured by the Government, and in such a case as this the Government might appeal with safety to the imperial authorities to support it in its rights against the people.

The Ecclesiastical Reservation.

Another hindrance to the full exercise of State rights, was the arrangement which was known as the Ecclesiastical Reservation. All ecclesiastical territories immediately holding of the Empire, which were in Catholic hands at the date of the Peace of Passau, in 1552, were to remain Catholic for ever. Not only, therefore, would the Bishops of the sees in question have it in their power to use all the means which were in their hands to proscribe the Protestant worship in their dominions; but, if the Bishops themselves should, by any chance, desert the cause of the Church, they would be forced to leave their subjects to the mercies of a more orthodox successor. By such an arrangement the temporal power, which was left in the hands of the ecclesiastics, was guaranteed, as has been the case at Rome in our own day, by external force.

Its injurious effects.

It is probably to this unfortunate stipulation, rather than to any other cause, that the miseries under which Germany suffered during so large a part of the following century are to be ascribed. By its means Protestantism was checked in its natural expansion, and it failed to obtain, while it was yet time, that superiority which would have enabled it to frustrate all attempts to repress it.

Geographical distribution of Protestantism in Germany.

A short study of the map of Germany will show how dangerous these ecclesiastical territories were to the independence of the Protestant Princes. To the north of the chain of hills, indeed, which runs from the western angle of the Bohemian mountains almost to the frontiers of Holland, the ecclesiastical principalities had scarcely any existence, and Protestantism reigned without a rival. But beyond these hills, the new doctrines had pressed forward over a territory which formed an irregular triangle, the apex of which reached within a few miles of the boundaries of Switzerland. Within this narrow space the chief Protestant Princes were the Landgrave of Hesse, the Margrave of Anspach, the Elector Palatine, the Duke of Wurtemberg, and the Margrave of Baden. To the east, they were hemmed in by the dominions of the Duke of Bavaria and by the hereditary possessions of the Austrian Emperors. On the west, the narrow slip of land which they could claim was bounded by the three Ecclesiastical Electorates, and by the Bishoprics which still remained in the hands of the Catholics. The occupants of these sees rested not only upon the agreements which had been made at Augsburg, but, with far greater confidence, upon the Spanish troops which garrisoned the Netherlands in their rear.

Nor was it only upon the two sides of their territory that, if the conflict were renewed, the Protestant Princes would have to fear from the encroachments of the enemy. Excepting for a few miles, the Bishoprics of Bamburg and Wurzburg stretched across the whole breadth of their territory, so that it would be possible for an army to march from Bavaria into the Spanish dominions without leaving at any time, excepting for a few hours, the lands of one or other of the Ecclesiastical Princes. Such an arrangement isolated the Protestants of the south from their brethren in the north, and threatened to leave them exposed whenever hostilities should once more break out.

Catholic reaction.

Bound by these unhappy stipulations, the German Protestants were obliged to look on whilst their adversaries were drawing the net around them more closely every day. At the time when the religious peace was drawn up, there was scarcely one of the Catholic Princes amongst whose subjects the new opinions had not found their way. Before the first five years of the next century were past, these opinions had been resolutely stamped out in every direction. The Protestants witnessed the operation with helpless indifference. They knew that their opponents had the law in their favour, and that they had, at least after the death of Maximilian II., in 1576, the whole organization of the Empire on their side. Nor was it only indifference which kept them quiet. Whilst their opponents were thus preparing a basis for further operations, the Protestants were occupied in quarrelling amongst themselves, and the mutual persecutions to which Calvinists and Lutherans subjected one another went far to encourage the common enemy of both.

At last their eyes were opened to the true nature of the fate which was prepared for them. In 1606 a Catholic Abbot insisted on passing in procession through the Protestant city of Donauworth. It was in vain that the magistrates warned him to desist. The consequence was, that those who formed the procession were attacked by the populace, and were obliged to take refuge in the monastery from which they came. The town was placed under the ban of the Empire, and the Duke of Bavaria, Maximilian I., was authorized to execute the sentence. As the leading man of the Catholic party, he was ready enough to take vengeance for the insulted Abbot. He

CH. X. 1606. took possession of the city, and, contrary to all law and justice, put a stop to the exercise of the Protestant religion within the walls. In order not to allow the work of conversion to be interrupted, he took care to keep the place in his own hands, on the plea that he had a right to do so until his expenses had been paid.

1608. The Union. Alarmed by this flagrant violation of the laws, and by the declarations of the Jesuits, who began to deny the validity of the religious peace, after they had themselves made use of it so long for the purpose of keeping their opponents from all interference with their projects, the Protestant Princes turned a ready ear to those who invited them to forget their mutual differences, and to form an alliance for defence against the aggressions of the Catholics. Foremost amongst those who had long been urging such a course was the Elector Palatine, Frederic IV. Cut off as his own dominions were by the ecclesiastical territories from the Protestant north, he was the first to feel the danger, and had been calling in vain for many years to his brethren to join him in a defensive league. Unhappily, the Lutherans, with the powerful Elector of Saxony at their head, turned a deaf ear to his advances, on the plea that his Calvinistic opinions excluded him from the society of the orthodox. As soon, however, as the news of the capture of Donauworth was spread abroad, his difficulties were at an end, and, although the Elector of Saxony still refused to follow the lead of the head of a rival house, a considerable number of the Princes of both confessions agreed to form a union for defence against the Catholics.

1609. The League. In the following year, the step which they had taken was met by the formation of a Catholic League, at the head of which was Maximilian of Bavaria. It was plain that the two parties could not long remain in such antagonistic positions without coming to blows. As yet, however, the Catholic League was the weaker of the two associations. With the exception of the Duke of Bavaria, not a single secular Prince had joined it, and neither the resources nor the character of the Bishops fitted them for carrying on military operations. Events had recently occurred in Austria which made it doubtful how far Maximilian would meet with the support of the Austrian Government. Ferdinand of Gratz, indeed, the cousin of the Emperor Rudolph II., still held his ground for the Pope and the Jesuits in his own dominions, which comprised Styria, Carniola, and Carinthia; but a successful revolution had recently put Austria, Hungary, and Moravia into the hands of the Emperor's brother Matthias, whilst Rudolph himself retained Bohemia alone. Both Rudolph and Matthias, weakened by the competition in which they had engaged, were forced, sorely against their will, to grant religious freedom to the estates of their several provinces.

Under these circumstances, Maximilian was obliged to turn to Spain for help. He found that the Spanish Government was inclined to assist him, although it was jealous of his personal influence in Germany. It was finally agreed that the King of Spain should furnish a sum of money, on condition that he should be named director of the league.

Death of the Duke of Cleves.

A few months before the formation of the league, an event had occurred which was calculated to bring about a collision between the rival confederacies. On the 25th of March, John William, Duke of Cleves, died without male heirs, and left his dominions exposed to all the evils of a disputed succession. At such a time, the succession to any one of the numerous States of Germany could not fail to be treated as a party question. But there was not one of all those States, the possession of which was of equal importance to that of the territories which were now in dispute. It was not merely that the successful candidate would be possessed of the acknowledged right of imposing his own religion upon the inhabitants of an extensive and flourishing district, but that he would be able, if war should again break out, to command a position of the greatest strategical importance. The dominions of the late duke were an aggregate of petty states, which had been brought into his family by a series of well-timed marriages, and which formed a tolerably compact territory, lying along the banks of the Rhine, excepting where they were interrupted by the

Importance of the disputed succession.

CH. X. 1609.

narrow strip of land belonging to the Elector of Cologne. In the hands of the last duke, who had been a Catholic, they not only connected the outlying bishoprics of Munster, Paderborn, and Hildesheim with the Ecclesiastical Electorates and the Spanish Netherlands, but, by their command of the Rhine, they served to interrupt the communications of the Protestants of Central Germany with the Dutch Republic. In the hands of a Protestant all these conditions would be reversed; and it happened that the only claimants, whose pretensions were not absolutely ridiculous, were Protestants.

Pretenders to the succession.

The eldest sister of the last duke had married the Duke of Prussia, and had died without male heirs. Her eldest daughter, who had married the Elector of Brandenberg, was also dead, and her title had descended to her son, the Electoral Prince. The second sister of the late Duke of Cleves, on the other hand, was still alive; and her husband, the Count Palatine of Neuburg, declared that the younger sister, being alive, was to be preferred to the descendants of the elder sister, who was dead. The whole case was still further complicated by a number of Imperial grants and marriage contracts, the stipulations of which were far from coinciding with one another. It was upon one of these that the Elector of Saxony founded a claim, which he hoped to prosecute successfully by the help of the Emperor, as he had carefully held aloof from the proceedings of the Princes of the Union. There were also other pretenders, who asked only for a portion of the land, or for an equivalent sum of money.

The Elector of Brandenberg and the Palatine of Neuburg take possession.

At first, it seemed not unlikely that the Elector of Brandenberg and the Palatine of Neuburg would come to blows. They both entered the duchy in order to take possession. They were, however, induced by the Landgrave of Hesse and other Protestant princes to come to a mutual understanding, and they agreed that Cleves should be governed in their joint names until the controversy between them could be decided.

The Archduke Leopold seizes

It was not likely that the Catholic party would look on quietly at these proceedings. At their request, the Emperor cited the pretenders before his court, and no

1609.

Juliers in the name of the Emperor.

notice having been taken of this citation, he put the Possessioners, as they were called, to the ban of the Empire, and ordered the Archduke Leopold, who, as Bishop of Strasburg and Passau, had an interest in resisting the encroachments of the Protestants, to take possession of the territory until the question was settled.

The Possessioners refused to admit these pretensions. Not only was the Emperor's Court notoriously partial in questions of this kind, but it was supposed that he was determined to set aside the grants of his predecessors, and that he would himself lay claim to Cleves as a fief vacant by default of male heirs. The Archduke, supported by a force which he had raised with the assistance of the League, obtained possession of the town of Juliers, by means of the treachery of the commander of the garrison, but was unable to advance further in the face of the forces of the Possessioners. These princes, on the other hand, appealed to Foreign Powers for aid in a struggle by which the interests of the whole of Western Europe were affected.

The Possessioners supported by the King of France,

The King of France had already declared himself in their favour. When he first heard of the death of the Duke, he at once said that he would never permit such an important position to fall into the hands of the House of Austria. He openly declared that he was ready to assist the Possessioners, not because he cared who obtained the inheritance, but because he would not allow either Austria or Spain to establish itself at his gates.* At the same time he ordered his troops to march towards the frontier, in order to assure the German Protestants that he did not intend to desert their cause.

and by Holland and England.

The assistance of the Dutch, in a cause which interested them so deeply, might certainly be counted upon; and, although the matter in dispute was of less immediate importance to England, yet it might fairly be expected that James would not be content to look on when Protestant Germany was assailed by Austria and Spain. He was, perhaps, the more ready to give his help as he foresaw that the forces on the other side were

* Carew to Salisbury, April 5, 1609, *S. P. France*.

CH. X. 1609. utterly unable to offer a prolonged resistance. The divisions in the Austrian family had rendered the Emperor powerless for the time, and Spain was engaged in the suicidal operation of expelling from her territory the descendants of the conquered Moors, who were, not without reason, suspected to be wanting in attachment to the faith of their Christian oppressors. James, therefore, who knew that the independence of Central Germany was the best guarantee for the permanent peace of Europe, consented to send a force to the assistance of the Princes; but he prudently declared that, as the French and Dutch were far more interested in the question than he could possibly be, he considered that they should be the first to move.

Projects of Henry IV. He was the more unwilling to engage precipitately in the war, as the King of France seemed to be hanging back, under pretence of waiting for the meeting of the Princes of the Union, which was appointed to take place in January, at Hall in Swabia. It was supposed in England that this delay was caused by his unwillingness to engage the arms of France in the support of a Protestant cause.

The English Government was mistaken. Henry was thoroughly in earnest. He saw, with the instinct of genius, that an opportunity was presented to him of freeing Europe for ever from the leaden domination of the House of Austria. If Spain were allowed to proceed quietly with the expulsion of the Moors, and if the Austrian territories were again united under one vigorous hand, it might be too late. It was still possible to avert, by one or two short but decisive campaigns, the storm of war which was hanging over the Continent. As far as we are able to judge of the King's intentions, he had made up his mind, as soon as the war of Cleves was at an end, to throw himself boldly upon the Archduke's dominions in the Low Countries. At the same time he hoped to secure Lorraine by negotiating a marriage between the Dauphin and the eldest daughter of the Duke, who had no sons to inherit his possessions; and he calculated that there would be little difficulty in driving the Spaniards from Franche Comté. Still greater importance was attached by him to the campaign which he projected in Italy. For the first time since Charles VIII. had crossed the Alps, a monarch was upon the throne of France who was aware that Italy would be more valuable as an ally than as a conquered province. On the other hand, Charles Emmanuel, the Duke of Savoy, an able but unscrupulous prince, had spent the greater part of his reign in a fruitless endeavour to extend his dominions on the side of France. He had now learned, by a bitter experience, that he could have no hope of success in that direction; and he was ready to turn his energies against the Spanish possessions in the Milanese. There was, therefore, no difficulty in establishing an understanding between the two powers; and negotiations were commenced, which resulted in a treaty by which they bound themselves to join in the conquest of Milan.* The Spanish territory was to be annexed to the Duke's dominions, with the exception of a portion which was to be the price of the cooperation of the Republic of Venice. Although in the treaty the French only stipulated for the destruction of the fortress of Montmeillan, by which Savoy was commanded, it is probable that there was an understanding that, in the event of complete success, the whole of Savoy should be ceded to France.† It was also agreed that the Prince of Piedmont should marry the eldest daughter of the King of France. A large army was collected, in the course of the spring, on the Italian frontier, under the Duke's old opponent, Marshal Lesdiguieres, and a force was prepared to assist the Moriscos in defending their homes in Spain, in order to prevent the Spanish Government from sending any assistance to Milan. The King himself was to command the army which was to assemble in Champagne.

It is not probable that under any circumstances Henry would have been able to carry out the whole of his plans. But if he had succeeded in establishing a strong barrier on the Lower Rhine between the Spanish Netherlands

* Dumont, Corps Diplomatique, v. 2, 137.

† See, besides the French authorities quoted by Martin, *Hist. de France*, xii. 153. Beecher to Salisbury, Nov. 21, 1609; Feb. 2, 9, and 18; March 19; April 10; May 3, 1610, *S. P. France.*

CH. X. 1610.

and the Catholic States, and had placed the Milanese in the hands of the Duke of Savoy, he would have conferred inestimable benefits upon the whole of Europe. By such means he would have isolated Spain from Austria, and Austria from the Netherlands. The links which bound the unwieldy fabric together would have been broken, and its power for evil would have been at an end. It is not too much to say that if Henry had been able to carry out his views, the Thirty Years' War, with all its attendant horrors, would never have devastated the face of Europe —a blessing which, as no real existing nationality would have been endangered, would have been cheaply purchased by some extension of the territory and influence of France.

Preparation for the war.

Whilst Henry was engaged in preparation for the campaign in the spring, he had the satisfaction of knowing that in Germany everything was going on in accordance with his wishes. The Princes of the Union met at Hall in January, and decided upon taking up the cause of the Possessioners. The forces which they agreed to furnish were to be placed under the command of Prince Christian of Anhalt, who had earned a considerable reputation both in diplomacy and in war. The Dutch promised to send four thousand men, and England was to furnish an equal number. The latter force was to be taken from amongst the English and Scotch who were in the pay of the United Provinces, and who were to return to their old service after the conclusion of the war. It was to be placed under the command of Sir Edward Cecil, a son of the Treasurer's elder brother, the Earl of Exeter.

On their part, the Catholic Princes had given up all hope of being able to resist the forces which were being brought against them. There seemed at one time a prospect that Spinola's veterans would throw themselves on the French line of march; but even if the position of the Court of Brussels between France and Holland had been less dangerous than it was, its want of money was so great that there was reason to fear that a mutiny would break out in the army as soon as it was brought into the field.* Under these circumstances resistance

* Trumbull to Salisbury, April 18, 1610, *S. P. Flanders.*

was impossible, and the Archduke was obliged to submit to the humiliation of granting permission to the French to pass through the territory of the Netherlands on their way to Juliers.

CH. X.
1610.
Murder of Henry IV.

The courier who carried this permission was still on his way to Paris when the knife of Ravaillac freed the House of Austria from its fears. The murder of the great King as he was setting out to join the army was greeted with a shout of exultation from every corner of Catholic Europe. Those who were endangered by his far-sighted policy knew well that he had left no successor who was capable of carrying out his designs.

James at once declared * that, though he would be glad of the cooperation of the French, he was determined to fulfil his engagements to the German Princes. He sent Sir Thomas Edmondes, who had already served with distinction in several important diplomatic employments, to Paris, in order to learn what was likely to be the consequence of the death of Henry IV. On his arrival, Edmondes found that the late King's widow, Mary de Medici, was quietly in possession of the government, as Regent, in the name of her son Louis XIII., who was still a child. It was not to be expected that she would attempt to carry out her husband's designs. Even if she had had the power, she was far from having the inclination, to enter upon a general war. Educated as she had been at a petty Italian Court, she had learned from her childhood to look with awe and admiration upon the grandeur of the Spanish monarchy.

At the time when the negotiations which led to the Truce of Antwerp were in progress, the proposal which had been formerly made to Henry, on behalf of the King of Spain, for a double marriage between their children had been repeated. Henry IV., who had no wish to desert his allies, had again refused to have anything to do with such a scheme. The Queen had never forgiven his rejection of the proposal, and now that power had unexpectedly fallen into her hands, she was anxious to

* Instructions to Edmondes, May, *S. P. France.* The Council to Winwood, May 18, 1610, *Winw.* iii. 165.

carry out the plan which had failed to obtain the approval of her husband.

The new government decide upon sending forces to Juliers.

Yet even under the influence of these feelings, the Regent was unable to refuse to carry out that part, at least, of her husband's plan which consisted in sending troops to the siege of Juliers. It was impossible that any ruler of France should allow the House of Austria to extend its dominions upon the Rhine. It was therefore in vain that the Nuncio at Paris* exercised all his influence in endeavouring to divert her from her purpose. After a short delay, it was announced that Marshal de la Châtre would be ready to march on the 5th of July.†

The siege.

Before, however, De la Châtre arrived at Juliers, the siege had already commenced. The English and Dutch contingents came up on the 17th of July,‡ and they felt themselves strong enough to do without the assistance of the French. They were the more eager to reduce the place with all possible speed, as they were not without apprehension that the Regent might be intending to play them false. It was to no purpose that the French pressed for a delay.§ The works were carried on vigorously, under the superintendence of Prince Maurice, who was in command of the Dutch troops; and when De la Châtre arrived, on the 8th of August, he found that the siege was already far advanced.

On the 22nd the garrison surrendered. The commander, in hopes of obtaining better terms, opened negotiations with De la Châtre. He was anxious to put the place into the hands of the French. This was, of course, refused by the allies, and Juliers was placed under the charge of the Princes of the Union.

Winwood's negotiations.

The reduction of Juliers had been accomplished without any great difficulty. Winwood, who had been despatched to Dusseldorf, in order to conduct, in conjunction with the French ambassador Boississe, the

* Nuncio at Paris to the Nuncio at Prague, May $\frac{20}{30}$, $\frac{\text{May } 23}{\text{June } 2}$, 1610, *Winw.* iii. 171, 176.

† Edmondes to Winwood, June 14, 1610, *Winw.* iii. 182.

‡ Winwood to Salisbury, July 22, 1610, *S. P. Hol.*

§ Winwood to Salisbury, July 27, 1610, *S. P. Hol.*

negotiations which were to decide upon the disputed succession, had a far more impracticable task before him. The Elector of Saxony had thrown himself into the hands of the Emperor, and had succeeded in obtaining his good will. He now came forward with a demand that the whole matter in dispute should be referred to the Emperor, and that, in the meanwhile, he should be admitted to share in the possession of the disputed territories. This proposal was considered by the other two claimants to be inadmissible. They, on their part, offered to submit to the arbitration of the Princes of the Empire, who were not likely to decide in favour of any claimant who was supported by the Emperor.* Under such circumstances, all hope of coming to an agreement was at an end. The negotiations were broken off, and Winwood returned to the Hague, leaving all the important questions which were connected with the Cleves succession still unsettled.

Treaty with France.

Whilst the armies were occupied with the siege of Juliers, the English Government signed a treaty† with France, by which the two Powers engaged mutually to furnish one another with troops, if either of them should be attacked by a foreign enemy. It was now more than ever important to England to retain, if possible, the Government of France in the alliance against Spain, or, at least, to prevent the French from taking open part with the common enemy. A stipulation was also inserted, that if the merchants of either country should suffer wrong in the dominions of any third Power, both Governments should join in making reprisals upon the subjects of the offending State.

The case of the English merchants in Spain.

Emboldened by this stipulation, and by the general position of Continental affairs, Salisbury determined upon a step which he ought to have taken long before. The grievances of the English merchants in Spain, which had moved the compassion of the House of Commons in 1607, were still substantially unredressed. Cornwallis had been most active in supporting their

* Winwood to Salisbury, Sept. 12, 26, Oct. 12, 26, 1610, *S. P. Hol.*
† Rymer, xvi. 691.

CH. X. 1609. claims. He had pressed them in every possible way upon the attention of the Spanish Government, and had at his own expense employed advocates to maintain them in the courts of law. When he returned to England in 1609, he left behind him his secretary, Cottington, who was to act as agent for the King of England until the appointment of another ambassador. Cottington took up the cases immediately, and left no stone unturned to obtain justice.* At last, on the 1st of December, 1609, a judgment was given in the case of the Trial. The vessel was to be restored to its owners, but nothing was said about the value of the merchandise, or about reparation for the inhuman treatment inflicted upon the crew. Nor was it easy to obtain restitution even of the vessel itself. The Duke of Feria, who had been Viceroy of Sicily when the seizure was effected, was dead, and his son, who had succeeded to his title, was far too powerful a personage to pay any attention to the sen-
1610. tence of an ordinary court. Cottington complained that, in spite of all his efforts, nothing was done. At last, three days after the signature of the treaty with France,† Salisbury wrote to him, ordering him to present his complaints formally before the Spanish Government, and to intimate that if justice were still denied, he was directed to return home at once, to give an account of the treatment to which English subjects were exposed.

Effect of Cottington's remonstrance. The effect of this was immediate. He was told indeed that in the case of the Trial, nothing could be done for the present, as the Duke of Feria was in France, and it was necessary to wait for his return. Orders were, however, given him, commanding the various tribunals to proceed expeditiously in the other cases of which he complained. These orders he received on the 20th of October, and on the 10th of April in the
1611. following year‡ he was able to report not only that he had at last obtained several decisions in favour of the merchants, but that those decisions had actually been

* The despatches in the *S. P.* are full of details on this subject.

† Salisbury to Cottington, Aug. 21, 1610, *S. P. Sp.* The treaty was signed on the 19th.

‡ Cottington to Salisbury, April 10, 1611, *S. P. Sp.*

carried into effect. Still, the more important cases remained undecided, and these were left to the advocacy of Sir John Digby, who was to come out as ambassador in the course of the summer. CH. X. 1611.

Salisbury's foreign policy.

To those who read history as alone it ought to be read, and who know what are the momentous issues which depend upon the wisdom or the folly of the actors upon the scene, there is something indescribably sad in the events which have been just narrated. Whatever may be the true explanation of the pension which Salisbury was still drawing from Spain, and of the demand for additional payments which he put forward shortly after the signature of the Truce of Antwerp, there can be no doubt that under his guidance England was taking up her position on the side of the liberties of the independent States of the Continent.* In spite of the mistakes which had undoubtedly been committed, and of the deplorable indecision which had too frequently characterized the counsels of the Government, Salisbury's foreign policy had been marked by a steady progress in the right direction. Avoiding all rash and hazardous enterprises as unsuited to the poverty of the Exchequer, and to the defective military organization of the country, he had yet succeeded in interposing the weight of his influence wherever he thought that it could be put forward with any prospect of success on behalf of those who were engaged in resistance to the House of Austria. Yet what hope was there that this policy, right as it was in itself, could possibly be crowned with success? It was evident that for the future, if it was to be continued there would be need of constant watchfulness and of fresh exertions in the common cause of Europe. It was no less evident to all impartial observers that, if England was to intervene in Continental affairs, her intervention could only prove effectual if it was carried out by a Sovereign who was able to dispose of all the resources which the nation would readily put into the

* This is the simple fact. I cannot reconcile the actions of the man with the increased desire for Spanish gold shown in Digby's letters in App. III., except by supposing that he was playing with Spain. For certain information we must wait till the archives of Simancas have been ransacked.

CH. X. 1611.

Its dependence upon the maintenance of a good understanding with the House of Commons.

hands of one in whom they could place their confidence. Salisbury knew well that the success of his foreign policy depended entirely upon the maintenance of a good understanding with the House of Commons. We know that he pleaded the state of the Continent as a means to induce the Commons to come to terms with the King. There can be little doubt that he employed similar arguments with James in order to induce him to give way to the demands of the Commons. Of the close connection between the Treasurer's domestic and foreign policy James understood nothing. When on the 5th of November he sent the message which virtually put an end to all chance of a good understanding between himself and the Lower House, he would have been astonished if any one had told him that he was striking a blow as effective as that which had been dealt by the arm of Ravaillac, in favour of the pretensions of Spain and of the Pope. Under the guidance of James, the vessel of State was, amidst all outward signs of prosperity, steering directly upon the rocks. It had become a mere question of time how soon its course would be arrested, and he would be compelled by sheer necessity to leave the Continent to its fate.

The Court of Wards.

At home, some feeble attempts were made to win the good opinion of the nation. Instructions were issued forbidding the officers of the Court of Wards to accept irregular payments from the suitors. Salisbury declared that he was ready to renounce all the personal profit which he derived from his office of Master of the Court, and resigned his emoluments to the King.* Negotiations were also entered upon with the several counties, in which hopes were held out to them that all claims to purveyance would be surrendered in consideration of a fixed payment,† a scheme which before many years

* Instructions, Jan. 9, 1611, *S. P. Dom.* lxi. 6. Pembroke to Edmondes, *Court and Times*, i. 132. According to Walter Yonge (*Diary*, 19), it had been proposed in the House of Commons to grant £20,000 as compensation to the Master, and £10,000 to the other officers 'during their lives.'

† Justices of Hertfordshire to Salisbury, April 1, 1611, *S. P. Dom.* lxiii. 1. See also Gray to Salisbury, Sept. 5, 1611, *S. P. Dom.* lxvi. 9. I have taken it for granted that the proposal was general. In the Calendar the negotiation is said to have been for a composition for tenures, which is a mistake.

elapsed was adopted by the majority of the counties. But it was in vain that Salisbury applied himself to the task of reducing the expenditure. If he imagined that James had at last become conscious of the absolute necessity of practising the strictest economy, he must soon have been undeceived. In less than a month after the King had declared his intention of dissolving Parliament, he thought fit to present to four of his Scottish favourites no less a sum than £24,000, for which they had rendered no services whatever.*

CH. X.

1611.

Salisbury's vain attempt to reduce the expenditure.

Carr created Viscount Rochester.

The dissatisfaction which was felt throughout the country at the dissolution of Parliament can hardly have failed to gather new strength as soon as it became known that, for the first time since his accession, James had raised one of his countrymen to the English Peerage. On the 25th of March, Sir Robert Carr was created Viscount Rochester. He had been naturalised by Act of Parliament, so that there was nothing illegal in the proceeding. But he had long been known in no favourable manner to the English people, as holding the most prominent place among the detested race of Scottish favourites, who, without any merits of their own, had succeeded in acquiring so large a share in the confidence of their master. He was descended from the well-known family of the Kers of Ferniehurst, and had, as a boy, attended the King in Scotland, in the capacity of page. Upon James's accession to the English throne, he had been dismissed from his post, and had sought to push his fortunes in France. Having failed of success upon the Continent, he returned to England, when he attached himself to the service of Lord Hay. He had not been long at Court before he had the good fortune to break his leg at a tilting match in the presence of the King. James was attracted by his demeanour, and from that moment his success was certain. In him those requirements were found together which James always looked for in his favourites. His strong animal spirits and his comely proportions gave him a real superiority to which the weak nature of the King could

* Warrant, Feb. 1, 1611, *S. P. Warr. Book*, ii. 191.

CH. X. 1611.

cling, whilst his want of intellectual culture and of social position enabled James to represent to himself that he was in reality standing far above the man whom he had raised from the dust, and whom he was able at any moment to hurl back from the splendid position in which he had placed him. Step by step the man who had arrived in England as a penniless youth, rose in the royal favour, till, to the disgust of all who thought that the peerage should be a reward of merit alone, he took his place among the old nobility of the realm.

Raleigh and the manor of Sherborne.

In the midst of this life of festivity and splendour, the favourite would have been greatly surprised if he had been told that there was one amongst his heedless actions by which his name would be handed down to the scorn of posterity, by the mere fact of its having brought him into collision with a far greater man than himself. Amidst the wreck of his fortune, Raleigh had succeeded in inducing the King to make over the manor of Sherborne to trustees who were to hold it in behalf of Lady Raleigh and her eldest son during his lifetime. Immediately upon his death, it would descend to his son, in virtue of the conveyance which he had signed in the days of his prosperity. A few months after this arrangement had been made, he was horrified by the news that a flaw had been discovered in the conveyance, which would after his death place the whole property at the King's disposal. He immediately wrote to Salisbury, begging him to come to his help, and requesting that the deed might be laid before Coke and Popham, in order that he might know what the real state of the case was.* His request was acceded to. Unhappily, there could be no doubt whatever as to the fact. The words omitted were of such importance that Popham could do nothing but declare that, as a legal document, the conveyance was worthless. He added, however, that he believed the error had arisen from the fault of the clerk who had engrossed the deed.†

1604.

Discovery of a flaw in the conveyance of the land.

1605.

* Raleigh to Cranborne. Late in 1604, or early in 1605. Add. MS. 6177, fol. 311.

† Popham to Salisbury, June 7, 1605, Add. MS. 6177, fol. 393. Much indignation has been thrown away upon this opinion, which was given at Raleigh's own request, and which, as will be seen, could not possibly have

As soon as it was known how the case really stood, Lady Raleigh lost no time in imploring the King not to take advantage of his legal rights to ruin her innocent children. James at once consented to waive all pretensions to the reversion of the land, and directed Salisbury to prepare a grant of it to Lady Raleigh and her children.* It would have been well for James's good name if these directions had been carried out. There are no means of knowing with certainty what the inducement was which caused him to draw back. It is possible that the foolish rumours which reached him shortly afterwards of Raleigh's participation in the Gunpowder Plot,† caused some delay, and that when those rumours proved to be without foundation, some new influence had obliterated his good intentions from his facile mind.

CH. X.
1605.
The King promises to give up his claim.
James retracts his promise.

In the summer of 1606, Raleigh even entertained a hope that he might recover his liberty.‡ He supposed that the King of Denmark, who was on a visit to his brother-in-law, might be induced to plead his cause.§ When these expectations proved to be without foundation, Lady Raleigh, in despair, made her way to Hampton Court, where she threw herself on her knees before the King. James passed her by in silence.‖

1606.

Another year passed away, and the King had taken no steps to call Raleigh's conveyance in question. But before the close of 1607 a temptation was presented to him which he was unable to resist. Carr was rapidly rising in favour, and James was anxious that he should become a landed proprietor. He was, however, preparing at that time to entail the greater part of his own lands upon the Crown, and had, probably, already come to the

1607.
And determines to procure the manor for Carr.

been given in favour of the validity of the document. In 1608, the Attorney-General, Hobart, said, in the Court of Exchequer, that 'the sentence that should have appointed the said Sir W. Raleigh, his heirs and assigns, or such as had estate in the same premises to stand and to be seized thereof to the intended uses, was all wanting' (App. II. 1). See also an extract from a letter of Coke's, Add. MS. 6177, fol. 391, the date of which should apparently be June 7, 1605.

* Add. MS. 6177, fol. 323. The date 1603 in the copy is clearly wrong. The petition was probably sent and answered in the autumn of 1605.

† Add. MS. 6178, fol. 469, 553. Hoby to Edmondes, Nov. 19, 1605. Add. MS. 4176, fol. 34 b.

‡ Examination of Cottrell, Feb. 4, 1607, *S. P. Dom.* xxvi. 42.

§ Carleton to Chamberlain, Aug. 20, 1606, *S. P. Dom.* xxiii. 10.

‖ Whyte to Shrewsbury, Sept. 24, 1606, *Lodge*, iii. 186.

CH. X. 1608. determination to grant away no more manors excepting those which might fall into his hands by forfeiture.

In this difficulty he cast his eyes upon Sherborne. Early in 1608, an information was exhibited in the Exchequer, calling upon Raleigh to show the title by which his heirs held the reversion of the manor. He could only produce the conveyance which, as he knew, would not bear the scrutiny of the court. In order that he might have fair play, the judges assigned him counsel. The lawyers who were thus appointed, after consultation amongst themselves, refused to argue the case, as it would be impossible to find any line of defence to which the court could be induced to listen. It was not, however, till the 27th of October that judgment was finally pronounced in favour of the Crown.* James had already bought up for £5,000 the interest which, by his grant in 1604, Lady Raleigh possessed in the estate during her husband's lifetime.† If, therefore, he determined to present it to Carr, the new owner would be able at once to enter into possession, without waiting for Raleigh's death.

Judgment in the Exchequer in favour of the Crown.

The manor granted to Carr.

A letter has been preserved in which Raleigh, a few weeks after the decision of the court was known to him, begged Carr to do him justice, and implored him not to build his rising fortunes upon the ruin of an innocent man.‡ Lady Raleigh, too, made one more attempt to move the compassion of the King. Taking with her young Walter and the boy who had been born to her in her hour of sorrow in the Tower, she again threw herself at James's feet and begged for mercy. It is said that his only answer was, 'I maun have the land, I maun have it for Carr.' On the 9th of January the grant was passed by which the estate, which Raleigh had received from Elizabeth in the days of his prosperity, came into the possession of a worthless favourite.§

1609.

* App. II.

† Devon. *Issues of the Exchequer*, p. 99. The first instalment was not to be paid till June 1609, though the writ for its payment was dated March 13, 1608. This may have been in order to leave the rents in the hands of Lady Raleigh's trustees till the decision was given in the Exchequer.

‡ Raleigh to Carr, Dec. 1608, Cayley's *Life of Raleigh*.

§ Pat. 6 James I., part 32, *P. R. O.*

Compensation to Raleigh.

In preferring Carr to Raleigh, James had given to the world an additional evidence of his own folly. He had, however, no intention of taking the land from Raleigh without allowing him compensation for his loss. He therefore ordered a survey to be taken of the lands, and, as a guarantee that it would be fairly carried out, he allowed the name of Raleigh's follower, Keymis, to appear amongst those of the Commissioners by whom the survey was to be made.* A negotiation was entered into with Sir Arthur Throckmorton and the other feoffees to whom the estate had been conveyed by the deed which had been lately proved to be invalid, which ended in the renunciation† of the £5,000 which was to have been paid to Lady Raleigh for her interest in the land, and in the grant by the King of a pension of £400 a-year, to be paid during her own life and that of her eldest son. To this was added a sum of £8,000 in ready money.

According to our notions, James's conduct in taking advantage of the flaw in the conveyance would be inexcusable, even if he contented himself with making use of it only to force the sale upon equitable terms. But at that time it was a matter of every day occurrence for the Crown to make a profit out of defects in the titles by which lands were held, though it would have been considered to be tyrannical to exact, in such cases, the full penalty of the law.

In order to judge, therefore, what was the extent of the wrong done to Raleigh, it is necessary to know what

* Keymis to Salisbury, Sept. 23, 1609, *S. P. Dom.* xlviii. 5 A, printed in the *Literary Gazette,* new series, No. 18. The survey is also referred to in the *Exchequer Depositions,* 7 James I. Mich. Term. No. 24, *P. R. O.*

† This may, I suppose, be taken for granted, as the payment to Lady Raleigh of the interest due upon the £5,000, which had been retained in the King's hands, was made on the 13th Jan. 1610 (*Issue Book of the Exch.*), and the two patents assigning the pension on the two lives, are dated on the 16th of the same month (Pat. 7 James I., part 13, *P. R. O.*). Nothing further is heard of the £5,000. The £8,000 was paid over to Keymis on the 23rd Dec. 1609. During the year 1609 a second information had been exhibited in the Exchequer, calling upon Raleigh to produce any other title by which the land might be claimed from the Crown. He had been heard to speak of an earlier conveyance which he had made in 1598, of the ninety-nine years' lease which he held. As he was unable to produce it, and no witness could be found to speak to its contents, judgment was given against him, on Nov. 23, 1609.—App. II. 2.

CH. X. 1609.

was the precise money value of the land which was taken from him. Unfortunately, it is not very easy to obtain this information. Raleigh, indeed, writing in 1604, under circumstances in which it was his interest to calculate the value of his property as low as possible, made it out to be considerably under £400 a year.* But in 1612 the payments on account of the manor amounted to a little more than £750,† and there is other evidence which makes it probable that this was in reality the amount of revenue derived from it at that time. As the ordinary value of land in the reign of James was calculated at sixteen years' purchase,‡ this would give £12,000 as the total value of the estate, which would be about equivalent to the £8,000, with the £400 pension § which was granted. If this calculation be admitted, it would appear that Raleigh obtained a fair payment for his property, and that the wrong that was done him consisted only in the compulsion which was used to force him to sell it—a wrong the hardship of which was considerably lessened by the known fact that he had long been anxious to find a purchaser.‖

There is, however, undoubted evidence in existence which conflicts strangely with the result of these calculations. When, shortly after Carr had received the manor, he resold it to the King, he obtained £20,000;

* Appendix II., Nos. 3 and 4.

† On the 15th of March, 1614, R. Connock, bailiff of the manor of Sherborne, paid money into the Exchequer as part of £754 11*s.* 10½*d.*, as arrears of his office due at Michaelmas 1612, which time Sherborne was the property of Prince Henry. I suppose this is the amount of the rents of the year, which would agree with Chamberlain's statement that Sherborne, 'besides the goodly house and other commodities, is presently worth £800 a year, and in reasonable time will be double' (*Court and Times of James I.* 426). It might be supposed that this is inclusive of the rent paid to the Bishop; but I can find no payment to the Bishop in the Issue Books.

‡ Bacon, in his Essay on Usury, speaks of this as if it were the ordinary rate, and this is confirmed by a note in Sir Julius Cæsar's hand-writing appended in 1612 to a calculation of the revenue derived from the estate of Lord Vaux of Harrowden: 'After sixteen years' purchase, the common rate of sale there,' &c.

§ It is sometimes stated that this pension was very irregularly paid. This charge seems to have arisen from the difficulty she had in obtaining payment on one occasion, apparently shortly after her husband's execution. Lady Raleigh to Cæsar.—Lansd. MS. 142, fol. 282, and note at fol. 280.

‖ Raleigh to Cecil, Add. MS. 6177, fol. 281. Raleigh to Cranborne, Add. MS. 6178, fol. 457.

and when, in 1615, he bought it back again, it was, according to a statement made by Bacon, valued at £25,000.* Either, then, the value of the house and pleasure grounds must have been expressed by this very great difference, or the expectations, which do not appear to have been realised,† of a great increase in the future income to be derived from the land, raised its value in the market. Whether this or some other explanation be the true one, it would seem that the difference between the actual value of the estate and the ordinary market value of the revenue derived from the estate at the time, will give the amount of which Raleigh was mulcted.

Such is the true story of the transfer of the manor of Sherborne‡ from Raleigh to Carr. As it stands it is bad enough, but it is needless to say that this is not the story which has obtained credence for more than two centuries. Posterity has revenged itself upon James by laying to his charge sins of which he was guiltless, and by exaggerating those which he in reality committed. The value of the lands was swollen, in the imaginations of men, to an enormous amount, and it has been believed by one of Raleigh's biographers after another, that James threw to the man from whom he had, by means of a sentence procured in a corrupt court, wrenched an estate worth £5,000 a year, a pittance which barely

* Bacon to Villiers, Nov. 29, 1616 (*Works*, ed. Montagu, xii. 238). The sum actually paid into the Exchequer in 1615 by Somerset was only £20,000, but £4,000 more may be accounted for, as the King owed him that sum at the time. Perhaps the remaining £1,000 was wiped off in the same way.

† By the account in App. II., No. 5, it appears that in the time of the Commonwealth the gross annual value of the property was £1,302 6*s.* 8*d.*; but of this £286 stand for the Prebend which had been bought since the land came into Digby's hands, and for certain new purchased grounds. For the purposes of comparing the value of the property at the two periods, Raleigh's outgoings of £334 13*s.* 0*d.*, must also be deducted, leaving £681 13*s.* 8*d.*, or less than the value in 1612. Of course, land may have been sold, but of this there is no trace, at least in Hutchins' *Dorsetshire*.

‡ An accusation was brought against Raleigh about this time, by John More, of having offered him a bribe to give false evidence concerning the conveyance. Mr. Sainsbury, who published More's letter in the *Literary Gazette* (New Ser. No. 18), together with the enclosed letter of Raleigh's offering the bribe, pronounces the latter to be a forgery. His suspicions derive confirmation from a sentence taken from a letter of Raleigh's written to Cecil in 1601 (Add. MS. 6177, 187). He there says that More 'writes any hand so perfectly as I can not any way discern the difference.'

CH. X. 1610. exceeded the annual rental of the lands. Everything might be believed of a Sovereign whose blindness and stupidity were so gross that he could find no place out of the walls of a prison for such a man as Raleigh.

Raleigh remains in prison.

Worn out with weariness and sickness, the old hero continued from time to time to send forth piteous cries to those who, like the Queen, were ready to sympathize

1611.

with him. But towards his enemies he bore himself as proudly as ever, as Northampton found to his cost, when he attempted to extract from him some information of which he was in need.* Poor Raleigh paid for his outspoken language by being placed in closer confinement than before;† but it is hardly likely that, if he could have known what was coming upon him, he would have consented to purchase a remission of the rigours of his imprisonment by flattering Northampton. He consoled himself as best he could with his books and his chemical experiments. It is to his enforced leisure that we owe the 'History of the World;' but we may be sure that he would willingly have surrendered all his fame as an author for one whiff of fresh air in the western seas.

With Carr all things as yet went smoothly. Little dreaming that for him too the Tower gates would one day open, he fancied that life offered nothing more than an unbroken round of folly and amusement. When his highest ambition had been crowned by the honours of the English peerage, it might well seem to him, as he looked round him from such an eminence, that the whole world was beneath his feet.

Death of Archbishop Bancroft.

During the first months of 1611, whilst Carr was looking forward to the honours which were in store for him, and Salisbury was regarding with despair the empty treasury over which he was doomed to preside, James was called upon once more to choose an occupant for one of the most important positions in the kingdom. On the 2nd of November Archbishop Bancroft died. Excepting when he was called upon to stand forward as the champion of the clergy against what he considered

* Northampton to Rochester, July 12, 1611, *S. P. Dom.* lxv. 26.
† Bennet to Carleton, July 15, 1611, *S. P. Dom.* lxv. 32.

the encroachments of the House of Commons or of the judges, the latter years of his life had been passed for the most part in the unostentatious exercise of the duties of his office. After carrying his point at Hampton Court, and seeing the Nonconformist clergy ejected from their cures, he found occupation enough in endeavouring to make those who had submitted more worthy of the position which they held. His efforts were not unattended with success. It is undeniable that, within the limits which had been prescribed by the Elizabethan system, the clergy were advancing under his superintendence in intelligence and vigour. He succeeded in winning over some who by less skilful treatment would have been driven into opposition. The unmeasured violence with which he had met those whom he looked upon as the confirmed enemies of the Church passed away when he had to deal with men whose course was yet doubtful. To such he was always kind, and he spared no labour in inducing them to surrender opinions which he regarded as erroneous.

Expectation that he will be succeeded by Andrewes.

The man who was recommended by the Bishops as the fitting successor of Bancroft was Launcelot Andrewes, at that time Bishop of Ely. Of all those whose piety was remarkable in that troubled age, there was none who could bear comparison for spotlessness and purity of character with the good and gentle Andrewes. Going in and out as he did amongst the frivolous and grasping courtiers who gathered round the King, he seemed to live in a peculiar atmosphere of holiness, which prevented him from seeing the true nature of the evil times in which his lot had fallen. James, indeed, reverenced and admired him, and was always pleased to hear him preach, the more readily, perhaps, because his sermons were not such as were likely to be of any real use to him. What was needed in that Court was the fearless tone and the unbending righteousness of a Latimer or a Knox to rouse the giddy crowd into a sense of the solemn realities in the midst of which they were living. The piety of Andrewes was of too feminine a character for such a work. The ritual observances and the intellectual subtleties in which he delighted, and which in reality conveyed a sense of the Divine presence to his devotional mind, had no power to move the hearts of his thoughtless hearers, who went away interested but unchanged. Those who have the greatest admiration for the sermons which he preached before the Court cannot but feel, when they remember what the audience was to which they were addressed, that one stirring appeal in the mouth of a man who could reason of righteousness, of temperance, and of judgment, would have been worth them all.

He would have been unhappy in the office.

There is no reason to regret that Andrewes was passed by. Few will be found who still believe with Clarendon that his appointment would have turned back the rising tide of Puritanism. Even if his mind had been sufficiently comprehensive to lead him to pursue the conciliatory path in which his kindly disposition would have inclined him to walk, he would have found an insuperable obstacle in the King. He would himself undoubtedly have suffered by the change. The wearing anxiety of the office would have preyed upon his spirits, and he would have found himself but ill at ease when called upon to repress the howling storm of party dissension, which was so soon to test the stability of the edifice which at so great a sacrifice had been raised by Whitgift and his successor.

Selection of Abbot by the King.

After some delay, the King announced that his choice had rested upon George Abbot, the Bishop of London. He had formerly been chaplain to the Earl of Dunbar, through whose hands the greater part of the King's Scottish business passed. He had accompanied him in his visit to Scotland in 1608, and had been serviceable to him when there. It was upon Dunbar's death, in January 1611, that James declared that he had determined to show respect to his memory by promoting Abbot to the Archbishopric. Reasons, however, were not wanting which would have inclined James to turn his thoughts in this direction, independently of the motive by which he professed to be actuated. He was at this time placing himself in strong opposition to the Papal system upon the Continent, and he had been inclined, since the murder of Henry IV., to look with favour upon those who were most opposed to it at home. At the same time, there was a lull in the Puritan controversy. Bancroft's measures had been attended by at least a temporary success, and James may easily have been led to think that the question of Nonconformity was settled for ever. CH. X. 1611.

Under these circumstances, Abbot would seem to be the very man for the vacant post. Thoroughly imbued with the Calvinistic theology, he had made it the business of his life to oppose the doctrines and principles of the Church of Rome. At the same time, he had no wish to see any change in the Church of England, and he was prepared to defend the authority of the Sovereign in ecclesiastical matters, in the maintenance of which he saw the strongest bulwark against Popery and heresy. Nor was he wanting in other qualities more entitled to respect. His piety was deep and real, and his thorough conscientiousness was such that it might safely be predicted that, whatever mistakes he might make in his new office, neither fear nor interest would induce him to swerve for a moment from what he considered to be the strict line of duty. His merits,

These merits were balanced by faults which would have been far more conspicuous than they were, if the management of Church affairs had been left more completely in his hands than James allowed it to be. It was observed of him that he had never had personal experience of pastoral duties, and that, when in 1609 he became a Bishop, he had not been fitted for the exercise of his office by any practical knowledge of the difficulties and trials of the parochial clergy. It may, however, be fairly questioned whether any experience would have given him that knowledge of men and things which was required in order to fulfil satisfactorily the duties of his new position. His mind was deficient in breadth and geniality, and he never could have acquired the capacity for entering into the arguments and feelings of an opponent, which is the first requisite for public life. His theology was the theology of the Puritans, and Puritanism failed to show itself to its best advantage till it had been filtered through the minds of men who were engaged in the active business of life. In his hands, if and defects.

CH. X. 1611.

he had been allowed to have his will, the Church of England would have become as one-sided as it afterwards became in the hands of his opponents. Practices which many pious Christians loved would have been rigorously prescribed, and doctrines which seemed irrefragable to a large and growing section of the clergy would have been checked by the stern exercise of authority. If he was not allowed to carry out his theory into practice, he unfortunately brought with him a temper which boded ill for the prospects of peace. It is said that under his administration the sentences of the High Commission acquired a harsher tone, and that his eagerness to repress heresy and vice led him far beyond the limits which Bancroft had imposed upon himself in the punishment of offenders.

The High Commission Court.

The new Archbishop, upon taking possession of his see, found himself already involved in a quarrel with Coke upon the interminable question of the prohibitions.

Chancey's case.

A certain Sir William Chancey had been charged before the High Commission with adultery, and with having expelled his wife from his house without providing for her maintenance. The Commissioners, after hearing the case, ordered him to support his wife, and to make submission for his offence; and upon his refusal to obey, they committed him to the Fleet. He applied to the Court of Common Pleas for a habeas corpus. The judges unanimously decided that the Commission had no power to imprison for adultery, and that the order to Chancey to find 'a competent maintenance' for his wife was too vague to justify a committal. They therefore ordered that the prisoner should be set at liberty, though they took bail for his future appearance in order that they might have an opportunity of conferring with the Archbishop before they came to a final decision.*

Abbot appeals to the Council against Coke.

Upon hearing what had happened, Abbot, who was as little inclined as Bancroft had been to submit to any diminution of the privileges of the clergy, appealed to the Council.† In consequence of this complaint, the judges were sent for in order that the arguments might

* *Rep.* xii. 82.

† Lansd. MS. 160, fol. 410.

be heard on both sides of the question. Coke, in the name of the four judges of the Court of Common Pleas, produced a treatise which he had drawn up in support of the doctrine that the Commission had no right to fine and imprison excepting in cases of heresy and schism.* A few days later, the judges of the Common Pleas were sent for alone, and every effort was made by the Chancellor to shake their resolution. Finding that it was all in vain, the other judges were sent for, who at once declared that, in their opinion, Coke and his colleagues were in the right. One more attempt was made. The judges of the King's Bench, and the Barons of the Exchequer, were summoned before the King himself, whilst the judges of the Common Pleas were this time excluded from the conference. Before this ordeal some of those who were consulted gave way. When Coke was at last admitted, he was told that the other judges differed from him, and that the King would take care to reform the Commission so as to obviate the objections which had been brought against it. Coke answered that he would reserve his opinion on the new Commission till he saw it, and that, however much he regretted that his brethren differed in opinion from him, he was still more grieved that he had not been allowed to set forth his views in their presence.†

A new Commission issued, in which the judges refuse to take part.

The new Commission, in which the jurisdiction in cases of alimony was omitted,‡ was issued in August. Amongst the names of the Commissioners appeared those of Coke and of six others of the judges, apparently under the idea that they would be tempted to acknowledge the legality of proceedings in which they were themselves called to take a part. The members of the Court were invited to meet at Lambeth in order to hear the Commission read. With the intention of showing that he refused to acknowledge its legality until he had heard the terms in which it was couched, Coke refused to take his seat until the reading of the document was concluded. In this course he was followed by the other judges. As

* 4 *Inst.* 324; Cott. MS., *Faust.* D., vi. fol. 3-11. Lansd. MS. 160, fol. 412.
† *Rep.* xii. 84.
‡ Bacon (*Works*, ed. Montagu), vii. 401.

CH. X. 1611.

soon as the reading was over, they, with one voice, protested against it, as containing points which were contrary to the law of England. Upon this, Abbot had recourse to a scheme which he had planned as being likely to convince even Coke of the advantages which the country would derive from the maintenance of the Court. He ordered two men, who are described as blasphemous heretics, to be introduced, in the expectation that their language would be sufficiently alarming to turn the tide in his favour. He did not know the man with whom he had to deal. In spite of the Archbishop's ingenious device, the judges left the room without having taken their seats in a tribunal which was directed to inflict fine and imprisonment beyond the limits authorized by the law.*

Abbot, however, though flouted by the judges, gained his point. He was sure of the support of the King in maintaining the pretensions of the Court; but he little knew that he was forging a weapon for the hands of the man whom, above all others, he cordially detested, and who would be sure to use it in defence of a system which he himself regarded with the deepest abhorrence. That man was William Laud, at that time a fellow of St. John's, at Oxford. He had frequently come into collision with him in the University, and had done everything in his power to throw obstacles in the path of one who boldly professed his adherence to a very different system of theology from that in which he had himself been trained.

Opposition between Abbot and Laud at Oxford.

It was in Laud that the reaction against Calvinism reached its culminating point. It was inevitable that, in a vigorous nation such as England was, minds should be found who would not be content with the beaten track; it was also inevitable, that those amongst the clergy who were most attached to the institutions of the Church of England, should work out for themselves some system of thought other than that which owed its origin to the Church of Geneva. It was time that a spirit should be breathed into the dry bones of the

* *Rep.* xii. 88. The name of Bancroft is, of course, inserted in this report by mistake for that of Abbot.

Elizabethan Church. Whatever might be the result of their inquiries, it was better that men should seek for Divine truth as the ground on which they founded their ecclesiastical pretensions, than that they should be content to rest them upon maxims of State expediency. From the time of the appearance of Hooker's great work, two theological and ecclesiastical systems were in the field, each appealing for their credentials to Divine authority, and forsaking the lower ground of Acts of Parliament and Royal favour.

The two systems

Even those who have the clearest perception of the evils which arose from the collision between the two systems, may yet be willing to acknowledge that this was a step in advance. The work of Henry VIII. and of Cranmer had accomplished its ends. The authorities of the State were everywhere predominant over the authorities of the Church. The clergy did not dare to stir beyond the limits which might be traced out by the lay Government. Every dream of an independent ecclesiastical authority was at end. But there was a danger lest the Church should subside into a mere tool of the State. It was impossible that men should long preserve their moral dignity, who, when the most prominent institutions of their Church were assailed as unchristian, could only answer that they were content to live under them until they were abolished by an Act of the legislature.

From henceforth all this was at an end. Each of the two rival systems would stand upon its own basis; each would summon men to an investigation of truth; each would declare that it was the duty of the Government to give free scope to the development of the Church, and to assist it in carrying out its principles, instead of regulating its institutions and controlling its actions in obedience to the reasonings and interests of politicians.

The whole theory and practice of the Calvinists circled round the profound conviction that God makes himself known to man by entering into a direct communication with his spirit. The whole theory and practice of their opponents circled round an equally profound conviction that God makes himself known by means of operations external to the individual Christian. Starting from this point, they were ready to ascribe an importance, which appeared to their adversaries to be little short of idolatry, to everything which could speak to the senses and the imagination. With them the place, which in the Calvinistic system was occupied by the preaching of the word, was filled by the sacraments which spoke of a reliance upon God which was not based upon the growth of the understanding or the feelings. Men were to be schooled into piety by habitual attendance upon the services of the Church. At those services nothing unseemly or disorderly was to be permitted by which the mind of the worshipper might be distracted. Uniformity of liturgical forms and uniformity of ecclesiastical ceremony would impress upon every Englishman the lessons of devotion which were to sustain him in the midst of the distractions of the world. This uniformity was to be preserved by the exercise of the authority of the Bishops, who were divinely appointed for its maintenance. The men who held these opinions naturally threw themselves eagerly into the study of the writers of the third and fourth centuries. It was there that they saw the principles prevailing which they had adopted, and it was from thence that they drew arguments by which their cause was to be defended.

counter-balance one another.

It is evident that each of these systems supplied something which was not to be found in the other. At the same time, it was evident that a considerable time must elapse before they would agree to tolerate one another. For some time to come, a violent controversy was to be expected: uncharitable accusations would be made, and fiery words would be flung about from every pulpit in the land; but if the Government would be content to maintain order between the contending parties, no great harm would be done. The great body of the laity would refuse to listen to the violence of noisy partisans. Something would be learned from the more moderate on either side. Puritanism, with its healthy faith and manly vigour, would long have continued to supply the muscle and sinew of English religion, but its narrow severity would have given way to the broader and gentler teaching of the disciples of Hooker and of Andrewes. The storm would have been followed by a calm very different from the stagnation of the eighteenth century.

Danger of Government interference.

If, on the other hand, the Government should determine to interfere, and to lend its aid to establish the unchecked supremacy of either party, the most disastrous consequences would inevitably ensue. Armed with powers sufficient to enforce their own principles upon the whole Church of England, those who were fortunate enough to gain the ear of the King would goad the whole nation into resistance, from which the Sovereign himself would hardly escape scathless.

Character of Laud.

Of those to whom Calvinism was distasteful, Laud was the most decided in his opposition. Of all men then living he was the least fitted to be entrusted with political power. No less conscientious than Abbot, he was still more riveted to the system which he had adopted. To him the words might have been applied which were afterwards used of Robespierre: 'This man will go far, for he believes every word he says.' His thorough belief in the unbounded efficacy of external forms and institutions, combined with his complete ignorance of human nature, would be sufficient to goad to madness any nation which might be subjected to his control. Within the limits which his system allowed him he was all that could be desired. He was ever anxious to do good, and was unwearied in his labours for what he considered to be the cause of God, of the Church, and of his country.

His theory of the divine right of Episcopacy.

The question which brought Laud into collision with the Calvinists at Oxford was one which placed the principles of the contending parties in distinct relief. In his exercise for the degree of Bachelor of Divinity he maintained not only that Episcopacy was of Divine origin, but that no congregation could be considered to form part of the Church which was not under the government of a Bishop. It was objected to him that, in that case, he unchurched the whole body of the foreign Protestants.*

* This answer has, I think, been misunderstood by those who reply that if Laud's theory was true, it was to no purpose to urge that it led to unpleasant consequences. It was an *argumentum ad absurdum*. The consequences are manifestly false, therefore the theory cannot be true.

He might have answered, if he had chosen, that Abbot's theory unchurched St. Anselm and St. Bernard; for Abbot would acknowledge no Church excepting where what he considered to be pure doctrine was preached. From that time Laud was regarded as a mere Papist by the Calvinist party, which was in the majority amongst the elder members of the university. This he certainly was not, though he looked at many questions from the same point of view as that from which they would be regarded by the Catholics. He doubtless found consolation in the support of that large number of the younger members of the university who supported him in his opinions.

He is elected President of St. John's.

Towards the end of 1610, Abbot's friends were thrown into dismay by hearing that Laud was likely to acquire an influential position at Oxford. It was known that Buckeridge, the President of St. John's, was to be appointed to the vacant see of Rochester, and that he was using all his influence with the fellows to induce them to appoint Laud as his successor. News of the apprehended danger was carried to Abbot, who immediately waited upon Ellesmere, who had been at Bancroft's death elected Chancellor of the University, and persuaded him to represent to the King the danger of allowing a man so deeply tainted with Popery to occupy a post of such importance. Laud, however, found an advocate in his patron Neile, the Bishop of Coventry and Lichfield, and the election was allowed to proceed. On the 10th of May, 1611, he was chosen President; but as there was some irregularity in the proceedings, an attempt was made to set the election aside. The King, whose intervention was asked, referred the matter to Bilson, who, as Bishop of Winchester, was the Visitor of the College. Bilson reported that the irregularity certainly existed, and suggested that James should take advantage of it to claim the nomination for himself. James begged him to let him know whether the error in the proceedings had been intentionally committed. In the end, he summoned the parties before himself, and, after an examination which lasted for three days, he decided that the election was to stand good, as there was reason to suppose that the mistake had resulted simply from a misunderstanding of the statutes. He refused to take advantage of Bilson's suggestion, which would, as he said, be a bad example for the future.*

Controversy of James with Vorstius.

Abbot was more successful in directing the current of the King's indignation against the learned Conrad Vorstius, who had recently been appointed professor of theology in the University of Leyden. His opinions concerning the nature of God † were such as in our own days would certainly disqualify him from holding such an office in any Christian University. Connected as Holland and England then were, in the defence of their common religion, there would have been nothing strange if James had contented himself with offering a friendly remonstrance to the States. Such a course, however, would not have satisfied him. He threw himself into the quarrel with all the zeal of a theological controversialist. He had on his side Maurice and the greater part of the Dutch clergy. On the other hand, the statesmen of Holland, and the mercantile aristocracy which they represented, were on the side of toleration. Their opposition brought down upon their heads a whole torrent of protests and invectives from the Royal theologian. It was only after a long resistance that the fear of alienating the King of England from their cause, induced them to give way, and Vorstius was ordered to resign his professorship.

Burning of Legate and Wightman.

Whilst this controversy was still in progress, James found an opportunity for the establishment of his reputation for orthodoxy nearer home. An unfortunate man, named Edward Wightman, was convicted by Bishop Neile of holding several distinct heresies. About the same time a question arose in London as to what was to be done with a man named Bartholomew Legate, who professed Arian opinions. Legate had frequently been brought into the presence of James, who had finally, upon his confessing that he had ceased to pray to

* Laud's *Diary*. Answer to Lord Say's speech, (Laud's Works, iii. 34; vi. 88.) Bilson to the King, June 14, 1611. The King to Bilson, June (?) and Sept. 23, 1611, *S. P. Dom.*, lxiv. 35, 36; lxvi. 25.

† *Winw.* iii. 294.

CH. X. 1612. Christ for seven years, driven him out of his presence. He was then brought before the Consistory Court of the Bishop of London, by which he was committed to Newgate. Having been released, he had the imprudence to threaten to bring an action against the Court for false imprisonment, and he was again arrested, in order to be brought once more to trial.

Unfortunately, James was in the full flush of his controversy with Vorstius. It was not to be borne that the heresy against which he was contending in Holland should rear its head in his own dominions. Elizabeth had burnt two heretics, and why should not he do the same? There was, however, some doubt as to the legality of the proceedings which were contemplated; and it was necessary to take the opinion of at least some of the judges. Coke, as was known, believed that the proposed execution was illegal. Abbot was therefore directed to write to Ellesmere, requesting him to choose some among the judges who were to be consulted on the point, and informing him that the King would not be sorry if Coke were excluded from the number.*

It must not, however, be imagined that Coke had any scruples on the score of humanity; it was with him, like everything else, a mere question of law, and he never had the slightest doubt that it was perfectly lawful to burn a heretic; but he believed that it was necessary to obtain a conviction before the High Commission before a writ could issue out of Chancery for the execution. Hobart and Bacon, together with the judges who were consulted, declared that a conviction before the Bishop's court would be sufficient.†

Upon this it was determined to proceed against Legate

* Abbot to Ellesmere, Jan. 21 and 22, 1612, *Egerton Papers*, 447.

† The Act of Elizabeth, it was agreed, abolished all statutes concerning the burning of heretics. Coke held that, previously to the reign of Henry IV., heretics had been burnt by Convocation alone, and that the judicial powers of Convocation were now vested in the High Commission. The other lawyers held that Bishops had exercised jurisdiction over heresy before the reign of Henry IV., and that they consequently retained those powers, though they could no longer make use of the Act of Henry IV. to require the sheriff to burn the heretic. It would now be necessary to obtain a writ *de heretico comburendo* out of Chancery.—3 *Inst.* 39; *Rep.* xii. 56, 93; Hale, *Pleas of the Crown*, part i. chap. 30.

in the Consistory Court. As even the judges, who held that such a course would be legal, thought it would be advisable to cite the prisoner before the High Commission, the only explanation of the course which was taken is, that James was anxious to show that he was able to override the opinions of Coke.

The conviction followed as a matter of course, and the writ was issued out of Chancery without remonstrance from any quarter; and, on the 18th of March, the wretched man was burnt at Smithfield. A few days later, Wightman suffered a similar fate at Lichfield.

It seems strange to us that not a word was uttered against this horrible cruelty. As we read over the brief contemporary notices which have reached us, we look in vain for the slightest intimation that the death of these two men was regarded with any other feelings than those with which the writers were accustomed to hear of the execution of an ordinary murderer. If any remark was made, it was in praise of James for the devotion which he showed to the cause of God. Happily, if men of education failed to regard these acts of tyranny in their true light, there was a spirit abroad amongst the common people which warned the King that there was nothing to be gained by a repetition of the experiment which had been tried. When, a few years afterwards, a Spanish Arian was convicted of heresy, he was allowed to linger out the rest of his life in prison. This was bad enough, but it was at least a step in advance. Since the judicial murder of Wightman, no such atrocity has again disgraced the soil of England.*

The Princess Elizabeth.

If nothing had been done during the year which followed upon the dissolution of Parliament to win the confidence of the nation by any wise course of domestic policy, Salisbury took care that, as far as lay in his power, the English Government should not recede from

* Fuller, v. 418, *State Trials*, ii. 727. I have no doubt that the Spaniard mentioned by Fuller is the one whom James proposed, in 1618, to send back to his own country by way of showing mercy to him. It is to be hoped that Fuller's account of his perpetual imprisonment is correct, and that, at all events, he did not fall into the hands of the Inquisition.—Brent to Carleton, Feb. 14; Chamberlain to Carleton, Feb. 28; Herbert to Carleton, March 20, 1618, *S. P. Dom.* xcvi. 16, 37, 68.

CH. X.
1611.

the position which it had occupied abroad after the death of Henry IV. It was his anxious wish that the alliance with the enemies of the House of Austria might be strengthened by the marriages of the King's children.* The Lady Elizabeth had grown up, far from the frivolities and dissipations of the Court, at Combe Abbey, under the watchful care of Lord and Lady Harrington. No better school could have been found for her than a country house, presided over by a master and mistress who gained the respect and the love of all who knew them. From them she learned the religion, free from fanaticism or superstition, which was at no distant date to support her under no ordinary trials. In the spring of 1611, she had not completed her fifteenth year, but she was already noted for a grace and discretion beyond her years. She was the darling of her brother Henry, and she won golden opinions from young and old at her father's Court, to which she was now transferred.† Young as she was, proposals had already been made for her hand. Amongst them had been one on behalf of the youthful heir to the throne of Sweden, who was afterwards to be so well known as the great Gustavus Adolphus. All these suitors, however, had on various grounds been rejected, and it was not till the beginning of 1611 that an offer was made which James thought worthy of being taken into consideration.

Proposed marriage with the Elector Palatine.

The Elector Palatine, to whose wisdom and firmness the Protestant Union owed its existence, had died in the previous year, leaving his son, Frederick V., a minor. Not long before his death, the old Elector had made advances to the English Court, with a view of obtaining the hand of Elizabeth for his heir. They had been not unfavourably received, but they do not appear to have assumed the form of a definite proposal. The idea was taken up, after the death of the Elector, by his widow, daughter of the great William of Orange, and by her brother-in-law, the Duke of Bouillon, one of the leaders of the French Protestants. In January 1611, Bouillon

* Elizabeth was now again James's only daughter. The two children, Mary and Sophia, who had been born after his accession to the English throne, had both died in their infancy.

† Green, *Princesses of England*, vol. v.

met Edmondes in Paris, and sounded him as to the reception which a proposal for such an alliance would obtain in England.* Edmondes wrote home for instructions. The answer was satisfactory. He was to inform the Duke that no formal reply could be given till a formal demand had been made. He was, however, to understand that the prospect of such a match was regarded by the King with a favourable eye. Bouillon communicated what he had done to the Electress, who highly approved of his proceedings. It was, however, impossible to send a formal proposal at once, as it would be necessary to secure the consent of the three guardians of her son, Count Maurice, the Prince of Anhalt, and Count John of Nassau.†

Offer made on behalf of the Prince of Piedmont.

Another offer had already been made. A few days after the letter was written in which the Government expressed their approbation of the match with the Elector, the Spanish Ambassador asked whether James would be willing to give his daughter to the eldest son of the Duke of Savoy. The Duke had by this time discovered that he had no hope of obtaining the French Princess who had been promised by Henry IV. to his son, and was anxiously looking about for a new alliance. It was impossible that such a marriage could find favour with the English people. The Duke, indeed, was by no means likely at any time to prove a subservient follower of his brother-in-law the King of Spain; but he was not strong enough to stand alone, and unless he were supported by France, he could hardly be expected to play an independent part against the master of the Milanese. The only object which he had in view during the whole of his stirring life, was the extension of his scanty territory; and even if James could bring himself to send his daughter into exile to a land where the religion which she had learned in her childhood was unknown, policy would forbid him from contracting a close alliance with a Prince who was too weak and too distant to afford any aid to England.‡

* Council to Edmondes, Feb. 7. Edmondes to Salisbury, Jan. 19, 1611, *S. P. Fr.*

† Edmondes to Salisbury, April 24, 1611, *S. P. Fr.*

‡ These and similar arguments were used by Raleigh a few weeks later,

CH. X.
1611.

The Duke of Savoy proposes a double marriage.

James, however, though he did not look upon the proposal with favour, was not inclined to throw away a chance which might be useful if the negotiations with the Electress Palatine failed. He accordingly gave orders that the Count of Cartignana, who was to come as Ambassador from the Duke of Savoy, should be allowed to lay his proposals before the Council. To the astonishment of the English Government, he asked that not only should the Princess be given to his master's son, but that a marriage should be contracted between the Prince of Wales and a daughter of the Duke of Savoy. He added that he had no authority to treat for one match without the other. He was at once told that the King would enter into no negotiations upon such a basis. He replied that it would be necessary for him to return home, but that it was possible that he might come back with proposals for a single marriage. Before he went, he was informed that although the King would not refuse to consider the propriety of bestowing the hand of his daughter upon the Prince of Piedmont, such a match could only be taken into consideration if the Duke were prepared to guarantee to her the free exercise of her religion.*

The Spanish Ambassador proposes that the Prince of Wales shall marry the Infanta.

When Cartignana left England, Salisbury probably hoped that, before he returned, all the difficulties which lay in the way of a complete alliance with a Protestant power would be removed. Not many days, however, had passed after his departure, before the Spanish Ambassador informed the Government that he was now instructed to propose an alliance which he had already recommended at various times in an informal manner. If the King of England, he said, were willing to make a proposal on behalf of the Prince of Wales for the eldest daughter of the King of Spain, the Infanta Anne, such an offer would not meet with a refusal at Madrid. It was not the first time that such a scheme had been heard of since the negotiations had been broken off in 1606, in consequence

in his 'Discourse touching a Marriage between the Lady Elizabeth and the Prince of Piedmont,' which he wrote at the request of the Prince of Wales. —Works, viii. 223.

* Salisbury to Winwood, April 3, 1611, *Winw.* iii. 271.

CH. X. 1611.

of the ill feeling which existed between the two countries after the detection of the Gunpowder Plot. In 1607, hints had been thrown out to Cornwallis, that Spain would be glad to see the subject again brought forward. In the following year nothing more was heard of these suggestions, as the Spaniards were at that time employing the Infanta as a bait to induce Henry IV. to retire from his alliance with the Dutch Republic. These hopes proving fruitless, they determined once more to try what could be done with James. At the very time when the signature of the Spanish plenipotentiaries was being affixed to the Truce of Antwerp,* a most extraordinary proposal was made to Cornwallis. The Ambassador who represented the Duke of Savoy at Madrid came to him one day, and told him that he was empowered by the King of Spain to offer to the Prince of Wales the whole of the Netherlands as a dowry with the Infanta, provided that James would join the Spaniards in a stratagem by which it was hoped that the reduction of the rebellious provinces might be effected. Cornwallis at once answered that his master would never listen to any such proposal.

Digby directed to demand the Infanta.

When the offer of an alliance was repeated in 1611, Salisbury probably suspected, what was really the case, that the King of Spain never had any intention of giving his daughter to an English Prince.† James, however, was unable to resist the bait held out to him, and directed Sir John Digby, the new Ambassador, who was on the point of setting out for Spain, to demand the Infanta for the Prince, if he found that the Spaniards were in earnest and were willing to agree to reasonable conditions.

* In April, 1609. These details are derived from two undated and anonymous papers preserved among the *S. P.* in the Spanish correspondence of 1611. They were evidently written by Cornwallis at a much later date.

† In 1613, Digby procured copies of the instructions to the Spanish Ambassadors, extending over some years, and discovered that there had never been any intention to do more than, by amusing James, to obtain freedom of action for the Catholics in England. It was hoped that they would grow in strength, and that a Spanish party would thus be formed (Digby to the King, June 4, 1613, *S. P. Sp.*). It is here that the valuable series of extracts from the Archives of Simancas commences, which has been published by M. Guizot, in the *Revue des Deux Mondes* (July 15, 1862). They have come most opportunely to me, and have enabled me to make

CH. X.
1611.
The Spanish Government draws back.

Fortunately, when Digby arrived, he found that the Spanish Government was by no means anxious for the alliance. In all probability, instructions had been sent to the Spanish Ambassador in London to make propositions of this kind, without the remotest idea that James would ever think seriously of accepting them. By this means he might be induced to look upon the King of Spain as his friend, and something might be gained for the English Catholics, and for the anti-Protestant cause in Europe. When Digby presented himself to the King of Spain, and made the request which he was authorized to lay before him, he caused no little confusion in the Court of Madrid. Accordingly, Philip passed Digby on to Lerma, who, as soon as he saw him, began to make excuses. He said that, although he should be glad if such a marriage could take place, the difference of religion was an obstacle which could only be removed by the Pope; and that if the King thought that his daughter would be drawn away from her faith, he would not consent to see her married to a heretic if it were to save his kingdom.* In spite of these obstacles, however, the matter should be taken into consideration, and in due time an answer should be given. The fact was, as Digby soon learned, that the Queen-Regent of France had proposed that the double marriage, to which she had been unable to obtain her husband's consent, should now be

some additions to my narrative. On the other hand, M. Guizot, not having had the advantage of a perusal of the English correspondence in the Record Office, has been led to attribute to James, in these early negotiations, a far greater eagerness to begin the negotiations than I believe to have been the case. He takes the view put forward by the Spanish Government, that James on the occasion took the initiative, 'rattachant sa proposition aux paroles prononcées à Londres par les ambassadeurs de sa majesté catholique.' Digby's correspondence shows plainly that a direct intimation was given by the Spanish Ambassador that his master was ready to listen to a proposal for his daughter's hand. It is in some respects difficult to explain his doing so, but of the fact there can be no doubt. Further on, M. Guizot gives us a series of papers relating to the discussions in Spain in 1614. He seems, however, not to have been aware of the resumption of the negotiations in 1615, and has consequently been led to give an erroneous interpretation to the facts connected with Lord Hay's mission in 1616. It is thus that historical evidence starts up in various places generally incomplete in itself, but combining with other portions of evidence elsewhere in existence.

* Digby to — Birch, *Life of Henry Prince of Wales*, 530. Instructions to Digby, April 7, 1611; Digby to Salisbury, June 18, 1611, *S. P. Sp.*

contracted; and that the Spaniards rightly judged that an alliance with a Catholic sovereign was more likely to prove lasting than one with Protestant England. Some weeks later, Digby was informed that the Ambassador in England had exceeded his instructions, and that the Infanta Anne was to become the wife of the young King of France. If, however, the Prince of Wales would be content with her sister Maria, Spain would be ready to negotiate on the subject. In reporting this conversation, Digby begged the King to give up all thought of a Spanish match for the Prince. The Infanta Maria, he told him, was a mere child, not yet six years of age, and it was certain that the Spaniards were only desirous of playing upon his credulity.* Salisbury was delighted with the turn matters had taken. The Prince, he said, could find roses elsewhere, he need not trouble himself about this Spanish olive.† James, perhaps ashamed of having been deceived so thoroughly, was only anxious to let the matter drop. But the Spanish Government thought that it would be still possible to keep up the delusion. They continued to send messages to induce him to listen to their proposal, telling him that the King of Spain would be ready to agree to the marriage with his younger daughter, if only matters of religion could be accommodated. Upon this, James asked what they meant when they talked about accommodating matters of religion? Lerma had the insolence to answer, that they expected that the Prince of Wales should become a Catholic. After this, it is needless to say that the negotiation came to an end.

James consents to the marriage of the Princess with the Elector.

In November Cartignana returned to England with instructions to ask for the Princess alone.‡ But he soon discovered that his journey had been to no purpose. The remonstrances of Salisbury, backed as he was by the great majority of the nation,§ had not been ineffectual, and the treatment which James had received from the

* Digby to the King, Aug. 9, 1611, *S. P. Sp.*
† Salisbury to Winwood, *Winw.* iii. 239.
‡ Chamberlain to Carleton, Nov. 13, 1611, *Court and Times of James I.* i. 144.
§ Tidings from England, Dec. 1611, *S. P. Dom.* lxvii. 118.

CH. X. 1611.

King of Spain* was not likely to influence him in favour of his nephew. He was, however, unwilling to give a decided answer in the negative till he was certain that the Electress was in earnest. In December, he discovered that there could be no further doubt upon that point, and he at once gave up all thought of assenting to the Savoy alliance.† Cartignana returned home, complaining of the indignity which had been put upon his master in placing him in the balance with a German Elector.

1612. Treaty of alliance with the Union.

To show that something more than a merely family alliance was intended, James directed Winwood to attend the meeting of the German Protestants at Wesel, in the beginning of the ensuing year, and to assent to a treaty,‡ by which the King of England and the Princes of the Union agreed upon the succours which were mutually to be afforded to one another in case of an attack by the common enemy. The envoys who brought this treaty to England for ratification were empowered to make a formal demand for the hand of Elizabeth; and, on the 16th of May, in the presence of Bouillon, who had come over on a special mission from the Queen Regent, the marriage contract was signed.§

Signature of the marriage contract.

Salisbury's illness and death.

Amongst the signatures, the name of the man who more than any other contributed to this result is wanting. Worn out with labours which through the fault of others had brought no reward with them, Salisbury, though he had not yet completed his forty-ninth year, had grown prematurely old. Even as early as at the opening of the session in which he called upon the Commons to assist him in bearing the financial burdens which weighed so heavily upon him, he seems to have felt a presentiment that his life would not last much longer. But it was not till the close of the following year that he was overtaken by disease. In December 1611, he had an attack

* The proposal to substitute the younger for the elder sister had already been made. The final insult of demanding that the Prince should become a Catholic was not offered till the following spring.

† Edmondes to Salisbury, Dec. 21; Salisbury to Edmondes, Dec. 26, 1611, *S. P. Fr.*

‡ Signed March 28, Rymer, xvi. 714.

§ Rymer, xvi. 722.

of rheumatism in his right arm. Towards the end of the month, it had almost entirely passed away.* A few weeks later he was seized with an ague, which was accompanied by symptoms which indicated that his whole system was breaking up.† From this condition he rallied, and it was supposed that the danger was at an end. In the second week in March he was able to walk in his garden, and began to apply himself to the business of his office. A few days later it was given out that he was completely recovered, and that his illness had never been serious.‡ The change did not last long. The physicians were unable to discover the nature of the disorder which was again settling upon him. Towards the end of April, he made up his mind to try the Bath waters, though he was told that the place would only prove injurious to him. He was anxious to be quiet, and to lose sight of the men who, as he well knew, were only waiting for his death to scramble for his offices. Before he went, he twice dragged himself to the Council Table, and on each occasion spoke for no less than two hours.§ He remained at Bath for sixteen days. At first he revived a little, but afterwards he rapidly grew worse. His mind was troubled by the remembrance of the plotters in London, and he could not rest satisfied without making one more effort to show them that he was still alive. In this determination he was strengthened by his dislike of what he called the suffocating sulphurous air of Bath. Summoning the last remains of his strength, he set out for London. He never accomplished his journey. On the 24th of May he breathed his last at the parsonage house at Marlborough.‖

When the dying statesman left Bath, his steps had

* Chamberlain to Carleton, Dec. 4 and 18, *Court and Times*, i. 151.

† More to Winwood, Jan. 25, and Feb. 17, 1612, *Winw.* iii. 331, 337.

‡ Chamberlain to Carleton, Feb. 26, March 11 and 21, 1612 (*Court and Times*, i. 135, 137; *S. P. Dom.* lxviii. 78). Here, as in several instances, the editor of the valuable collection published as the *Court and Times of James I.*, has misplaced the letters, having forgotten to alter the date with the change in the commencement of the year.

§ Chamberlain to Carleton. March 25, *Court and Times*, i. 162, April 29, 1612, *S. P.* lxviii. 104.

‖ Chamberlain to Carleton, May 27, *Court and Times*, i. 168; Finett to Trumbull, May 28, 1612, *Winw.* iii. 367.

CH. X. 1612.

been hastened by a desire to show himself once more in London, to the discomfiture of his rivals. Before he reached Marlborough, all such thoughts seem to have left him for ever. If he expressed any anxiety, it was that his children might live virtuous and religious lives. When he spoke of himself, his words were those of a man who had been too much occupied with the affairs of life to know much about theological questions. Whatever his faults were, and they were many, he had in the main striven to do his duty to his country. Whatever may be the truth concerning the dark intrigues with the Spanish Ambassador, or concerning those more private vices with which rumour delighted to blacken his fame, to all appearance, at least, he died as one who was aware of having committed many faults, but who was ignorant of any deed which might weigh down his conscience in the hour of death, and who had kept the simplicity of his faith intact. The victories and the defeats of the world were all forgotten now. Quietly and calmly the last of the Elizabethan statesmen went to his rest.*

Unpopularity of Salisbury.

The news of the Treasurer's death was received in London with satisfaction. The heartless Northampton and his followers fancied that the time was now come when they might rule England unchecked, and might divide the spoils of office amongst themselves. Bacon believed that a free field would now at last be open for the exercise of his talents and for the reforms upon which he had meditated so long. James had long been weary of the yoke, and was by no means sorry to be rid of his monitor. Nor was it only at Court that the dead man's name was regarded with aversion. The popular party, which was daily growing in strength, looked upon him as the author of the hated impositions. Many who cared little about politics, only knew him as the great man who had kept the reins of government in his own hands, and who himself was rich whilst the Exchequer was lying empty. Other causes have made posterity unjust to his memory. The system of government which he upheld was deservedly doomed, and when

* Observations of Mr. John Bowles, Peck's *Desiderata Curiosa*, 205.

it had passed away, it was hard to believe that anyone could innocently have taken part in practices which a later age condemned as oppressive and injurious to the welfare of the nation. It was still harder to imagine that the man who succeeded whilst Essex and Raleigh, Northumberland and Bacon, failed, could have prospered except by the most unscrupulous treachery.

Defects of his character.

No doubt he had faults enough upon which such accusations could fasten themselves. That he stood alone, as he did, proves that there was some radical defect in his character. For steady application to business, and for moderation in action, he was unrivalled amongst his contemporaries. But he was too apt to look upon his own character as if it were the only type in which the mind of a statesman should be cast. The irregularities of genius simply perplexed him. He had no sympathy with the fervid imagination of Raleigh, or with the grand schemes of Bacon. Whilst Elizabeth lived all was well, she kept her Secretary firmly in his post to do the work for which he was most fitted, and she gave ear, as occasion served, to other counsellors who could tell her things of which the sober Cecil never dreamed. But when James came to the throne, all this was at an end. In his head there was no room for more than one side of a question at a time. If he was to be guided by Cecil at all, he must be guided by him altogether. There is no need to imagine conscious deceit in the successful minister: of himself and of his own policy he believed eveything good; of Raleigh and his policy he believed everything bad. He only told James what he thought. When the catastrophe came, Cecil fully believed that his rival was capable of the crime of which he was accused, and half believed that he had committed it. He did his utmost to secure him a fair trial, but, when the jury pronounced against him, he left him to his fate. As it was with Raleigh, so it was with Bacon. Bacon, he thought, would throw everything into confusion with his schemes of reform. It would be better to keep him at a distance.

As it always happens, with these motives were mingled others of a baser character. Unconsciously, no doubt,

CH. X. 1612.

the love of power grew upon him with the use of it, and he began to think that it was only in the natural course of things that all the business of the Government should pass through his hands.

Salisbury's want of sympathy with the foremost men of his own generation prevented him from attracting round him the rising talent of the next. He founded no political school; he left behind him no watchword by which the leaders in the great conflict which was so soon to break out could arouse the flagging energies of their followers; he threw no light upon the questions which were for such a length of time to agitate the minds of his countrymen; he stood alone whilst he lived, and when he died there were few to mourn his loss.

Causes of his failure not in himself,

And yet, strange to say, it was not to the defects of his character that his failure as a statesman is to be attributed. Bacon spoke truly of him when he said that he was fit to prevent affairs from growing worse, though he was not fit to make them better. James, in his reply, let it be known that he thought that Salisbury had failed in preventing his affairs from growing worse. The statement was true, but it was not true that the fault lay at Salisbury's door. It was James, whose extravagance had driven the Treasurer to the necessity of laying the impositions which raised such ill-feeling between the nation and the Crown. It was James, whose ignorance and self-will brought about the failure of the great contract by which all causes of dissatisfaction would have been removed. If Salisbury had been allowed to take his own way, all would have been well. If he could have kept affairs from growing worse, everything would have been gained. There can be no doubt that, even as late as in 1610, if he had been left to himself, he would have restored the old relations which existed at the death of Elizabeth between the Government and the Commons. The reforms which the nation demanded would never indeed have originated with him. He did not feel their necessity, and probably looked with suspicion upon such sweeping innovations. But as soon as he saw that the House of Commons was bent upon obtaining them he gave way. He had been brought up in the

but in the King.

school of Elizabeth, and he had learned to prize the doctrine, that though the executive Government was never to submit to the direct interference of the Lower House, nothing could be more dangerous than a policy which was likely to lead to a permanent disagreement between the Crown and the representatives of the people. He may well have felt sad during the last years of his life, knowing, as he did, that he might have saved the monarchy, if the Sovereign had not stepped in to frustrate his attempt.

His foreign policy.

If his foreign policy has been praised at the expense of his domestic, it has been because he had freer scope, and that it was not till after his death that James strayed from the right path. It was marked by the same peculiar characteristics: want of originality, and a tendency to indecision as fresh complications arose, were his besetting sins. But they were almost redeemed by the readiness with which he applied himself to master the real circumstances of the case, and the good judgment with which he almost invariably chose the right course at last. Of the great blot of his life, his acceptance of the Spanish pension, it is difficult to speak without knowing the peculiar circumstances under which he permitted himself to decline so far from the paths of rectitude. But even under the most favourable construction it betrays a want of sensitiveness in his character to the distinction between right and wrong, which is almost enough to make us forget the services which he undoubtedly rendered to his country.

His industry.

Of his unwearied industry it is needless to speak.* His presence at the Treasury breathed at once a new spirit into the financial administration. Nothing was too small to escape him. He succeeded without difficulty in raising the revenue to an amount which would have filled Elizabeth with admiration, though it was all too little for her successor. All the while he was carrying on the business which came thickly upon him in the office of Secretary, which he continued to hold; but

* A good sketch of what he effected in his office will be found in Sir Walter Cope's Apology, printed in Gutch's *Collectanea Curiosa*, i. 119.

CH. X. 1612.

however ably he discharged the duties of his place, it could hardly be expected that the aspirants for office could look on with satisfaction whilst he engrossed the whole work and credit of government. It remained to be seen whether those who were so eager to occupy his seat would be able to imitate his wisdom.

The Treasury put in Commission.

It was generally expected that the white staff of the late Lord Treasurer would be placed in the hands of Northampton; but Northampton was by no means eager at such a time to take upon himself the responsibilities of the office. The Treasury was therefore entrusted to the charge of Commissioners. Their names were not likely to inspire confidence in their skill. The only man amongst them who had any practical acquaintance with finance was Sir Julius Cæsar, the Chancellor of the Exchequer, and even he had no abilities above those which might be possessed by any experienced clerk. The high-sounding names of the Earls of Northampton, Suffolk, and Worcester, and of Lords Zouch and Wotton, only served to fill up the list.*

Candidates for the Secretaryship.

Far more eagerness was shown to obtain the Secretaryship, which did not entail the labour of watching over an empty Exchequer. The post was coveted by a large number of persons, each of whom imagined that he had the best claim to succeed to the deceased statesman. Gradually, however, the numbers of those who had any chance of obtaining the object of their desires diminished; and at last it was rumoured among the courtiers that the choice lay between Sir Henry Wotton, Sir Thomas Lake, and Sir Henry Nevill.†

Sir Henry Wotton.

Sir Henry Wotton was supported by the influence of the Queen, and at first even by that of the Prince of Wales. He was looked upon as a man likely to walk in the path which had been traced out by Salisbury. It was reported that before his death Salisbury had intended to resign the Secretaryship in his favour. He was a man of integrity and ability, and had won the regard of James as well by his reputation for learning as by a service

* Chamberlain to Carleton, June 17, 1612, *Court and Times*, i. 173. Lord Wotton was a brother of Sir Henry.

† Chamberlain to Carleton, June 11, 1612, *Court and Times*, i. 171.

which he had rendered him before his accession to the English throne. There was something in him of that steadiness and solidity of character for which Salisbury had been distinguished, and it is certain that he would never have been the advocate of any rash or extreme measures; but it is hardly likely that he would have succeeded as a statesman. Even if he had been naturally qualified to act as the guide of a nation, which requires in its leaders sympathy with its noblest aspirations, his long absence from his native land was sufficient to create a wide gulf between himself and his fellow-countrymen. Since he had completed his education, he had spent the greater part of his life in Italy, at first by choice, and latterly as Ambassador at Venice. The opposition which had been aroused by nine years of misgovernment found no echo in his breast. He had only heard of the errors of his Sovereign through the medium of a distant correspondence. If he had learned in Italy to be tolerant of differences of opinion, he had also learned to think less of that great cause of Protestantism for which England, if she remained true to her principles, would soon be called upon to do battle once more.*

Sir Thomas Lake.

Sir Thomas Lake was a man of a very different character. He had no pretensions to be anything more than a diligent and ready official. No scheme of policy, domestic or foreign, was ever connected with his name. Of the three rivals he is the only one of whom we hear that he offered a bribe to obtain the post which he coveted. His promotion would hardly have given pleasure to any one, excepting perhaps to Northampton.

Sir Henry Nevill.

The candidate whose selection would have given most satisfaction to the nation, was undoubtedly Sir Henry Nevill. In the reign of Elizabeth, he had served with credit as Ambassador at Paris. He was in London at the time when Essex was planning his foolish and unprincipled rebellion, and had unfortunately been made acquainted with a portion at least of the schemes of

* The manifest dislike which he felt for his embassy to Holland in 1614–15 is enough to show how he felt in this matter. Winwood would never have begged to be removed to Italy or Spain. I have taken my view of Wotton from his voluminous unpublished correspondence in the Record Office.

CH. X. 1613.

the conspirators. There was no reason to suppose that he sympathized with them in the slightest degree; but either from thoughtlessness, or from regard for his informants, he omitted to give information to the Government of what he had heard. As this amounted to misprision of treason, he was committed to the Tower, from which he was only released at the accession of James, in company with Southampton and the other conspirators who had escaped the scaffold. In the Parliament which met in the following year he sat for Berkshire, and although he refrained from taking any prominent part in opposition to the Government, there was never any doubt that his sympathies were with the popular party. A little before the end of the first session of 1610, he took an opportunity of stating to the King, in the plainest possible terms, what the demands of that party were, and of pressing upon him the necessity of giving way. It is evident that the elevation of such a man to the secretaryship would have been equivalent to a declaration on the part of the King, that he was willing to retrace his steps, and in future to govern in accordance with the wishes of the House of Commons. The members of the last Parliament who happened to be in London, came flocking round their candidate. Southampton came up from the country, hoping that the time was now come when the friends of Essex might be admitted to power, and did all he could to forward his prospects.

James determines to be his own secretary.

Even if James had been otherwise disposed to look upon Nevill with favour, all this would have been sufficient to move his jealousy. Although, from some unexplained motive, Rochester gave his support to the popular candidate, the King at once declared against him, saying that he would have no secretary imposed upon him by Parliament.* He let it be known that he had no thoughts, for the present at least, of making an appointment at all. He imagined that he was perfectly capable of acting as his own secretary, and of directing the complicated machinery of the domestic and foreign policy of the Government himself. Lake would

* Chamberlain to Carleton, June 11 and 17, July 2, 1612, *Court and Times*, i. 171, 173, 179.

be sufficiently capable of receiving and sending out the despatches and other necessary documents. If he needed any assistance beyond this, Rochester, who had recently been raised to the dignity of a Privy Councillor, would be with him. Rochester, no doubt, had no very close acquaintance with state affairs, but he had at least the qualities which would make him a useful tool, and there was no reason to suppose that, owing everything, as he did, to the bounty of James, he would ever be otherwise than devoted to his master. In the same spirit the King chose Sir George Carew* out of many competitors for the Mastership of the Court of Wards; apparently on the principle that a candidate who was in no way distinguished amongst his contemporaries was more likely than an abler man to submit without questioning to the bidding of his Sovereign. James never learned that, by refusing to admit ability and genius into his service, he cast the greatest reflection upon himself.

Quarrel between Maxwell and Hawley.

The position which Rochester had been for some time gradually assuming was not likely to conciliate the good will of the English towards his countrymen. Indeed, it was not without difficulty that James succeeded in keeping the peace. At the festivities with which the Duke of Bouillon and the German Commissioners had been received, the ill-feeling between the English and the Scotch nearly led to actual violence. Amongst those who were present on one occasion, was a gentleman named Hawley, a member of the Temple. He gave some slight offence to one of the gentlemen ushers, a Scotchman of the name of Maxwell. Maxwell, instead of remonstrating, seized him by the ear to drag him out of the palace. Next day, all the Inns of Court were talking over the outrage, and the members came in crowds to Hawley, offering to support him in the quarrel. His first step was to send a challenge to Maxwell. Here, however, he was stopped. The King, who had heard what had happened, sent for him. Such was the feeling against the way in which James supported his countrymen, that Hawley purposely kept out of the way, in

* The Sir George Carew who had been Ambassador in France, a different man from the two of the same name who had served in Ireland.

CH. X. 1612.

order not to receive the message, which would, as he supposed, only lead to his being subjected to fresh insults at Court. James was actually obliged to send for the Benchers of the Temple, and to assure them that, if Maxwell were in the wrong, he would give him no support. Upon this Hawley came forward, and Maxwell was with some difficulty induced to make a proper apology.

Murder of Turner by the order of Lord Sanquhar.

A few days before this quarrel occurred, a murder was committed in London, under circumstances of no ordinary atrocity. About seven years previously, Lord Sanquhar, a Scottish baron of the ancient family of Crichton, had lost an eye in playing with a well-known fencing-master of the name of Turner. He fancied that the injury had been inflicted by design, or, at least, through culpable negligence; and, from that time forward he bore a grudge against Turner for what he had done. As soon as he recovered from the effects of the wound, he went into France, and whilst he was there Henry IV. saw him, and inquired into the cause of his disfigurement, and thoughtlessly or mischievously asked whether the man still lived who had done the deed. Not long afterwards Sanquhar returned to England, determined to take vengeance for the injury which he had received. He brooded over his loss till he was ready to become a murderer, fancying all the while that he was only acting in accordance with the dictates of the laws of honour. For some days he tracked his victim up and down London in vain. On his return from a visit to Scotland, he renewed the search. It was at this time that he descended a step lower in his career of baseness. He was aware that he was well known in Whitefriars, where Turner's fencing school was situated, and that, if he set upon him in his own house, it would be almost impossible for him to escape detection. He therefore agreed with two of his countrymen to play the part of the assassin in his place. He himself went to France, in order to be out of the reach of the law, when the deed was done. For some time he waited for the news in vain. Either the two men had never intended to execute his orders, or their hearts failed them when the time came. When Sanquhar came back to London once more, Turner was still alive and well. This time, two of his own servants, Gray and Carlisle, undertook to accomplish the villany. But Gray's heart failed him, and he fled away, intending to take refuge from his master in Sweden. Upon this Carlisle assured Sanquhar that he should not be disappointed, as he was himself ready to carry the project into execution. He accordingly took with him a friend, named Irwin, and going at once to Turner's house, shot him dead with a pistol. Carlisle succeeded in escaping to Scotland, but his accomplice was taken. Irwin was examined, and gave reason to believe that Sanquhar was, in some way or another, implicated in the deed, and the suspicions against him were strengthened by the fact that he had been keeping out of sight for three or four days. The King took the matter up warmly, and issued a proclamation offering a reward for his apprehension, as well as for that of Carlisle. Before the proclamation appeared, Sanquhar surrendered himself to the Archbishop at Lambeth. He protested his innocence, and apparently thought that he might escape punishment as he had had no direct dealings with Irwin, and the only witnesses who could speak of his guilt from personal knowledge had made their escape. In this hope he was doomed to disappointment. Gray was intercepted at Harwich as he was going on board ship, and made such revelations as were sufficient to drive Sanquhar to a full confession of his guilt. Carlisle was afterwards taken in Scotland, and brought up to London. Both he and Irwin were convicted without difficulty, and were immediately executed.

Trial and execution of Sanquhar.

On the 27th of June, Sanquhar was indicted in the Court of King's Bench, for procuring the murder of the unfortunate Turner. He pleaded guilty, acknowledging in general terms that he had acted wrongly; but it was evident that he still believed that he was justified in what he had done, at least by the laws of honour. He concluded his confession by asking for mercy. James was not inclined to interfere with the sentence of the law. Sanquhar, though a Scotchman, was not one of his favourites, and there was no motive, in this case, to pervert his sense of justice. The wretched man was

CH. X. 1612.

accordingly left to his fate. On the morning of the 29th he was hanged in front of the great gate of Westminster Hall. Before his execution he expressed his sorrow for his crime, and ended by declaring that he died in the faith of the Roman Catholic Church. It is characteristic of the time that the compassion of the bystanders, which had been moved by his acknowledgment of his offence, visibly abated when this last statement was made.*

James determines to carry out the contract between Elizabeth and the Elector Palatine.

The most important subject which engaged the attention of James during the summer of 1612 was the marriage of his children. Salisbury's death made no change in his determination to carry out the contract which was already signed. The ill-treatment which he had received from the Court of Spain had been too recent to allow him as yet to think again of an alliance with that country, although he knew that it was probable that overtures would be made for the hand of the Princess by the King of Spain, who had become a widower in the course of the past autumn. Such a marriage, it was well known, would give great pleasure to the Queen, who was in secret inclined to the Roman Catholic religion, and who would gladly have seen her daughter upon the Spanish throne; but James never allowed his wife to interfere with politics, and in this case there never could have been any probability that she would succeed in obtaining the object of her wishes. It must have been from her that the Ambassador Velasco obtained the strange information which he forwarded to his master. It was actually believed in Spain, not only that the King would in all probability obtain the Princess as soon as he chose to ask for her, but that she was ready to forsake the Protestant faith in which she had been brought up.†

Rumours that the King of Spain intends to ask for the Princess.

Zuniga's mission to England.

Under these impressions, the Spanish Court decided upon despatching a special mission to England. Zuniga, who was chosen for this service, had formerly resided in

* *State Trials*, ii. 743. Chamberlain to Carleton, May 20, July 2, 1612, *Court and Times*, i. 166, 179.

† The important part of Digby's despatch of the 4th of Jan., is printed by Mrs. Green, *Lives of the Princesses*, v. 178.

England as ambassador, and was therefore well qualified, by his knowledge of the court to which he was accredited, to fulfil the delicate service entrusted to him. Ostensibly he was only sent to give explanations concerning the French marriages; but in Spain, nobody doubted that he was empowered to demand the Princess for his master, if, upon his arrival, he should have reason to believe that the offer would be accepted. As soon as he had time to discover what the King's real intentions were, he found that the marriage with the Elector was irrevocably decided upon, and that there was as much probability of the King of Spain turning Protestant as there was of the Princess Elizabeth deserting the religion of her childhood. Accordingly, when James granted him an audience, he contented himself with giving explanations on the subject of the negotiations with which the two courts had been occupied in the past year. As soon as he had finished, the King asked him if he had nothing more to say, and on his replying in the negative, dismissed him with evident signs of anger.* It can hardly be doubted that he was eager to return in kind the insult which he had received in the preceding year, and that he was vexed at being baulked of an opportunity of venting his indignation. As soon as Zuniga was gone, James told his councillors what had passed, and assured them that nothing should ever induce him to allow his daughter to marry a Papist.†

The reception of the Elector in England.

But although the marriage articles had been signed in May, there were still many points to be settled, and it was not till September that the negotiations were sufficiently advanced to allow the young Elector to

* Zuniga's despatch, Aug. 2, 1612, *S. P. Sp.* Mrs. Green (v. 179) supposes that James wished to receive a proposal, and was disappointed in not getting one. I do not think this is possible. If he had still any desire for the connection, he would not have allowed the contract to be signed in May. At that time he knew perfectly well that Zuniga was coming. Besides, his conduct ever since the German alliance had been suggested by Bouillon was that of a man who wished to see it accomplished. Perhaps too much has been made of his anger on this occasion; he had a very bad toothache at the time, which will account for a good deal of it.

† He had other reasons for distrusting Zuniga. A few days before, he had discovered that the ambassador had brought large sums of money with him for the purpose of corrupting the courtiers. Abbot to the King, July 22, 1612, *S. P. Dom.* lxx. 11.

CH. X. 1612.

set out to visit his affianced bride. When it was known that the vessel in which he sailed had arrived in safety at Gravesend, the enthusiasm in London was unbounded. As his barge passed up the river to Whitehall, he was welcomed by the thousands who had come out to see him arrive. James received him cordially, and even the Queen forbore to give expression to her dislike. It was not long before he was able to assure himself that he had won the heart of Elizabeth as well as her hand. The impression which he made upon all who conversed with him was favourable, and even those who, before his arrival, had spoken slightingly of the match, were obliged to confess that, as far as his personal appearance went, he was worthy even of Elizabeth herself.

The marriage favoured by the Prince of Wales.

Of all those who had favoured the Elector's suit no one had been more deeply interested in its success than the Prince of Wales. His attachment to his sister had ripened into the warmest affection during the few years which had passed since she had left Lord Harrington's roof. He had been deeply vexed when he learned that there was a prospect of an offer being made to her by the King of Spain, and had publicly declared that, in his eyes, whoever favoured such a match was a traitor. He believed that the only aim of the Spaniards was to get the succession to the English throne into their hands, and that, as soon as they had possession of the Princess, they would immediately clear the way for her accession by murdering himself and his brother. He was proportionably delighted when he knew that his father had irrevocably declared in favour of the Elector.

Question of the Prince's marriage. Proposed alliances with Savoy or Florence.

Whilst James was engaged in concluding the arrangements for his daughter's marriage, he was also busy in deliberating with his councillors upon the equally important question of providing a wife for the Prince. He knew that the Duke of Savoy was anxious to obtain the hand of the heir of England for his daughter, and that the Duke of Florence was desirous of securing the prize for his sister. As soon as the final rupture of the negotiations with Spain was made public, the two Italian potentates lost no time in making known their wishes.

CH. X. 1612.

The Duke of Florence, however, thought it well to make an attempt to secure the consent of the Pope to the marriage of his sister with a Protestant. The question was seriously debated at Rome, and he was told that such a union would not meet with the approbation of the Church.* The Duke did not allow himself to be altogether deterred by this rebuff from pursuing the object which he had at heart, but there can be no doubt that the course which he had adopted was not such as was likely to conciliate the goodwill of James and his advisers. The Duke of Savoy, who was desirous of freeing himself from the chains of Spanish domination, was more bent upon securing a political ally than upon obtaining the approbation of the Pope. He offered to give his daughter a dowry of seven hundred thousand crowns,† and engaged that she would be content if she were allowed the exercise of her religion in the most private manner possible. This marriage was warmly supported by Wotton, who had passed through Turin on his return from his embassy at Venice. His fondness for Italian society rendered him blind both to the political objections to the match, and to the domestic unhappiness which was likely to ensue if such a man as Prince Henry were to be condemned to live with a wife who would find it impossible to sympathise with him in any one of his feelings.

At first Wotton contrived to carry the Prince with him. It was not long, however, before his good sense told him that such a marriage would conduce neither to his own welfare nor to that of the country. Yet, in spite of this feeling, he determined to keep quiet, in order not to provoke his father by untimely opposition to a plan which might never be actually presented to him for his acceptance. James, indeed, had not confined his attention to the two Italian Courts. When the Duke of Bouillon was in England in the spring, he had taken an opportunity of bringing before the King the advisability of entering into a close alliance with France, and he even hinted that it

A marriage with a French Princess suggested.

* Carleton to the King, June 19; the Count of Vische to ——, July 14, 1612, *S.*

† Northampton to Rochester, Oct. 7, 1612, *S. P. Dom.* lxxi. 1.

CH. X. 1612. was not impossible that, after all, the Spanish marriage might come to nothing, and that in that case the Regent would gladly bestow the hand of her eldest daughter upon the Prince of Wales. If this should not prove to be the case, there would be no difficulty in obtaining her sister, the Princess Christina. James, upon making inquiry, found that Bouillon had no authority for giving any hopes of the elder Princess, and was for a time disposed to give up all further thoughts of the alliance, as Christina was a mere child in her seventh year.*

A week or two later he changed his mind. The French alliance would be worth having, in the state in which Europe then was. The mere fact of such an overture having come from France showed that the Regent was not disposed to place herself unreservedly in the hands of Spain. In truth, though she was glad enough to obtain the support of the Spaniards against her enemies, foreign and domestic, she had no idea of joining in a crusade against Protestantism. She wanted to be quiet, and she thought that an alliance with her great neighbour would be likely to preserve her from foreign war, and to overawe her turbulent nobles at home. If she could gain an influence in England as well as in Spain, so much the better; it would be one chance the more for peace. With such guarantees as these, she would surely be able, when the time came when she would be called upon to deliver over the government to her son, to boast that in her hands France had not been exposed to the miseries of war.

Arguments in its favour.

James, too, loved peace, but as yet he looked for peace in a close alliance between all the powers that, from any cause, were opposed to the ambitious projects of the House of Austria. A proposal which might, if it were accepted, help to free the French Court from the subserviency to Spain which had lately characterized its policy was not to be lightly rejected. He therefore ordered Edmondes to discuss the matter in an unofficial manner with the French minister Villeroi, and to ascertain under what conditions the Regent would agree to

* The King to Edmondes, June 1612, *S. P. Fr.* Christina was born on the 10th of February, 1606.

the match.* After all, if the Prince should be willing to consent to defer his marriage for so long a time, the extreme youth of the Princess might not be an objection. If the Regent could be persuaded to part with her daughter at once, she might be educated in England, and would, in all probability, be induced to embrace the religion of her future husband. CH. X. 1612.

Edmondes accordingly made his proposal to Villeroi, and expressed his hope that if the marriage were agreed to the Princess would be sent into England before the end of the following year. In consequence of that minister's illness, it was not till the 25th of September that he was able to forward an answer to James. Villeroi assured him that the Regent was most anxious for the conclusion of the marriage, but that she begged for a little longer time, in order that her daughter might be fully instructed in her religion before she left her home. Edmondes, however, stated that it was his belief that the French Government were so desirous of obtaining the marriage, that if they were pressed upon this point, they would certainly give way; and in fact, on the 7th of November, he was able to write that Villeroi had informed him that the Regent was ready to consent to part with her daughter at the time proposed by James.†

The question submitted to the Prince.

By the King's command, Edmondes' despatch of the 25th of September was forwarded by Rochester to the Prince, with a request that he would give his opinion upon a matter which concerned himself so deeply. The Prince did not give any decided answer. The Savoyard Princess, he said, would bring with her a larger dowry than the daughter of the Queen of France. On the other hand, the French marriage would give far greater satisfaction to the Protestants abroad. If the offer of the Regent was to be accepted, it must be understood that the Princess was only to be allowed the exercise of her religion in private, and it must be expressly

* Edmondes to the King, July 21, 1612, *S. P. Fr.*

† Edmondes to the King, Sept. 25 and Nov. 7, 1612, *S. P. Fr.* The first of these despatches is endorsed with a wrong date, which may mislead anyone who is in search of it. The true date will be found at the end of the despatch itself.

CH. X. 1612.

stipulated that she should be sent over before the end of the following year at the latest, in order that there may be a reasonable prospect of her conversion. If he seemed indifferent, his father must remember that he knew little or nothing of State affairs, and that the time for making love, which was his part in the matter, was not yet arrived.*

Raleigh's pamphlet.

The French alliance had the support of no less a man than Raleigh. In a treatise which he wrote at this time† he went once more over the arguments against the Savoy match which had been urged by him when the Princess's marriage was being discussed in the preceding year. A marriage with a German lady would, he said, be equally undesirable, as the friendship of Protestant Germany was already secured. On the other hand, it was of the utmost importance that France should be won over as soon as possible to the cause of European liberty. He saw at once that the present friendship between France and Spain could not last for ever, and that, if Spain should renew her aggressions, France would of necessity be found sooner or later in opposition to her natural enemy.

The Prince not satisfied.

It is evident that in spite of these arguments the Prince was ill at ease. He knew that if he expressed his real sentiments to his father he would only draw down upon himself a torrent of argument. After all, even if the Princess should be sent over at an early age, it was not certain that he would succeed in converting her, and 'he was resolved,' as he afterwards expressed it, 'that two religions should never lie in his bed.'‡ He was secretly meditating a scheme of which, as yet, he did not breathe a syllable to anyone; he would accompany his sister to Germany, when there, he would fling politics to the winds, and choose a wife for himself.

* Rochester to the Prince, Oct. 2; the Prince to Rochester, Oct. 5, 1612; Birch's *Life of Henry, Prince of Wales*, 308.

† A Discourse touching a Marriage between Prince Henry of England and a Daughter of Savoy. (Raleigh's Works, viii. 237.) The date, 9 Jacobi, is evidently erroneous, and must have sprung from some confusion with the treatise on the marriage of the Princess Elizabeth in the preceding year.

‡ Wake to Carleton. Undated, 1612 (*S. P. Ven.*). Wake derived his information from Newton, to whom the Prince spoke of his designs upon his deathbed.

This plan of his was destined never to be accomplished. For some weeks he had been far from well. During the summer he had neglected to take the most ordinary precautions for the preservation of his health. In the hottest season of the year he had allowed himself to take far too violent exercise. Like his father, he was fond of fruit, and had partaken of it in unusually large quantities. He had even indulged in the imprudent practice of swimming immediately after supper. CH. X. 1612. The Prince's illness,

Though he had complained of feeling unwell during the whole of the autumn, it was not till the 10th of October that he was actually attacked by illness. A violent cold was attended with other symptoms of disease. Two days afterwards he recovered to some extent, and insisted, in opposition to the advice of his physicians, upon going out. For some days he kept up, but he looked pale and haggard. On the 24th he foolishly played at tennis, in which he exposed himself in his shirt to the chilly air of the season. The next day the fever was upon him, and he was forced to take to his bed.

On the 1st of November he was somewhat better, and the King, the Queen, and his brother and sister, as well as the Elector, were admitted one by one to his bedside to see him. They left him hoping that he might yet recover. The amendment was not for any length of time; he grew worse and worse, and the physicians lost all hope. On the 6th he was evidently dying. The Queen, who had often derived benefit from Raleigh's prescriptions, sent off, as a last resource, to the prisoner in the Tower for help. He immediately prepared a medicine, which was given to the dying Prince. It was all in vain; before the day was over, the sufferer was no more. and death.

Of all who knew him, the one who felt his loss most deeply was his sister Elizabeth. Since her visit to his sick room on the 1st, she had made repeated efforts to see him, and had even attempted to penetrate to his apartments in disguise. She was, however, not allowed to pass, as, by that time, it was considered that his disease was infectious. Nor had he forgotten her: the

CH. X. 1612.

last words he uttered in a state of consciousness were, 'Where is my dear sister?'*

Universal grief.

Throughout the whole of England the sad news was received with tears and lamentations. Never in the long history of England had an heir to the throne given rise to such hopes, or had, at such an early age, inspired every class of his countrymen with love and admiration. They were not content with sorrowing over his memory, they vented their affection in the foolish outcry that their beloved Prince had been murdered. Sometimes it was Rochester, sometimes it was Northampton, who was supposed to have administered the poison which carried him off. Nor was there any lack of suspicions more horrible still: grave men actually whispered to one another that James himself had a hand in the imaginary murder of his son.

If the Prince had lived, he certainly would not have thrown the reins of government into the hands of the leaders of the House of Commons. He would not have anticipated the result of the inevitable struggle by giving way in what he would have considered to be his rights; he would have had his own views on every question as it arose, and he would have striven by every means in his power to carry them out. Northampton was right, as far as he and such as he were concerned, when he said that 'the Prince, if ever he came to reign, would prove a tyrant.' He would have made short work with the men and measures which Northampton regarded with approval.

Irreparable loss to England.

But it does not follow that the reign of a popular King would have thrown obstacles in the way of the liberties of England. Experience has shown us that it is not by submission to a ruler whose views are in accordance with the noblest instincts of his people that nations are enslaved; it is when ignorance and folly are banded together in an unholy league with power that every day eats more deeply into the vigour of a nation, and renders it more difficult to throw off the burden of tyranny. Nothing of this sort was to be

* Cornwallis, *Life of Prince Henry*, Somers' Tracts, ii. 231; Chamberlain to Carleton, Nov. 12, 1612; *Court and Times*, i. 202.

dreaded from the Prince who had been so suddenly snatched away. He would have ruled in accordance with the noblest feelings of the nation; he would have kept England at the head of the great Protestant League, and would have resisted to the uttermost the encroachments of the House of Austria. At home he would have been of one mind with the House of Commons on the great ecclesiastical question of the day. He would certainly not have fulfilled the expectations of his Puritan admirers, by overthrowing Episcopacy and reducing the Church of England to the measure of the Presbyterian Churches; but he would undoubtedly have seen with pleasure limits imposed upon the power of the Bishops, and would have given free liberty to those preachers whose mouths had been stopped for Nonconformity. Nor would he have found any difficulty in coming to an understanding with the Commons on such questions as were those of the tenures and the impositions. Once more at unity with itself, the nation would have taken its true place upon the Continent. Nor would the postponement of the domestic conflicts have been otherwise than beneficial in the end. When the time came for renewed resistance to the Crown, the Commons would be far better prepared even than they were in the reign of James or of his younger son. Many questions which were still considered to be doubtful, would have been settled in favour of the nation, once and for ever. It would have become a habit in the Commons at least to tender their advice in times of difficulty on many points upon which they had never before been consulted. Above all, under the mild sway of religious toleration, the House of Commons would have escaped alike all the evils of the theological partisanship and of the gross immorality which afterwards, at different periods, cast a stain even upon its noblest achievements. But these are dreams, and those who know best the difficulty of attaining to an accurate knowledge of events which actually happened will be the first to shrink from an investigation of probabilities which were never realised.

Bayley's sermons.

Northampton was not long in discovering that his opposition to the cause to which the Prince had devoted

CH. X. 1612.

himself had rendered him, and those who agreed with him, intensely unpopular. A little more than a week after the Prince's death, one of his chaplains, named Bayley, preached a sermon, in which he told his congregation that religion was lying bleeding, and that there were members of the Council who attended mass, and told their master's secrets to their wives, by whom they were betrayed to the Jesuits.* Bayley was reprimanded by the Archbishop, but he only repeated his accusation, in a more distinct form, on the following Sunday. Similar insinuations were made by other preachers, who took care not to bring any direct accusation which could be laid hold of by the Government. A few days later, Northampton heard that it was a matter of common conversation that, after he had published the speech which he had delivered at Garnet's trial, he had written secretly to Bellarmin, beseeching him to take no notice of what he had said, as he only spoke as he did in opposition to the Papal claims for the sake of pleasing the King and the people. The story obtained credit the more easily as, in all the controversial works which had appeared upon the Catholic side, not a word had been said of Northampton's speech. Still no proof was ever brought of the correctness of the rumour, and it is possible that Bellarmin may have abstained from attacking him simply from unwillingness to offend a man whose voice in the Council was likely to be raised against the Protestant Alliance. However this may have been, it is certain that Northampton took the very worst course which was open to him, if he wished to vindicate his fame. He summoned before the Star Chamber six unlucky persons, who had been detected in spreading the report, and sent them away smarting under heavy fines. As might be expected, such a proceeding, though it rendered the newsmongers of the day more cautious in what they said, had no effect in changing their opinions.†

Star Chamber fines imposed on six persons for slandering Northampton.

* This, I suppose, referred to Suffolk.

† Chamberlain to Carleton, Nov. 19, Dec. 17, 1612, *Court and Times*, i. 206, 213; *State Trials*, ii. 862. The story of Abbot's producing the letter can only refer to this trial, and is quite irreconcilable with the facts given us upon contemporary authority. If another trial had occurred later, we should surely have heard of it.

Betrothal of the Princess.

But if Northampton was allowed to inflict punishment upon his personal opponents, he was not allowed to influence the policy of the Government. Hopes had been entertained, by those who were interested in breaking off the marriage of the Princess, that James would be less willing to carry out his design now that, by the death of her brother, she was a step nearer to the throne. He was determined to show that he had set his heart upon the match by directing the signature of the final marriage articles upon the 17th of November, and by ordering that the ceremony of betrothal should take place on the 27th, as the marriage itself was necessarily postponed on account of the Prince's death.

The solemnity of the betrothal was almost marred by Sir Thomas Lake, who was directed to act as Secretary for the occasion. In that capacity he was called upon to read the contract in French, in order that the young couple might repeat the words after him. His translation, however, was so bad, and his pronunciation so detestable, that those who were present could not refrain from laughing, till the Archbishop, whose whole heart was in the scene before him, broke in with the solemn words, 'The God of Abraham, of Isaac, and of Jacob, bless these nuptials, and make them prosperous to these kingdoms and to His Church.' *

Question of the Secretaryship.

Although Lake was allowed to act as Secretary on this occasion, it was generally understood that, in spite of his Parliamentary antecedents, Nevill was now the candidate most likely to obtain the post, if the King should determine to fill it up. In the beginning of January the Council petitioned him to name a Secretary.†

* Chamberlain to Carleton, Dec. 31, 1612, *Court and Times*, i. 215; *Rymer*, xvi. 725.

† Chamberlain to Carleton, Jan. 7, 1613, *Court and Times*, i. 218. Wotton was out of favour at this time, as James had just heard of his celebrated inscription in the Album at Augsburg, 'Legatus est vir bonus peregrè missus ad mentiendum Reipublicæ causâ.' The difficulty of the ordinary explanation has often been felt. It is impossible that he should have meant to make a joke which is unintelligible excepting in English, a language which was not understood at Augsburg. Is it not possible that the interpretation, 'An ambassador is a good man sent to lie abroad for the sake of his country,' was a happy thought which first occurred to him as a good excuse to make, when he was taxed by James with what he had done?

CH. X. 1613.

With his usual impulsiveness, James had at first thrown himself into the business of the office, and had read and answered despatches with commendable regularity. But he had soon grown tired of the labour, and complaints were heard that business was often at a standstill for want of his application to the duties which he had voluntarily undertaken. James promised to consider the advice of his Council; but he was too desirous of keeping power in his own hands to take any steps in the matter. Nevill, however, was in hopes of being able to bring with him into office his friend Winwood, who had been a special favourite of the King ever since he had shown his zeal in carrying out his instructions in the dispute with Vorstius. If James could have been induced to listen to advice, no more fortunate event could be conceived for the country than that the direction of home politics should be entrusted to the hands of Nevill, whilst foreign affairs were committed to the charge of Winwood. Under their auspices a bold and dignified foreign policy would have advanced hand in hand with a spirit of concession at home, which would have won the confidence of the House of Commons. Englishmen who look back at the opportunity which was lost must feel inclined to forgive Rochester all his many follies, when they remember that it was he who favoured this arrangement.

Marriage of the Princess.

But whatever might be the King's decision on this point, he threw no obstacles in the way of the solemnization of the marriage to which all good Protestants were hopefully looking forward. The ceremony was performed with all possible pomp and splendour on the 14th of February. Even the Queen herself condescended to be present, though she had long looked with displeasure at the alliance, and had hitherto refrained from showing any sign of favour to the Elector. His frank and hearty manners seem to have won her over, and to all appearance she was perfectly contented with her daughter's lot. None of those who were present at that gay scene had the slightest foreboding of what that lot would be. If it was to be sad and stormy, at least it was to be without shame.

CH. X.
1613.

It was not long before the shadows of Elizabeth's future life began to fall upon her. The expenses connected with her marriage amounted to more than £60,000.* Such a burden would have been severely felt at any time; but in the disordered condition in which the finances were, it was almost insupportable. James was accordingly obliged, as a mere matter of necessity, in less than a month after the wedding, to dismiss the greater number of the attendants who had been appointed to wait upon the Elector during his stay in England. The Princess felt the slight put upon her husband deeply.† It was not the last time that James would be forced to turn his back upon her from want of means to help her.

The Princess and her husband leave England.

On the 10th of April the Elector and his bride left Whitehall. They travelled slowly, as if Elizabeth were loth to take leave of the land in which she had spent so many happy days. When they reached Margate they were detained by the state of the weather, and it was not till the 25th that they set sail for Holland.‡ Both she and her husband were young to face the storms which were before them, neither of them having yet completed their seventeenth year.

The States join the Union.

Before he left her, in order to make preparations for her reception in the Palatinate, he was called upon to take part in a ceremony which was of no slight importance to himself. On the 6th of May the States, at the request of the King of England,§ signed a treaty with the Princes of the Union, by which the two parties engaged themselves for fifteen years to give mutual succour to one another in case of need. Attempts had been made in vain to induce the French to join the League. There was, however, one point upon which France still made common cause with England: when at the commencement of 1612 the Imperial throne became vacant by the death of Rudolph II., both countries had strenuously resisted an attempt on the part of Spain to

The French refuse to do so.

* This includes all the expenses of the Elector's household during his stay in England, as well as the expenses of the journey to Heidelberg. The Princess's portion was £40,000 in addition.

† Chamberlain to Carleton, March 11, 1613, *Court and Times*, i. 232.

‡ Chamberlain to Carleton, April 29, *S. P. Dom.* lxxii. 120; Green's *Princesses*, v. 221.

§ The King to Winwood, April 1, 1613, *S. P. Hol.*

CH. X. 1613.

obtain the election of the Archduke Albert,* and had done everything in their power to promote the success of Matthias. Spain was now renewing the attempt to favour the brother-in-law of Philip III., and the French Government again declared that they would use every means in their power to hinder the election of Albert to the dignity of King of the Romans.†

James at the head of the Protestant Alliance.

James was now in close alliance with Holland and with Protestant Germany, and upon friendly terms with France. The position which England had thus taken up promised to place him at the head of the league which was forming against the Catholic powers. Already his voice had been heard even in the far north, and his ambassadors had been successful in mediating a peace between Denmark and Sweden, and in putting an end to a war between two Protestant States, in which the genius of the young Gustavus had maintained an unequal struggle against the superior forces of the King of Denmark.

* Beaulieu to Trumbull, June 29, 1612, *Winw.* xiii. 375.

† Edmondes to the King, April 24, 1613, *S. P. Fr.*

CHAPTER XI.

RESULTS OF IRRESPONSIBLE GOVERNMENT.

1613.

Relations between England and Spain.

It would have been strange if the attitude assumed by the English Government had not made a difference in its relations with the Court of Spain. As long as there had been any hope that the overtures of that Court would meet with a favourable reception in England, Digby had found that the ministers of Philip III. were not indisposed to redress the grievances of which he was instructed to complain. As soon as he could obtain a hearing, he presented a memorial, in which the wrongs done to the English merchants were set down in detail,* and he threatened the Spaniards with the severe displeasure of his master if justice were not done. He was met with abundant promises of compliance, and orders were immediately given that the cases should be brought to a speedy decision. In some of the more recent ones, where the tribunals had not yet taken cognizance of the supposed offences, commands were issued that the goods which had been seized by the King's officers should at once be restored to their owners.

The merchants' grievances.

December 1611.

Digby investigates the causes of the evils complained of.

Digby was not content, as Cornwallis had been, with merely demanding justice, and reporting his good or bad success from time to time to his Government. Immediately upon his arrival at Madrid he set himself to investigate the causes of the evils complained of, and did his best to devise a remedy against their recurrence. He was not long in discovering that they were the almost inevitable result of the Spanish judicial system. Whenever, in consequence of a real or supposed infringement of the customs' laws, sentence was given in the local

* Digby to Salisbury, Dec. 29, 1611, *S. P. Sp.*

courts against a merchant, the property in question was immediately confiscated and divided into three equal parts, which were assigned respectively to the King, the judge, and the informer. Thus it happened that the interest of the judge would frequently lead him to pronounce sentence for the Crown whenever the case was sufficiently doubtful to give him an excuse for doing so. It was true that an appeal lay to the Courts at Madrid, and that not only were these courts notorious for their integrity, but, as a matter of fact, scarcely a single instance had occurred since the peace, in which an Englishman had appealed to them without obtaining a sentence in his favour. But their forms of procedure were extremely wearisome, and it was seldom that a case was before them for less than two or three years. Such a delay, involving as it did the residence at Madrid of the merchant himself, or of his representative, in order to watch the proceedings, caused an expense which none excepting the most wealthy traders could afford. Nor were the difficulties of the merchant at an end even when he had obtained a favourable sentence: as his goods had been divided immediately after the original decision had been given against him. The informer was sure to be a beggar, who had spent long ago all that had fallen to his share. The judge had probably been removed to some distant station, perhaps in Africa or America, and if he were still to be found where the wrong had originally been done, it was no easy matter to put the law in force against a great man presiding in his own court. The King's third was the only one which there was a chance of recovering, but so low was the Treasury that the Royal warrants for satisfying claims of this nature scarcely ever obtained payment in less than two or three years.

Remedies agreed to.

To remedy these evils Digby proposed two changes, which the Spanish Government at once promised to adopt. In future, whenever an appeal was made against the decision of the local court, it was to be heard before a special commission, which would be able to hear and determine the matter at once. The second concession was of still greater importance: the goods were no longer to be confiscated by the inferior judges, but bonds were to be given, by which the owners engaged to pay their value, in case of the rejection of their appeal. In order to show his willingness to oblige the English, the King directed, a few days after these arrangements had been made, that several Englishmen, who were prisoners in the galleys, should immediately be set at liberty. 1612.

Consuls.

Lastly, Digby had long been pressing upon his Government to appoint consuls. It had often happened that the English traders had, either through ignorance or wilfulness, broken the Spanish laws, and that they had afterwards made complaints, as if they had themselves been wronged when they were called in question. Digby justly thought that many of these unfortunate occurrences would be prevented, if an experienced person were on the spot to warn them of the consequences of their actions, and that he would himself be provided with intelligence which would prevent him from advocating at Madrid the causes of men who had no one but themselves to blame if they had been subjected to punishment or loss. The Government at home fully agreed with his suggestion, and appointed a person named Lee to act as Consul at Lisbon. They also sent out Cottington to reside in the same capacity at Seville, in order to take a general supervision of the interests of the English merchants in the southern ports.*

A few months later, the Spanish Government began to assume a very different tone. When all hope of diverting James from the alliance with the German Protestants was at an end, they were in no hurry to fulfil the engagements which they had made. Nothing was done about the appointment of a special tribunal to hear appeals.† A steady resistance was opposed to the admission of the new consuls. At last, after a delay of 1613.
a twelvemonth, Digby was informed that, though Lee would be permitted to act at Lisbon, no one who was not a Catholic would be allowed to fulfil the duties of a Consul in Andalusia.‡

* Digby to the Council; Digby to Salisbury, Jan. 19, 1612, *S. P. Sp.*
† Digby to Salisbury, May 30, 1612, *S. P. Sp.*
‡ Cottington to Lake, Jan. 5; Digby to Lake, Jan. 18, 1613, *S. P. Sp.*

CH. XI.
1613.
The Spanish Government dissatisfied with England.

For some time it was even thought to be possible that Spain might venture upon a declaration of war. The Virginian Colony had long been a thorn in the sides of the Spanish Government, and long and anxious deliberations were held at Madrid upon the expediency of sending an expedition against it.* The ill feeling in Spain was increased by the return of several vessels which had gone out to take part in the Spitzbergen whale fishery, from which they had been driven by the crews of the ships belonging to the English Muscovy Company, which claimed the exclusive right to the lucrative employment in which they were engaged.† Nor was the treatment which the recusants were now receiving at the hands of James such as was likely to conciliate the goodwill of a Catholic nation. The oath of allegiance had become a mere contrivance for filling the pockets of courtiers. In 1611 a proclamation had been issued commanding that the oath should be administered according to the law.‡ At first, two or three wealthy persons, who refused to take it, had been thrown into prison, and had only been released upon payment of large sums. It was, however, soon discovered that it was not necessary to go through these forms; it was enough to intimate to the persons who were supposed to be unwilling to take the oath, that unless they were ready to pay for their immunity, proceedings would be taken against them.‡ This course was never known to fail. The money, almost invariably, went directly, without even passing through the Exchequer, into the hands of some hanger-on of the court, who had managed to secure a share of the booty. The treatment which the ordinary recusants received was equally harsh. The number of the persons whose lands were seized was considerably greater than

* Digby to the King, Sept. 13, 1612, *S. P. Sp.* In his despatches of the next six months, he frequently mentions the feelings of the Spaniards with respect to Virginia.

† Digby to Lake, Sept. 4, 1613, *S. P. Sp.*

‡ Proclamation Collection, No. 18, *S. P.*

§ Cæsar to the King, Aug. 14, 1612, Lansd. MS. 153, fol. 46 a. There are in the same volume several letters from recusants, offering compositions for taking the oath, foll. 78—87. In the *S. P. Dom.* lxx. 9, is a list of seventy persons to be called upon to take the oath, dated July 18, 1612.

it had been in the earlier years of James's reign. The new fine which had been imposed by Parliament upon persons whose wives refused the oath, pressed hardly upon Catholic ladies. Many of them were obliged to leave their husbands' houses in order to remain in concealment.* CH. XI. 1613.

Fear of invasion in England.

In the first days of 1613 the English Government were in expectation of a Spanish invasion. They knew well where their weakness lay. An order was issued for an immediate search of the houses of the recusants for arms, and directions were given that none should be left in their hands beyond that which was sufficient for the defence of themselves and their families.† It was not long, however, before all apprehension was at an end. If the disorderly state of the English finances had, for a moment, led the Spanish Government to imagine that an appeal to arms would terminate in their favour, they must speedily have remembered their own poverty, and a little reflection must have taught them that there was no surer means to fill the Exchequer of the King of England than an unprovoked aggression of a foreign enemy. They persuaded themselves that the colony in Virginia would certainly die out of itself, and they resolved to take no active measures to hasten what they considered to be its inevitable fate.‡ The defence of the English recusants must be postponed to a more convenient season. In the meanwhile they determined to replace their ambassador in England by one of the ablest diplomatists in their service, Don Diego Sarmiento de Acuna, better known to us by his later title as the Count of Gondomar. He was instructed to watch events, but to take no active steps in favour of the persecuted Catholics.§

Arrival of Sarmiento in England.

For the intelligence which Digby was able from time

* Lewknor to —— (Tierney's *Dodd*, iv. 145). Many particulars in this letter are demonstrably gross exaggerations, but the facts of the persecution are probably in the main true. See also the account given by Lady Blount, March 1613, in the same volume.—App. 188.

† Council to Sheriffs, &c., Jan. 10, 1613 (Tierney's *Dodd*, iv.; App. 188). The date given here is the true date.

‡ Digby to the King, Sept. 3, 1613, *S. P. Sp.*

§ Instructions of Sarmiento, sent with Digby's despatch of the 27th of May, 1613, *S. P. Sp.*

CH. XI. 1613.

Spanish despatches come into Digby's hands.

to time to transmit to England, he was indebted to something more than the ordinary means of obtaining information which are at the disposal of an ambassador residing in a foreign country. He had not been long in Spain before he discovered that it was possible with a very little money to obtain access to the most treasured secrets of the Government. There was not a despatch of any importance which passed between the Spanish embassy in England and the Court of Madrid which did not find its way into Digby's hands.

He becomes aware that English officials are in the receipt of Spanish pensions;

In May, 1613, he got into his possession the instructions which Sarmiento was to take with him. As he read them he discovered that the Spanish ambassadors had long been in the habit of obtaining intelligence in London by the same means as those which he was using with such success at Madrid. As yet, however, he had no reason to suppose that anything worse had happened than that some of the minor officials about the court had been induced to repeat the gossip of Whitehall. Yet even this was not a matter to be neglected. He determined to give himself no rest till he had tracked out the secret. In August he was able to inform the King that he had heard of a paper which contained the names of all the English pensioners of Spain.* Such a paper was of course difficult of access, and it was some time before he could procure a copy of it. In the beginning of September, however,† he obtained some documents in which the pensioners were, in various ways, referred to; but the names were disguised under fictitious appellations. He thought he could make out that a pension had been given to Sir William Monson, the Admiral in command of the Narrow Seas. There was one name about which there could be no mistake. To his astonishment and horror, that one name was that of the late Lord Treasurer the Earl of Salisbury. In December, he, at last, procured the long-desired key to the whole riddle.‡ He was thunderstruck at the disclosures which awaited him. One by one he read the names of men whose loyalty had

and, at last, discovers the names of the pensioners.

* Digby to the King, Aug. 8, 1613, *S. P. Sp.*
† See Appendix III.
‡ Digby to the King, Dec. 24, 1613, *S. P. Sp.*

never been suspected, and who occupied the highest posts in the Government, and were in constant attendance upon the person of the King. He hoped, indeed, that some of the persons indicated might have refused to accept the offered bribe, but, even after the utmost allowance had been made, enough remained to fill him with astonishment and disgust. 1613.

1614. Obtains leave to return to England with the information he had acquired.

The secret was of far too high importance to be entrusted to paper. Digby, therefore, at once asked permission to return home on leave of absence, in order that he might acquaint the King, by word of mouth, with the discoveries which he had made. The request was, of course, granted, and in the spring he set out to carry the important intelligence to England. The precautions which he took have prevented us from knowing the full extent of the evil which he discovered. It is certain, however, that Northampton and Lady Suffolk were in the pay of Spain, whilst it is no less certain that Suffolk* himself and Rochester had kept aloof from these practices.

1613. Warning given to James by these revelations.

What James's feelings were on the receipt of this startling intelligence we have no means of knowing, as his answers to Digby's despatches have not been preserved. We may, however, be sure that he neglected to draw the only inference from the terrible tidings which could alone have saved him from further disgrace. In fact, such revelations as these are the warnings which are invariably given to every Government which persists in separating itself from the feelings and intelligence of the nation which it is called to guide. The immorality in high places which had just been brought to light was only the corruption which naturally festered round a system from which life had departed. Was it wonderful that a Sovereign whose only idea of political wisdom lay in the preservation of his own authority, by repressing the free utterance of the thoughts which were everywhere

* Suffolk's innocence is, I think, established by his appointment to the Treasurership, even if my interpretation of the cypher in Digby's despatch should be incorrect. Although no letters have been preserved on the subject, it is impossible to believe that James would have taken such a step without communicating with Digby.

CH. XI. 1613. fermenting around him, should be surrounded by men who had accepted office rather in the hope of obtaining wealth and honour for themselves than from any wish to devote themselves heart and soul to the service of their country? When selfishness, however much it might be disguised even from himself, was the ruling principle with the King, it could not be long before it showed itself in his ministers.

Yet, if the discovery, rightly viewed, was humiliating to James, it offered an excellent opportunity of escaping from the false position in which he was placed. He had only to declare publicly what he had learnt, and to throw himself upon the unbought loyalty of the nation, to become the most popular Sovereign who had ever sat upon the English throne. At such a moment it would have been easy to come to terms with the House of Commons, and to put an end for ever to the causes which had led to his estrangement from his subjects.

But it must be confessed that not one Sovereign in a thousand would have had the moral courage to break thus openly with the past, and to acknowledge that the policy pursued for so many years had been a blunder as well as a fault; and of all the Sovereigns who ever lived, James was the least likely to grow wise by experience.

Position assumed by Rochester.

If James refused to throw himself upon the loyalty of his subjects, there was but one course open to him. As soon as he learned that there were those in his Council upon whom he could place no dependence, there was no help for it but to take the conduct of affairs more entirely into his own hands. Accordingly, the members of the Council were made to feel that their authority was slipping away from them. They were still allowed to discuss public business, but upon all points of importance James reserved his decision till he had had an opportunity of talking them over in private with Rochester.* The favourite was now more than ever regarded as the instru-

* 'The Viscount Rochester, at the Council Table, showeth much temper and modesty, without seeming to press or sway anything, but afterwards the King resolveth all businesses with him alone.' — Sarmiento's despatch, sent home by Digby, Sept. 22, 1613, *S. P. Sp.*

ment through whom James intended to carry out his wishes, and to establish his authority above that of his ministers.

It was a dangerous position for both of them. If James could be certain that the favourite would never swerve from his duty to himself, could he expect that a giddy young man would remain untainted by the moral atmosphere in which he breathed? And even if he could himself be secure of keeping aloof from the follies of his most intimate companion, would they not involve him in the disgrace which was their natural consequence? Was it possible for men who deliberately refused to recognize the intelligent opinion of the country to avoid for any length of time the commission of some act which would outrage its moral feeling?

The politics which these two men met to discuss in private were not such as were likely to elevate or refine the mind. There are men in whose hearts devotion to a noble cause leaves no room for vice or folly to enter in, but neither James nor Rochester was one of these. All James's thoughts circled round himself, and there was nothing in the petty arrangements and small contrivances which he called wisdom to hinder him from being led away by every gust of passion or of feeling. Rochester was even in a more perilous position than his master. He had come to England avowedly for the purpose of making his fortune, and, if he had succeeded above his utmost expectations, he was only the more likely to regard what he had gained as furnishing him with means of ministering without restraint to his own enjoyments.

The time would come when the question of Rochester's true character would force itself upon the attention of James; but, as yet, no doubt seems to have crossed the mind of the King that whatever the favourite did was right. During the course of the very year in which he had been admitted, to the exclusion of all others, to the fullest confidence of his master, he had been engaged in an affair by which, although he obtained the complete approbation of the King, he had drawn down upon himself the contempt of every man of right feeling in

CH. XI. 1606.

England; and there were secrets yet to be disclosed which would complete the scandalous history of the man whom James was pleased to honour.

Marriage of the Earl of Essex and Lady Frances Howard.

When James first came to England, he was anxious to put an end to those personal disputes between the leading men by which the later years of his predecessor had been troubled. He hoped to accomplish this by bringing about marriages between the great families. The Earl of Suffolk had two daughters who would, as he thought, serve his purpose. The elder was destined for Lord Cranborne, the only son of the Earl of Salisbury; the younger was to become the wife of the young Earl of Essex, who would, as it was hoped, forget his father's fate in this new alliance with the Howards and the Cecils.* It was no obstacle to the King's benevolent intentions that the bride and bridegroom by whose union such great things were to be accomplished were mere children. On the 5th of January, 1606, they were called upon to pronounce those solemn vows of which they little knew the import. Essex was only fourteen, and Lady Frances Howard was a year younger than the husband who had been chosen for her; but by a doctrine which the ecclesiastical law of England had accepted without examination from the jurisconsults of more southern climes, they were held to be of full age for the purpose of taking upon themselves the engagements of married life. Great were the festivities by which the auspicious event was celebrated. Ben Jonson did his best to produce a masque worthy of the occasion, and Inigo Jones gave his talents to construct the machinery and the decorations which were to amuse the frivolous crowd. The hollowness of the ceremony which had been witnessed by the admiring spectators must have betrayed itself by the necessity of separating the boy bridegroom from his wife. Two years after his marriage the Earl was sent to travel on the Continent, and it was not till some time after he had attained the

* It is also said that the match was proposed by Salisbury. The idea, probably, occurred to both of them. It is no argument against James's participation in the affair that he afterwards inveighed against early marriages.

age of eighteen that he returned, apparently shortly after Christmas, 1609, to claim his bride.*

Conduct of Lady Essex to her husband.

If upon his return he looked for a faithful and loving wife, he was doomed to a bitter disappointment. He soon discovered that she regarded him with the deepest repugnance. Under the most favourable circumstances this ill-assorted pair could never have lived together with any degree of comfort. The sterling qualities which Essex possessed, and which had already gained for him the respect of Prince Henry, were shrouded from the eye of the thoughtless observer by the heaviness and imperturbability of his outward demeanour. Of all women then living, the young girl of seventeen who bore the name of Countess of Essex was the least capable of appreciating his virtues. Headstrong and impetuous by nature, she had received but an evil training at the hands of her coarse-minded and avaricious mother. The Court in which she had been bound to her child-husband was no place for the cultivation of the feminine virtues of modesty and self-restraint.† She had already attracted the notice of the rising favourite, at that time still Sir Robert Carr, and if that unhallowed marriage had not stood in the way, she might have become his wife innocently enough, and have left no records of her butterfly existence with which history would have cared to meddle.

She was startled from her dream of enjoyment by the

* The date is proved by the statement in the libel (*State Trials*, ii. 785) that Essex had lived with his wife for three years before the divorce case began, and after he had arrived at the age of eighteen. The date of his baptism was the 22nd Jan. 1591 (Devereux, *Lives of the Devereux*, i. 211), consequently he must have been eighteen in January, 1609. Lady Essex's reference to 'the winter' in her letter to Mrs. Turner, *State Trials*, ii. 93, probably refers to the winter of 1609—10.

† It is difficult to pronounce with certainty upon the extent to which the Court immorality went. It is evident, from the circumstances which are known to us, that it was bad enough; but I believe that Mr. Hallam's comparison of the Court of James with that of Charles II. is considerably exaggerated. Would it be possible for a series of letters, such as that of Chamberlain, containing so little of a scandalous character, to have been written after the Restoration? I have omitted, as will have been noticed, the well-known story of the drunken scene at Theobalds, during the King of Denmark's visit, not because I doubt its accuracy, but because it would leave an impression that such scenes were of constant occurrence. Whereas it is only on very rare occasions that anything of the sort is heard of.

sombre figure of the man who claimed her as his wife. At first she refused to live with him; but she was at last forced by her parents to treat him as her husband, and finally to accompany him to his country seat at Chartley. The whole truth of her miserable life for the next three years can never be known; but enough has been told to repel even the most callous investigator of history. It is enough to say that the wretched woman set her heart upon remaining a wife only in name, and upon preserving herself for the man to whom she had given her affections. She called in the aid of Mrs. Turner, a widow of abandoned character, in whom she had found a confidant. With the aid of Doctor Forman, one of those quack doctors, half physician and half sorcerer, who were the pests of that age, these two women proceeded to administer drugs to the unconscious husband. Partly by such means as these, and partly by the forbidding demeanour which the Countess assumed towards him, she succeeded in repelling his advances.*

She thinks of procuring a divorce.

At the beginning of the year 1613, three years had passed away since the return of the Earl from the Continent. With the completion of this period a new hope awoke in the breast of Lady Essex. It was now possible to obtain a declaration of the nullity of the marriage, if she could persuade a court to believe her declaration that her husband was incapacitated by a physical defect from entering into marriage; and she may have thought that, in his eagerness to escape from a connection which had brought him so much misery, he would allow her statements to pass without any strict examination. She succeeded in gaining the support† of her father and of his uncle, Northampton, to whom she probably told only

* The Earl's account of the matter is probably that which is at the basis of the paragraphs in Wilson's *History* relating to the divorce.

† In February a curious episode occurred. One Mary Woods accused the Countess of bribing her to procure a poison for the Earl. This made the Howards for a little time hesitate about proceeding with the divorce (Chamberlain to Winwood, May 6, 1613, *Winw.* iii. 452). There are several examinations in the *S. P.* taken on the subject, but nothing can be made of them, as it is difficult to say whether it is more probable that Mary Woods invented the whole story, or that Lady Essex in reality tried to poison her husband.

as much of the story as suited her convenience. Nor were they insensible to the advantages which would accrue to them from a close alliance with Rochester. They had no doubt that a marriage with him would follow immediately upon the divorce. Lady Essex had renewed her intimacy with the favourite, and although there is no positive proof against her in existence, it is not improbable that she was already engaged in an adulterous intercourse with him. To the Howards, at that moment, such an alliance would be most welcome. For some months they had encountered the opposition of Rochester, and they had found, by experience, that Rochester's opposition was fatal to their endeavours to influence the policy or to share in the exercise of the patronage of the Government.

The Howards found little difficulty in gaining over the King. He would naturally be pleased with any prospect of bringing about a reconciliation between the two factions which were so troublesome to him. It is not likely that he was acquainted with the darker side of the story, and it is probable that he was blind to much which a man of clearer moral perception would have detected at once. Nor should it be forgotten that he may well have been desirous of repairing the ruin of which he could not but feel that he had himself been, in no small degree, the author.

Meeting of the friends of the parties.

In May a meeting was held at Whitehall, to consider upon the course which was to be pursued. The Earls of Northampton and Suffolk appeared for the lady, whilst her husband was represented by the Earl of Southampton and Lord Knollys.* It was found that Essex was determined to admit of no assertion which would throw any obstacle in the way of his own remarriage; and both Suffolk and Northampton knew that they could not prove their case without his consent. They were consequently compelled to allow that, though the Earl was incapable of being the husband of his present wife, there was nothing to prevent him marrying another. Accordingly, the way having been thus

* Lord Knollys was married to a third daughter of the Earl of Suffolk.

CH. XI. 1613.

Appointment of a Commission to try the case.

smoothed, a Commission was issued on the 16th for the trial of the case, to Archbishop Abbot, Bishops King, Andrewes, and Neile, Sir Thomas Parry, and Sir Julius Cæsar, together with the civilians, Sir Daniel Dun, Sir John Bennet, and Doctors James and Edwards.

As the case* proceeded the Howards found that they were likely to meet with an unexpected obstacle in the unyielding conscientiousness of the Archbishop. Supported as they were by the King, they had met with willing instruments in some of the Commissioners, especially in Bishop Neile and Sir Daniel Dun. But the more Abbot heard of the evidence the less he was satisfied with the part which he was expected to play. With incredible effrontery, Lady Essex allowed her counsel to argue that her husband was bewitched, though we may be sure that she took care that Doctor Forman's name was not mentioned in court. Abbot had grave doubts concerning the probability of such effects being produced by witchcraft, and these doubts were shared by the more respectable members of the Commission, and, as it appeared, even by the lawyers who pleaded on behalf of the lady. He was still more struck with the manner in which the proceedings were hurried over, and with the apparent shrinking on the part of Lady Essex's counsel from entering into the particulars of the case. Nor did it escape him that, even if the alleged facts were true, such a precedent would open a wide field for future evil, and that the proceedings of the Commissioners would be quoted by every couple who happened to be without children, and who were anxious to obtain a divorce by means of collusive proceedings.

Abbot's reasons for dissatisfaction with the Countess's case.

After some time had been spent in hearing the evidence which was produced, and in listening to the arguments of the lawyers on either side, it was found that the Commissioners were equally divided in opinion.† Abbot, who knew that the King was bent upon obtaining a

* *State Trials*, ii. 785.

† Chamberlain to Carleton, Aug. 1, 1613 (*Court and Times*, i. 260). In this letter four Commissioners only are mentioned as pronouncing against the nullity. Doctor James, however, though probably absent at that stage of the proceedings, would have joined them if they had actually come to a vote.

declaration in favour of a divorce, took an opportunity of an interview with him to press him to release him from his ungrateful task. James seemed much affected by the arguments which he used, and showed no signs of being displeased with him for the course which he had taken. But after the Archbishop had left him, and he was once more in the hands of Rochester and the Howards, he was again induced to take up their cause more warmly. The equal division of the members of the Commission gave him an excuse of adding to their number, and he allowed himself to take the unjustifiable step of appointing Bishops Bilson and Buckeridge, who could only be regarded in the light of partisans, to sit amongst the judges.

The number of the Commissioners increased.

Abbot's letter to the King.

Abbot determined to write a letter to the King. It was a great opportunity, and if he had been content to set down the arguments which he was prepared to maintain when his opinion was asked amongst the other Commissioners,* he would at least have left on record an unanswerable defence of the course which he had taken, even if he had failed in producing any lasting effect upon the mind of James. But, unfortunately, the Archbishop had an unlucky knack of committing blunders, when it would seem that he could hardly have avoided taking the right step. Incredible as it appears, he contrived, in the letter which he wrote, to omit the slightest mention of any one of the points upon which the strength of his case rested, and to substitute for them a number of most questionable propositions. To the deficiency of evidence, and to the danger of the precedent, he did not even make a passing allusion. But he argued at some length that there was no express statement in Scripture bearing upon this case, and that although it was perfectly possible that the effects attributed to witchcraft might have been produced by that means in the times of darkness and of Popish superstition, yet that it was impossible that the devil should be possessed of such power where the light of the Gospel was shining. He had not heard that either Lord or Lady Essex had taken measures against the supposed witchcraft, either by applying themselves to

* In the speech prepared, but never delivered. *State Trials,* ii. 845.

CH. XI. 1613.

prayer and fasting, or by using medical remedies. He concluded by appending to his letter a string of totally irrelevant quotations from the works of celebrated Protestant divines.*

Answer of James.

It can hardly be a matter for astonishment that James refused to admit such reasoning as this. In the answer which he wrote,† he had evidently the better of the Archbishop, at least so far as the grounds were concerned upon which Abbot had based his reasoning. But he was not content with demonstrating that the arguments used in the letter were untenable. Proud of his own logic, he called upon Abbot to withdraw such insufficient reasonings, and to rest his faith for the future upon the unerring judgment of a Sovereign who was not without some skill in divinity, and who was undoubtedly impartial in the present case.

The Commissioners pronounce for the divorce.

Abbot did not take the advice thus tendered to him. When the day came for pronouncing the decision of the Commissioners, the votes of the new members made it no longer doubtful which way that decision would be given. On the 25th of September there were seven votes given in favour of the divorce, against which the Archbishop, with four others, protested in vain.‡ In order to prevent the arguments of the protesters from being heard, an express order was brought from the King that the Commissioners should content themselves with giving their decision without adding the reasons by which they were influenced.§

Conduct of James,

Of the conduct of James, it is difficult to speak with patience. He acted as a mere partisan throughout the whole affair, and it was never doubted that his influence contributed materially to the result. Nothing could well have been more prejudicial to the interests of justice than his meddling interference at every step, which did even more harm than the appointment of the additional

* *State Trials*, ii. 794.

† *State Trials*, ii. 798, 860.

‡ Bishops Bilson, Andrewes, Neile, and Buckeridge, with Sir Julius Cæsar, Sir Thomas Parry, and Sir Daniel Dun, were in the majority. The minority was composed of the Archbishop, Bishop King, with Doctors Edwards, James, and Bennet.

§ Chamberlain to Carleton, Oct. 14, 1613. *Court and Times*, i. 275.

members. Yet it may reasonably be doubted whether he was conscious of doing anything which bore even the resemblance of an error. He was thrown almost entirely amongst men whose interests led them to influence him in one direction, and, utterly unprotected as he was by any real knowledge of what justice was, he probably looked with complacency upon an act which, at all events, freed two wretched persons from a life of misery, and was hardly inclined to investigate closely the evidence upon which the opinion which he formed was based, or to be debarred from doing what he fancied to be right by any regard to the future consequences of his actions. That it was improper for a Sovereign to meddle with the proceedings of a court once constituted, was an idea which certainly never entered into his head.

and of Andrewes.

There was one man who took part in these proceedings whose character for truthfulness and honesty of purpose is of far greater importance than that of James. Before the commencement of the sittings of the Commission, Andrewes had pronounced an opinion unfavourable to the divorce; and yet, soon after he had taken his seat, he changed his view of the case, and steadily adhered to the opinion of the majority. Suspicions could not fail to arise that he had given way before the influence of the Court, and these suspicions derived some importance from the fact that he made no use of his intimate knowledge of the canon law, but, with rare exceptions, remained silent during the whole course of the proceedings. All that can be said is, that against such a man it is impossible to receive anything short of direct evidence, and that it is better to suppose that he was, by some process of reasoning with which we are unacquainted, satisfied with the evidence adduced, though he must have felt that there was that in the conduct of Lady Essex which prevented him from regarding the result of the trial with any degree of satisfaction.*

Unanimous condemnation

For four months the trial had formed the general topic of conversation wherever men met together in

* In the Harl. MS. 39, fol. 416, is a paper drawn up by Dr. Dun, which will give all that was to be said by those who were in favour of the divorce.

CH. XI. 1613. Reception of the sentence throughout the country.

public or in private. The effrontery of the Countess, the shameless meddling of the King and of his courtiers, the truckling subserviency of Neile and his supporters, were discussed with a remarkable unanimity of abhorrence in every corner of the land. In the whole course of James's misgovernment, nothing had as yet occurred which had exposed him to such well-deserved unpopularity. The sober stood aghast at his disregard for the decencies of life, whilst the light-hearted laughed at the easy credulity with which he took for granted all the tales of a profligate woman. It may be doubted whether his rupture with the House of Commons contributed so much to widen the breach between himself and his subjects as his conduct on this occasion.

General expression of dislike at the conduct of Bilson.

The bitterest shafts of ridicule, however, were reserved for Bilson. Better things were expected of his known talents and learning; and those who thought it only natural that men like Neile should wallow in the mire for the sake of Court favour, were ill-pleased to see the Bishop of Winchester following his unworthy example. Bilson himself was not ill-satisfied with what he had done, and was gratified by the honour of knighthood which was conferred by the King upon his son. He was not long in discovering the unpopularity which he had incurred. His son was immediately nicknamed, by some wag, Sir Nullity Bilson, and the appellation stuck to the unfortunate man for the remainder of his life. His own son-in-law refused to live in his house, because he could not endure the jeers of his companions, who used to remind him that he only held his wife on the Bishop's sufferance, who would be able at any time to declare that his marriage was a nullity.*

Popularity of Abbot.

Abbot's conduct throughout the whole affair, on the other hand, made him the most popular man in England. The country was delighted to find that in that corrupt Court there was at least one who could hold his ground in opposition to the King's wishes, when a matter of conscience was at stake.

When the long expected sentence was pronounced,

* *State Trials*, ii. 833.

CH. XI.

1613.

Sir Thomas Overbury.

Lady Frances Howard, now no longer Countess of Essex, was once more free from the bonds under which she had writhed so long. The prize for which she had played the desperate game, and for the sake of which she had thrown away all feminine modesty, was within her reach at last; the man for whose sake she had braved the scorn of the world, and had submitted to make her name the subject of unseemly jests, was now ready to make her his wife. But even those whose sense of her degradation was the deepest had failed to measure the full extent of her guilt. They did not know that, whilst she was receiving the congratulations of all who believed that her smile would light them on the road to wealth and honour, she was carrying about with her the consciousness that in an instant the edifice of her fortunes might crumble into dust, and that she was liable at any moment to be dragged off from the bright scenes which she loved too well, to take her place in the felon's dock as a murderess.

The story of the tragedy, in which the proud beauty enacted so fearful a part, will in all probability never be known in all its details with anything approaching to certainty. The evidence upon which it rests has only reached us in a mutilated state, and even that which is in our hands is in such an unsatisfactory condition that it is impossible to come to any definite conclusion on the greater part of the questions which may be raised. But amidst all these uncertainties one fact stands out too clearly to be explained away. The guilt of Lady Essex is proved by evidence of which no reasonable doubt can, by any possibility, be entertained.

Overbury's connection with Rochester.

Amongst those who had attached themselves to the rising fortunes of the favourite was Sir Thomas Overbury, a young man of considerable talents, and, as his published writings prove, not without some nobleness of character. He was not long in obtaining an ascendancy over the inferior mind of Rochester, who submitted to be instructed by him in the wiles by which he hoped to make good his footing at court.* It is difficult to say

* The nature of the relations which existed between the two men comes out strongly in the letters printed in Appendix IV.

CH. XI. 1613.

how far Overbury was actuated by any feeling higher than a desire for personal aggrandisement. It was probably through his means that Rochester adopted Neville as his candidate for the Secretaryship, but it is difficult to determine whether, in making the selection, he had any thought of the political principles which were involved in the choice. The position in which he was placed was not one to develope whatever virtues he may have originally possessed. Even if he had not been naturally of a self-satisfied and overbearing disposition, he could hardly have continued for any length of time to supply Rochester's deficiencies without contracting a habit of treating him with an arrogance which would, sooner or later, become intolerable. The inevitable breach was only hastened by the efforts which he made to deter his patron from the ill-advised course which he was pursuing with regard to Lady Essex. As it is certain * that in earlier times he had assisted Rochester to compose the letters with which he courted that lady, it is difficult to explain the abhorrence with which he regarded the proposed marriage. It is possible that whilst he was ready to wink at an adulterous connection with another man's wife, he was startled by a proposal which would result in making a marriage possible, and which would bring with it a reconciliation between his patron and the Howards. If it had been through his influence that Rochester had placed himself in decided opposition to the powerful Earls of Suffolk and Northampton, he may well have dreaded lest he should be the first to fall a sacrifice as soon as a reconciliation with them was effected. But however this may have been, it is certain that he employed all his energies in deterring Rochester from the step which he was about to take, and that he let no opportunity slip of blackening the character of the lady upon whom his patron had set his affections.

His opposition to Rochester's proceedings with regard to Lady Essex.

As the time drew on for instituting the proceedings for the purpose of procuring the divorce, Overbury's language became more than ever annoying to Rochester,

* This could not be believed on anything short of his own evidence. Overbury to Rochester, *Winw.* iii. 478.

who was by no means inclined to give way to his follower's instructions, coupled as they were by insinuations that he owed all his advancement to his assistance.* Even if Overbury knew no more than what was soon to be laid before the Commissioners, his behaviour was likely to lead to a rupture. It is, however, difficult to avoid the conclusion that he had heard something which would enable him to put a stop to the divorce if he pleased. Rochester was not the man to keep a secret, and if he had only told Overbury, in a moment of confidential intercourse, one half of the stories which he must himself have heard from Lady Essex, of the way in which she had treated her husband, he must have known that he had entrusted him with a secret which, if he should determine to reveal it, would make it impossible for the most subservient judges to pronounce in favour of the divorce.†

The King jealous of Overbury's influence with Rochester.

If this conjecture be correct, it becomes at once intelligible why all who looked hopefully for a sentence of divorce should be anxious to get Overbury out of the way, at least till the proceedings were at an end. It was not long before a golden opportunity presented itself of accomplishing their purpose. Some one or another told James that it was commonly reported that, whilst Rochester ruled the King, Overbury ruled Rochester. Upon hearing this James, who looked with jealousy upon the man who had defeated his intention of keeping the favourite altogether in his own hands, determined to prove his independence.

He proposes to him a diplomatic appointment.

He accordingly directed Abbot to suggest to Overbury, as from himself, the propriety of his accepting a diplomatic appointment upon the Continent. Overbury had no wish to leave England, where he knew that the road to advancement lay. He therefore requested Rochester to do what he could to save him from this banishment. From the uncertain evidence which we possess, it is difficult to make

* Peyton's Examination, *State Trials*, ii. 978.

† This seems a much more probable explanation than that Overbury was acquainted with some secret which would ruin Rochester, such as his supposed complicity in the imaginary murder of Prince Henry, of which not a shadow of proof has ever been adduced.

CH. XI. 1613. out precisely what Rochester's conduct was.* It is possible that at first he had been ready to assent to the expatriation of Overbury, but that when he discovered how unwilling he was to leave the country, he changed his plan, and encouraged him in resisting the King's wishes, foreseeing that he would be committed to prison in consequence. An imprisonment of a few months would keep his mouth shut till the proceedings were over, and it is not unlikely that Rochester may have looked with favour upon a course which would enable him to retain the services of Overbury, whilst he would secure his attachment more completely by appearing in the light of his liberator.

Overbury refuses to accept it, and is committed to the Tower.

The King was not to be baffled in this manner. He sent Ellesmere and Pembroke to Overbury, with a formal offer of the appointment. As soon as Overbury perceived that excuses were of no avail, he boldly refused to comply, and added that neither in law or justice could he be compelled to leave his country. James was, of course, enraged with what he considered to be an insolent reply, and called upon the Council to vindicate his honour. They immediately summoned Overbury before them, and committed him to the Tower for contempt of the King's commands.†

In giving his assent to Overbury's imprisonment, Rochester was, no doubt, acting in concert with Northampton. As far as we can arrive at any probable conclusion as to their intentions, there is no reason to suppose that they meant anything more than to get him

* The want of evidence is here felt the more, as the two reports of the trial of the Earl of Somerset differ in a material point. In one Somerset (which was the title which was afterwards conferred upon Rochester) is represented as saying that Overbury asked him to take upon himself the refusal of the embassy; in the other, as acknowledging that he hindered Overbury on purpose to procure his imprisonment (Amos, *Great Oyer of Poisoning*, 105, 151). Overbury's own letters, as well as the evidence given at the trial, corroborate the latter statement; but Sir D. Digges gave evidence that Overbury once told him that he meant to undertake the employment, but that he afterwards sent him a message that he had changed his mind (Amos, 88). I have attempted to give an explanation which finds room for both statements, but of course it is nothing more than a mere conjecture. Compare Wotton's letter to Sir Edmond Bacon, April 22, 1613.—*Reliq. Wott.*

† Chamberlain to Carleton, April 29, 1613, *S. P. Dom.* lxxii. 120. The date of the committal was the 21st of April.

CH. XI.
1613.

out of the way for a time.* Orders were given that he should have no communication with anyone beyond the limits of his prison; and, though his health was failing, he was not permitted to have a servant with him. So strictly were these orders interpreted by Sir William Waad, the Lieutenant of the Tower, that although Rochester sent every day to inquire after the health of the prisoner, the bearers of the messages were never allowed to see him, or even to deliver a letter which, on one occasion, they had brought with them.

Sir G. Helwys appointed Lieutenant of the Tower in the place of Sir W. Waad.

This was not what was intended. If Overbury should be released without feeling a sense of obligation to Rochester, the first thing he would do upon leaving the Tower would be to disclose the secrets which he was so anxious to keep from the public ear. Waad must therefore be removed.† It was not difficult to trump up charges against him. He was accused of carelessness in guarding his prisoners, and especially of allowing too much liberty to Overbury. He had also permitted the Lady Arabella to have the use of a key, which might, as it was alleged, prove serviceable to her if she had any design of effecting her escape.‡ A successor was found in Sir Gervase Helwys, who was likely to be more complaisant.

Helwys's agreement with Rochester and Northampton.

It is plain that Helwys, upon his appointment, entered into some kind of compact with Rochester and Northampton. Of its nature there is no sufficient evidence But it is probable that he did not go farther than to agree

* Mr. Amos thinks that on the whole it is probable that Rochester was innocent of the crime imputed to him. It would be needless to repeat the arguments which will be found in his work (see especially pp. 349–356). It may, however, be added that it is unlikely that, if Rochester and Northampton had determined on poisoning Overbury, they would have had him committed to the Tower. Poison could have been administered far more easily in Rochester's own house, and even if they could foresee that they would be able to substitute a dependent of their own for Waad, their doing so would only be likely to draw attention to their proceedings. The strongest part of the evidence in favour of Rochester will be found in the progress of the narrative.

† I need not remind the reader that this explanation is purely conjectural. Of course the ordinary explanation is that Waad was not likely to be complaisant enough to overlook the murder.

‡ Waad's account of his dismissal, Sept. 1615, *S. P. Dom.* lxxxi. 84; Somerset's speech, Amos, 109.

Ch. XI. 1613.

to take care that their letters reached Overbury, whilst he would be at hand to supply whatever comments might be required, without allowing any suspicion to arise that he was acting from other motives than those of kindness to an unfortunate prisoner.*

Feelings of Lady Essex towards Overbury.

Whilst the confederates were calmly embarking in this scheme, there was one person who was not content with such half measures. To Lady Essex the language which Overbury had used was not merely a danger against the recurrence of which it might be necessary to take precautions, it was an intolerable insult, which cried aloud for vengeance.† With the same fixity of purpose with which she had for three years pursued the object which she had in view, she determined that Overbury should die before he left the Tower. She had already, whilst he was still at liberty, attempted in vain to induce a man who had a quarrel with him to waylay him and assassinate him.‡ She now resolved to accomplish her design by means of poison. Mrs. Turner was at hand to give her every information on the subject of the drugs which it would be necessary to use. Everything, however, depended upon the character of the man to whom was assigned the office of taking the immediate charge of the prisoner. Lady Essex's choice fell upon Richard Weston, who had for many years been a servant of Mrs. Turner, and who had lately been employed in carrying messages between the Countess and her lover. She accordingly used her interest with Sir Thomas Monson,§

She procures the appointment of Weston to be his keeper.

* This conjecture seems to derive some strength from the letters in Appendix IV.

† A difficulty certainly occurs here. Is it likely that Lady Essex, who was preparing for a marriage with Rochester, and who had perhaps already committed adultery with him, would not have informed her lover of her intention? It is not a difficulty to be lightly disposed of, but it must be remembered that Sir David Wood had already offered to murder Overbury if Lady Essex could obtain Rochester's promise to obtain pardon for him. When he came again, she told him that it could not be (Amos, 87). Either Lady Essex had been afraid to speak to Rochester on the subject, or he had refused to consent, or, if consenting, he had refused to compromise himself. In any of the three cases, she would avoid making him her confidant on such a subject in future.

‡ Examination of Sir David Wood, Oct. 21, 1615, *S. P. Dom.* lxxxii. 84.

§ Here again, why should Monson have been employed if Helwys had been appointed with the express purpose of poisoning Overbury? Surely Helwys would at once have been told to employ Weston.

CH. XI. 1613.

the Master of the Armoury at the Tower, who, in turn, persuaded Helwys to admit Weston as one of the keepers, and to give him the immediate charge of Overbury.

Requires Weston to poison him.

Weston had not been long in charge of the prisoner, when he was summoned by Mrs. Turner to attend upon Lady Essex at Whitehall. As soon as he was admitted into her presence, she told him that a small bottle would be sent to him, the contents of which were to be given to Overbury. This bottle she had obtained from an apothecary named Franklin. At the same time she warned him not to taste any of the liquid himself. She added, that if he acted according to her orders, he should be well rewarded.

Weston stopped by Helwys.

Soon after this conversation, Weston received the poison. As he was on his way with it to Overbury's lodgings, with the intention of mixing it with the soup which was to be sent up to him, he met the Lieutenant, and supposing him to be aware of what was going on, showed him the bottle, and asked him if he should give it to Overbury then. Helwys, as soon as he discovered what the keeper's meaning was, persuaded him to desist from the wicked action which he was intending to commit. Weston put the bottle aside, and the next day emptied it into the gutter.*

They do not reveal the secret.

Unhappily for himself and the other instruments in this abominable plot, Helwys had not the moral courage to denounce the culprit. Unless he could obtain credit for his tale, such a step would be certain ruin to himself, and he could not know how far the Countess's secret was shared by the powerful members of her family. Even if they were themselves innocent, they would undoubtedly be able to do many ill offices to him, if by his means the shame of Lady Essex were published to the world.

He therefore thought it better to hush the matter up

* Weston's Examination, Oct. 1. Helwys to the King, Sept. 10, 1615. Narrative of Helwys's execution (Amos, 178, 186, 213). Helwys and Weston agree in all important particulars, and the way in which Weston's confession was forced out of him makes this agreement valuable, as it shows that there had been no collusion between the two. Besides, is it likely that Overbury would have lived if the poison had been really given him so long previously?

CH. XI. 1613.

than to attempt to bring the powerful criminal to justice. However much the information may have shocked him at first, he soon grew to view it merely as it affected his own position. Even whilst he was arguing with Weston, upon Weston's telling him that he should have to administer the poison sooner or later, he allowed himself to reply, that it might be done provided that he knew nothing of it. It was finally agreed that Weston should inform Lady Essex that the poison had been given, and should describe the supposed effects of it upon the health of the prisoner.

Overbury's health suffers from his imprisonment.

Weston had the less difficulty in doing this, as Overbury was in reality far from well. He was ailing when he first entered the Tower,* and the sudden disappointment of his hopes had worked upon his mind. Every day which passed without bringing an order for his release increased his despondency. Whilst he was in this state, he suggested to Rochester that he should procure him an emetic, in order that, as soon as he heard that he had taken it, he might attempt to work upon the King's compassion by representing him as suffering from the effects of his confinement. Such treatment was not likely to improve his health. We may well believe that Rochester did not press the King very urgently to liberate the prisoner, even if he mentioned the subject to him at all. James consented to allow Overbury to receive the visits of a physician, but he was too much incensed at his presumption to give any heed to his request for freedom.†

Lady Essex persists in her attempts.

Whether the course of the unhappy man's disease was assisted by poison is a question to which it is impossible

* That there was some truth in the statement which he made of his ill-health, in order to excuse himself from being sent abroad, is shown by the first letter in Appendix IV. Still he was to all appearances a healthy man at that time.

† Rochester to Craig. Northampton to Helwys (Amos, 166). Mr. Amos remarks that these papers show that Rochester was willing that Overbury should be visited by a physician. Sir R. Killigrew's letter in the Appendix proves beyond doubt that Rochester asked him for an emetic for himself. A later letter of Lidcote's proves that Rochester sent other medicines to Overbury. It is, to say the least of it, extremely improbable that, if he intended to poison Overbury, he would bring suspicion upon himself, by sending him harmless medicines at the same time. The same remark applies to the sending of the tarts, &c., afterwards mentioned.

to give more than a very uncertain answer. Amidst contradictory evidence and conflicting probabilities, all that can be made out is, that Lady Essex did not desist from her design. Rochester was in the habit of sending tarts, jellies, and wine to the prisoner, by means of which he contrived to smuggle in the letters which he addressed to him. Lady Essex, if we are to believe a story which both she and Helwys afterwards admitted to be true, took advantage of this to mix poison with the food which was thus conveyed to him. This, however, as Helwys stated, was never allowed to reach the prisoner. It cannot however be proved whether the food thus provided was in reality kept back or no, excepting in so far that it is highly improbable that it should have reached him, and that he should, after partaking of it, have continued to live. There are even strong grounds for suspecting that no poison was ever put into the tarts at all. What is certain is, that Overbury* grew gradually

* The letter printed in Appendix IV., No. 23, was used at the time to prove the poisoning of the tarts, &c., and, together with the admissions of Helwys and Lady Essex, it certainly gives strong reasons for suspicion. The interpretation then given was that the word 'letters' in it signified 'poison.' But are there not reasons which make this interpretation, to say the least of it, very doubtful? The writer sends a tart to be changed 'in the place of his that is now come.' This is not very clear. Does it mean that Overbury had returned one? Possibly. She then promises to send a tart at four, and contemplates the possibility of Overbury's sending the tart and jelly and wine to the Lieutenant's wife, and warns her not to eat the tart and jelly because there are 'letters' in them. Does it seem likely that when Weston was at hand, and, as she believed, still faithful to her, she would poison jellies and tarts which she was uncertain whether Overbury would ever touch? If we read this in the light of Overbury's letter, printed in Appendix IV., No. 6, the difficulty becomes still greater, for we there see that Overbury made a practice of sending the jelly, &c., back to the Lieutenant, which Lady Essex appears to have known. If Lady Essex really meant 'letters' when she wrote the word, all becomes clear. Helwys may afterwards have stated that 'letters' meant 'poison' in mere desperation, and when the lady confessed the same, she knew that her case was desperate, and had probably meant to plead guilty. When, therefore, the examiners came to question her as to whether Helwys's statement was true, she may have allowed it in order to be quit of them, knowing well that it would not do her much harm, as the evidence against her was strong enough already. It must not be forgotten that she afterwards retracted some statements made in the lost confession, in which she first stated that 'letters' meant poison (Bacon's *Works*, ed. Montagu, vi. 234, and in the confession in Appendix IV. 24), and that if the second report of the trial be correct, she had only said that 'she meant, perhaps, poison' (Amos, 145). It seems to me much more probable that the tarts went backwards and forwards as media of a correspondence, and that Helwys invented the theory of the

CH. XI. 1613.

worse. In writing to Rochester, he became more and more importunate. Rochester seems to have represented to him that Suffolk was an obstacle to his release. He accordingly wrote to Suffolk, protesting that if he regained his liberty he would use all his influence with his patron in favour of Suffolk. About the same time Overbury wrote to Northampton, assuring him that he had never spoken dishonourably of Lady Essex, and promising to abstain from all reflections upon her for the future.

Proceedings of Rochester and Northampton.

From the stray fragments which have reached us of Overbury's correspondence, it seems as if both Rochester and Northampton were still encouraging him in the belief that they were straining every nerve for his delivery, and that Helwys was acting as their agent in bringing him to a sense of the obligations which he was supposed to be under to them. That Northampton, at least, received with pleasure the news of Overbury's illness and probable death, there can be no doubt; but there is no evidence to prove that he was aware of his niece's proceedings, though, on the other hand, there is no proof that he was kept in ignorance of them;* and Mrs. Turner certainly stated shortly before her execution that he was as deeply involved in guilt as any of the rest.

At last Lady Essex could bear the suspense no longer.

poison, in order to conceal his breach of trust in permitting it to go on through his hands, and to magnify his own merits in stopping the poison from arriving.

The warrant in Appendix IV., No. 25, shows that Somerset was anxious Overbury should be visited by others besides the physician.

* Here, again, the two reports of the trial are very perplexing. In the printed trial Northampton's letter to Rochester is quoted thus: 'I cannot deliver with what caution and discretion the Lieutenant hath undertaken Overbury. But for his conclusion I do and ever will love him better; which was this, that either Overbury shall recover, and do good offices betwixt my Lord of Suffolk and you . . . or else, that he shall not recover at all, which he thinks the most sure and happy change of all' (Amos, 25). In the other report the important words are: 'Overbury may recover, if you find him altered to do you better services; but the best is not to suffer him to recover' (Amos, 141). In quotations from written documents, the printed report seems to me to be the better authority, wherever they are not intentionally garbled. Does not all the constant correspondence with Overbury look as if it was expected that he would be free some day? Of what use was all this trouble if it was intended to poison him? Letter 22, in the Appendix, does not appear to be written by one confederate to another.

Whatever may have been the cause of Overbury's illness, he was at last not without hopes of recovery.* She was tired of Weston and his protestation that he had done all in his power, and had given enough to Overbury to poison twenty men. She found that a French apothecary named Lobell attended upon Overbury in the absence of the King's physician, Dr. Mayerne. If we can venture to rest anything upon the uncertain evidence before us, we may come to the conclusion that an assistant of Lobell's was bribed to administer the fatal drug. On the 14th of September, he succeeded in accomplishing his purpose by means of an injection. On the following day the prisoner died, the unhappy victim of a woman's vengeance. His death took place only ten days before the judgment was delivered by the Commissioners in the case of the divorce, by which his murderess received the prize which she had stooped so low to win.†

* Appendix III., No. 22. There is no date, but it must be subsequent to the letter to Suffolk of the 24th of August.

† Mr. Amos's book is too well known to make it necessary for me to refer to anything more than the leading points of the evidence. He suggests that Lobell may have been the poisoner, and seeks to connect this with his supposition that the King may have been at the bottom of the crime, though he supposes that Lady Essex may have also formed an independent plot against Overbury (pp. 162, 494). Dr. Rimbault, the editor of Overbury's Works, goes further, and boldly states that Lobell administered the fatal clyster (*Life of Overbury*, prefaced to his Works, p. liii.). Of this there is no satisfactory evidence whatever. Weston stated in his examination of the 1st of October 1615 (Amos, 180), that Helwys ordered 'that none should come . . . but the former apothecary,' i.e. Lobell, . . . 'or his man, and that no other came at any time, or gave any clyster to Sir Thomas Overbury,' and on the 6th of October (Amos, 182), that 'little before his death, and, as he taketh it, two or three days, Overbury received a clyster given him by Paul de Lobell.' The clyster by which death was caused was not administered two or three days before, but the very day before the death of Overbury. The only evidence of any kind against Lobell is derived from Rider's examination (Amos, 168). From this it appears that Rider met Lobell in October 1615, and talked to him of the rumours of Overbury's having been murdered. Lobell asserted that he died of consumption, and that the clyster which was said to have caused his death was prescribed by Mayerne, 'and that his son had made it according to his direction.' A week afterwards Rider met him again walking with his wife, and told him the poison was given by an apothecary's boy, meaning by this young Lobell's servant. Upon this Mrs. Lobell said to her husband, 'Oh! mon mari, &c.'—'that was William you sent into France.' Upon this Lobell trembled and exhibited signs of great discomposure. It does not, however, follow that he had known of the servant's act. He knew that his sending him away would bring suspicion upon himself, and Mr. Amos knows better than any one else that innocence might well tremble at the prospect of being tried in an

CH. XI.
1613.

Commission to inquire into the state of the navy.

It can hardly be considered to have been merely an accidental circumstance that these scenes of wickedness and immorality in high places were contemporaneous with the first of a series of legal proceedings, the object of which was to defend the prerogative from the assaults of hostile criticism. The growing unpopularity of the Government made men more ready than they had hitherto been to inquire into the limits of its powers; and James knew no other way of meeting such assaults than by imposing silence upon his assailants.

In the course of the preceding winter,* a commission had been issued to inquire into the abuses which were said to exist in the management of the navy. A similar inquiry had been made a few years previously, which had resulted in little more than in the production of a voluminous report by Sir Robert Cotton.† In spite of the poverty of the Exchequer, money had always been forthcoming for the maintenance of the navy. If the ships were not in good order, it was the fault of the officers who were charged with keeping them in repair, or of the system of management which prevailed in the dockyards.

The renewal of the inquiry was felt by Nottingham as a personal affront offered to him in his capacity of Lord High Admiral. He was a brave man, and had won the honours which he enjoyed by his services, when in the hour of danger he had led the mariners of England against the Armada, but he was not possessed of that energy of character, or of those administrative abilities,

English Court at the beginning of the seventeenth century. There is no improbability in Lobell's own account that the boy's parents asked him to give him an introduction to some friends in France, which he did the more readily, as he knew his master used him hardly. The argument against Lobell acquires weight from the fact that he was not put on his trial. It should, however, be remembered that it was the interest of the prosecution to keep the whole history of the apothecary's boy in the background. He was out of England, and if it had been proved that he was the real murderer, all the other prosecutions would fall to the ground at once; as an accessory could not be prosecuted until a verdict was obtained against the principal. I have omitted all reference to Franklyn's evidence, as no weight whatever can be attached to the assertions of so unblushing a liar.

* I have been unable to find the commission amongst the patents. Perhaps, in consequence of the opposition it received it was never enrolled. It does not appear to have been acted upon.

† *S. P. Dom.* xli.

which were alone capable of making head against the evils which prevailed in the department over which he presided; and, as usually happens, he was the last to perceive his own deficiencies.

Opposed by Nottingham and Mansell.

He determined, therefore, to oppose the inquiry to the utmost. He directed Sir Robert Mansell, who, as Treasurer of the Navy, was equally interested with himself in frustrating the proceedings of the Commissioners, to obtain a legal opinion upon the validity of the Commission under which they acted.

They obtain from Whitelocke an opinion against its legality.

Upon this Mansell applied to Whitelocke, who had been brought into notice by his great speech on the impositions, as a man eminently fitted to deal with the legal questions by which the prerogative was affected. He obtained from him, without difficulty, a paper in which were set down the objections to the Commission which presented themselves to his mind. Whitelocke's paper has not been preserved; but, as far as we can judge from the report of the proceedings to which he was afterwards subjected, he declared, at once, that the Commission was illegal, as it contained directions to the Commissioners to 'give order for the due punishment of the offenders.' Such directions, he urged, were contrary to the well known clause of Magna Charta, which provides that no free man shall be injured in body or goods, except by the judgment of his peers or by the law of the land.

This paper found its way into the King's hands. Whitelocke, however, had taken the precaution of not signing his name to it, and probably had not allowed it to leave his chambers in his own handwriting. Although, therefore, he was strongly suspected of being the author of it, no steps were for some time taken against him.

Whitelocke's argument in Chancery.

Whilst he was thus exposed to the displeasure of the King, he drew down upon himself the anger of the Lord Chancellor, by an argument which he delivered in the course of his professional duties. Having occasion to defend a plaintiff whose adversary appealed to the Court of the Earl Marshal, he argued that there was no such Court legally in existence, and succeeded in convincing the Master of the Rolls, and in obtaining an

CH. XI. 1613. order from him by which the defendant was restrained from carrying his cause out of Chancery. A few days later an attempt was made to reverse this order. As May 17. soon as the Chancellor had read it he burst out into an invective against Whitelocke. It was in vain that the sturdy lawyer stood his ground, and proceeded to quote the precedents and Acts of Parliament upon which he rested the conclusion to which he had come. Ellesmere only inveighed the more bitterly against him and the other lawyers who troubled themselves about questions concerning the prerogative. He told him that he himself knew nothing about the precedents to which he had referred. The question was too great for him. He would acquaint the King with what had passed, who could judge of the whole matter.

It was to no purpose that Whitelocke protested that he had not questioned the power of the King to grant commissions under which a Marshal's Court could be held, but had only argued that, as a matter of fact, no such commission had been issued. On the following day Ellesmere told his story to Northampton and Suffolk, who, as Commissioners for executing the office of Earl Marshal, were personally interested in the question. These three together carried their complaints to the King, and aggravated the supposed offence by reminding him that Whitelocke had not only been one of the leaders of the opposition to the impositions in the late Parliament, but that he was, in all probability, the author of the exceptions to the Commission for the Reform of the Navy, which had so greatly excited his displeasure.

He is committed to the Fleet.

May 18.

James directed that the offender should be brought before the Council. The three lords, well satisfied with their success, obtained an order that very afternoon to summon the obnoxious lawyer to appear. After he had been examined, he was immediately committed to the Fleet, where Mansell was already in confinement.

Mansell and Whitelocke charged before the

About three weeks after his imprisonment, he was again summoned before the Council to answer for the contempt which he was said to have committed, in the opinion which he had given upon the Navy Commission.

1613.

The charge against him on account of his argument in the Court of Chancery was dropped, in all probability in consequence of the discovery that he was right in point of law. At the same time Mansell was called upon to answer for the part which he had taken in acting as agent between Nottingham and Whitelocke, though, to save appearances, it was given out that Nottingham's name had been improperly used in the affair.

Council with their proceedings in reference to the exceptions to the Commission on the Navy.

Argument of Hobart and Bacon.

Hobart and Bacon appeared against Whitelocke. After objecting to the unceremonious language in which he had spoken of a document proceeding from the Crown, they charged him with making false statements in the opinion which he had given. It was not true, they said, that the Commissioners were empowered to inflict punishment themselves upon the offenders. It was never intended that they should do more than refer the offences to the ordinary course of justice. How far this explanation was warranted by the facts, we have no means of judging. It is, at all events, probable that the words of the Commission were, at least, ambiguous on this point. But the Crown lawyers took care not to rest their argument upon a mere question of fact which, however important to the parties themselves, would fail to command any general interest. They proceeded to argue that, even if the facts were as Whitelocke asserted them to be, he would still have been in the wrong. In the first place, the officers who were subjected to the Commission were the King's own servants, and were therefore liable to punishment by him in his capacity of master, as well as in that of sovereign. This, however, was not enough, they declared that there was nothing in Magna Charta which made it unlawful for the King to issue commissions with power to imprison the bodies, or to seize the lands and goods of his subjects without any reference to the ordinary courts of law. They affirmed that, in requiring a condemnation by the verdict of a jury or by the law of the land, Magna Charta included the case of proceedings before courts which existed in virtue of the King's prerogative for the trial of cases in which political questions were involved. To deny this, they said, would be 'to overthrow the King's

CH. XI. 1613.

martial power, and the authority of the Council-table, and the force of His Majesty's proclamations, and other actions and directions of State and policy applied to the necessity of times and occasions which fall not many times within the remedies of ordinary justice.' The same reasoning might be used to prove the illegality of the precautionary imprisonment which was a matter of necessity whenever resort could not be had, at a moment's notice, to the decision of a jury.

Submission of Whitelocke and Mansell.

As soon as these arguments were completed, Montagu, who, upon Doderidge's promotion to the bench, had succeeded him as King's Serjeant, followed with charges of a similar nature against Mansell. The statements of the lawyers were, of course, supported by the Council itself, followed with charges of a similar nature against Mansell. There was nothing for it but submission to the opinion of men with whom it was in vain to reason.

They are released, June 13.

Both Whitelocke and Mansell acknowledged the justice of the censure passed upon them, and requested the lords to assist them in an appeal to the clemency of the King.* On

* Whitelocke's *Liber Famelicus*, 33-40, 113-118. There is a report in Lansd. MS. 160, fol. 17, of the proceedings, which shows how much Bacon's speech must have been corrected before it was published (Bacon's *Works*, ed. Montagu, vii. 281; Chamberlain to Carleton, June 10, 1613, *Court and Times*, i. 241). Whitelocke's submission is worth reading, partly because it was corrected by Bacon, who was anxious to save him from any punishment, but still more because it shows, as in the case of Selden, how far a thoroughly honest man would go in renouncing the opinions which he still held. In fact, submissions of this kind were regarded as mere formalities.

'Whereas your most humble subject hath justly and worthily been convented before the Right Honourable the Lords of Your Majesty's Privy Council, and the principal judges of the realm, for his great error and misdemeanour in his rash and unadvised delivery of his opinion against your Majesty's Royal Commission, a matter too high and weighty for your subject to intermeddle withal, and wherein he confesseth, being now better instructed by that he hath heard as well from your learned counsel as from the lords and judges, that he had no just ground of exception: which offence your subject freely acknowledged before your lordships, professing himself most heartily sorrowful and penitent for the same.

'It may, therefore, please your most excellent Majesty, of your natural goodness, clemency, and princely disposition, to vouchsafe to accept from your dutiful subject this his humble submission and acknowledgment of that his offence, by which he hath most worthily drawn your Majesty's heavy displeasure upon him, and hereby is more afflicted in his own soul and conscience than he can be by any other calamity of this world.

'He therefore humbly prostrateth himself at your Majesty's feet, for your grace and pardon therein; entreating your Majesty to remove from him that your just displeasure conceived against him, and to accept from your subject this assurance and protestation in the faith and loyalty of a the following day it was announced that the King had accepted their submission, and both the prisoners were set at liberty.

Judicial irresponsibility claimed by the Government.

These proceedings are of no small importance in the history of the English Revolution. They drew forth a declaration from the Crown lawyers, which was endorsed by the Privy Council, without any protest from Coke and the other judges who were sitting by. That declaration went so far as to assert that, if only it could be shown that there was some political question involved in the case, it was an offence even to question the legality of the exercise of judicial powers by persons appointed by the Crown to act without the intervention of a jury. Such a declaration was the counterpart of the judgment of the Exchequer in the case of the impositions. The Government, which had acted upon that judgment, had done its best to make its authority independent of the votes of the House of Commons. It now declared its adhesion to a principle which would make it independent of the verdict of a jury.

Nor was the composition of the existing courts, or of those which might afterwards be created, less liable to objection than was their total want of responsibility. The same men who exercised the executive authority sat as a judicial body in the Star Chamber, with no check upon their governmental prejudices, except that which might be afforded by the presence of a few of the judges who held their positions at the pleasure of the Crown.

It is strange that James should have flattered himself that he would be able to maintain himself in such a position. It is still stranger that he should have imagined

subject that he will not only circumspectly for ever hereafter seek to avoid the offending of your most excellent Majesty, but will actually employ the whole endeavours of his life to deserve admission to your Majesty's favour, always applying himself to this rule of duty between your Majesty and himself, Tibi summum rerum arbitrium Dii dederunt: nobis obedientiæ gloria relicta est.

'Your Majesty's most submissive and obedient subject,

'JAMES WHITELOCKE.'

Council Register, June 12, 1613.

CH. XI. 1613.

that he could exercise the authority which he claimed through such instruments as Rochester and the Howards.

Part taken by Bacon in these proceedings.

There was, however, one man who took part in these proceedings whose conduct has been a mystery to succeeding generations. So perfectly have Englishmen become convinced, by the additional experience which they have acquired in the course of two centuries and a half, that a government which lays claim to freedom from responsibility is on the high road to its own ruin, that it is almost impossible for us to understand how Bacon could have lent the support of his mighty intellect to such a system. To those who venerate the memory of the champions who, in the hour of danger, stood firmly round the great cause of English constitutionalism, and who know what is the value of the victory which was won at the cost of so much blood and suffering, it is hard to look back with calmness upon the man who put forth all the powers of his unrivalled genius to overthrow the principles upon which the liberties of his country repose. To those who do not perhaps love Bacon less, but who love England more, the conclusions to which so many investigators have come seem to be unassailable. Not daring to dispute the intellectual powers of the man, they have been driven to push to the extremest verge of possibility their belief in his moral turpitude, until it has become almost an universally accepted article of historical belief that the great political reformer was actuated in the course which he took by considerations drawn from the very basest motives of which human beings are capable. It was only to be expected that from time to time voices should be raised protesting against such a conclusion, but they have failed in obtaining more than a limited acceptance, because they have persisted in attempting to prove too much, and have shrunk from asserting at the outset, what is undoubtedly the fact, that Bacon's political principles were as false in theory as his political actions were ill-considered and unconstitutional in practice.

His theory of government.

Bacon has not, indeed, left on record any sketch of what he considered to be the most perfect form of government. But there can be no difficulty in arriving at his real views on the relations which ought to subsist between the government and the representatives of the people.* His speeches and actions in political life all point in one direction, and they are in perfect accordance with the slight indications of his feelings on this most important subject which are scattered over his writings, and with his still more expressive silences. There can be no doubt whatever that his ideal form of government was one in which the Sovereign was assisted by councillors and other ministers selected from among the wisest men of the kingdom, and in which he was responsible to no one for his actions within the wide and not very clearly defined limits which, as he supposed, separated the ordinary rights of the Crown from its political prerogative. The House of Commons, on the other hand, was called upon to express the wishes of the people, and to enlighten the Government upon the general feeling which prevailed in the country. Their assent would be required to any new laws which might be requisite, and to any extraordinary taxation which might be called for in time of war, or of any other emergency. The House of Lords would be useful as a means of communication between the King and the Commons, and would be able to break the force of any collision which might arise between them. In order that the Government might preserve its independence, and that, whilst giving all due attention to the wishes of its subjects, it might deliberate freely upon their demands, it was of the utmost importance that the Sovereign should have at his disposal a revenue sufficient to meet the ordinary demands upon the Treasury in time of peace, and that he should be able to command respect by some means of inflicting punishment on those who resisted his authority, more certain than an appeal to the juries in the courts of law. According to the idea, however, which floated before Bacon's mind, such interferences with the ordinary courts of law would be of rare occurrence. The Sovereign, enlightened by the wisdom

* *De Augmentis*, viii. 3. But it is noticeable that even here he only says, 'Venio jam ad artem imperii, sive doctrinam de Republicâ administrandâ.' Of constitutional theory, not a word.

CH. XI. 1613. of his Council, and by the expressed opinions of the representatives of the people, would lose no time in embodying in action all that was really valuable in the suggestions which were made to him. He would meet with little or no opposition, because he would possess the confidence of the nation, which would reverence in their King their guide in all noble progress, and the image of their better selves.*

Not unnatural in one who had lived in the reign of Elizabeth.

It is impossible to deny that in such a theory there is much which is fascinating, especially to minds which are conscious of powers which fit them for the government of their fellow-men. In fact, it was nothing else than the theory of government which had been acted on by Elizabeth with general assent, though in her hands it had been modified by the tact which she invariably displayed. It was, therefore, likely to recommend itself to Bacon, who had not only witnessed the glories of that reign, but had been connected with the Government both by the recollection of his father's services, and by his own aspirations for office.

They are favoured by the bent of his genius.

The glories of the reign of Elizabeth, however, would have failed to exercise more than a passing influence over a man of Bacon's genius, if the tendencies of his own mind had not led him to accept her theory of government even when it reappeared mutilated and distorted in the hands of her successor. The distinguishing characteristic of Bacon's intellect was its practical tendency. In speculative as well as in political thought, the object which he set before him was the benefit of mankind. 'Power to do good,' as he himself has told us, he considered to be the only legitimate object of aspiration.† His thoughts were constantly occupied with the largest and most sweeping plans of reform, by which he hoped to ameliorate the condition of his fellow-creatures. No abuse escaped his notice, no improvement

* I do not know any better illustration of the proverb, that one man may steal a horse whilst another may not look over the hedge, than is to be found in the treatment which modern writers have bestowed upon two men whose political actions and opinions coincided so completely as did those of Ellesmere and Bacon. It has always seemed impossible that Bacon could make a mistake about anything.

† In the essay 'Of Great Place.'

was too extensive to be grasped by his comprehensive genius. The union with Scotland, the civilization of Ireland, the colonisation of America, the improvement of the law, and the abolition of the last remnants of feudal oppression, were only a few of the vast schemes upon which his mind loved to dwell.

He had more hope in the Privy Council than in the House of Commons.

With such views as these, it was only natural that he should fix his hopes upon the Sovereign and his Council, rather than upon the House of Commons. It was not to be expected that the Commons would adopt with any earnestness schemes which, except where they touched upon some immediate grievance, were so far in advance of the age in which he lived, that even after the lapse of two centuries and a half the descendants of the generation to whom they were addressed are still occupied in filling up the outline which has been sketched by the master's hand. Nor, even if the House of Commons had possessed the will, were they at that time capable of originating any great and comprehensive legislative measure. It was as yet but an incoherent mass, agitated by strong feelings, and moved by a high and sturdy patriotism, ready indeed to offer a determined resistance to every species of misgovernment, but destitute of that organization which can alone render it possible for a large deliberative assembly, without assistance from without, to carry on satisfactorily the work of legislation. The salutary action of a ministry owing its existence to the support of the House, and exercising in turn, in right of its practical and intellectual superiority, an influence over all the proceedings of the legislature, was yet unknown. To Bacon, above all men, a change which should make the House of Commons master of the executive government was an object of dread; for such a change would, as he imagined, place the direction of the policy of the country in the hands of an inexperienced and undisciplined mob.*

* What the faults of the House of Commons were when they did obtain the highest place in the State, has been shown in the precious fragments of Lord Macaulay's posthumous volume. His narrative is enough to convince us that though the suspicions of those who thought with Bacon were unfounded, they were certainly not absurd.

CH. XI. 1613.

Bacon's desire to free the executive from restrictions.

Nor was it only on account of its superior capability of deliberation on involved and difficult subjects that Bacon's sympathies were with the Privy Council; he looked upon it with respect from the mere fact of its being the organ of the executive government, by means of which those measures of improvement by which he set such store were to be carried out. He had always before him the idea of the variety of cases in which the Government might be called to act, and he allowed himself to believe that it would be better qualified to act rightly if it were not fettered by strict rules, or by the obligation to give an account of its proceedings to a body which might be ignorant of the whole circumstances of the case, and which was only partially qualified to judge of the wisdom of the measures which had been taken. His own intellectual superiority made him impatient of being fettered by general rules, and he was too ready to forget that it was better to leave a wise and beneficial work undone, than by his example to open the floodgates to the folly of lesser men.

His feelings with regard to the House of Commons.

Whilst, however, he was desirous to restrain the House of Commons within what he considered to be its proper bounds, he had the very highest idea of its utility to the State. Whenever occasion offered, it was Bacon's voice which was always among the first to be raised for the calling of a Parliament. It was there alone that the complaints of the nation would make themselves fully heard, and that an opportunity was offered to the Government, by the initiation of well-considered remedial legislation, to maintain that harmony which ought always to exist between the nation and its rulers.

His mistakes.

Englishmen do not need to be told that this theory of Bacon's was radically false; not merely because James was exceptionally unworthy to fill the position which he occupied, but because it omitted to take into account certain considerations which render it false for all times and for all places, excepting where no considerable part of the population of a country are raised above a very low level of civilization. He left out of his calculation, on the one hand, the inevitable tendencies to misgovernment which beset all bodies of men who are possessed of irresponsible power; and, on the other hand, the elevating operation of the possession of political influence upon ordinary men, who, at first sight, seem unworthy of exercising it.

Causes of them.

We can hardly wonder, indeed, that Bacon should not have seen what we have no difficulty in seeing. That Government owes its stability to the instability of the ministers who, from time to time, execute its functions, is a truth which, however familiar to us, would have seemed the wildest of paradoxes to the contemporaries of Bacon. That the House of Commons would grow in political wisdom and in the power of self-restraint when the executive Government was constrained to give account to it of all its actions, would have seemed to them a prognostication only fit to come out of the mouth of a madman. That the strength of each of the political bodies known to the constitution would grow, not by careful demarcation of the limits within which they were to work, but by the harmony which would be the result of their mutual interdependence, was an idea utterly foreign to the mind of Bacon.* Even if such a

* Mr. Spedding, in his preface to the 'True Greatness of Britain' (*Works*, vii. 42) quotes from the *Commentarius Solutus* the following brief notes:—'Limiting all jurisdictions more regular;' 'new laws to be compounded and collected;' 'lawgiver perpetuus princeps,' and observes that these were both measures 'on which Bacon was always harping.' The mind which took such an interest in drawing limits between jurisdictions was not likely to think much of a change of system which would at all events, at first, lead to a less definite line between the chief authorities in the State. Bacon would probably have approved as theoretically perfect the relations existing at present between the Emperor of the French and the Legislative Assembly. And yet every Englishman has long instinctively perceived them to be founded on a mistake, and they are rapidly becoming practically untenable.

The following extract from Mr. Ellis's preface to Bacon's Philosophical Works (*Works*, i. 62) is interesting, as showing that Bacon's speculative errors were precisely the same in kind as those which lay at the bottom of his political mistakes:—'Bacon . . . certainly thought it possible so to sever observation from theory, that the process of collecting facts, and that of deriving consequences from them, might be carried on independently and by different persons. This opinion was based on an imperfect apprehension of the connection between facts and theories; the connection appearing to him to be merely an external one, namely, that the former are the materials of the latter.' According to Bacon's view of the Constitution, the House of Commons were the collectors of facts, the Privy Council were those who were to derive consequences from them, and the connection between the two bodies appeared to him to be merely external. Ranke gives

CH. XI. 1613. thought had ever occurred to him, at what a cost of all that he valued most in his better moments would it have been realized! The supremacy of the representatives of the people over the executive Government would undoubtedly be accompanied by an indefinite postponement of those reforms upon which he had set his heart, and, to him, the time which must be allowed to elapse before the House of Commons was likely to devote itself to those reforms, must have seemed likely to be far longer than it would be in reality—if, indeed, he did not despair of any satisfactory results at all from such a change. In this, no doubt, he was mistaken; but it must be remembered that, unlike the continental statesmen who have in our own day fallen into a similar error, he had no beacon of experience to guide him. England was then, as she has always been, decidedly in advance, so far as political institutions are concerned, of the other nations of Europe. She had to work out the problem of government unaided by experience, and was entering like Columbus upon a new world, where there was nothing to guide her but her own high spirit and the wisdom and virtue of her sons. On such a course as this even Bacon was an unsafe guide. Far before his age in his knowledge of the arts of government, in all matters relating to the equally important subject of constitutional law, he, like his master, 'took counsel rather of time past than of time future.'

It is easy for us to be wise after the fact. We have seen that the Government, after it relinquished its independence, retained all its powers for good. But the question, as it presented itself to Bacon's mind, was whether or not the House of Commons should obtain

in a few words the true explanation of Bacon's attachment to the prerogative: 'Bacon war einer der letzten, die das Heil von England in der Ausbildung der monarchischen Verfassung, oder doch in dem Uebergewicht der Berechtigung des Fürsten innerhalb der Verfassung sahen. Die Verbindung der drei Reiche unter der verwaltenden Autorität des Königs schien ihm die Grundlage der künftigen Grösze Groszbritanniens. An die Monarchie knüpfte er die Hoffnung einer Reform der Gesetze von England, der Durchführung eines umfassenden colonial Systems in Irland, der Annäherung der kirchlichen und richterlichen Verfassung von Schottland an die englischen Gebräuche. Er liebte die Monarchie, weil er grosze Dinge von ihr erwartete.'—*Geschichte von England*, i. 596.

such a pre-eminence in the State as to sweep before it all opposition, and to domineer over every institution and even interest which was not its own.

Bacon's moral failings

But, after all, it is impossible to account for Bacon's political errors merely by considerations drawn from the imperfections of his mighty intellect. If he had been possessed of fine moral feelings he would have instinctively shrunk from all connection with a monarch who proposed to govern England with the help of Rochester and the Howards. But there was something in the bent of his genius which led him to pay extraordinary reverence to all who were possessed of power.* The exaggerated importance which he attached to the possession of the executive authority led him to look with unbounded respect to those who held in their hands, as he imagined, the destinies of the nation. The very largeness of his view led him to regard with complacency actions from which a man of smaller mind would have shrunk at once. His thoughts flowed in too wide a channel. They lost in strength what they gained in breadth. An ordinary man, who has set his heart upon some great scheme, if he fails in accomplishing it, retires from the scene and waits his time. But whenever Bacon failed in obtaining support for his views he had always some fresh plan to fall back upon. He never set before himself any definite object as one for which it was worth while to live and die. If all his plans were rejected, one after another, there would be at least something to be done in the ordinary exercise of his official duties; and the mere pleasure of fulfilling them efficiently would blind him to the rottenness of the system of which he had made himself a part.

connected with the comprehensiveness of his mind.

His admiration of the prerogative.

To Bacon the Royal prerogative was the very instrument most fitted for his purpose. To act as occasion might require, without being bound by the necessity of submitting to an antiquated, and, it might be, an absurd

* The feeling with which Lord Chatham regarded George III. is another example of the extent to which active minds are sometimes overawed by the possessors of power. Chatham's loyalty was probably sharpened by his dislike of the Whig aristocracy, as Bacon's was by his opposition to Coke and the lawyers of his class.

CH. XI. 1613.

restriction of the law, was the very highest privilege to which he could aspire. He could not but regard the Sovereign who had it in his power to admit him to share in wielding this mighty talisman as a being raised above the ordinary level of mortals, and he was ever ready to shut his eyes to the faults with which his character was stained.

His weakness.

How far he did this voluntarily it is impossible to say with certainty. No doubt, in his time, the complimentary phrases which he used were looked upon far more as a matter of course than they would be at the present day. It is only to those who are unaccustomed to the language of Bacon's contemporaries that his flattery appears at all extravagant. In many points, too, in which we condemn the conduct of James, that conduct would appear to Bacon to be not only defensible, but even admirable. Where, on the other hand, he was unable to praise with honesty, he may have been content to praise out of policy. To do so was the only manner in which it was possible to win the King's support, and without that support he knew that he would be powerless in the world. Some allowance must also be made for his general hopefulness of temper. He was always inclined to see men as he would have them to be, rather than as they were. Nothing is more striking in his whole career than the trustful manner in which he always looked forward to a new House of Commons. He never seemed to be able to understand what a gulf there was between his own principles and those of the representatives of the people. Whatever cause of quarrel there had been, was in his eyes always the result of faction. He was sure that, if the real sentiments of the gentlemen of England could be heard, justice would be done him. It would seem as if he regarded the King as he regarded the Parliament; both had it in their power to confer immense benefits on England, both, it might be hoped, and even believed, would do their part in the great work.

Nor can it be denied that if he loved office for the sake of doing good, he also loved it for its own sake. He was profuse in his expenditure, and money therefore never came amiss to him. His impressionable mind was open to all the influences of the world; he liked the pomp and circumstance of power, its outward show and grandeur, the pleasant company and the troops of followers which were its necessary accompaniments. His mind was destitute of that pure sensitiveness which should have taught him what was the value of power so acquired. The man who could find nothing better to say of marriage than that wife and children are impediments to great enterprises, was not the man to look upon life from its ideal side. He learned the ways of the Court only too well. Of all the sad sights of this miserable reign, surely Bacon's career must have been the saddest. It would have been something if he had writhed under the chains which he had imposed upon himself. Blind intellectually and morally to the one thing which it most imported him to know, he thought he was working for the benefit of mankind, when he was in reality working for the Rochesters and the Buckinghams —for the scaffold of Charles I. and the exile of James II. The meanest member of the popular party in the House of Commons was doing better than he for the cause of reform which the great statesman had most at heart.

Sutton's hospital.

Those who are desirous of investigating the causes of Bacon's political errors would do well to study with particular attention a letter which he wrote to the King upon a subject which, in the spring and summer of 1613, was dividing the attention of the public with the great divorce case and the imprisonment of Overbury. Thomas Sutton, a London citizen of great wealth, was one of that class of moneyed men which had risen into importance with the rising commercial prosperity of the country in the reign of Elizabeth, and which was already claiming a position of its own by the side of the old county families of England. He had no children to whom to leave his accumulated stores, and, in consequence, his property was looked upon with longing eyes by all who could urge any claim to succeed to a portion of it at his death. An attempt was even made to induce him to name Prince Charles as his heir, who was at that time a younger son, to whom an estate, worth at least

CH. XI. 1613.

six thousand a year, would be no unwelcome gift. To this proposal, however, Sutton steadily refused to listen. He was more inclined to pay attention to those who, like Joseph Hall, afterwards so well known as successively Bishop of Exeter and Norwich, invited him to devote his money to some pious or charitable object. After some consideration, he determined to erect a school, and an hospital for old and decayed gentlemen, at Hallingbury, in Essex, and, in 1610, he obtained an Act of Parliament giving him the powers which were requisite to enable him to carry out his intentions.

In the year after the Act had passed, however, he purchased from the Earl of Suffolk the buildings of the old Carthusian monastery near Smithfield, then, as now, commonly known as the Charter House, and obtained from the King letters patent authorizing him to transfer the institution to that site. A few months after the grant of the patent he died, in December, 1611, leaving it to others to complete the work which he had begun.

Question of the validity of the foundation decided in its favour.

Scarcely was he in his grave when it was known that the heir-at-law had determined to dispute the validity of the patent to which the institution owed its origin. The case was argued at length on various technical grounds, before the judges in the Exchequer Chamber, and, to the great joy of all who were interested in seeing that the generous intentions of the founder were carried out, judgment was finally pronounced, in June, 1613, in favour of the rising foundation.*

Bacon's letter to the King.

Bacon had been employed in arguing the case for the heir-at-law. He probably owed his selection for this duty to the knowledge that he was opposed to the erection of the institution upon other grounds than those upon which he was compelled to rest his case in arguing before the judges. It was, probably, immediately after Sutton's death that he wrote a letter † to the

* Herne, *Domus Carthusiana*, 37-95.

† *Works*, ed. Montagu, v. 374. The letter can hardly have been written later, unless we are to charge Bacon with coolly throwing his client overboard. After the trial was over he could scarcely have made the proposal contained in the letter, and even if he had, he would certainly have referred to the judgment.

King, in which he objected to the proposed application of Sutton's wealth, and advised that it should be employed in other ways, which were likely to be more beneficial to the country. There is not one of the arguments by which he supported his conclusion which does not deserve the greatest attention, even from those who disagree with his reasoning. But that which is most characteristic about the letter is the coolness with which he took it for granted that it was in the power of the King to annul the disposition of private property. This astounding interference with the most important of the rights of the subject does not seem to have caused the slightest scruple to Bacon. He evidently considered that, as soon as he had demonstrated that Sutton's money could be more profitably employed than if his own wishes were carried into execution, he had done all that was required of him, and that it was unnecessary even to expend a passing word upon this part of the question.

Importance of this letter as evidence of Bacon's character.

This letter of Bacon's is the more important as it points, with evidence which cannot be resisted, to what was the real defect in his intellect. There is no room here for the supposition which is made in almost every other case in which he committed a mistake. In this case it was not any moral weakness which bore down the correctness of his judgment, as he had no reason to suspect that he was anticipating the wishes of James. In granting the patent for the transfer of the foundation to London, James had shown that he gave his approval to Sutton's scheme, and he never took any step which could give rise to a suspicion that he had changed his opinion.* It was Bacon's own utter inability to comprehend that it was better that six thousand a year should be squandered upon unworthy objects, than that men should have reason to believe that they would be deprived of the protection of the law in the disposal of their property, which led him astray on this and similar occasions.

* After the trial was over, Sutton's executors took care to retain the good will of James, by presenting him with £10,000, under the pretence that in reimbursing him for his expenses in the building of the bridge at Berwick-upon-Twsed they were carrying out the intentions of Sutton, who had left a large sum to be conferred upon objects of general utility.

CH. XI.
1613.
Wealth and independence of the London citizens.

Sutton was not the only man amongst the citizens of London whose wealth and independence of character might have served to give a warning to James that his system of government would soon become untenable, and that the time was rapidly approaching when the leaders of commerce would join with the country gentlemen in demanding, in tones which could no longer be resisted, a larger share in the exercise of their due influence upon the political destinies of the country.

Hugh Myddelton.

It was to the energy and persêverance of Hugh Myddelton that London was indebted for all those priceless advantages which accompany the enjoyment of a copious stream of pure water. The supply had long been deficient, but, although complaints had been constantly heard, and even an Act of Parliament* had been obtained in 1606, authorizing the corporation to supply the deficiency by bringing in a stream from the springs at Chadwell and Amwell, no steps had been taken to carry out the designed operations. Vexed at the sluggishness of his fellow-citizens, Myddelton stood forward and declared that if no one else would do the work he would take it upon his own shoulders. His proposal was thankfully accepted. He had already paid considerable attention to the subject, as a member of the committees of the House of Commons before whom the recent Acts had been discussed.

The New River commenced.

The first sod upon the works of the proposed New River was turned upon the 21st of April, 1609. With untiring energy he persevered in the work which he had undertaken, in spite of the opposition of the landowners through whose property the stream was to pass, and who complained that their land was likely to suffer in consequence, by the overflowing of the water. In 1610 his opponents carried their complaints before the House of Commons, and a committee was directed to make a report upon their case as soon as the House reassembled in October. When they met again, the members had more important matters to attend to, and Myddelton's hands were soon set free by the dissolution.

* 3 Jac. I. cap. 18, explained by 4 Jac. I. cap. 12.

The King joins in the undertaking.

Although, however, he had no longer any reason to fear any obstacle which might be thrown in his way by Parliament, the opposition of the landowners was so annoying, and the demands which were made on his purse were, in all probability, increasing so largely in consequence of them, that he determined to make an attempt to interest the King in his project. James, who, with all his faults, seldom turned a deaf ear to any scheme which involved the improvement of the material welfare of his subjects, readily consented to take upon himself half the expense of the undertaking, on condition of receiving half the profits. Under the sanction of the royal name the works rapidly went forward, and on Michaelmas day, 1613, all London was thronging to Islington in order to celebrate the completion of the undertaking.*

Bacon's prospects of promotion.

The time was now come when Bacon might reasonably look forward to some reward for the services which he had rendered as Solicitor-General. Towards the end of the preceding year he had applied in vain for the Mastership of the Court of Wards, which had again become vacant by the death of Sir George Carew. He had counted upon success so far as to order the necessary liveries. For some reason or other he was disappointed. Perhaps he omitted to offer the accustomed bribe to Rochester. At all events, the place was given to Sir Walter Cope, a man of integrity, but of no great abilities. The wits made merry over the Solicitor's discomfiture. Sir Walter, they said, had got the Wards, and Sir Francis the Liveries.

He receives a promise of the Attorney-General's place.

It is possible that the knowledge which in the course of the summer of 1613 was acquired by James of the intrigues which so many of his ministers were carrying on with the Spanish Ambassador, may have led him to esteem more highly a man who, like Bacon, was thoroughly devoted to the cause of the prerogative. It was probably, however, before any information on this

* Smiles' *Lives of Engineers*, i. 107–132. It is often stated that Myddelton was made a knight in reward for his services. This was not the case; he received no honour whatever till he was made a baronet, many years afterwards.

CH. XI.
1613.

subject had reached him, that he gave him a promise* that he should succeed Hobart as Attorney-General at the next vacancy of that office. Soon after the promise was given, Hobart was taken ill, and Bacon wrote to remind the King of his engagement. The Attorney, however, soon recovered, and Bacon's promotion seemed as far off as ever, when, on the 7th of August, the death of Sir Thomas Fleming, the Chief Justice of the King's Bench, opened the way for his advancement.

Vacancy in the Chief Justiceship of the King's Bench.

Bacon at once wrote to the King, and begged him to appoint Hobart to the post. In case of his refusal he asked that he might himself be selected.† It was not long, however, before he thought of a plan which he immediately communicated to the King, by means of which James might show the weight of his authority, whilst he gratified Bacon, by inflicting an intense mortification upon the man whom he disliked more than any one else in England. Coke's resistance to the King on the subject of the proclamations and the prohibitions had never been forgotten; and Bacon knew that James would eagerly grasp at an opportunity of showing the great lawyer that he was not altogether independent. He therefore reminded him that such an opportunity had now arrived. The Chief Justiceship of the King's Bench was indeed a more honourable post than that which Coke now held, but it was far less lucrative, and it was well known that Coke would be unwilling to pay for the higher title with a diminution of his income. His selection as Fleming's successor would be universally regarded as a penal promotion, which would deter others from offending in a similar manner. Room would be thus made for Hobart in the Common Pleas. As for himself, he would take care to put forth all his energies as Attorney-General in defence of the prerogative. It was an office the duties of which he was better able to fulfil than his

* Referred to in Bacon's letter to the King (*Works*, ed. Montagu, xii. 121). The promise must have been given after the writing of the letter printed at p. 96 of the same volume, which must have been written shortly after the promotion of Doderidge and Nichols on the 25th and 26th of November, 1612.

† Bacon to the King (*Works*, ed. Montagu, xii. 286).

predecessor had been, who was naturally of a timid and retiring disposition.* CH. XI. 1613.

Legal promotions.

Bacon's advice was followed. Coke, sorely against his will, was forced into promotion. Hobart became Chief Justice of the Common Pleas, and Bacon stepped into the place vacated by Hobart. The Solicitorship was given to Yelverton, whose opinions in most points coincided with those of Bacon, and whose speech in defence of the prerogative, in the debate on the impositions, had not been forgotten. As a compensation for the loss of the post to which he was so much attached, Coke was made a Privy Councillor; and it was hoped that, in taking part in the administration of the Government, he would be less inclined, than he had been before, to oppose the prerogative of the Crown. Even this honour, however, was not sufficient to conquer his repugnance to the promotion which had been forced upon him. The first time he met Bacon, after these alterations were concluded, he could not avoid showing what his feelings were: 'Mr. Attorney,' he said, 'this is all your doing; it is you that have made this great stir.' 'Ah, my lord,' was the ready answer, 'your lordship all this while hath grown in breadth, you must needs now grow in height, else you will prove a monster.'†

Marriage of the favourite.

The year, which had been marked by so many crimes and follies, was worthily brought to a close by the festivities which accompanied the marriage of the favourite. The ceremony was performed on the day after Christmas day at the Chapel Royal. In order that the lady might not lose her title of Countess, Rochester had, a few weeks previously, been created Earl of Somerset. As far as he was concerned, he showed the good taste of not appearing surrounded by any extraordinary pomp. Lady Frances attracted attention by appearing with her long hair flowing down over her shoulders, a costume which was at that time reserved for virgin brides. The couple were married by the same Bishop who had done a similar service to the bride six

Rochester created Earl of Somerset.

* Bacon's *Works* (ed. Montagu), vii. 340.
† Bacon's Apopthegms, *Works*, vii. 169.

CH. XI. 1613.

Gifts presented at the wedding.

years previously. All who had to gain anything from the royal bounty pressed round the newly married pair with gifts in their hands. Nottingham and Coke, Lake and Winwood, did not think it beneath them to court the favour of the man who stood between them and their Sovereign. The City of London, the Company of Merchant Adventurers, and the East India Company, were not behindhand. Bacon prepared a masque to celebrate the marriage. He declared that, although it would cost him no less a sum than £2,000, he would allow no one to share the burden with him. A day or two after the marriage, Winwood had the opportunity of paying a still more delicate compliment to the bride.

Entertainment at Merchant Taylors' Hall.

Jan. 4, 1614.

The King had sent for the Lord Mayor, and had intimated to him that it was expected that he should provide an entertainment for Lord and Lady Somerset. The Lord Mayor, however, desired to be excused from entertaining the large company which might be expected to come in their train. He accordingly pleaded that his house was too small for the purpose. He was told that, at all events, the City Halls were large enough. He accordingly appealed to the Aldermen, who consented to take the burden off his shoulders, and directed that the preparations should be made in Merchant Taylors' Hall. It was arranged that the guests should make their way in procession from Westminster to the City, the gentlemen on horseback and the ladies in their coaches.

The bride was, naturally enough, anxious to appear on such an occasion in all due splendour. Her coach was sufficiently magnificent to attract attention, but, unluckily, she had no horses good enough for her purpose. In this difficulty she sent to Winwood to borrow his. Winwood immediately answered, that it was not fit for so great a lady to use anything borrowed, and begged that she would accept the horses as a present.*

Conduct of the courtiers.

When we remember what Lady Somerset was, there is something revolting to our feelings in the attentions which she received from all quarters. And yet it would

* Chamberlain to Lady Carleton, Dec. 30, 1613. Chamberlain to Carleton, Jan. 5, 1614, *Court and Times*, i. 284, 287.

be unfair to judge those who paid court to her by the standard of our own times. Some of them, at least, were not mere sycophants. They had been accustomed to see in the favour of the Sovereign the only road to advancement, and they had become callous to the means by which that favour was to be won, provided that they were not required themselves to commit directly any immoral act. The whole political system was out of joint, and the utmost that can be said is, that these men had not sufficient discernment to detect the causes of the evil, or sufficient determination to preserve their independence at all hazards. It is only on rare occasions that men can be found to protest against misgovernment when they profit by its continuance.

Silent protest of the Archbishop.

It was, however, well for the credit of human nature that one man should be found who would refuse resolutely to worship the idol. Whilst, in the persons of Coke, and Bacon, and Winwood, the most learned lawyer, the deepest thinker, and the most honest official statesman of the age combined with deans and bishops to do her homage, Abbot stood resolutely aloof. He appeared, indeed, in the chapel at the time of the marriage, but he refused to take any part in authorizing what he considered to be an adulterous union. If conscience retained any sway over the heart of the giddy young bride, she must have been awed by the stern features of the man who was regarding her with no friendly eyes. To us, who know what the future history of England was, there is something ominous in this scene. It was, as it were, the spirit of Calvinism which had taken up its abode in that silent monitor; the one power in England which could resist the seductions of the Court, and which was capable of rebuking, at any cost, the immorality of the great. Abbot was not a great man, but on that day he stood in a position which placed him far above all the genius and the grandeur which was around him.

As yet Lady Somerset had the world at her feet. Two years of dissipation and of enjoyment were yet to be hers; and then the final catastrophe was to come, with all its irretrievable ruin. For the present, not a shadow

CH. XI. 1613. Somerset's wealth and influence.

crossed her path. Her husband was at the height of his power. Exercising more than the influence of a Secretary, without the name, he shared in all the thoughts and schemes of the King. Nor was there any want of means for keeping up the dignity and splendour of his position; there was no need now to ask the King for grants of land or of ready money; every suitor who had a petition to present must pay tribute to Somerset if he hoped to obtain a favourable reply. What he gained in this way was never known. But it was calculated that, though his ostensible revenue was by no means large, he had spent no less than £90,000 in twelve months.

Prevalence of duelling.

The system under which a mere courtier could attain to the highest honours of the State was one which could not fail to be attended by mischievous consequences of every kind. Amongst the evils which were beginning to attract the attention of those who were anxious to provide some remedy for the moral disorders of the age, was the increasing prevalence of the practice of duelling. The death of Lord Bruce of Kinloss, who had lately succeeded to the title of his father, the late Master of the Rolls, and who was slain in a duel with Sir Edward Sackville, the brother of the Earl of Dorset, brought the subject more immediately before the notice of the King. He exerted himself successfully to stop a threatened combat between the Earl of Essex and Lord Henry Howard, the third son of the Earl of Suffolk, arising out of the ill-will which prevailed between the two families in consequence of the divorce of Lady Essex. A proclamation was issued to put a stop to duels for the
1614. future. Bacon was employed to prosecute in the Star-Chamber two persons who were intending to engage in single combat, and he declared that similar proceedings would be taken against all who, in any way whatever, committed any act which was connected with the giving or receiving a challenge.

Inefficiency of the remedies adopted.

No doubt, it was well that Government should take up the matter energetically. But the evil lay too deep to be reached by Star-Chamber prosecutions. In the earnest days of the Reformation, duels had ceased to be resorted to by men who had sterner work on hand. It was when the national struggle for independence had ended in victory that they were once more heard of. If James wished to cleanse the land of bloodshed, it was necessary for him to change his own nature. If he would put himself at the head of the serious thought of England, there would soon be work enough for the young nobility, in which they would be proud to join, instead of wasting their courage upon their own miserable quarrels. If the Court and the Council Board had been filled with the men who were the natural leaders of the nation, and if the nation itself had been admitted to share in their deliberations, a healthy public opinion would soon have been created, which would have chastised alike those who plunged heedlessly into quarrels, and those who gave the provocation by unbridled licentiousness of speech and action.

CHAPTER XII.

THE PARLIAMENT OF 1614.

CH. XII. 1612. Financial difficulties.

IF James was blind to the intellectual inferiority of the men of whom his Privy Council was composed, as compared with those who had sat at the Board during the reign of his predecessor, and to the moral scandals which were the sure symptoms of the disease which is, sooner or later, the invariable accompaniment of irresponsible Government, there was one warniug, at least, to which it was impossible for him to shut his eyes. In every country where a Government has been erected in defiance of the laws of nature, financial embarrassment is the inevitable scourge which, sooner or later, awaits the rulers; but in England, the institutions which render it necessary to obtain the consent of Parliament, at least to all internal taxation, were certain to accelerate the crisis and to bring the culprit face to face with the consequences of his errors almost as soon as they had been committed. Since Salisbury's death efforts had been made, with only a very partial success, to bring the expenditure to a level with the revenue. In June, 1612, the Chancellor of the Exchequer, Sir Julius Cæsar, informed the King* that the ordinary expenditure of the Crown exceeded the revenue by no less a sum than £160,000, and that the debt had risen to £500,000 from the £300,000 at which it stood at the opening of the session in the Spring of 1610. Upon this a Sub-Committee, of which Bacon as well as Cæsar were members, was appointed to report to the new Commissioners of the Treasury upon the state of the finances. The result of their labours was a plan which was actually carried into

* Cæsar's notes, Lansd. MS. 165, fol. 223.

CH. XII. 1612.

effect, by which the deficit might be reduced by about £35,000, leaving the £125,000 still unprovided for, to say nothing of the extraordinary expenses which were certain to arise from time to time. What the amount of these extraordinary expenses was may be calculated from the fact that in the two years which ended at Michaelmas, 1613, although many claims upon the Government were left unpaid, it was necessary to borrow £143,000, of which a great 1613.
part was raised by a new issue of Privy Seals;* and that, in addition to the money thus obtained, no less a sum than £388,000 had been paid into the Exchequer on account of payments, many of which were not likely to be repeated, and none of which could be considered as forming part of the regular revenue of the Crown. Some of this, no doubt, was expended in providing for outstanding claims; but, in spite of all the efforts of the Government, the debt, as has been seen, continued to increase. It must, however, be said that it was upon the report of this committee that James, for the first time, showed a desire to economize; and though he could not at once withdraw the pensions and annuities which he had heedlessly granted, or reduce in a moment the scale of expenditure which he had authorized, he did what he could in checking his propensity to give away money to every one of his courtiers who asked him.

In the year which ended at Michaelmas, 1613, the difficulties were especially great. In addition to the ordinary expenditure, a part at least of the expenses connected with the marriage of the Princess had to be met within the year. Those expenses amounted to more than £60,000, to which £40,000 had to be added for the portion of the bride. £16,000 was wanted towards defraying the outlay at Prince Henry's funeral. Other extraordinary charges were pressing for payment, and

*	
Subsidies and fifteenths in 1611–12	£24,423
Do. in 1612–13	9,261
Sale of Crown property in 1611–12	46,986
Do. in 1612–13	19,555
Extraordinary payments in 1611–12	118,462
Do. in 1612–13	169,901
	£388,588

(See the financial tables in the Appendix.)

CH. XII. 1613. amongst them, £105,000 was required to pay off a loan which had fallen due.

No effort was spared to meet these demands. The Earl of Northumberland was forced to pay £11,000 on account of his fine in the Star-Chamber,* which, under other circumstances, would, in all probability, have been left in his pocket. £65,000, which had long been owed by the French Government, was extracted from the King of France. The repayment of the debt which the Dutch had contracted with Elizabeth commenced in 1611, and was still continuing at the rate of £40,000 a year. £57,000 was produced by Baronetcies in the two years, and all other means which could be thought of were resorted to without scruple. Privy Seals were again sent out to a select few who were supposed to be capable of sustaining the burden, although the last loan had not been repaid, and £6,000 was borrowed from other sources. On one occasion, when the Exchequer was all but empty, Rochester produced £24,000, which he requested the King to accept as a loan until the present difficulty was at an end.† It was all in vain. Recourse was again had to the sale of lands and woods. By this means a sum of £65,000 was realized.

Necessity of calling a Parliament,

Such a method of extricating the Exchequer from its difficulties must have an end. Already the entail of 1609 had been broken into, and lands had been parted with which were intended to be indissolubly annexed to the Crown. £67,000, moreover, of the revenue of the following year had been levied in anticipation, so that the prospect was more than ever hopeless. Under these circumstances, it is not strange that the idea of the necessity of calling a Parliament was accepted even by those who had been most opposed to such a measure.

advocated by Nevill and Bacon.

There were two men who had always consistently recommended the summoning of Parliament. Immediately upon Salisbury's death Bacon wrote to the King,

* It is generally supposed that the Star-Chamber fines formed a large portion of the King's revenue. This is by no means the case. The large fines were almost invariably remitted.

† Receipt Book of the Exchequer. In Chamberlain's letter to Carleton, April 29, 1613 (*S. P.* lxxii. 120), the sum is erroneously given as £22,000; £20,000 was repaid within the year.

advising this course, and offering to suggest measures which might lead the way to a settlement of the differences between him and the House of Commons.* Some months before, Nevill had a conversation with James on the same subject, in which he had given his opinion strongly in the same direction†. It was not, however, till the summer of 1613 that James was willing to admit the idea of appealing once more to the representatives of the people, who had been dismissed by him so summarily.

Nevill's memorial.

It was probably about this time that a memorial was drawn up by Nevill, which at once stamps its author as a statesman who was fitted above all others to mediate between James and his people, and to watch over the development of the new order of things, which was certain, sooner or later, to take the place of the existing system.‡ His opinion was, that all the schemes which had been suggested for raising money in any way except by Parliament, would prove in the end to be failures. It was no mere question of money. The ill-feeling which had been caused by the dissolution of the last Parliament had not been confined to its members. From them it had spread over every constituency in the kingdom. All Europe knew that the King and his subjects were at variance, and the enemies of England would be emboldened to treat with contempt a nation where there was no harmony between the Government and the people. If James wished to maintain his position amongst the Sovereigns of the Continent he must prove to them that he had not lost the hearts of his subjects; and there was no better way of accomplishing this than by showing that he could meet his Parliament without coming into collision with it.

Advises the summoning of a Parliament.

Objections answered.

It might indeed be said that the Commons would still

* Bacon to the King, May 31, 1612, (*Works*, ed. Montagu, xii. 281.)

† *C. J.* i. 485. The conversation at Windsor there mentioned took place in July, 1611. But the mention of projects in the memorial looks as if it had been drawn up at a later date. It is, perhaps, a repetition of arguments formerly presented.

‡ The memorial is printed in Appendix V. The copies which are among the *State Papers* are all anonymous. But Carte (*Hist.* iv. 17), who had another copy before him, speaks distinctly of the memorial as being Nevill's, and the internal evidence all points in the same direction.

CH. XII. 1613.

be unwilling to give money under any conditions whatever, or that, even if they consented to grant supplies they would clog their concessions with unreasonable demands. To these objections Nevill replied that it was a mistake to suppose that the opposition in the last Parliament arose from factious motives. He had himself lived on familiar terms with the leaders of the opposition, and he was able to affirm without fear of contradiction that they bore no ill-will towards the King. He was ready to undertake for the greater part of them that, if the King would act fairly by his people, he would find these men ready to exert themselves in support of the Government. It was true, indeed, that it would be necessary to grant certain things upon which those who would be called to pay the subsidies had set their hearts. It remained to be considered what these concessions should be.

Concessions to be made.

It was difficult, he said, for any one man to set down the requirements of all the members of the House, but from what he knew of the leading men of the last Parliament, he had ventured to draw up a list* of concessions which, as he thought, would prove satisfactory to them. In this paper, which was appended to his memorial, Nevill set forth certain points in which he thought that the law pressed hardly upon the subject. None of them, however, were of much importance. He undoubtedly attached greater weight to the eight concessions which James had offered to the Commons shortly after the breach of the contract. These he copied out, and, adroitly enough, refused to give any opinion on them, taking it for granted that they still expressed the opinions of the King. Amongst them was a renunciation of the right of levying impositions without consent of Parliament.

Conduct recommended to the King.

Having thus laid before James a list of the points which it would be advisable to yield, Nevill proceeded to urge that Parliament should be summoned immediately. Let the King avoid the use of any irritating speeches, and let him do his best while he was on his

* I have not printed this list in the Appendix, as it consists chiefly of dry details. It will be found among the *State Papers, Dom.* lxxiv. 46.

progress to win the good-will of the country gentlemen. Let orders be given to the Archbishop to allow no books to be printed, or sermons preached, which reflected upon the House of Commons. Let the grievances presented in the last Parliament be examined, and, if the King were willing to yield on any point, let him do it at once, without waiting for the commencement of the session. Above all, let him see that all promises of reformation which he had made were actually carried out. There can be little doubt that if Nevill had been called upon to speak more plainly he would have pointed to the ecclesiastical grievances as those which it was most necessary to redress. It is equally clear that if James had accepted his advice, and had met Parliament with some concession on the ecclesiastical question and with a renunciation of his claim to levy impositions, he would have had no difficulty in obtaining any supplies which he might choose to demand.

CH. XII. 1613.

No less wise were the practical suggestions which were offered by Nevill as to the best mode of conducting the business of the House of Commons. He saw, as every one must have seen, who had sat in that House since Salisbury's elevation to the Peerage, that the system of communicating the King's wishes through members of the House of Lords did not work well. He therefore recommended that the King should make any proposals which he wished to lay before the Commons, either by his own mouth, or by such of his ministers as were members of the Lower House, and that he should call upon them themselves to nominate a committee which might confer with him on all points on which any difference of opinion existed between them.

Bacon's letters. Jan. 1614.

It is melancholy to descend from this statesmanlike memorial to the letters which were written about six months later by Bacon, on the same subject.* In the first of the two letters which he wrote he began by referring to those who, like Nevill, had offered to be serviceable to the King in the new Parliament, but who,

* Bacon to the King, Cott. MS., Tit. F. iv., fol. 328. The mention of bonfires in the first letter shows it to have been written shortly after the 9th of January, 1614.

CH. XII. 1614.

He advises James not to sell his favours.

reasonably enough, had told him that unless he would make concessions which were likely to satisfy the House, it was impossible for them to be of any use to him. Bacon warned James not to become a merchant of his favours. If, indeed, there was anything among the proposals of these men which it was advisable to carry into execution, they should be allowed to have the credit of their own skill in drawing up their scheme. If this was not the case, they should have something better given them to bring into shape. The King might be sure that he had not lost the affections of his people. If he had heard the bells ringing in London, and witnessed the bonfires burning at the announcement of the birth of his grandson, who had just been born at Heidelberg, he would have had little doubt that he was still in possession of the hearts of the English people. Such advice as this was far inferior to that which Nevill had given when he called upon James to take the lead himself in carrying out the measures which were likely to satisfy his subjects. But it was in another letter, which he wrote a few days later,* that Bacon showed clearly how great was the difference between the man whose heart beat in unison with the better feeling of the Parliamentary opposition, and the man who, in spite of the acknowledged greatness of his intellect, was unable to see in the majority of the House of Commons anything more than a set of men who had been induced by factious motives to shout for a policy for which, in their hearts, they cared little or nothing.

Argues for the probability that the Parliament will support the King.

The first argument by which he supported his opinion that the Parliament would be likely to look upon the King's demands with favour was sufficient to show how far he had mistaken the character of his countrymen. He actually stated his belief that it was so long since the old grievances had been produced that they would now be forgotten, and that, as the Government had not lately done anything unpopular,† James was not likely

* Bacon to the King, Cott. MS., Tit. F. iv., fol. 332. The notes at fol. 329 are evidently those from which this letter was drawn up.

† 'I do not find since the last Parliament any one action of estate amongst your Majesty's proceedings that hath been harsh or distasteful, and, therefore, seeing the old grievances (having been long broached) cannot but wax

to be annoyed by their revival. After having thus measured the retentive powers of his countrymen's memories, he went on to say that Lord Sanquhar's execution had produced a conviction that the King was now impartial in dealing justice to Scotchmen and Englishmen alike; that the deaths of the Earls of Salisbury and Dunbar had rid him of the odium which, as he imagined, was attached to their persons; and that the leaders of the House of Commons had found out by this time that nothing was to be gained by opposition, and would at last, through hope of the King's favour, be ready to support him in his demands.* He concluded this part of his letter by charging Salisbury with having supported, in an underhand manner, the opposition to his own measures in the last Parliament.† It is difficult to understand how Bacon could for a moment have believed in the truth of such a charge as this, were it not for the intense dislike which he felt for the cousin who had so long barred his way to promotion.

Advises the King how to meet the Parliament.

In meeting his Parliament, Bacon again urged, the King must avoid all appearance of any wish to strike a bargain with the House. He must not ask for too much at once; he must give out that he had called the members together for some other reason than in order to obtain a grant of money, and tempt them by propounding some of those great schemes which Bacon would so gladly have recommended to the consideration of the House. He must tell them that he would be able, in time, to supply his own wants without their assistance,

dead and flat, and that there hath been no new matter either to rub up and revive the old, or to give other cause of discontent, I think the case much amended to your Majesty's advantage.'

* 'That opposition which was, the last Parliament, to your Majesty's business, as much as was not *ex puris naturalibus*, but out of party, I conceive to be now much weaker than it was, and that party almost dissolved. Yelverton is won. Sandys is fallen off. Crew and Hyde stand to be Serjeants. Brock is dead. Nevill hath hopes. Berkeley will, I think, be respective. Martin hath money in his purse. Dudley Digges and Holles are yours. Besides, they cannot but find more and more the vanity of that popular course, especially your Majesty having carried yourself in that princely temper towards them as not to persecute or disgrace them, nor yet to use or advance them.'

† 'I cannot excuse him that is gone of an artificial animating of the negative, which infusion or influence now ceasing, I have better hope.'

CH. XII. 1614. and that he called upon them in order to anticipate the conclusion of his efforts rather than from any absolute necessity.

A paper,* which contains the notes which probably formed the basis of a third letter, now lost, in which he entered further into particulars, stands in still more striking contrast with the manly advice given by Nevill. Such questions as the following were, according to Bacon, to be matters for the consideration of the King. How the subject of the impositions could be settled so as that no more might be heard about the matter?—how the House could be induced to put off the investigation of the grievances of the nation until the supply had been voted?—what project it would be advisable to put forward as the one to be held in terror over the Commons, as affording a ready resource in case the House should prove contumacious?—what measures are to be taken in hand so as to win popularity?—what laws were actually to be propounded to Parliament in order to give content to the people? The last suggestion was well enough, but Bacon does not long continue in this strain; he begins immediately to consider how the lawyers can be won over to the King's side, and how the different classes of men who together constituted the House might be gained. This, however, is far from being the worst. He suggests that the more popular members should be intimidated or flattered, and that the judges themselves should be tampered with, lest they should decide in a manner adverse to the Crown any points of law which might come before them.† Care must be taken to influence the elections whenever it can

* Headed, 'Incidents of Parliament,' Cott. MS., Tit. F. iv., fol. 330. The first paragraph is 'The impositions, and how that matter may be buried and silenced.' I have given the most favourable interpretation. The words might mean 'How it can best be kept out of sight.' But at its best, there is no recognition of the real worth of the arguments of the opposition.

† 'What course may be taken with that combined body . . . which made the popular party last Parliament, for the severing of them, intimidating of them, or holding them in hopes or the like, whereby they may be dissolved or weakened or won? What course may be held to engage and assure the judges *in omnem eventum* for any points of law or right which may be foreseen as likely to come in question in Parliament?'

be done by fair means. There were the Cinque Ports, more or less under the influence of their warden, the Earl of Northampton; there were other boroughs where the Chancellor of the Duchy of Lancaster could do much; and there were not a few where a word from one or other of the Lords of the Council would not be thrown away. Everything, however, must be sedulously avoided which bore the appearance of packing the Parliament. The King would merely avoid the mistake of leaving everything to chance. By allowing the legitimate influence of the Government to be felt, he would have a Parliament which was really free. It was the opposition leaders who were attempting to pack the Parliament with their followers. In Nevill's advice, that the Government should be represented by officials sitting in the Lower House, Bacon, of course, concurred.

Character of Bacon's recommendations.

Such language as this speaks for itself. It is the language of a man who believed that the Crown was right in its attempt to maintain its prerogatives unimpaired, and that in so doing it would obtain the support of the people of England, if they did not allow themselves to be led astray by men who were influenced by factious motives. It is also the language of a man who believed that, in order to obtain the object at which he aimed, it was allowable to make use of means from which others, who were possessed of a more delicate sense of right and wrong, would shrink, and who had little idea of the injury which, if he had been successful, he would have inflicted upon the morality of the nation by obtaining its support by other than the most straightforward means, and by influencing its leading men by offers of the favour, or by the threats of the ill-will, of the Government.

Bacon's advice palatable to James.

Unfortunately, there was little doubt that James would choose the programme of Bacon in preference to that of Nevill. The grievances and the impositions would have been a bitter pill to swallow, and he was naturally inclined to take Bacon's hopeful view of the feelings of the country, and to be satisfied with the theory that the opposition with which he had hitherto met had been merely a factitious movement arising from the ill-humour of a few individuals.

CH. XII. 1614.

He decides upon summoning a Parliament.

The proposal to summon Parliament had long been resisted by Northampton. In September, when the question was debated in the Council, he had told the King that to do so would only be to call together an assembly of his enemies,* and James assured him, after the conclusion of the discussion, that he believed that he was in the right. A few months, however, made a change even in Northampton's views. He submitted, as a matter of necessity, to what he considered to be the indignity of applying for help to the House of Commons.† On the 16th of February, the Council informed the King that they had taken the matter into consideration, and that they were of opinion that the only course to be pursued was the summoning of Parliament.‡

Amount of the debt.

It was high time. In spite of the enormous sales of land, it had been found impossible to obtain money enough to defray the necessary expenses of the Government. The garrisons in the cautionary towns were ready to mutiny for their pay. The ambassadors were crying out for their salaries and allowances. The sailors who manned the navy were unpaid, and the fortifications by which the coast was guarded were in urgent need of repair.§ Lord Harrington, who had a claim upon the King for £30,000, which he had spent upon the establishment of the Princess, was put off with a patent giving him a monopoly of the copper coinage of the country. In every department there was a long list of arrears which there were no means of satisfying, and which amounted on the whole to £488,000. To repay the money borrowed upon Privy Seals £125,000 would be needed, and the £67,000 which had been levied by anticipation from the revenues properly belonging to the following year, must in some way or other be made good. Altogether, the King's liabilities now amounted to £680,000,‖ to say nothing of a standing deficit which, after including the extraordinary expenditure, was certain to exceed £200,000 a-year.

The Council took Nevill's advice so far as looking

* Digby to the King, Sept. 22, 1613, *S. P. Sp.*

† Northampton, to [Somerset], Cott. MS., Tit. F. iv., fol. 325, 327.

‡ Council to the King, Feb. 16, 1614, *S. P. Dom.* lxxvi. 22.

§ Speeches of Winwood and Cæsar, *C. J.* i. 461, 462.

‖ Lansd. MS. 165, fol. 257. The statement is dated May 2, 1614.

over the grievances was concerned; but they went no further. On no single point did they think proper to give way. They also examined his list of concessions, and the offers which had been made by the King after the breach of the contract in 1610. From these they selected some which James consented to lay before Parliament, in order to show that he was willing to give way in matters where he considered that his subjects were hardly treated. The concessions were not unimportant in themselves, but they were altogether unconnected with the points in dispute. The impositions, as might have been expected, were not even named.

Proposed concessions.

For the first time within the memory of man, the country was subjected to the turmoil of a general election, in which a great question of principle was at stake. Under these circumstances, the Government were induced to take steps to procure a favourable majority, to which they had thought it unnecessary to resort ten years previously. How far they went it is difficult to say, with the scanty information which we possess. Nevill, indeed, had offered to undertake, on behalf of the future House of Commons, that if the King would concede all the chief points in dispute, the House would not be niggardly in granting the supplies which he required. It seems, however, that there were some who went beyond this very safe assertion, and who were allured by promises of Court favour to engage to do what they could to obtain the return of members who were likely to favour the prerogative. Whoever they may have been, they were certainly not men of any great importance, and it is not probable that they offered to do more than to influence a few elections here and there.*

A contested election.

The Undertakers.

* Compare Bacon's estimate of them, in his letter just quoted, with the following extract of a letter from Suffolk to Somerset, written about the end of March: 'The last night, Pembroke came to me in the garden, speaking in broken phrases, that he could not tell what would come of this Parliament, because he found by the consultation last day that my lords had no great conceit that there would be any great good effected for our master: divers of my lords having spoken with many wise Parliament men, who do generally decline from the Undertakers, only Pembroke and myself were the hopeful believers of good success, two or three petty Councillors more seemed to be indifferently conceited, but so as my Lord of Pembroke is much unsatisfied that they are no more confident in his

CH. XII. 1614.

Unimportant as the whole affair was, the Government soon discovered that they had only injured their own chances of success by meddling with such intrigues. Rumour magnified the matter into a conspiracy to procure a whole Parliament of nominees. The Undertakers, as they were termed in the phraseology of the day, had dared to speak in the name of the whole Commons of England. It was not long before the most discouraging reports reached the Council of the reception which the Government candidates were everywhere meeting with.* It was in vain that lords and great men wrote to every borough and county where they had any influence. Constituencies which had never before raised an objection to the persons who had been pointed out to them, now declared their determination to send to Westminster men of their own selection. It frequently happened that the Court candidates were flatly told that no votes would be given to any man who was in the King's service. The pressure which was put upon the electors, whilst it failed in the object for which it was intended, only served to strengthen the belief that an attempt had been made to pack the Parliament. So strong was the feeling against the Government in the city of London, that Sir Henry Montagu, who had represented the city in the last Parliament, and who had served as Recorder for many years, was rejected, in memory, no doubt, of his speech in favour of the impositions; whilst Fuller, the strenuous asserter of the principles of the popular and Puritan party, was elected without difficulty. Not one of the men who had distinguished themselves on the

The elections are unfavourable to the Government.

friends. . . . . We are appointed to meet again on Saturday. Pembroke and I have undertaken to bring to my lords the demands that will be asked of the King this Parliament, and that they shall be moderate for the King, and yet pleasing to them. Which we affirm to my lords we conceive will be attractive inducements to get the good we look for, and what this shall work at our next meeting you shall know as soon as it is past. But I must make you laugh to tell you that my Lord Privy Seal soberly says to me, "My Lord, you incline before the Council too much to these Undertakers." This troubles me nothing, for if we may do our master the service we wish by our dissembling, I am well contented to play the knave a little with them, which you must give me dispensation for following your direction.'—Cott. MS., Tit. F. iv. fol. 335.

* Lake to ——, Feb. 19, 1614. Nichols' *Progresses*, ii. 755. Chamberlain to Carleton, March 3, March 17, 1614, *Court and Times*, 300, 235. The last letter is misplaced.

popular side during the debates in 1610 was without a seat. Sandys and Hakewill, Whitelocke and Wentworth, were all there once more to defend the liberties of England. The scanty ranks of the defenders of the prerogative were headed as before by Bacon and Cæsar; and the four candidates for the Secretaryship, Nevill and Winwood, Wotton and Lake, were all successful in obtaining seats. One of the most remarkable features of the new House was the number of those who appeared for the first time within the walls of Parliament. Three hundred members, making nearly two-thirds of the whole assembly, were elected for the first time. The fact admits of an easy explanation: the constituencies in their present temper would be on the look-out for men who represented the determined spirit of the nation even more strongly than the members of the late Parliament had done. Amongst those who were thus elected were two men who were to set their mark upon the history of their country. Sir Thomas Wentworth, a young man of twenty-one, and heir to a princely estate in Yorkshire, represented the great county of the north; John Pym, a Somersetshire country gentleman, nine years older than Wentworth, was sent to the House of Commons by the little borough of Calne. We may be sure that neither Wentworth nor Pym were unobservant spectators of the events of the session; but, as far as our information extends, neither of them took any part in the debates.*

CH. XII. 1614.

1613. Necessity of choosing a Secretary.

The unfavourable character of the elections made it more than ever necessary that a Secretary should be chosen who could speak with authority in the name of the Government, and who could make use of any influence which he might possess as a member of the House of Commons to frustrate the expected opposition. As late as in September in the preceding year Nevill was still confident of success.† But he had great difficulties to contend with. The Howards had no cause to be satisfied with him, as he had never taken care to conceal his dislike of the divorce. Northampton, besides, had reason

* At least, I have been unable to discover his name in the pages referring to the debates of this session.

† Chamberlain to Carleton, Sept. 9, 1613, *Court and Times*, i. 271.

CH. XII. 1613. to look askance upon him, as he suspected him of having some connection with the scheme by which Mansell had hoped to overthrow the Commission for the Reformation of the Navy, in which Northampton took a peculiar interest.* Above all, the King never could forget the part which he had taken in the last Parliament, and the plain words in which he had set forth the grievances of the Commons. In October, Nevill discovered that his hopes were destined to be disappointed. It was generally believed that the favourite would continue to act in that confidential capacity to the King in which he had hitherto been employed, and that Lake, as the nominee of the Howards, would be admitted to perform the subordinate duties of the Secretaryship.† In order to console Nevill for his disappointment, Somerset‡ proposed to purchase for him the office of Treasurer of the Chamber. Nevill at once replied, that he would take neither money, nor anything bought for money, at the hands of a subject, and gave him to understand that, though he was ready to act as Secretary, he would not put up with any lower place.

1614. In February, hopes of success were given him once more. It was intimated to him by Suffolk that he was selected for the appointment; but that, as the King was still displeased with him for his conduct in the former Parliament, he must expiate his misdemeanors before he could hope to be promoted.§ If this was anything more than a mere trick on the part of Suffolk, to secure his services during the session, either James must soon have changed his mind, or Nevill must have refused to make the required submission. On the 29th of March, Winwood took the oaths as Secretary. Lake, as some compensation for his disappointment, was admitted to the Privy Council on the same day.

Appointment of Winwood.

His qualifications for the post.

In many respects, if Nevill was not to have the place, it was impossible to have made a better selection. Winwood had served, with credit to himself, as ambas-

* Whitelocke, *Liber Famelicus*, 46.

† Chamberlain to Carleton, *Court and Times*, i. 277.

‡ He was still only Rochester, but it is perhaps better to avoid confusion by giving the title by which he was known in 1614.

§ Suffolk to Somerset, Cott. MS., Tit. F. iv., fol. 335.

sador in Holland for many years. His whole heart was in the opposition to Spain and the Catholic powers. It was by him that all those treaties had been negotiated which bound England to support the Dutch Republic and the Princes of the German Union against the House of Austria. In the Council he would be sure to side with Abbot and Ellesmere in denouncing the entanglements of a Spanish policy. Nor was his good sense likely to desert him in dealing with the domestic difficulties with which the Government was beset. On many points he shared the opinions of the majority of the House of Commons, and if he had been allowed to shape the policy of the Crown, he would have had little difficulty in giving satisfaction to the nation. In some respects, indeed, he was less fitted than his friend Nevill to act as leader of the House. He had, with the exception of occasional visits, been absent from England for many years, and he was hardly aware how completely the feeling of his countrymen had changed since the death of Elizabeth. Nor had his position at the Hague tended to soften down the asperities of his somewhat unconciliatory temper. He was also at the further disadvantage of being altogether untried in Parliamentary life, and of being destitute of that peculiar experience which is a necessity to those who attempt to guide the deliberations of a large public assembly. It was probably this very circumstance which recommended him to James. His name brought with it no reminiscences of Parliamentary opposition, nor did it revive the remembrance of the time when Somerset and the Howards were at deadly feud, and when Nevill and Lake were the rival candidates, supported by the two parties who were struggling for power. Nor must it be forgotten that James still sympathized with the bold foreign policy of which Winwood was the acknowledged representative. As to the home government, it was well understood that it was the business of the Secretary to carry out the directions given to him, and not to prescribe the mode in which political difficulties were to be met.

Winwood, indeed, was one of a class of diplomatists

CH. XII. 1614.

He was one of a class of diplomatic statesmen.

in which James and his son would henceforward find the most valuable, if not always the most trusted of their ministers. It was rapidly becoming impossible for any man living in England, who was not either animated by corruption or ambition, or utterly incapable of understanding the requirements of the time, to attach himself to the service of the Crown. But with many of the ambassadors the case was very different; they were accustomed, from long habit, to receive orders from the Sovereign, which they were bound implicitly to follow. On their return home, they continued to look upon the King in the light of an employer, with whom it was allowable to remonstrate, but whom it was impossible to disobey. They were accordingly prepared to support the prerogative, not because they deliberately disregarded the rising influence of the House of Commons, but because it was an element which had never entered into their calculations. If the Sovereign for a moment was straying from the right path, they were contented to wait for a happy change, just as they would have been contented to execute the orders which might be sent to them, during their embassies at Paris or the Hague, although those directions might not altogether accord with their own ideas.

The King's speech at the opening of the Session.

Certainly Winwood's position was not to be envied. He had to induce a hostile House of Commons to grant supplies, at the same time that he would have to refuse those concessions upon which their hearts were set. It was not long before he had to make his first essay in the art of guiding the House. The session was opened on the 5th of April by a speech from the King. James told the two Houses that he had called them together for three reasons: he was anxious that, by their support, religion might be maintained, the future succession to the Crown provided for, and his necessities relieved by the grant of a supply. He commended to their consideration the increase of Popery, which was spreading in spite of the exertions which he had used to combat it both with his tongue and with his pen. He had no wish for any more rigorous laws against recusancy, but he hoped that some means might be contrived for executing more

April 5.

He speaks of the recusants,

strictly those which were already in existence. He then referred to the events which had taken place in his own family since he had last met his Parliament. God had taken his eldest son from him, but He had just given him a grandson in his place, and he looked to Parliament to settle the succession, in case of the failure of heirs through Prince Charles, upon this child and the other children who might be born to the Electress. He had chosen a husband for his daughter out of a Protestant family, in order that, if his own issue male should fail, the future Kings of England might be brought up in the Protestant faith.

of his daughter's marriage,

Thus far, he must have carried with him the sympathies of every man amongst his audience. He now entered upon more dangerous ground. The extraordinary charge connected with the marriage had emptied the Exchequer, and there were other expenses which pressed heavily upon him. He would, however, speak plainly to them. He would not bargain with them for their money. He would see what they would do in their love. He had shown them that he relied upon their affection, by having recourse to them rather than to his own prerogative. He must, however, clear himself on one point: it had been rumoured that he relied upon some private Undertakers 'who, with their own credit and industry, would do great matters.' This he declared to be false: he would rather have the love of his subjects than their money.*

and demands supplies.

* *Parl. Hist.*, i. 1149. James is generally accused of deceiving his hearers on this point; and it is said that in 1621 he acknowledged that 'in the last Parliament there came up a strange kind of beasts called Undertakers, a name which in my nature I abhor.' In this, however, there is no necessary contradiction with what he said in 1614. There were, no doubt, men in 1614 who were called Undertakers; but the question is, how far the King availed himself of their efforts. We have seen that Bacon and Northampton laughed at the scheme, though there were a few among the Council who encouraged them. We do not know enough about their proceedings to say what it was that they proposed to do, but the rumour appears to have been that they offered to influence the returns to such an extent as to procure a Government majority. Such a rumour was absurd in itself, as James said in his speech of the 8th, 'If any had been so foolish as to offer it, yet it had been greater folly in me to have accepted it.' No doubt he knew that letters had been sent by the Lords of the Council and others to influence the electors; but he may have held that such letters did not amount to interference with elections. Besides, influence of this kind was used on both sides.

CH. XII. 1614. April 8. The King's second speech.

Three days later, James again addressed the Houses. This Parliament, he said, was to be a Parliament of love. The world was to see his own love to his subjects, and the love of his subjects to their King. God was loved for the gift which He gave, and he, who as a King represented God, would begin by offering them a gift, and he expected from them cheerfulness in retribution for his favour. He then went over the heads of his former speech. He again denied that he had attempted to 'hinder or prompt any man in the free election,' and asserted that he had never 'put any confidence in a party Parliament.' He declared that he would begin this Parliament by making offers of concessions which would soon be laid before them. As to their grievances, it would be better that each member should present them on behalf of his own constituency; 'to heap them together in one scroll like an army' would 'but cast aspersion upon' him and his 'government, and' would 'savour more of discontent than of desire for reformation.' He was unwilling to give up any of the honours and flowers of the Crown, but he would not stretch the prerogative further than his predecessors had done. He never intended his proclamations to have the force of law, but he thought that they ought to be obeyed, until Parlia-

The following extract from Whitelocke's *Liber Famelicus* (p. 40) gives an insight into the manner in which elections were conducted:

'I was returned a burgess for the town of Woodstock, in the county of Oxon, where I was recorder, and was elected, notwithstanding the town was hardly pressed for another by the Earl of Montgomery, steward of the manors, and keeper of the house and park there.

'There was returned with me Sir Philip Cary, younger son to Sir Edward Cary, master of the jewels. He was nominated in the place by Sir Thomas Spencer, who, being steward of the town, refused to serve himself, but commended that gentleman.

'I was returned burgess also for the borough of Corfe Castle, and that was by the nomination of . . . the Lady Elizabeth Coke . . . I gave her thanks for it, and yielded up the place to her again, and in it was chosen Sir Thomas Tracy.

'My worthy friend, Sir Robert Killigrew, gave me a place for Helstone, in the county of Cornwall, and I caused my brother-in-law, Henry Bulstrode, to be returned for that place.'

The fact, probably, was that, whilst the recommendations of the influential landowners were generally in accordance with the feeling of the electors, the recommendations of the Court Lords were not. That James had made a bargain with certain persons to return members favourable to him, has not been proved. What he did do was, probably, in conformity with Bacon's advice given in the letters before-mentioned.

ment could meet to provide a remedy for the evil in question. He once more denied having made any bargain with the Undertakers, and declared that he relied altogether upon the love of his subjects.

CH. XII. 1614.

What is most remarkable in this speech is the air of self-satisfaction which pervades the whole of it. James had evidently no idea that anyone besides himself was competent to judge what grievances ought to be redressed, or in what degree his prerogative was injurious to the interests of the nation.

Question whether the Attorney-General might sit.

The first question taken up by the House was raised by a member who doubted whether Bacon could take his seat, as there was no precedent for the election of an Attorney-General. The matter was referred to a committee, who were ordered to search for precedents. The House finally decided that Bacon might be allowed to sit, but that for the future no Attorney-General might take his seat in the House. On the 11th of April, Winwood rose to move the grant of supplies, and read over the list of concessions which the King was prepared to make. The next day, when the House was about to take up the subject, Myddelton rose and said that these promises chiefly concerned the country gentlemen, and offered to the House a Bill concerning the impositions. Other members followed, bringing forward one by one the old list of the ecclesiastical grievances. It was in vain that Winwood rose and spoke at length upon the necessities of the public service, and that he panegyrized the foreign policy of the King; that Cæsar entered into details of the misery which was inflicted upon the debtors of the Crown, and that Bacon appealed to the House to consider the state of the Continent, where war might break out at any moment. The House was unwilling to grant the supply until the rumours relating to the Undertakers had been inquired into.*

A supply demanded.

It is postponed.

The grievances referred to a committee.

A few days later Sandys moved that the grievances which had been presented to the last Parliament should be referred to the Committee on Petitions. It had already become evident that the House would not be satisfied with the instalment of justice which had been offered

* *C. J.* i. 456–463.

CH. XII. 1614. them by the King, and that if James hoped to obtain supplies the only course open to him was to follow the advice which Nevill had given him.

The House receive the Communion. On the 17th of April the whole House received the Communion together. They chose St. Margaret's, the church of the parish in which they were sitting, in preference to Westminster Abbey, 'for fear of copes and wafer-cakes.'* It is from this day that the peculiar connection of St. Margaret's with the House of Commons dates. The object of the members in thus solemnly taking the Communion together was partly the expectation that they would thus be able to detect any recusant who might have slipped in amongst them. When the day arrived it was found that there was not one of them who absented himself from the church.

The Bill on Impositions. The next day the Bill on Impositions was read a second time. It was ordered that it should be considered in Committee of the whole House, in order that, as Hakewill said, the three hundred new members might hear the arguments, and that, understanding the true state of their right, they might leave it to their posterity.

Monopolies. The House had other grievances in view. A patent had been granted for the manufacture of glass, which they regarded in the light of an injurious monopoly, whilst the Government looked upon it as an encouragement to native industry. A company had been recently established for exclusive trading with France, which was liable to the same objections under which the Spanish Company had sunk. Undertakers. On the 2nd of May the question of the Undertakers was again before them, and in spite of Bacon's† attempt to persuade them to be content with a protest, they directed that the suspected Undertakers should be strictly examined. After a long investigation, the Committee were unable to obtain any evidence whatever of any corrupt bargain having been struck. At last a paper was produced, which was owned by Sir Henry Nevill. He said that he had written it more than two years before, as containing the heads of the advice which

* Chamberlain to Carleton, April 14, 1614, *S. P. Dom.* lxxvii. 7, *C. J.* i. 463.

† Bacon's *Works* (ed. Montagu), vi. 13.

he then offered to the King. As there was no reason why he should not have done his best to persuade the King to call a Parliament as soon as possible, and as his advice was clearly wise in itself, the House had nothing to do but to express its satisfaction in the course which he had taken; and finding that its search was likely to prove fruitless, it allowed the matter to drop.*

Impositions.

The arguments which were used in the Committee on the Impositions for the benefit of the new members have not been preserved. It was, however, determined that a conference with the Lords should be demanded, and that they should be requested to join in a petition to the King, and the parts were assigned which each manager was to take.†

Owen's argument from the laws of foreign countries.

On the 21st, the House took the subject again into consideration, before sending to the Lords to demand a conference. In the argument which the managers were directed to put forward there was, unluckily, one point which was sufficiently doubtful to offer a hold to the supporters of the prerogative. One of the managers was Sir Roger Owen, the member for Shrewsbury, a man who, with no real claim to distinction, chose to consider himself an authority upon the constitutional law of the nations of the Continent as well as upon that of England. He had, in the last Parliament, argued strongly‡ that the right of imposing, without the consent of the three estates, was not allowed by the law in any European monarchy. He was now instructed to enforce this argument upon the Lords. Such a theory was entirely irrelevant to the question at issue, and it involved a long discussion upon the principles upon which foreign constitutions were founded, to which the Lords could hardly be expected to have the patience to listen. Wotton saw his opportunity. He knew very well that, as a matter of fact, foreign

Answered by Wotton and Winwood.

* *C. J.* i. 485. Chamberlain to Carleton, May 19, 1614, *S. P.* lxxvii. 26. Lorkin to Puckering, May 28, 1614, *Court and Times*, i. 314. The paper may possibly be the same as the one printed in the Appendix. A few days before, Sir Thomas Parry, the Chancellor of the Duchy of Lancaster, had been detected in interfering in the Stockbridge election. He was expelled the House, as well as the sitting members. The King sequestered him from the Privy Council.

† *C. J.* i. 481, 486.

‡ *Parl. Deb.* in 1610, 112.

CH. XII. 1614. Sovereigns did succeed in obtaining money which had not been voted by their estates, and he was not inclined to inquire too closely into the methods by which this power had been acquired. He accordingly, after expressing a hope that Owen would look well to the ground upon which he was treading, asserted his own belief that the power of imposing belonged to hereditary but not to elective monarchs. He was supported by Winwood, who after declaring that he had no wish to maintain the right of imposing, added that his opinion was that the foreign princes in question imposed in right of their prerogative. Owen, he said, had made several assertions, but had proved absolutely nothing.

Reply of Digges, It was high time to draw back from the ground which Owen had so inconsiderately taken up. Sir Dudley Digges accordingly put the matter upon its right footing. The ground upon which the House rested its claim, he said, was that which Englishmen had received from their ancestors:* *Nolumus mutare leges Angliæ.* All else was merely illustrative of the main argument, and was used as an answer to those who urged the King to imitate the Kings of France and Spain, if he wished it to be thought that he was not inferior to those monarchs.

of Sandys, Still there was something more to be said. The contrast, which had been insisted upon so strongly between the elective and the hereditary monarchies of the Continent, admitted of very different inferences from those which had occurred to Wotton and Winwood. They had argued that hereditary monarchs had the right of imposing; others might come to the conclusion that if Kings were not to impose, it was necessary that they should hold their crowns by a tenure which was not altogether independent of the consent of their subjects. This seems to have been the ground which was taken up by Sandys, as far as we can judge from the very imperfect notes of his speech which have come down to us. It is certainly unfortunate that his words have not been preserved in full, as it would have

* 'That the first ground that we have received from our neighbours, *Nolumus*,' &c. should evidently be 'from our ancestors,' *C. J.* i. 493

been interesting to trace the first dawning of the idea that, in order to preserve the rights of the subject intact, it would be necessary to make some change in the relations between the authority of the Crown and the representatives of the people. He began, apparently, by referring to the enormous burden of taxation which had been imposed upon France by the sole authority of Henry IV. He reminded the House that it was not merely the right of laying impositions which was claimed by those hereditary sovereigns of which they had heard so much; they exercised also the right of making laws, without the consent of their estates. What could come of such a state of things but tyranny, from which both Prince and people would suffer alike? The origin of every hereditary monarchy lay in election. If, on every occasion of the demise of the Crown, the new Sovereign does not go through the formalities of an election, he must remember that the authority which he holds was, in its origin, voluntarily accepted by the people; and that, when the nation gave its consent to the authority which he is called to exercise, they did so upon the express understanding that there were certain reciprocal conditions which neither King nor people might violate with impunity. A King who pretended to rule by any other title, such as that of conquest, might be dethroned whenever there was force sufficient to overthrow him.* He concluded by denying the validity of the argument that the King of England might do whatever the King of France might do, and by moving that Owen might be called upon to substantiate his doctrine.

and of Went-worth.

It would have been well if the debate had come to an end here. Though the doctrine of the original contract thus propounded by Sandys will not stand before the researches of modern historical inquiry, it was, nevertheless, a far closer approximation to the truth than any rival theory which was at that time likely to be opposed

* This is, I suppose, the meaning of the brief notes, 'No successive King, but first elected. Election double, of person, and care; but both come in by consent of people, and with reciprocal conditions between King and people. That a King by conquest may also (when power) be expelled.' *C. J.* i. 493.

CH. XII. 1614.

to it. He was, however, followed by Wentworth, the Puritan lawyer, who sat for the city of Oxford. He had given offence in the last Parliament by the freedom of his language. He was one of those men who are always to be found in times of political excitement, and who, whilst they generally succeed in speaking to the point, are careless of the decencies of expression under which the real leaders of the movement are accustomed to veil their opinions. On this occasion his speech was in strong contrast to the calm argument of Sandys. The Spaniards, he said, had lost the Low Countries by attempting to lay impositions. All the power of the greatest of the French monarchs had not saved them from dying like calves upon the butcher's knife. Princes who taxed their people as they had done should remember that, in the prophecy of Ezekiel, in the description given of the future state of the Holy Land, a portion of the soil is assigned to the Prince, in order that he may not oppress the people. Kings who refused to profit by this example might read their destiny in Daniel's prediction that there should stand up a raiser of taxes in the glory of the Kingdom, but that within a few days he should be destroyed.*

The House of Lords refuse to confer.

As soon as the debate was at an end, Winwood carried up to the House of Lords the message demanding a conference. The Lords, after some consideration, resolved to consult the judges. The judges were by no means inclined to allow themselves to be entangled in such a dangerous question. Coke adroitly answered, in their name, that they were unwilling to give any opinion, as they might have to decide judicially upon the points involved, and they did not think it well to become partisans of either side, by delivering an extrajudicial sentence.† Upon this a discussion arose as to the answer which was to be given to the Lower House; and it was finally decided that, on the ground that the Lords had not had time to acquaint themselves with all the records

* Chamberlain to Carleton, May 26, 1614, *Court and Times*, i. 312.
† *L. J.* ii. 706.

upon which the case rested, they should refuse to meet the Commons, at least for the present.*

The division in the Lords.

The request which had been made by the Commons was virtually equivalent to a demand that the Lords would take up their true position, as leaders of the nation, in asking for justice from the King. As yet the Lords were unwilling to occupy this ground, but an examination of the division must have been reassuring to all who did not despair of some day seeing the two Houses fighting the battle of the constitution side by side. Of the seventy-one peers who were present, at least thirty † voted in the minority. Of the majority, sixteen were Bishops, Matthew, Archbishop of York, being the only one who voted for conferring with the Lower House. Amongst the twenty-five lay peers who voted with the majority were the two Scotchmen, Somerset and Lennox, who had recently been raised to the English Earldom of Richmond. There were nine Privy Councillors present; so that it appears that if, as is probable, they all voted against the conference, it was impossible to find more than eleven independent lay peers who would vote with the Government, and of these at least four or five were in some way or other under obligations to the court.

Speech of Bishop Neile.

Annoying as this refusal must have been to the Commons, they felt themselves to be still more deeply aggrieved when they heard of some words which had fallen from one of the speakers in the debate in the House of Lords. Of all the sycophants who sought for power and place during the reigns of James and of his son, Bishop Neile was justly regarded as the worst. He had lately been notorious as the one amongst the Commissioners sitting in the case of Lady Essex who had been most active in pushing on the divorce with indecent haste. As soon as the sentence was pronounced, he put forth all his efforts in attempting to ruin the Archbishop, and although he did not succeed

* C. J. ii. 707, 708; Cott. MS., Tit. F. iv. 257. Petyt's *Jus Parliamentarium*, 340.

† Chamberlain gives the numbers as thirty-nine and thirty. According to the Journals, there were seventy-one present. I have, therefore, supposed the division to be forty-one and thirty. The difference of two votes is not of much importance.

CH. XII. 1614. in this as he desired, he ingratiated himself with James sufficiently to obtain for himself the Bishopric of Lincoln, which had been originally destined for Abbot's brother Robert, who had done the King no small service in his controversy with Bellarmin. Neile now stood up to vilify the House of Commons. The matter, he said, on which the Lords were asked to confer with the Lower House was one with which it had no right to meddle. No man who had taken the oaths of supremacy and allegiance could, with a good conscience, even join in a discussion upon the question of the impositions. Not only were the Commons striking at the root of the prerogative of the Crown, but they would, if they were admitted to argue their case, be sure to give utterance to seditious and undutiful speeches, which would be unfit for the Lords to listen to, and which would tend as well to a breach between the two Houses as between the King himself and his subjects.*

May 25. Indignation of the Commons. The next day the whole House of Commons was in an uproar. One member called for a Bill confiscating to his Majesty's use the profits of the Bishopric of Lincoln for the next seven years. Another said that Neile's head ought to be set upon Tower Hill. A third declared that banishment was the fitting punishment for lesser offences than this. Those who treated the subject more calmly were doubtful whether it would be preferable to make their complaint to the King or to the House of Lords. A Committee was appointed to take the question into consideration.

May 26. On the following day, the committee reported that they had decided by a small majority to recommend that an immediate reference might be made to the King, and that no other business might be taken up till an answer was received. As soon as the report had been made, Sandys rose to hinder the House from the suicidal step which it was advised to take. He told them that by complaining to the King of words spoken in the House of Lords, they were not only insulting the Peers, and placing the King in a position of great difficulty, but they

* *L. J.* ii. 709.

were cutting at the root of their own most cherished right of freedom of speech. If the Commons might appeal to the King to punish a Peer for words uttered in the House of Lords, it was clear that they could never again protest against any claim which might be put forth by the King to a similar jurisdiction over the House of Commons. This reasoning carried conviction with it, and in spite of the opposition of Sir Roger Owen and a few others who were afraid that justice would not be done by the Peers, it was decided to ask satisfaction from the Lords. It was also resolved, that until satisfaction had been given to the House no business should be proceeded with.

The King's letter.

The King had long been watching the debates in the House of Commons. He could now have little doubt that the House would take up the position which they had occupied at the close of the last session. They had already shown that they were determined to carry their point in respect to the Impositions before they consented to a grant of money. They were only waiting till the Committee had finished its labours to present a petition of grievances as objectionable to him as that from which he had turned aside four years before. On both of these points he had made up his mind not to give way. He accordingly wrote a letter to them, objecting to their resolution to abstain from business till they had obtained satisfaction from the Upper House, and telling them that it did not belong to them to call or dissolve assemblies. They sent in reply a deputation of forty members, with the Speaker at its head, which was directed to inform him that they had never claimed any such right, but that they intended merely to forbear from entering upon matters of moment, as they were unfit to treat of such subjects until they could clear themselves from the imputations which had been cast upon them.*

The Lords' reply concerning the Bishop's speech.

On the 30th of May, the Lords sent down an answer to the effect that they should always be sorry to hear any aspersion cast upon the other House, but that as the

* *C. J.*, i. 500. Chamberlain to Carleton, June 1, 1614, *Court and Times*, i. 318.

CH. XII. 1614.

accusation against the Bishop was grounded simply upon common fame, they did not think it right to entertain it. If, however, they had any express charge brought before them, they would be ready to do justice.* The excuse was manifestly frivolous. The Commons had appealed from common fame to those who were present when the speech was delivered. It would no doubt have been better to have ignored the whole affair; and the Lords might very well have refused to discuss with any external body words which had been spoken within their own walls. If they had done this, the Commons would probably have drawn back, for fear of damaging their own claims. But it was impossible for the Commons to accept the excuse which was made. They replied by sending Sir Roger Owen with a paper containing the words which had been uttered by the Bishop, as closely as they could gather them. Upon this, the Lords called upon the Bishop to explain his words. He seems to have been frightened at the position into which his rash, headlong temper had brought him. He protested, with many tears, that he had been misconstrued, and that he never meant to speak any evil of the House of Commons. The Lords acquainted the Commons with what had passed, and added, that though they had taken care to give them contentment in this matter, they wished it to be understood that in future they would not allow any member of their House to be called in question on the ground of common fame.†

The Bishop excuses himself.

Here the Commons ought to have stopped. Instead of this, the speakers urged more eagerly than ever that some steps should be taken against the Bishop. One member declared that Neile had once given a false certificate of conformity to a recusant. The House could not resist the temptation of inquiring into the Bishop's misconduct, and, without perceiving that they were lowering themselves by indulging in personal recriminations, determined that the charge should be examined.‡ Upon this the King, who was in no good humour with them before, lost all patience. He sent them a message that,

The King threatens to dissolve.

* *L. J.*, ii. 711. † *L. J.*, ii. 713. ‡ *C. J.*, i. 504.

unless they proceeded forthwith to treat of supply, he should dissolve the Parliament.

Parliament dissolved.

Upon the receipt of this message, some of the members were willing that something should be done to satisfy the King. But it was too late for this. The House felt instinctively that they had no chance of obtaining the objects upon which they had set their hearts, and did nothing to check the more violent amongst the members. Christopher Nevill, a younger son of Lord Abergavenny, poured forth a torrent of strong language against the courtiers, and declared that they were 'spaniels to the King, and wolves to the people.' Hoskins boldly entered upon the more tender subject of the Scottish favourites, and even went so far as to put them in mind of the possibility of an imitation of the Sicilian Vespers.* James waited two or three days longer, and then on the 7th of June dissolved the Parliament, which had sat for little more than two months. Not a single Bill received the Royal Assent. The Parliament was, in consequence, nicknamed by the wits, 'The addled Parliament.'†

Up to the unfortunate episode of the speech of Bishop Neile, the proceedings of the House of Commons had been all that could be desired. They were undoubtedly right in refusing to grant supplies until the questions of the impositions and of the grievances had been settled in their favour. There might indeed arise upon the Continent, at any moment, dangers which would call upon them to support the Crown even at the cost of postponing to a future time the demand for justice which they put forward on behalf of themselves and of their children. But that time had not yet come. The visions of war which Bacon had called up before them were not as yet realities, and the Commons wisely decided to provide for the dangers which were at hand, rather than to supply James with means of defence against perils which were still in the future. Even the violence of their behaviour during the last few days of the session admits of some excuse. They knew that the refusal of

* Chamberlain to Carleton, June 9, 1614, *Court and Times*, i. 320.
† Lorkin to Puckering, June 18, 1614, *Court and Times*, i. 323.

CH. XII. 1614.

the House of Lords to hold a conference was the death knell of their hopes. There could not be the slightest doubt that in thus rejecting their demand they were acting in concert with the King; and the Commons, perceiving that all their labours had been in vain, would have been more than men if they had not felt indisposed to treat with deference those who were doing their best to bring ruin upon their common country.

Exasperation of the King.

These, however, were not the feelings of James. Not having ever grasped the idea that he had asked the Commons to surrender points upon which it was impossible for them to give way, he was proportionately exasperated at their steady refusal to give up their claims. His first act was to summon before the Council those members who had been appointed to take part in the conference with the Lords, and to order them to deliver up all the notes and collections which had been prepared to assist them in conducting their argument. All these papers were immediately burnt in the presence of the Council.* After this was done, four members who had distinguished themselves by the violence of their language, Wentworth, Hoskins, Christopher Nevill, and Sir Walter Chute, were sent to the Tower. All this while James was sitting in a neighbouring room, amusing himself by looking through an opening in the hangings, in order to see the effects of the childish folly which he was perpetrating.

Four members imprisoned.

Treatment of other members.

On the same day, Sandys and four other members were ordered not to leave London without permission. In a few weeks, however, they were allowed to return home, though Sandys was required to give bonds for his appearance whenever he might be called for.† Sir John Saville, Sir Roger Owen, Sir Edward Philips, and Nicholas Hyde, were put out of the commission of the peace.‡ Of the four members who were

* 'To have made the victory secure,' observes Mr. Bruce, 'His Majesty should have thrown into the conflagration the records from which the martyred arguments were derived' (Preface to Whitelocke's *Liber Famelicus*, p. ix.). Would it not have been necessary to burn the men as well?

† Privy Council Register, June 8, 9, 15, 29, and July 10.

‡ Whitelocke, *Liber Famelicus*, 43.

sent to the Tower, Wentworth was allowed, on the 19th of June, to go out for a few days to visit his wife, and was finally released on the 29th of June. Neville was set free on the 10th of July, and Chute on the 2nd of October.* Hoskins did not escape so easily. When he was questioned as to what he meant by threatening the Scots with a Sicilian vesper, it appeared that he had no clear notion of the meaning of the words which he had used, as he had not studied history very deeply. On being asked where he got his information, he said it was from Doctor Sharp, a clergyman, who had pressed him to animate the House against the Scots, and had assured him that, in so doing, he would have the protection of Sir Charles Cornwallis, the late Ambassador in Spain, and even of the Earl of Northampton himself.† Cornwallis declared that he had nothing to do with this speech of Hoskins, though he had procured the election of another member, by the help of a letter from Northampton, and had given him notes of a speech which he was to deliver, complaining of the recusants and the Scots. This speech, however, he said was never delivered. Sharp, on the other hand, declared that Cornwallis had promised to give Hoskins £20 for the loss of his practice during the session, a piece of evidence which was denied by Cornwallis. The Government chose to consider the whole matter as a conspiracy to frustrate its objects by hiring members to stir up the passions of the House.‡ Both Cornwallis and Sharp were committed to the Tower, from which they were only liberated, together with Hoskins, at the expiration of a twelvemonth.§

Release of the imprisoned members.

Examination of Cornwallis and Sharp.

In the step which James had thus taken, he had engaged himself still more deeply in the conflict which was now inevitable. In fact, the existing position of the Sovereign towards the House of Commons had already

Importance of the step taken by James.

* Privy Council Register of the above mentioned dates. Chamberlain writing to Carleton on the 30th of June (*Court and Times*, i. 325) was mistaken in supposing that Wentworth was still a prisoner.

† Wotton to Sir Edmund Bacon, June 16, 1614, *Rel. Wott.* ii. 434.

‡ Chamberlain to Carleton, June 30, 1614, *Court and Times*, i. 325. Cornwallis to the King, June ?, 1614, *S. P.* lxxvii. 43.

§ On the 8th of June, 1615. Privy Council Register of that date.

CH. XII. 1614.

become untenable. No political truth has been more completely demonstrated by experience than that which declares the impossibility of the coexistence, for any long time, of an hereditary sovereign and a representative legislature, wherever no right of control is recognized as existing either in the legislature itself, or in the nation which it represents. James might choose one of two courses; he might attempt to deprive the Parliament of its representative character, by refusing to allow it to express the wishes of the nation, or he might give it a control over the executive government. No middle way was possible. Supported by his Council, by his own ideas of his rights as a King, and by a few precedents from the reign of Elizabeth, he chose the former alternative. To this step of his there could be but one reply. Misgovernment had been met by the Commons with refusal of supplies. Imprisonment of their members, it might safely be predicted, would be answered, whenever they met again, by impeachment of the ministers of the Crown.

There was one man who must have looked on with sadness at what was going on. Sir Henry Nevill had taken no prominent part in the angry discussions which he had done his best to avert. He did not live to see the growing evils which came thickly upon the country in consequence of the rejection of his advice. He died in the summer of 1615, regretted by all those who knew how to value a man of his integrity and worth.

Death of Northampton.

If the unpalatable measure of summoning another Parliament was to be postponed for any length of time, it would be necessary to provide some means for filling the empty Exchequer. The first thing to be done was to appoint a Treasurer who might be responsible for the state of the revenue. Northampton had long been looking forward to promotion to this high office. The investigations conducted by the Commissioners who had been appointed after Salisbury's death, had relieved him from any fear that he would be held accountable for a deficit which would plainly not be of his making. In these investigations he had taken part, and had shown no little diligence in conducting the inquiry. But just as he hoped to receive from the King's hands the great office which he coveted, Digby arrived from Spain, and James learned that Northampton had been for many years in receipt of a pension from the Spanish Court. Whether James informed the Earl of the discovery which he had made we do not know. He was already stricken down by sickness. During the whole of the session he was lying ill at Greenwich. On the day after the dissolution, he was well enough to come up to London. His strength, however, was not sufficient to bear a surgical operation to which he submitted, and on the 15th of June he died, unregretted by men of all classes and of all parties.*

CH. XII. 1614.

Suffolk appointed Treasurer.

Amongst those whose character had passed without a stain through Digby's investigations was Suffolk. It was therefore only natural that the vacant appointment should be given to him. On the 10th of July, the King informed him that he had made choice of him for no other reason than for his approved fidelity and integrity. The office of Lord Chamberlain, vacated by Suffolk, was conferred upon Somerset. The King told him that he gave him the place which would bring him into such close relations with himself, because he loved him better than all men living.† The offices of the Lord Privy Seal and of the Warden of the Cinque Ports, which had belonged to Northampton, were to be kept vacant till some one could be found fitted to hold them. In the meanwhile, Somerset was to transact the business of both these places. Not very long afterwards, the Chancellorship of the Exchequer was given to Sir Philip Sydney's old friend, Sir Fulk Grevill, in place of Sir Julius Cæsar, who had been appointed Master of the Rolls.

Somerset Lord Chamberlain.

State of the revenue.

The new Lord Treasurer had no light task before him. The state of the finances had been slightly improved during the past year, but they still presented formidable

* Chamberlain to Carleton, June 30, 1614, *Court and Times*, i. 325.

† Chamberlain to Carleton, July 14, 1614, *S. P.* lxxvii. 64. Lorkin to Puckering, July 21, 1614, *Court and Times*, i. 335.

CH. XII. 1614.

obstacles to any Treasurer who was rash enough to entertain hopes of being able to balance the two sides of the account. From a statement* drawn up the day after Suffolk's accession to office, it appeared that the estimated annual expenditure of the Crown now amounted to £523,000, and that even by including the £40,000 which the Dutch were bound to pay every year until the whole debt was wiped off, the revenue could not be calculated at more than £462,000, leaving a deficit of £61,000. There were, as usual, extraordinary expenses to be taken into account, and a debt of about £700,000 was pressing on the King, who had no means of paying a farthing of it. James had certainly not chosen an opportune time for breaking with his Parliament.

A Benevolence offered by the Bishops and others.

At the time of the dissolution some of the Bishops made an offer to the King of the value of the best piece of plate in their possession, to help him out of his difficulties. The proposal was eagerly accepted, and in a few days all the great lords and officers of the Crown were following their example. Soon, every man who had anything to hope from the favour of the Court was bringing money to the Jewel House for the King's use.† The idea occurred to some one that it would be well to call upon all England to follow the example of the Bishops. The King, however, first wrote to the Lord Mayor to request a loan from the City of £100,000. The reply was that they would rather give £10,000 than lend £100,000.‡ If this offer was accepted, as there can be little doubt that it was, it may be considered as laying the foundation of the general Benevolence, as these voluntary gifts were called. A few of the gentlemen of the counties round London, and a few towns apparently in the immediate neighbourhood of the capital, followed the example of the courtiers. In this way the sum of £23,000 was collected before the 18th of July.

Appeal to the country.

But this was not all that was intended. The King was under the impression that the refusal of supplies by the House of Commons had proceeded merely from a

* Appendix VIII. No. 2.

† Chamberlain to Carleton, June 30, 1614, *Court and Times*, i. 325.

‡ Chamberlain to Carleton, July 7, 1614, *S. P.* lxxvii. 58.

factious opposition, and that a direct appeal to the country would be attended by the most favourable results. He was, indeed, stopped by Coke* from sending missives under the Great Seal, as had been originally intended; but the Council made no difficulty in writing letters to every county and borough in England, requesting them to send in their contributions. It was on the 4th of July that these letters were despatched. The Council began by acquainting the sheriffs and other magistrates to whom they were directed, that the late Parliament had not granted such supplies as might have been expected. Upon this many of the clergy, and the Lords of the Council, and others, had, of their own free will, presented to the King plate or money. Their example had been followed by the judges, by gentlemen of property in the adjacent counties, and by some cities and boroughs. The Council was, therefore, desirous that the gentlemen and other persons of the county or borough addressed should know what was being done, in order that they might show their love and affection to the King. Whatever was collected was to be sent to the Jewel House at Whitehall, together with a list of the names of the givers, in order that the King might take note of their good affection. The money thus paid was to be employed solely in the payment of debt, especially of that incurred on account of Ireland, the navy, and the Low Country garrisons.

Effect of this appeal.

It is possible that the Council meant to leave those whom they addressed free to give or to refuse; but, from the very nature of the case, it was impossible that those who were addressed should feel entirely at their ease. The concessions which had been offered by the King at the opening of the last session prove how completely he might have every gentleman in England at his mercy. Many of them were directly tenants of the Crown, and those who were not might easily be entangled in the meshes of a law which gave every facility to the Sovereign in prosecuting his extremest rights. In spite of this, however, the letters of the Council did not produce the

* Bacon's *Works* (ed. Montagu), vii. 404.

CH. XII. 1614.

effect which was anticipated. In every county the sheriffs were told that the King would have no difficulty in obtaining a supply, if it should please him to call a Parliament.* July, and then August, and then the first fortnight of September, passed slowly by, and not a single favourable answer had been vouchsafed to the letters of the Council.† Since the 18th of July a poor £500 was all the money which had been sent in to Whitehall.

Affairs in Cleves.

The Council determined to appeal once more to the country. By this time events had occurred in Germany which, as they hoped, would give weight to their demand for money in the eyes of all true Englishmen. The old quarrel of Cleves was threatening to break out once more with redoubled violence. In the previous November Wolfgang William, the young Palatine of Neuburg, had married a sister of the Duke of Bavaria. He had already secretly professed himself a convert to the Roman Catholic Church. A few weeks after his marriage he came down to Dusseldorf with the intention, it can hardly be doubted, of making himself master, sooner or later, of the whole of the disputed territory, with the help of the Archduke and the Catholic League.

Juliers in the hands of a Dutch garrison.

The Brandenburg party was not likely to remain long quiet under these apprehensions. Foreseeing that an attack would, some time or other, be made upon them, they determined to strike the first blow. An attempt to seize Dusseldorf failed, but they succeeded in getting into their hands the town of Juliers, which had, since the conclusion of the siege, been held by a garrison composed of troops in the service of both pretenders. As soon as he had gained his object, the Brandenburg commander invited Dutch troops into the place. This proceeding was approved of by the States, who gave out that they wished to preserve the peace between the irritated rivals.

The Palatine of Neuburg declares himself a Catholic.

The Palatine replied to this aggression by declaring his conversion to Catholicism, and by fortifying Dussel-

* Raleigh's 'Prerogative of Parliaments,' *Works*, viii. 218.

† The Council, in their letter of the 17th of September, say that they had had no answers. They would hardly consider the Devonshire reply, afterwards referred to, an answer at all.

CH. XII. 1614.

dorf, which had previously, like the other towns of the country, been held in common by the two Governments. He also appealed to the Court of Brussels to come to his help.

Spinola invades the Duchies.

The Archduke, having obtained the consent of the King of Spain, levied large forces, which he placed under Spinola. Some attempts were made to negotiate, but they were altogether unsuccessful. In August, Spinola set out with his army. On his way he restored the Catholic magistracy at Aix-la-Chapelle, which had been overthrown four years before by the Protestant majority of the citizens. In a short time he was master of all the towns in the Duchies on the left bank of the Rhine, with the exception of Juliers itself. He then passed the river, and, after a siege of four days, compelled Wesel to capitulate, on condition that he would evacuate the place whenever the States withdrew their garrison from Juliers. The Dutch, on their part, alarmed at the progress of Spinola, ordered their troops to enter the Duchies. Maurice accordingly took possession of Emmerich and Rees, and though he had orders not to break the truce by attacking the invading army, it was obvious that, unless some means were taken to arrange the questions in dispute, a collision between the two armies was imminent.*

Maurice at Emmerich and Rees.

Second letter of the Council to the sheriffs.

Under these circumstances, it was more than ever desirable that the English Treasury should be full enough to be ready for the worst. On the 17th the necessity of the King was again laid by the Council before the country. The sheriffs of the several counties were reminded of the letter which had been sent to them in July. They were told that the King's want of money was now more pressing than ever, in consequence of the dangers to which his allies were exposed. Spinola had gathered a large army, and there could be little doubt that he was in league with both the King of Spain and the Emperor. In the Duchies of Cleves and Juliers, he had seized upon all the towns which lay upon the

* Bentivoglio, *Relationi* (ed. 1650), 145. Wolf. *Geschichte Maximilians I.*, iii. 487.

CH. XII. 1614.

Rhine. By this aggression not only was the Elector of Brandenburg, his Majesty's ally, deprived of his possessions, but the Elector Palatine was placed in a position of considerable danger. Nor was it unlikely that an attack was intended upon England itself, or upon some other part of his Majesty's dominions. As a precautionary measure, orders had been given for a general muster. The navy was to be prepared for service, and all recusants were to be disarmed. The Council concluded their letter by expressing their surprise to the sheriffs that they had received no answer to their former letters, and by begging that they would lose no time in exerting themselves in a service which was so needful for the good of the country.

Smallness of the sum obtained.

It is, of course, impossible to say how far some of the counties were moved by such an appeal. But the smallness of the sum which was actually realized is sufficient to show that there was no general response to the request for money on the part of a King who had turned a deaf ear to the demands of the House of Commons. After every exertion had been made during nine months, the amount of money obtained barely exceeded £23,000. Then there was a pause. In November, 1615, the work of collection began again, and after eight months had been spent in pressing the people to contribute, a further sum nearly amounting to £15,000 was obtained. In the course of two more years a last payment of £9,000 was gradually raised. The whole sum thus obtained from the people of England was no more than £48,600. As £23,500 had already been paid by the City of London and by the Bishops and the courtiers previously to the general appeal, the total result of the Benevolence may be calculated at not much more than £71,000, or about two-thirds of the value of a single subsidy with its accompanying fifteenth.

Means used to obtain it.

No doubt care was taken not to utter a single word which might deprive these payments of their character of voluntary contributions. But the Council certainly allowed itself to give very strong hints that it would not be well with those who refused to pay. It was significant that the judges of assize were entrusted with the task of recommending payment. Those whom they addressed must have known well how probable it was that they might some day or other be dependent for at least some portion of their property upon these novel collectors of contributions. Several instances have been reported to us in which we can easily trace the spirit in which these free gifts were asked for. When Whitelocke, who had property in Buckinghamshire, came before the judges, they refused to receive his name, in hopes of being able to make a better profit of him if they could deal with him in London. As he had no wish to be cajoled in this manner, he put down his name on the roll for £2, whilst their attention was called away in another direction. Two of his acquaintances, however, were not so fortunate. Lord Knollys took the liberty of putting down their names, without their consent, for £5 apiece.* At the same time the Council kept a vigilant eye upon what was being done in various parts of the country. Having heard that Lord St. John, the Lord-Lieutenant of Bedfordshire, had been cool in the cause, they immediately wrote to him, telling him that his behaviour had been taken note of, and advising him to take care what he was doing. In some shires the resistance was more general. Even before the second letters had been written, the great western county of Devonshire had offered a remonstrance, and had declared that, however ready they were to assist the King in his difficulties, they were unwilling to injure their posterity by establishing such a precedent. A few weeks later Somersetshire appealed to the Act† of Richard III. against Benevolences. Similar protests were made by Nottinghamshire and Warwickshire.‡

Resistance in some counties.

The Council, upon this, summoned before them three or four of the Justices of the Peace, from each of the recalcitrant counties. Care was taken that no two counties should be heard on the same day, probably in order to prevent them from settling upon any common plan of action. As soon as these poor gentlemen were admitted, they were overwhelmed with a flood of records

Deputations summoned to London.

* Whitelocke, *Liber Famelicus*.

† 1 Ric. III. cap. 2.

‡ Privy Council Register, Nov. 2, 14, 16, 30; and Appendix VI. to this volume.

CH. XII. 1614. Overwhelmed with precedents.

and precedents which they were utterly unable to resist. Coke himself took part against them. The statute of Richard III., he said, was intended to prevent exactions passing under the name of free gifts; it was never meant to stand in the way of really voluntary contributions like the present. He had no difficulty in showing that Benevolences had been paid during the reigns of the first two Tudors, in spite of the statute of Richard III.* The bewildered men had nothing left but to acknowledge their error. The Council took care to follow their returning steps with a fresh letter urging the counties to go on with the good work.

Leicestershire contribution refused, as insufficient.

It was not long before it was discovered that even those counties which had not ventured upon open remonstrance were not always likely to give satisfaction to the Government. Leicestershire had notified that, after several meetings, a resolution had been come to to present the King with £1,000. But it was one thing to pass resolutions, and another thing to collect the money. After some time the Lord Treasurer was informed that no more than £400 could be obtained, as many who had promised had refused to pay. Upon this the

Feb. 5, 1615.

Council wrote to the sheriff and the justices of the peace, rating them for their backwardness, and telling them that so mean a sum could not be accepted. They accordingly admonished them to take the business in hand once more. When they had done their best they were to forward a perfect list, not only of the names of those who paid, but of the exact value of the sums subscribed. Another list was to be furnished containing the names of those who were able to pay, but had held back from contributing. A similar letter was written to the borough of Taunton, which had also sent a sum which was held to be inadequate.

In July, when the stream was flagging, another

* There is a report in the Lansd. MS. 160, fol. 118, of an argument of Coke's on the Benevolences, said to have been delivered on the 8th of November. In it he states that 'this Table hath done nothing contrary to the laws of this realm.' The story of Coke's opposition to the Benevolence must be founded on his dislike of the use of the Great Seal as savouring of compulsion. There is no evidence of anything more. The opinion in *Rep.* xii. 119 must have been delivered on some other occasion.

appeal was made to ten of the twelve Welsh shires. They had sent nothing, pleading their poverty. They were told that this was no excuse, as it was never intended that any but men of property should contribute, and there was a sufficient number of them to do something for the King. At the same time letters were written to those amongst the English counties which were most backward. Stafford, Durham, and Westmoreland had not furnished a single contributor. In Shropshire there had been found one, in Herefordshire two, in Sussex three. The clergy of the diocese of Durham were also visited with a letter. The result of these letters was that from three of the Welsh shires £394 was obtained, Cumberland sent £67, Westmoreland £85, Shropshire £95, the Durham clergy £126, whilst Sussex provided as much as £772. Staffordshire and Herefordshire remained impenitent to the last.*

The Welsh shires written to, and the most backward English counties.

At a time when the feeling in the country is running strongly on any subject, it generally happens that some one or other starts forward with an ill-considered and exaggerated expression of that feeling. On this occasion the person by whom this part was performed was Oliver St. John, a gentleman of Marlborough. As soon as the second appeal of the Council reached that town,

St. John's letter.

* *S. P. Dom.* lxxvii. 12. The sums mentioned are those paid after Oct. 10, 1615, but as the letters were written on the 21st of July, and as we know from the Receipt Books of the Exchequer that, with the exception of £100 paid in on the 26th of July, no money was received by the Exchequer till the 18th of November, we may be pretty sure that the sums given above are the whole of the payments made in consequence of the letters. The only certain instance I have found of direct ill-treatment in consequence of slackness in paying the Benevolence was in Lincoln diocese. On the 30th of June, 1615, Bishop Neile wrote to his clergy, telling them that in consequence of their having been backward in this respect, as well as for other reasons, they were no longer to be exempted from providing arms for the musters. —Neile to Lambe, June 30, 1615, *S. P. Dom.* lxxx. 123.

Probably, however, Whitelocke's statement of the reasons for which George Croke was omitted from the list of lawyers who were to be made Serjeants-at-law, refers to the Benevolence. 'It is not to be forgotten,' he says, 'that the Serjeants-at-law gave each of them £600 to the King . . . Mr. George Croke was left out because he refused to give the money, and offence was taken at his words, because he said he thought it was not for the King,' (p. 44). Mr. Foss (*Lives of the Judges*, vi. 3, 294) interprets these words as referring to a refusal to pay an ordinary gratuity expected from all persons elevated to the degree. The date, however, September or October, 1614, favours the other interpretation.

CH. XII. 1614. Oct. 11. the mayor applied to St. John, amongst the other residents, to know what he was willing to give. St. John not only refused to subscribe, but wrote a letter which he requested the mayor to lay before the justices of the county. In this letter, he declared that all such contributions were contrary to Magna Charta and other statutes, as well as to the well known Act of Richard III. It was also unreasonable that those should be called upon to supply the King who were unacquainted both with the extent of his necessities, and with the sums which might possibly be required to satisfy them. He concluded by charging the King with breaking his coronation oath, and added a declaration of his belief that all who paid the Benevolence were supporting their Sovereign in perjury.

He is brought before the Star-Chamber. After such a letter as this it can hardly be a matter of surprise that he was sent for to London by the Council, in order that he might be brought before the Star-Chamber, to answer for the contemptuous language in which he had spoken of the King. He was immediately committed to the Fleet, from which, after he had been examined, he was transferred to the Tower, but in consequence of the illness of the Lord Chancellor, it was not till the 29th of April that proceedings were commenced against him. As Attorney-General, Bacon took a prominent part in the prosecution.

Bacon's charge. To Bacon the feelings with which the great majority of patriotic Englishmen were animated in hanging back from contributing were utterly unintelligible. With the Parliamentary opposition to the Impositions he had no sympathy whatever, and if he agreed, to some extent, with those who asked for ecclesiastical reform, he looked upon the determination of the House of Commons to force their views upon the King as an unwarrantable interference with the Royal prerogative. The tendency of thought which isolated him from so many of his countrymen on these questions, made him blind to the objections which were commonly felt to the Benevolence. He regarded the dissolution of Parliament as an accidental circumstance arising from the bitterness of feeling produced by the Bishop of Lincoln's speech. Overlooking the growing divergence between the policy of the King and that of the House of Commons, he fancied that the House would in the end have granted the supplies required, even if a deaf ear had been turned to their complaints. He accordingly maintained that those who paid the Benevolence were only carrying out the intentions of the House of Commons. He had no difficulty in showing that no actual threats had been used by the Council to induce anyone to pay;* and he argued that the Benevolence was in reality, as well as in name, a free gift, and that it had nothing in common with those exactions which, in former times, had passed under that name. In this view of the case he was supported by Coke and by the other members of the Court. Coke, it is said, even went so far as to retract his former opinion against the legality of a Benevolence demanded by letters under the Great Seal.† St. John was sentenced to a fine of £5,000, and to imprisonment during the King's pleasure.‡ The fine was, as usual, remitted, but it was some time before he was set at liberty. After his release, he addressed a letter to the King, couched in terms of fulsome flattery, asking that the record of his punishment might be cancelled.§ From that time he drops out of sight.

St. John's sentence.

It happened with St. John as it had happened with Fuller seven years before. It is not the men who spring forth first to defend the cause of liberty who become its martyrs. It is those who suffer in silence till the time comes when they are no longer justified in forbearing to speak out, who endure the trial. Yet, setting aside the intemperate language which St. John allowed himself to

He is right in the main point.

* He even went so far as to say that there was 'no certifying of the names of any that denied.' This was true at the time when St. John wrote his letter, but it had since become untrue.

† *State Trials*, ii. 899. Charge against St. John, Bacon's *Works* (ed. Montagu), vi. 138. Bacon to the King, Feb. 7, April 29, 1615, xii. 133, 136.

‡ Bacon, *Works* (ed. Montagu), vii. 404.

§ Dixon's *Personal History of Lord Bacon*, 188. The letter is shown by internal evidence to have been written after Bacon became Lord Keeper, and also after St. John's release from the Tower; not, as Mr. Dixon seems to have thought, immediately upon his incarceration. On the 21st of October, 1618, a release from the fine inflicted was given to St. John (Pat. 16 Jac. I. Part 20), and it is very probable that this was an answer to the petition.

use, there cannot be a doubt that he was right on the main point. To a great extent, at least, the Benevolence was not a free gift. The small amount actually raised, and the slowness with which it came in, would be enough to prove this, even if we did not know that the Council, vexed at the neglect with which their entreaties were received, allowed themselves at last to give very strong hints of the mode in which they looked upon those who refused to pay. Can those who speak of the whole collection being voluntary, honestly say that they believe that more than a mere fraction of the amount obtained from the general subscription would have been realized if the subscribers had received the assurance that their names would never have become known to the Government?*

Raleigh writes 'The Prerogative of Parliaments.'

The question of the Benevolences called out an argument upon the King's financial position from a man of very different calibre from the malcontent St. John. Raleigh had been so long a prisoner that he had lost all reckoning of the currents of the political world. He imagined that James was personally innocent of the rank crop of abuses which was springing up on every side. He was ready to lay the blame upon the evil councillors who prevented the truth from reaching the ears of the King. In a Dialogue which he wrote at this time, and with which he hoped to regain† the favour of James, he called upon him to take up once more the policy of Elizabeth, to cast away all those unpopular schemes for raising money to which he had been addicted, and to throw himself unreservedly upon the love of his subjects. Such a book was hardly likely to find favour with James. Whatever the faults or merits of his government may have been, they were to be ascribed to him far more than to his Ministers. It was his own ignorance and wrongheadedness which had brought him into the collision with

* By 13 Car. II., cap. 4, the King was authorized to issue a Commission for accepting voluntary presents of a limited amount. The last clause of the Act is: 'And be it hereby declared that no commissions or aids of this nature can be issued out or levied but by authority of Parliament; and that this Act, and the supply hereby granted, shall not be drawn into example for the time to come.'

† 'The Prerogative of Parliaments,' *Works*, viii.

the House of Commons in 1610, from which Salisbury would have saved him. He was, not unnaturally, incensed by an argument which, in reprobating his councillors, proceeded to condemn the whole scheme of policy upon which he had, of his own free will, embarked. Raleigh, who had hoped to gain his freedom as a reward for the good advice which he had offered, was disappointed to find that the only notice taken of him was an order for the suppression of his work. CH. XII. 1615.

1614. Peacham's deprivation.

At the same time with the case of St. John, another affair was engaging the attention of the King and the Council, which owed all its importance to the excited state of feeling which prevailed in consequence of the levy of the Benevolence. Edmond Peacham, the Rector of Hinton St. George, in Somersetshire, was one of those who felt strongly on the subject of the ecclesiastical abuses of the time. Whether his temper had been soured by real or fancied ill-usage, it is impossible to say; but what we know of him is not of a character to prepossess us in his favour. His language was intemperate, and his conduct would lead us to imagine that his complaints against the authorities proceeded rather from personal rancour than from any settled principle.

The chief object of his dislike seems to have been the Ecclesiastical Court of his diocesan, the Bishop of Bath and Wells. He is first heard of as being in London, shortly before the dissolution of the last Parliament, as holding a conversation with Sir Maurice Berkeley about a petition which had been sent up from Somersetshire against the officials of the Ecclesiastical Courts.* At some time or other he committed to writing some charges against the Consistory Court,† which he followed up by bringing accusations of no light nature against the Bishop himself. The former production was not discovered by the authorities, but the latter having come before the notice of the Bishop, its author was at once sent up to Lambeth for trial before the High Com-

* Examination of Peacham, March 10, 1615, *State Trials*, ii. 877.

† The book mentioned in Yonge's *Diary*, p. 28, is, I suppose, the same as the 'Consistory Villanies,' spoken of by Bacon, *State Trials*, ii. 875.

CH. XII. 1614.

mission. After due investigation these charges were adjudged to constitute a libel, and he was sentenced to be deprived of his orders.*

He is committed to the Tower.

This sentence was delivered on the 19th of December. Ten days before, by order of the Privy Council, he had been transferred from the Gatehouse, in which he had hitherto been confined, to the Tower.† In searching his house, apparently for the missing papers which he had written against the Consistory Court, the officials came across some writings which they brought away with them. They consisted partly of loose papers, and partly of a composition in the form of a sermon, which had been carefully drawn up from materials which had first been jotted down on separate sheets. They were thought to be of sufficient importance to lay before the Council. They were there investigated, and it was decided that they contained treasonable matter.

Nature of the offensive composition.

As far as we can judge from the interrogatories which were administered to Peacham, the treatise was of a peculiarly offensive nature. It found fault with the Government in no measured terms. It touched upon all the stock objects of popular dislike, the misconduct of the officials, the prodigality of the King, and his refusal to subject the ecclesiastical to the temporal Courts.‡ The King might some day be smitten with a death as sudden as that which overtook Ananias or Nabal. It was possible that the people might rise in rebellion, on account of the oppression which they experienced, and of the heavy taxation which was imposed upon them. It was also possible that, when the Prince came to the throne, he would attempt to regain the Crown lands which had been given away, upon which those who were interested in retaining them would rise in rebellion, saying, 'Come, this is the heir; let us kill

* Sentence of deprivation, Dec. 19, 1614, *S. P.* lxxviii. 78. I do not understand that Mr. Dixon found a copy of the libel among the Wells MSS. He is probably right in describing the paper as having really borne a libellous character, but no inference is to be drawn from the fact that some of the judges 'lean to Puritan views,' and others 'incline towards Rome.' In a question of attack upon Church Courts, Abbot was likely to have been quite as forward as Neile, and probably more so than Andrewes.

† *Council Register*, Dec. 9, 1614.

‡ I suppose this is what is meant by 'his keeping divided Courts.'

him.' Peacham concluded his performance by saying that, when James had come to the throne, he had promised mercy and judgment, but that his subjects had found neither.

Peacham examined.

Peacham was sent for and examined. He acknowledged that he had intentionally aimed at the King, and justified his conduct by saying that it was proper that by the 'examples of preachers and chronicles, Kings' infirmities should be laid open.' He refused, however, to give any farther information.

Causes of the persistence of the Council in investigating the affair.

It cannot be a matter of surprise that James should have felt indignant at the discovery. Yet it is probable that, under ordinary circumstances, even a man of James's sensitiveness would have allowed the affair to drop into the oblivion which it deserved. Even if the fact of Peacham's notes having been copied out fairly could be accepted as a proof that they were intended either to be preached from the pulpit, or to be made public through the press, it was impossible that the stability of the throne should be in any way affected by the publication of such incoherent rubbish. But there were circumstances in the case which no doubt weighed with the Council in taking up the affair as a serious matter. They were aware that the levy of the Benevolence had caused great dissatisfaction in many parts of the kingdom, and that Somersetshire was one of the counties which had taken the lead in remonstrating against it. They were, therefore, anxious to discover whether Peacham stood alone, or whether he had acted at the instigation of any of the leading gentry of the county. So lately as on the 20th of November three Somersetshire gentlemen had been summoned before them to give account of the feeling prevailing in the county, and to hear the arguments of the Council in favour of the measure which had been adopted for raising money.* Of these three, they may perhaps

* *Council Register*, Nov. 2, 1614. This is an order for Sir M. Berkeley, Sir N. Halswell, and J. Paulet, Esq., to appear before the Council on the 20th. Though everyone who has occasion to go over this ground must thank Mr. Hepworth Dixon for drawing attention to many circumstances connected with Peacham's case, I am obliged, in justice to myself, to say that it is perfectly unintelligible to me how he succeeded in drawing out of

CH. XII. 1614. have known that Sir Maurice Berkeley had been in communication with Peacham at the time of the last Parliament, and they were certainly aware that John Paulet was the neighbour of Peacham in the county, and had presented him with the living which he held. Although, therefore, there is no direct evidence on the point, there can be little doubt that the Council imagined that Peacham's book was not a mere isolated piece of folly, but that it had been prepared as a signal of discontent, and perhaps of rebellion, in connection with the principal landowners of the county. As he resolutely refused to make any confession which would implicate others in the
1615. composition of his paper, directions were given that, if he still continued obstinate, he should be put to the torture. Winwood, as Secretary of State, accompanied by Cæsar, Bacon, Yelverton, Montagu, and Crew, together with Helwys, the lieutenant of the Tower, were ordered by the Council to renew the examination, and, if they should see fit, to 'put him to the manacles.'* The old man was accordingly tortured, in the vain expectation that he would reveal a plot which existed only in the imagination of the Councillors. He suffered in silence—either being unable to confess anything which might satisfy his persecutors, or being unwilling, as yet, to invent a story which might tell against himself in the end.†

Peacham put to the torture.

There was no reason to suppose that any of those

the *Council Register* a great part of the story which he tells. That register is not generally accessible to the public, and if I had omitted to notice the error, it would be impossible for more than a very few to be able to verify either of our conflicting narratives. Mr. Dixon quotes from the register the entries on Nov. 2, Dec. 9, 1614, Feb. 25, 26, 1615, to prove his story of the reasons why Peacham was tortured. The last two references of course prove nothing with respect to what passed previously to Jan. 18, the date of the order for the torture. The entry on Dec. 9 is a simple warrant for his committal to the Tower. Of course, the letter to the three Somersetshire gentlemen, written on the 2nd of Nov., can have no reference to charges made by Peacham subsequently to Dec. 9. The fact is, that of any charge made against Sydenham, before the torturing, there is no evidence whatever. Nor is there evidence of Berkeley's ever having been brought to town at all on Peacham's account. But there is, as will be seen, evidence that neither Peacham nor anybody else ever accused Paulet of any crime, and that consequently Peacham is entirely guiltless of any attempt to get his patron hanged.

* The letter is printed in Dixon's *Personal History*, 195, and in Jardine's *Reading on the Use of Torture*, 106.

† *State Trials*, ii. 871.

State of opinion on the subject of torture.

who were intrusted with this odious work imagined, for a moment, that they were doing anything wrong. Though the common law expressly rejected the use of torture, it was generally understood that the Council had the right of obtaining information by its means, whenever they might come to the conclusion that the evidence of which they were in search was sufficiently important to render it necessary to appeal to such a mode of extracting a secret from an obstinate person. The distinction then so familiar between the law which ruled in ordinary cases, and the prerogative by which it was overruled in matters of political importance, has happily passed away even from the memory of men. It is, therefore, not without difficulty that we are able to realize to ourselves a state of feeling which would regard proceedings of this kind as contrary to the law, and yet as being perfectly justifiable. And yet it is indubitable that such a feeling existed, and there can be little doubt that it was shared by all those who witnessed the horrible scene. If, however, we are reduced to conjecture what were the feelings of most of those who took part in inflicting the torture upon an unfortunate old man, there is no difficulty in discovering what Bacon thought about the matter. He disliked the use of torture, as he disliked everything that gave pain, but he believed it to be necessary in certain cases. There is no reason to suppose that on this point he felt in any way different from those who were associated with him.*

* His words in the letter of Jan. 21, are, 'Although we are driven to make our way through questions, which I wish were otherwise &c.,' do not seem to imply more than I have said above. Bacon's language in 1620 is explicit against the theory that he objected to the use of torture, but consented to share in it as an official duty: 'If it may not be done otherwise, it is fit Peacock be put to torture. He deserveth it as well as Peacham did.'—Bacon to the King, Feb. 10,1620, *Works* (ed. Montagu), vii. 369. In another place, he writes: 'By the law of England no man is bound to accuse himself. In the highest cases of treason torture is used for discovery, and not for evidence.'—'Of the Pacification of the Church,' *Works* (ed. Montagu), vii. 78. He means, I suppose, that torture was used for discovering facts against others, but that the evidence extracted is not used against the tortured man. This seems to have been the case here. It was evidence of a conspiracy which was wanted, not evidence to hang Peacham. If the book were treasonable, there was no more evidence wanted against the writer.

CH. XII. 1615.

Of all the transactions of Bacon's busy life, there is none of which it would be more desirable to have a full and accurate narrative than of the collision between him and Coke which followed. There cannot be the slightest doubt that he was thoroughly in the wrong, and that Coke was thoroughly in the right, through the whole course of the proceedings; and it is therefore of particular importance to know what were the exact circumstances under which his mistakes were made. Unfortunately, we have to pick our way amongst hints and allusions thrown out for the most part in the course of Bacon's own letters.

Bacon's first letter.

The first glimpse we have of what was going on is derived from one of Bacon's* letters to the King, written two days after the infliction of the torture. He writes as if he had fears lest he should be frustrated in obtaining the object which he had in view by the interference of some one from whom assistance was to be expected. 'Every man,' he says, 'must put too his helping hand, or else he must say as St. Paul said to the centurion, "Except these stay in the ship, ye cannot be saved." For my part,' he adds, 'I hold my opinion, and am strengthened in it by some records that I have found.' Interpreting these words in the light of what followed, they afford a clear insight into the cause of Bacon's confusion. The torture having proved to be a total failure, no conspiracy, or any shadow of a conspiracy having been detected, the Council, either spontaneously, or at the instigation of the King, had made up their mind to proceed directly against the prisoner. Whether the treatise had anything to do with the discontent which prevailed in Somersetshire or no, it at all events contained abuse against the King; and, as abuse of the King was likely to stir up dislike of his Government, which, in turn, might possibly end in rebellion, it might, without any very forced reasoning, be considered as a treasonable production. There is no reason to suppose that either Bacon or those who joined with him in condemning the book were saying more than they believed. A government is at all times liable to interpret the law of treason with

* Bacon to the King, Jan. 21, 1615 (*Works*, ed. Montagu, xii. 123).

considerable laxity; and it is notorious that its limits were at that time by no means strictly defined even by the judges themselves. It would therefore be with considerable vexation that Bacon heard that Coke had allowed it to be known that he had doubts as to the legality of the course upon which the Council had determined. Such feelings would find vent in the letter which he wrote to the King.

Explanation of his interference with the judges.

This supposition (for it does not pretend to be more) has the advantage of explaining what, in the accounts usually given of this affair, is perfectly inexplicable. In those accounts it is taken for granted that James, being doubtful of his case against Peacham, employed Bacon to tamper with the judges, in order that he might be sure of obtaining their assent to a legal doctrine which had not been argued before them. It has been forgotten that Bacon was only employed to influence the judges of the King's Bench, and that, as a matter of fact, when Peacham was at last brought to trial, not one of the judges of that Court had anything to do with the matter. Surely, if Bacon had wished to obtain an extra-judicial opinion in order to prejudicate the case, he would have been better employed in discovering who were the two judges who had been selected to ride the Western Circuit at the next assizes, and in expending all his energies on them.

Coke's opinion.

If, however, Coke had publicly given out that, in his opinion, there were no grounds for proceeding against Peacham on a charge of treason, Bacon's conduct becomes at least intelligible. He looks at his records, and finds in them, as he imagines, confirmation of his opinion that Peacham's book is a treasonable production. He is afraid to trust the two judges who are to go down to Somersetshire with a decision on a matter of such importance, if they are to be left under the impression that, in laying down the law against the prisoner, they will be acting against the settled judgment of the greatest lawyer of the day. At the same time, he has no great faith in Coke's opinion as being the genuine expression of his feelings. He had not been accustomed to be so squeamish in interpreting the law in his previous dealings

CH. XII. 1615.

with real or supposed traitors, and the most natural inference was that, consciously or unconsciously, he had been influenced rather by his dislike of the Attorney-General than by any calm conviction of the merits of the case.

Attempts to induce him to change it.

If these were the thoughts which passed through Bacon's mind, it is not difficult to understand how it happened that he eagerly accepted the proposal of the King, that Coke should be induced, in one way or another, to retract his opinion, shutting his eyes to the truth, that it was more important that even a real traitor should escape, than that a judge should give an opinion under the pressure of Government influences.

Consulting the judges separately.

If, however, an attempt was to be made to obtain from Coke an opinion contrary to that which he had already expressed, it would be necessary to have recourse to some unusual measures. That the Crown had a perfect right to consult the judges on points of law, even when they bore upon a capital case still undecided, was never doubted by any lawyer of that age, and least of all by Coke.* The plan, however, which was adopted by Bacon had at least the merit of originality. It was decided that each of the Judges of the King's Bench should be asked their opinion privately. In Bacon's eyes this was merely a course of arriving at the true opinion of the three puisne judges, by taking care that

* Coke's objection was not to the consultation of the judges by the King, but to their being consulted separately. On the 27th of January, Bacon writes, 'For the course your Majesty directeth and commandeth for the feeling of the judges of the King's Bench their several opinions, by distributing ourselves and enjoining secrecy, we did first find an encounter in the opinion of my Lord Coke, who seemed to affirm that such particular and (as he called it) auricular taking of opinions was not according to the custom of this realm.'—*Works* (ed. Montagu), xii. 124. Even here it is plain from the context that the stress is laid upon being consulted in private. In his letter of Feb. 11, Bacon puts it in a still clearer light. 'Coke,' he says, 'fell upon the same allegation which he had begun at the council table, that judges were not to give opinion by fractions, but entirely according to the vote whereupon they should settle upon conference; and that this auricular taking of opinions, single and apart, was new and dangerous.' At a later time, no doubt, Coke expressed himself against the propriety of the law-officers consulting the judges at all (3 *Inst.* 29), and quoted a conclusive precedent in his favour from the *Year-Books*; but this point was never moved on the present occasion. Luders, in his *Consideration of the Law of High Treason*, iii. 113, acknowledges that it was the practice to consult the judges together.

they were out of the reach of Coke's influence, and of intimidating Coke himself into pronouncing in favour of a view which he would certainly have arrived at of himself, if it had not been for his intolerable factiousness. It is unnecessary to say that, even if Bacon had been right in his mode of regarding the legal question at issue, he was opening the door to innumerable abuses. It is to no purpose that he tried to defend himself under the sophism that it was the judges' place to give counsel to the Crown whenever it might be asked. The Crown had no right to use its prerogative so as to induce any man to declare his opinion otherwise than freely and independently.

Coke's resistance.

Coke himself did not think it worth while to argue upon the disadvantages of the practice which his rival was introducing. He contented himself with saying, 'that such particular and auricular taking of opinions' was 'not according to the custom of this realm.' There can be little doubt that Coke was right. In Legatt's case, in 1611, indeed, Coke's name had been designedly omitted from those of the Judges who were to be consulted. But even then the three judges of the King's Bench had been consulted together. Shortly before Raleigh's trial, too, a case had occurred which, at first sight, supports Bacon in his proceedings. Chief-Justice Popham had been indeed consulted by the Government as to the mode in which they should proceed against the prisoner. But, in the first place, Popham was simply asked whether it would not be wise to drop certain charges which they had intended to bring; and, in the second place, there is no resemblance whatever between a question put to a judge, which he is at liberty to answer or not, and one which is designedly put in such a manner as to induce him to give a different reply from that which he would, under other circumstances, have given. Whether Bacon intended it or not, it is impossible to argue that he was doing otherwise than striking a severe blow at the moral independence of the judges.

Information was accordingly laid before the four judges separately on the point on which their opinion

CH. XII. 1615. The judges consulted separately.

was requested, and such records were put in their hands as would be likely to influence their decision. In the case of the three puisne judges who were consulted by the Solicitor-General Yelverton, and the two Serjeants, Montagu and Crew, there was no difficulty in obtaining a favourable opinion. Bacon, who had taken the Chief Justice upon himself, found that he had a harder task. Coke met him at once by protesting against the course which had been adopted. It was altogether a novelty. It was not according to the custom of the realm. Every feeling of the man and of the judge was roused against a proceeding which, whatever semblance it might wear in the eyes of Bacon, was, undoubtedly, a direct aggression upon the independence of the Bench. To Bacon, this resistance would seem to proceed merely from the angry passions of a man who had been disappointed in working mischief. No doubt, there was much that was personal in Coke's resistance; but, after all that can be said on that score, it must never be forgotten that Coke was decidedly in the right, and Bacon was as decidedly in the wrong.

Coke's opinion.

It was not without difficulty that Coke was induced even to take the papers which were offered to him. At last he consented to look over them, and told his rival that he would give him an answer in due time.* After some delay the answer arrived. As might be expected, it was by no means satisfactory to Bacon.† There were two grounds upon which the treasonable nature of Peacham's production might be questioned. The first was that the writing had never been published. The second was that, even if it had been published, it did not amount to treason. It does not appear whether Coke touched upon the former point at all; but he asserted boldly that no mere declaration of the King's unworthiness to govern amounted to treason,‡ and in this opinion he would have obtained the support of every lawyer who has lived since the Revolution.

* Bacon to the King, Jan. 27, Feb. 11, 1615, *Works* (ed. Montagu), xii. 124.

† Bacon to the King, Feb. 14, 1615, *State Trials*, ii. 875.

‡ 'Innovations of Sir E. Coke,' Bacon's *Works* (ed. Montagu), vii. 404.

In considering the course taken by Bacon it must be remembered that the theory of the law of treason which at that time prevailed was one which made it very easy for a man to go astray if his feelings were, from any cause, enlisted on the side of the prerogative. According to that theory, there was no question whatever whether Peacham's treatise were criminal or not. The only question was, whether it was sufficient evidence of a design to compass or imagine the King's death. It was not difficult for one who was half convinced already to fancy that the declaration of the King's unfitness to govern implied a belief that he ought to be deprived of the power of governing, and that the expression of such a belief in any way implied an intention to assist in bringing about such a catastrophe; and all lawyers were agreed that, to imagine the King's deposition, was equivalent to imagining his death.

Causes of Bacon's dissent.

In some sophistry of this sort, it would seem that Bacon allowed himself to be entangled. It never occurred to him to ask whether it was well that a man should be brought within danger of the gallows for writing a few disrespectful sentences concerning the King and his Government. Whether, if Bacon had never been brought within the atmosphere of the Court, he would have come to the same conclusion as that at which he now arrived, is a question which it is easy to ask, but which it is certainly impossible to answer. No man, indeed, could, at such a time, have occupied the position of Attorney-General with impunity. Imperceptibly he would contract ideas congenial to the office which he held. But there was nothing in Bacon's intellect which was likely to give him insight into the true nature of the fallacies by which he was led astray.

Although Bacon had secured three out of the four judges, he was uneasy lest Coke's opinion should get abroad. He did not scruple to advise that a false rumour should be deliberately spread, to the effect that the only difference of opinion had been on the question whether the publication of a treasonable writing was necessary to bring the writer under the penalties of treason; 'for that,' he said, 'will be no man's case.' These last words

His treatment of Coke's opinion.

CH. XII. 1615.

reveal his real thoughts about the matter. He was afraid lest, if Peacham's writings were not held to be treasonable, the country would be flooded with seditious writings; whilst little harm would be done by declaring that publication was necessary to constitute the offence, as it would seldom happen that such papers would be seized before they had been shown to anyone by the writer. It is evident that Bacon was not merely interested in securing the King's favour by taking vengeance upon the unlucky prisoner, but that it was the bearing of the case upon those who might hereafter be tempted to assail the authority of the Crown, of which he was chiefly thinking.*

Peacham accuses Sir John Sydenham.

On the 14th of February Bacon forwarded Coke's reply to the King. Ten days afterwards directions were given by the Council that Peacham should be sent down into Somersetshire for trial.† Either on that very evening or on the following morning, he told a tale which induced the Government to cancel the order for his removal, and to retain him for farther examination. As a last resource, in hopes of escaping from being sent down, as he supposed, to almost certain death, he charged Sir John Sydenham, the brother-in-law of his patron, Mr. Paulet, of Hinton St. George, with having suggested to him the objectionable words which had brought him into trouble.‡ Sydenham was immediately sent for,§ and on the next day Paulet was also directed to come up to London, bringing with him five of his servants, who were indicated by name.‖ As Peacham had brought no charge whatever against Paulet, it must be supposed that, as the words attributed to Sydenham were said to have been spoken while he was on a visit at Hinton St. George, it

* Bacon to the King, Feb. 28, 1615, *State Trials*, ii. 875.

† *Council Register*. Cancelled order, Feb. 24, 1615.

‡ Examination of Peacham, Aug. 31, 1615, *S. P. Dom.* lxxxi. The more important parts of this paper are printed in Dixon's *Personal History*, 200.

§ *Council Register*, Feb. 25, 1615.

‖ Council to Paulet. *Council Register*, Feb. 26, 1615. That there was no charge against Paulet appears from the following passage in the order allowing him to return:—March 26. 'Their Lordships have thought fit to dismiss the said Mr. Paulet, against whom there was no accusation at all, as also his servants afore-mentioned.'

was thought advisable to have the testimony of those who were in the house at the time.

Peacham examined by the Bishop of Bath and Wells.

In the meanwhile the Bishop of Bath and Wells was employed to examine the prisoner once more. Peacham stuck to his story about Sydenham, but declared that he had no new names to give up. When asked whether Paulet had ever said anything objectionable to him, he replied that he must take time to answer that question. Bacon, who was by no means satisfied that Peacham's book had not been part of an organized conspiracy amongst the Somersetshire gentry, recommended that Peacham should be told that he was to be sent down at once to take his trial, in order that he might be frightened into making farther disclosures relating to the secrets with which he was supposed to be familiar.*

What explanation Sydenham gave, we do not know. It is not improbable that he may have spoken, at some time or other, of the Government in no complimentary terms, which may have led Peacham to catch at the chance of saving his own life by bringing an accusation against an innocent man. But as he succeeded without difficulty in satisfying the Council that there was no truth whatever in the statement that he had anything to do with the compilation of Peacham's papers, we may be sure that the charge brought against him was a false one. After a detention of more than four weeks he was dismissed without a stain on his character. Two days later Paulet and his servants were also allowed to return home.†

He denies his handwriting.

The threat used to Peacham produced a different effect from that which had been expected. The Somersetshire conspiracy having no existence whatever, excepting in the fervid imagination of James and his Ministers, Peacham had nothing to tell; and when he found that his first invention was only met by an order to be ready to prepare for his trial, he saw that it was useless to persist. He accordingly took refuge in a device of another kind. He boldly denied that the papers were in his handwriting at all. If he had ever said so, it was

* Bacon to the King, Feb. 28, 1615, *State Trials.*

† *Council Register,* March 24 and 25, 1, ii. 875.

CH. XII. 1615.

because he was afraid of being again put to the torture. He stated his belief that the papers were in the handwriting of a namesake of his, who had been in the habit of frequenting his house.*

His trial and conviction.

Of course all this was a mere fabrication. But instead of seeing in it the natural result of the treatment to which the prisoner had been subjected, Bacon had no eyes for anything but the impudence of the falsehood. Although the Government were probably at last convinced that no conspiracy existed, they determined to send Peacham to Taunton for his trial. He was there convicted without difficulty, as the two judges who went down for the assizes were sure to lay down the law in accordance with the views of Bacon and the King.†

Shortly after his conviction, Peacham was again pressed to tell the truth. He made a statement that after his treatise had been written, he heard Sydenham use words which seemed to him 'a confirmation of that which he had formerly written,' and that he had meant nothing more than this when he charged him with being the real author of his seditious writings. He declared that he had never intended either to publish them or to preach them. His purpose was to make use of them as an assistance to him in conversation, as soon as he had taken everything that was objectionable out of them.

He is again examined.

It was unlikely that such an improbable story as this should find belief. A man does not jot down his thoughts on loose sheets, and then write them out fairly, with a text at the head of them, for such a purpose as this. But if Peacham was a foolish and untruthful man, he was none the less an object of an oppressive interpretation of the law. The sentence of death, indeed, which had been pronounced, was never executed. About

* Examination of Peacham, March 10, 1615.

† They were Chief Baron Tanfield and Serjeant Montagu. I do not know whether they were appointed in regular order, but it was, to say the least of it, an unlucky circumstance that Montagu should have had anything to do with the trial. He had not only been one of the law-officers of the Crown who had been employed to tamper with the judges, but, as the brother of the Bishop of Bath and Wells, who had been libelled by Peacham, he was unfit to be employed in the case.

seven months after his trial, he died in Taunton gaol. Gaols were by no means healthy places in those days; and his end was probably hastened by the sufferings which he had undergone. But this is mere conjecture. All that we know positively is the fact of his death.*

Owen's case.

The trial of Peacham was not the only case in which Bacon was brought, at this time, into collision with Coke. John Owen, a Catholic of Godstow, had used expressions to the effect that it was lawful to kill the King, being excommunicate. These words appear to have meant that it was lawful to kill the King, if he were excommunicated. Bacon held that the words were treasonable, as the very fact of putting such a hypothesis was evidence that the speaker assigned to the Crown a position of subordination to the Pope.† The judges of the King's Bench were consulted,‡ and were equally clear that the words used amounted to treason. But, much to Bacon's annoyance, though Coke came to the same conclusion with himself, he arrived at it by a different road. He argued that there was nothing hypothetical in the words at all; but that, as the Pope was accustomed once a year to include, under a general excommunication, all Calvinists, together with other heretics and schismatics, the King was undoubtedly an excommunicated person, and Owen's expression amounted to a direct assertion that it was lawful to kill him. Bacon, who had always an eye to the political consequences of a legal opinion, felt that it would never do to use such an argument publicly in court. If it should be generally understood that the King had been excommunicated by the Pope, the risk of assassination would be considerably increased. In spite of all that Bacon could do, however, Coke refused to give up his opinion, and in delivering his sentiments at the trial, he placed the legality of the proceedings on the ground

* Chamberlain to Carleton, March 27, 1616, *Court and Times*, i. 392.

† That Bacon retained his opinion on this subject is plain from his language in relating Sir William Stanley's case: 'History of Henry VII.,' *Works*, vi. 151.

‡ The King suggested that they should be consulted separately, as in Peacham's case; but Bacon told him that it was unnecessary, as the case was so clear.

CH. XII. 1615.

which alone appeared to him to render them justifiable. But whatever may have been the difference between the views of the Attorney-General and those of the Chief Justice, the prisoner reaped no benefit by it. The jury brought in a verdict of guilty, without troubling themselves about the arguments by which their verdict could be sustained,* and sentence of death was passed in due form. No steps, however, were taken to carry it out. Owen remained in close confinement for more than three years, when he was liberated at the request of the Spanish Ambassador, on condition of leaving the country.†

Commission for compounding for fines on buildings.

Undeterred by the mutterings of discontent to which the collection of the Benevolence had given rise, the Government, anxious to escape at any cost from its financial difficulties, had recourse to means which were not likely to increase its popularity in the City of London. The King's proclamation, by which he had hoped, in 1611, to restrain the increase of buildings in London and Westminster, had not been attended with any effect. He now determined to make one more effort to check what was considered to be the over-population of the capital. In October, 1614, an order was issued to the aldermen of London, and to the justices of the peace in the neighbouring counties, to report on the condition of the buildings.‡ In the following May a Commission was issued to the whole of the Privy Council, to whom some of the judges and other persons of note were joined.§ They were to summon before them all persons who had built new houses; or who, in rebuilding old ones, had constructed the fronts of wood, and to fine them for their offences. The same fate was to overtake those who had let part of their houses to lodgers, if hey thad not done so previously to Michaelmas, 1603. The obloquy which James brought upon himself by this attempt to help out his exchequer by such means was enough to induce him to issue a procla-

* Bacon to the King, Jan. 27, and Feb. 11, 1615, *Works* (ed. Montagu), xii. 124, 134. *State Trials*, ii. 879.

† Pardon of Owen, July 24, 1618, *S. P. Sign Manuals*, ix. 45.

‡ *Council Register*, Oct. 16, 1614.

§ May 15, 1615, Pat. 13 Jac. Part 1.

mation, two months later, in which he declared that he had never thought of his own profit, and that, in order to prove the sincerity of his statement, he had consented, not, as might be supposed, to remit the fines, but to give a positive and final order that nobody should build any more houses; in which case there would, of course, be no fines to levy.* The sum † obtained by the Commission was no more than £4,000, an amount which can hardly be regarded as sufficient to counterbalance the irritation which was caused by the mode in which it was obtained.

Oct. 16, 1614. The brewers.

On the same day as that on which the aldermen and justices were required to report on the growth of London, a letter was addressed by the Council to the Lord Mayor, requiring him to examine into the progress of an evil of an equally alarming description. It had reached the ears of the Government that the brewers of London were in the habit of brewing exceedingly strong beer, and thereby of breaking the laws which had been made for the purpose of preventing the unnecessary consumption of barley.‡ The Lord Mayor was to examine into the facts, and to make a report to the Council. This, however, was not the only point in which the Government was brought into collision with the brewers. The money owed for two thousand casks which had been taken for the King's household was still unpaid, and it was rumoured that there was an intention of laying an imposition of twopence a barrel upon beer. In these straits, the brewers discovered in the charter of the city of London a clause by which they were, as they fancied, exempted from purveyance, and on the strength of this they demanded immediate payment of the debt owing. The Council sent Bacon to prove to them that the King was not bound to pay ready money for any article above the value of forty shillings, and at the same time declared explicitly that the rumour of the intended imposition was a mere fabrication. The money owed should be paid immediately, and similar debts should in future be

* July 16, Proclamation Book, *S.P. Dom.* clxxxvii. 44.
† Appendix VIII. No. 5.
‡ *Council Register*, Oct. 16, 1614.

CH. XII. 1614. met at the close of every year.* With this the brewers were obliged to be content, and they were also forced to enter into bonds of £100 each that they would in future brew beer sufficiently weak to please the Lords of the Council.†

The question of Cleves and Juliers. The dissolution of Parliament, and the consequent impoverishment of the Exchequer, were certain to diminish any weight which James might otherwise have had in his interference with the conflict which seemed to be on the point of breaking out on the Rhine. There can be little doubt that the Spaniards were emboldened by the attitude of the House of Commons. As soon as the news of the dissolution reached Brussels, the agent of the English Government found himself in the midst of politicians who confidently predicted the speedy outbreak of a rebellion in England,‡ and though the event proved that they had miscalculated the extent of the national spirit of endurance, they would not be wrong in concluding that James would, at such a moment, find it impossible to send an army into the Duchies.

Wotton's negotiations. Some weeks before Spinola entered the disputed territories, James had sent Wotton to the Hague, in the hope of being able to settle the question by negotiation, and even after the invasion had taken place, he continued to direct him to do what he could to bring the quarrel to an amicable termination. Conferences were held at Xanten, at which the English and French Ambassadors appeared as mediators. An arrangement was at length come to on the 2nd of November, 1614, by which the two rivals agreed to share the revenue and other advantages of the Government between them, but to make a division of the territory, which should be valid till some final decision would be taken.§

The Treaty of Xanten.

It was not without difficulty that the claimants had been induced to submit to these stipulations. But a

* *Council Register*, Dec. 4, 1614. The story of the imposition is given by Chamberlain in a letter to Carleton of the 24th of November. Perhaps it originated in a proposal for a composition for purveyance, such as had been by this time pretty generally adopted in the counties.

† *Council Register*, Feb. 16, March 26, 1615.

‡ Trumbull to Winwood, June 30, 1614, *S. P. Fland.*

§ Dumont, *Corps Diplom.* v., part ii. 259.

still greater obstacle arose as soon as it was proposed that the Dutch and Spanish troops should evacuate the Duchies. Spinola proposed that both parties should agree never to enter them again. Maurice, who was afraid that the Elector of Brandenburg might be attacked by the German Princes of the Catholic League, would only declare that he would never return so long as the Treaty of Xanten was maintained intact. To make matters worse, Spinola received an order from Spain to hold Wesel until the King had made up his mind whether he would give his consent to the observance of the treaty or not. The conferences broke up, and the two armies remained face to face, each occupying the ground upon which they stood.

Difficulties between the Dutch and Spaniards.

1615.

Renewed negotiations.

During the whole of the early part of the following year, James was labouring indefatigably to find some form of agreement which would satisfy both parties. At last he obtained the assent of the Archduke to a form which permitted the Dutch to enter the territories in case war should break out.* To this the States-General demurred. They wished a clause to be inserted which would enable them to pass through the Duchies in case of an attack being made upon their other German allies. Here James refused to support them. To him it was a mere question of regulating an ordinary dispute relating to a definite portion of territory. To them it was only a part of the great quarrel which must sooner or later be brought once more to the arbitration of war. Between the two Governments, therefore, there was no possibility of agreement. The Dutch retained their hold upon the fortresses which were garrisoned by their soldiers, and kept the road to Germany open. James, after fruitless attempts to persuade them that they were unreasonable, and in the wrong, withdrew his Ambassador, in order to bring such fruitless negotiations to a close.

Recall of Wotton.

* Bentivoglio, *Relationi*, 186. Wotton's correspondence, Aug. 1614,—Aug. 1615, *S. P. Hol.* The form proposed was, 'Et promettons en oultre que les dicts gens de guerre ni aucuns dependants de nous ne rentreront à l'advenir dans les dicts pays pour y prendre aucune place soubs quelque nom ou pretexte que ce soit, sy non en cas qu'iceulx pays vinssent à tomber en nouvelle guerre ouverte ou invasion manifeste soit facte sur aucun de nos amis dedans les dicts pays.'—Add. MS. 17, 677, I. fol. 51 a.

CH. XII. 1615. Commercial rivalry between England and Holland.

Unfortunately, the question of the evacuation of the fortresses on the Rhine was not the only subject upon which a disagreement existed between the two Governments, at a time when it was above all things desirable that a good understanding should be maintained between the leading Protestant powers.

The whale fishery.

The claim which had been put forward by the English to the exclusive right in the Northern whale fishery could not possibly be acknowledged by the hardy Dutch sailors who had spent their lives in battling with the Polar seas. It was evident that, unless concessions were made, a collision would, sooner or later, ensue.

The East India trade.

It was of still greater importance to settle as speedily as possible the disputes which had already begun to arise out of the lucrative commerce of the East Indian seas. That commerce had, for almost the whole of the sixteenth century, been a monopoly in the hands of the Portuguese. But with the absorption of Portugal in the Spanish empire, and with the growing weakness of Spain itself, the thought of disputing this monopoly occurred to the merchants of other nations. In 1595, Dutch ships made their way round the Cape, and by degrees the Portuguese found themselves supplanted in their most valuable commercial stations. In 1602, the great Dutch East India Company was formed by the union of the smaller associations by which these original enterprises had been undertaken. Their ships were fitted out for fighting as well as for conveying merchandise. The Portuguese, emboldened by their long supremacy in those seas, had rendered themselves obnoxious to many of the native Princes by their overbearing demeanour. The Dutch skilfully availed themselves of this feeling, and constituted themselves the protectors of the natives. In this way they easily obtained permission to erect their factories, and even induced the Sovereigns whom they had defended to enter into contracts with them, by which they engaged to sell to them alone the most valuable produce of their territories. By these means the whole of the commerce of the finer spices which were produced in the islands of the Eastern Archipelago fell into their hands. What this trade was worth may be calculated from the fact that in 1602 an English vessel brought a cargo of cloves from Amboyna, which sold for more than twelve hundred per cent. upon its cost price. CH. XII. 1602.

1599. The English East India Company.

In 1599, a handful of London merchants applied to Elizabeth for permission to trade to the East Indies. At first she turned a deaf ear to their request, as the negotiations at Boulogne were in progress, and she was unwilling to do anything which might bring her into additional antagonism to the Spanish Government. But as soon as her hopes of peace were at an end, she expressed her readiness to listen to their proposals, and in the following year she granted them the charter which they desired. 1600. The English East India Company, thus founded, pushed on in the track of the Dutch sailors who had preceded it in those seas. Neglecting the great country with which its future history was to be indelibly associated, its first factories were erected at Acheen in Sumatra, and at Bantam in Java. It was not till 1608 that the agents of the Company reported that the cloths and calicoes of Hindustan were in request in Sumatra and Java, and suggested that if factories were established at Cambay and Surat, they might get into their hands the trade between the islands and that part of the Continent. It was not till 1612, however, that an attempt was made in this direction. The English ships which were engaged in opening the trade at Surat were attacked by an overwhelming force of Portuguese, who were unwilling to tolerate the presence of intruders on a coast which they had so long looked upon as their own, and which they overawed by means of a succession of fortified posts dependent upon the chief station at Goa. In spite of the superiority of numbers, however, they were doomed to disappointment. The English vessels, after a hard struggle, succeeded in driving off the enemy. The natives here, as everywhere else, looked upon the Portuguese as oppressors, and, in consequence of their victory, the English had no difficulty in obtaining permission to establish a factory at Surat.

Factories at Acheen and Bantam.

1612. Trade with Surat.

The factory at Surat.

In the following year one of the factors of Surat travelled to Ahmedabad. On his return, he reported that it would be advantageous to open a direct trade

CH. XII. 1612.

with the markets in the interior, and recommended that a resident should be sent from England, who might obtain the necessary facilities from the Mogul Emperor.

Sir Thomas Roe.

The person selected for this novel enterprise was Sir Thomas Roe. Like Sir Henry Nevill, he was one of those men who, if James had been well advised, would have been the very first to be selected for high office. In 1609 he had made a voyage to Guiana, and had sailed the broad waters of the Amazon. In 1614 he had taken his place in the House of Commons, and had given a firm but loyal support to the principles of Sandys and Whitelocke. He was thus admirably qualified to act with that body of men who were prepared to stand as mediators between the past and the future, and to show that the loyalty and patriotism of the Elizabethan age were not incompatible with the growing spirit of independence with which the nation was pervaded.

1615. His embassy to Agra.

With the dissolution all hopes of usefulness at home were at an end, and we may well believe that he now looked without dissatisfaction upon the distant and perilous employment which was proposed to him. He left England in the spring of 1615, and upon his arrival in India made his way without delay to the court of the Emperor Jehanghir at Agra. During his stay there he forwarded several wise suggestions to the Company. He advised them not to attempt to become a political power, or to waste their money, like the Portuguese, in building forts and batteries. This advice was undoubtedly the best which could be given at the time. As long as the whole of Northern India was in the hands of a powerful Sovereign, it was better that a body of traders should be able to show that they trusted implicitly to his protection. With that protection they were unable to dispense, as it would be hopeless for a handful of foreigners to maintain themselves in a corner of the empire by force of arms. The time when anarchy and weakness made a different course advisable had not yet arrived.

His advice to the Company.

In the same spirit, the Ambassador pointed out that his own mission was altogether a mistake. What was needed was a native resident who would represent their wishes in the same way as the wishes of any other body of traders might be brought before the Emperor. The authority with which a representative of the King of England was obliged to speak only made it more difficult to obtain privileges for those who, after all, were only merchants exercising their avocation on sufferance.*

1611. The Company dissatisfied with the loss of the spice trade.

But this extension of their trade did not compensate the Company for the loss of their commerce with the Spice Islands, of which they had been deprived by the encroachments of the Dutch. It was in 1611 that the English East India Company first laid its complaints before the Government. Their Dutch rivals had taken possession of all the posts which were most advantageous for trade, and their armed vessels and the fortifications which they had erected were sufficiently powerful to keep the English at a distance. Salisbury immediately forwarded to Winwood the complaint which had been laid before him, and directed him to lay it before the States-General.† The reply of the States was conciliatory, and promises were made that orders should be sent out to the Dutch merchants to desist from their proceedings. This was very well as far as it went; but it was exceedingly problematical whether such orders would meet with obedience on the other side of the globe.‡

In the meanwhile a proposal was made by the Dutch for an amalgamation of the two Companies.§ This proposal proving distasteful to the English Commissioners, of whom the celebrated Grotius was one, were sent over to London in the spring of 1613.|| The negotiation came to nothing; but towards the end of the following year James determined to take it up again, and accordingly directed Clement Edmondes, the Clerk of the Council, together with two other Commissioners, to 1614

* Bruce's *History of the East India Company*; Mill's *History of British India.*

† Petition of the East India Merchants, Nov. 1611, *S. P. East Indies*, No. 591. Notes of negotiations, 1613, *S. P. Hol.*

‡ Winwood to Salisbury, Jan. 31, 1612, *S. P. Hol.*

§ Winwood to Salisbury, March 10, 1612, *S. P. Hol.*

|| Negotiation, March 23—April 20, 1613, *S. P. East Indies*, No. 643.

CH. XII. 1612. betake themselves to the Hague, to treat upon the disputed points, under Wotton's superintendence. At the same time they were ordered to try to come to some terms on the subject of the disputed fishing grounds.

1615. Negotiations at the Hague. The Commissioners arrived at their destination on the 20th of January, 1615. The discussions were carried on till the beginning of April, when the negotiations were finally broken off. The English began by demanding that the principle of freedom of trade should be at once accepted, as the starting point of the deliberations. The Dutch replied that they had been at considerable expense in equipping fleets, by which the seats of the spice trade had been cleared of the Portuguese, and that the native princes who had been succoured by them were under contract to furnish the produce of their territories exclusively to them. It was not fair, therefore, that the English should share in the benefits which others had gained only after a considerable expenditure of men and money.

Upon this the English professed their readiness to bear their fair share in the defence of the islands against the Spaniards and Portuguese. This, however, was not sufficient for the Dutch. They declared plainly that the only condition on which the English could be admitted to an equality with Holland in the spice trade was an engagement to join in an aggressive warfare upon Spain, at least beyond the Cape. When the Eastern seas were swept of every remnant of Portuguese commerce, then the English and the Dutch might jointly exercise as complete a monopoly in the East Indies as that which was claimed by Spain in the West. To this proposal the English Commissioners gave a decided negative. The negotiations on this important question having come to an end, no attempt was made to continue the discussion which had been already commenced on the subject of the fishery.*

1613. It was not only in Holland that James met with a rebuff in the spring of 1615. Edmondes had, ever since Prince Henry's death, been busy at Paris discussing the

* Despatches and negotiations of Clement Edmondes, passim. Feb. 4—April 18, 1615. *S. P. Hol.*

terms upon which the French Government would consent to a marriage between his brother and the Princess Christina. The difficulties springing from religious differences caused the negotiations to drag on slowly. According to what rites the marriage was to be celebrated, how many priests were to be permitted to accompany the bride, in what kind of building they were to be allowed to officiate after their arrival in England, and in what ground the attendants of the Princess were to be buried after their death, were all questions which each Government wished to settle in its own way.*

CH. XII. 1615. Proposed marriage of Prince Charles with the Princess Christina.

1614.

At last, in February, 1614, after more than a year had been spent in discussing the subject, Edmondes came over to England, bringing with him the proposals of the French Government. Five months afterwards he returned, bearing the counter-proposals to which James was willing to agree.† To these, however, he received no immediate answer, and as the autumn drew on he was told that it was impossible to consider the subject until after the conclusion of the expected assembly of the States-General.

The fact was that the Queen Regent had no heart in the English alliance. It would, perhaps, be unfair to say that she allowed the English proposals to be listened to simply in order to content the princes of the blood, and the other great nobles who were dissatisfied with the Spanish marriages. She, no doubt, knew very well that it was advisable, for the interests of France, not to put herself unreservedly in the hands of Spain; but, at all events, it is plain that her sympathies were not with England.

It would be impossible to play this double game much longer. The States-General, which met in October, could hardly be dissolved without forcing her to declare her policy.

* Edmondes to the King, Jan. 9, July 29, 1613. *Réponse aux propositions*, &c., probably the paper mentioned in the last-named despatch. Edmondes to the King, Nov. 14, 1613, *S. P. Fr.*

† Instructions to Edmondes, July 1614, *S. P. Fr.* Amongst other things James said that the Princess should be allowed private worship, although he did not doubt that she would soon be induced to conform to the Church of England.

CH. XII. 1614. The States-General.

It is a strange and instructive contrast which meets the eye of anyone who glances over the records of those two assemblies which met on either side of the channel in the course of the same year. In Westminster, the Commons called upon the House of Lords to assist them against the King. In Paris, the Third Estate called upon the King to assist it against the other two. On both sides of the channel justice was on the side of the representatives of the people. But whereas in England the House of Commons represented the force as well as the rights of the nation, in France the Third Estate was powerless unless the Sovereign would lend it the strength of that organization which he alone could give. Between it and the privileged orders there was a great gulf, which it was in vain to attempt to bridge over. One day an orator from amongst the Third Estate spoke of the other orders as the elder brethren of the family to which his own class belonged. The nobles and the clergy shrank back with horror at the profanation, and the boy-King was brought down in state to bid the Third Estate ask pardon for the insult which it had offered.

There was not one of the points upon which the Third Estate insisted to which James, if he had sat upon the throne of France, would not have given his hearty concurrence. These men would have made Louis XIII. a king indeed. They called on him to withdraw from the nobility the pensions which were wrung out of the people, to take his stand against the encroachments of the Papal power by imposing an oath of allegiance, and to withdraw from the clergy certain privileges which were oppressive to the people. It was all in vain. The Regent had taken her side. Her son should be King of the nobles and the priests; he should not be the King of the people. The last States-General of monarchical France were dismissed abruptly, but not before the ominous words had been heard, 'We are the anvil now; the time may come when we shall be the hammer.'

1615. The negotiations at an end.

The quarrel between the Regent and the States-General could not fail to have its effect upon her relations with England. She hurried on the completion of the Spanish marriages, and she sent a reply to James's proposals which, in his eyes, was equivalent to a refusal.*

The Savoy war.

At the same time the opposition between the two Courts became manifest in another quarter. For three years the Duke of Savoy had been engaged in a war in which he bore the whole weight of the Spanish monarchy. In spite of frequent defeats, he was still unconquered. The English and the French Governments agreed in advising him to make peace with his formidable enemy. At the same time some of the French nobles prepared to raise a force to support him in case of the failure of the negotiations. The Regent forbade a single man to leave France for such a purpose. James sent him £15,000, a large sum for him to provide out of his impoverished treasury.†

* Answer of Villeroi, May $\frac{14}{24}$, 1615, *S. P. Fr.*

† Edmondes to Winwood, *S. P. Fr.*, April 14, 1615.

CHAPTER XIII.

THE TRIAL OF THE EARL OF SOMERSET.

CH. XIII.
1614.

Somerset's influence with the King.

It was in the autumn of 1614 that Somerset's influence reached its highest point. As Lord Chamberlain he was in constant attendance upon the King, and though he had not the official title of Secretary, he was treated as a confidential adviser far more than Winwood, through whom the correspondence with the ambassadors ostensibly passed. In spite of all his frivolity, there was something not altogether despicable in Somerset's character. It had been by his support that Nevill had hoped to obtain the Secretaryship, and Winwood had found his assistance not altogether unavailing. The feelings of respect with which he was regarded by such a man as Sir Robert Cotton will always tell in his favour. Although he took care to fill his own pockets with the money which was offered to him by men who wished to obtain the King's consent to their wants, at least no public scandal is to be traced to him. We never hear of any attempt, on his part, to interfere with the due course of the law, or to obtain assignments of duties upon commerce. In his dealing with his dependents, he frequently displayed a generosity for which we are hardly prepared. But his connection with the Howards ruined him. The most respectable members of the Privy Council, Ellesmere, Pembroke, and Worcester, began to look upon him not merely as an upstart, but as a man who was prepared to influence the King in favour of their rivals.

First appearance of Villiers

At this time, the attention of all who hated Somerset was turned upon a young man who had lately made his appearance at Court. It was at Apthorpe in the beginning of August, 1614, that George Villiers first presented himself before the King. He was a young man of singularly prepossessing appearance, and he was endowed not only with personal vigour, but with that readiness of speech which James delighted in.

He was a younger son, by a second marriage, of Sir George Villiers, a Leicestershire knight of good family. His mother, Mary Beaumont, was not inferior by birth to her husband, but in early life she had occupied a dependent position in the household of her relation, Lady Beaumont of Coleorton.* When she became a widow her means were once more straitened, and she was burdened with the charge of providing for a family which consisted of three sons and a daughter. George, her second son, was her favourite, and she determined to educate him for a courtier's life. As far as solid intellectual training was concerned, she did nothing for him; but she used every means in her power to perfect him in all external accomplishments.

When James first saw him he was in his twenty-second year. It was an anxious moment both for his mother and himself. If he did not succeed in impressing the King in his favour, no other career was open to him. Almost the whole of his father's property having descended to the children of the first marriage, all his fortune amounted to a miserable £50 a year, and his education had unfitted him for any of the ordinary means of raising himself in the world.

He comes to Court.

Fortunately, however, for him, at least as far as his more immediate prospects were concerned, James seems to have liked him from the first, and, if he did not himself invite him to Court, was by no means displeased to see him there. Those who wished ill to Somerset took him in hand, and instructed him how to gain the ear of

* Wilson calls her 'a young gentlewoman of that name allied, and yet a servant, to the lady' (Kennet, ii. 698), which is more probable than that she was a kitchen maid at her future husband's own house, which is Roger Coke's story. Weldon calls her (*Secret History of the Court of James I.*, i. 397) 'a waiting-gentlewoman;' if she had really served in a menial office, he would hardly have lost the opportunity of saying so.

CH. XIII. 1614.

the King. Sir John Graham, one of the Gentlemen of the Privy Chamber, gave him a piece of advice which he accepted without difficulty. He was attached to the daughter of Sir Roger Aston, and it is said that she would have been his wife if he had been able to scrape together the little sum which her parents required before they could prudently consent to the marriage. Graham advised him to think no more of entangling himself in such a manner, at the very beginning of his career. This advice he determined to take. If he felt any compunctions at the step, he managed to conceal them from the knowledge of the world.

In November, the supporters of Villiers were in hopes of obtaining for him a post in the bedchamber. Somerset, however, remonstrated, and the King, who as yet appears to have formed no intention of deserting his old favourite, gave the place to one of Somerset's nephews.* Villiers was obliged to content himself with the inferior position of a cup-bearer.

Somerset's behaviour to the King.

It was apparently a month or two after this that James began to take umbrage at Somerset's behaviour. Somerset's position had, no doubt, been long a trying one. It is plain from the manner in which the King is referred to in the letters which Overbury wrote from the Tower, that even at that time Somerset had no respect whatever for his patron. He had already accustomed himself to look upon the King's company as a necessary evil which must be endured on account of the benefits which were to be obtained through the Royal favour. He now became aware that there was a powerful league formed against him. He heard men muttering that one man should not for ever rule them all. Villiers' presence provoked him, and he treated him with studied insolence. As if it were not enough that he had alienated the affections of all excepting the family of the Howards, he now proceeded to do his best to offend the King. He seems to have thought that James was a mere plaything in his hands. He disturbed him at unseasonable

* Chamberlain to Carleton, Nov. 24, 1614, *S. P. Dom.* lxxviii. 61. Printed with a wrong date in *Court and Times*, i. 350.

hours by complaints of the factious conduct of his enemies. He even had the audacity to accuse the King of being in league with those who had combined to ruin him, and used language towards his sovereign, 'in comparison' of which, as James told him, 'all Peacham's book' was 'but a gentle admonition.'

1615. The King's expostulatory letter.

Somerset had made a great mistake. If he had played his cards well he might have maintained his position, at least till some unexpected event revealed the mysteries of the Tower. But James was not likely to submit to be bullied by one whom he looked upon as the work of his hands. He wrote to his favourite an expostulatory letter, which is perhaps the strangest which was ever addressed to a subject by a sovereign.* As for the factions, he wrote, of which Somerset complained, he knew nothing of them, and he certainly should refuse to give heed to any accusations against him proceeding from such a quarter. He had done all that was in his power to prove that his confidence was undiminished. He had made Graham, who had incurred Somerset's ill-will, feel his displeasure.† He had admitted Somerset's nephew to the vacant place which he demanded for him, though even the Queen had begged him to give it to another. He now told him that his behaviour was unbearable. His affection for him was great, but he would not be forced any longer to listen to the abusive language with which he had been wholly overwhelmed. Let Somerset only deal with him as a friend, there was nothing which he was not ready to grant him. But he was resolved not to put up with his present behaviour any longer. He concluded by reminding him that he and his father-in-law were in such positions that all suits of importance passed through their hands, so that they had no real reason to be discontented.

* James to Somerset. Halliwell, *Letters of the Kings of England*, ii. 126. The date of this letter is probably about January or February, 1615. The reference to Peacham's book makes it necessarily later than Dec. 9, 1614, and it must have been written before April 23, 1615, when Villiers was made Gentleman of the Bedchamber, as, after that, his appointment would have been expressly referred to as a grievance.

† No doubt as being a friend of Villiers.

CH. XIII. 1615.

The King's visit to Cambridge.

What was the immediate result of this letter, we do not know. On the 7th of March we find the King at Cambridge, which he visited to do honour to Suffolk, who had, upon the death of his uncle Northampton, been elected Chancellor of the University. Even in the midst of these festivities, signs were not wanting of the mutual hostility of the factions by which the Court was distracted. Suffolk, who entertained the company, had not thought proper to invite the Queen to partake of his hospitality, and it was noticed that not a single lady accompanied the Court who was not in some way or another connected with the Howard family.*

Intrigues against Somerset.

What were the exact relations between the King and Somerset during the six weeks which followed this visit to Cambridge we do not know; but it is not improbable that Somerset's ill-temper continued, and that the King began, in consequence, to think of replacing him by Villiers. It was on the 23rd of April that the new favourite gained another step. Somerset's enemies had long been on the watch for an opportunity of supplanting him, and they instigated the Archbishop to do his best to procure the assistance of the Queen. Abbot had good cause to wish for Somerset's disgrace. Not only had the favourite's connection with the divorce case indelibly impressed itself upon his memory, but he justly regarded his friendship with the Howards as an act of treason to the great cause of Protestantism which he himself so heartily supported. In his eyes, and in the eyes of the malcontent Privy Councillors who acted with him, the substitution of Villiers for Somerset was not a mere personal question. No doubt Villiers, to all appearance, was tractable enough, and his affability was in strong contrast to Somerset's arrogance. But the chief point of difference was this, that whilst Somerset acted as a man who had been selected by the King at a time when he was distrustful of his Council, Villiers, having achieved his position by the aid of the principal Councillors, would, as they fondly hoped, be content with

* It was on this occasion that the play of *Ignoramus* was acted, which gave such offence to the lawyers. Chamberlain to Carleton, March 16, 1615. Nichols, *Progresses*, iii. 48.

maintaining a good understanding between the Sovereign and his ministers. CH. XIII. 1615.

At first, Abbot found that the Queen was not altogether so willing as he had expected to forward his scheme. She had indeed no love for Somerset, but she had very little hope of improving her position by the substitution of one favourite for another. She knew her husband's character well, and she told Abbot, in words which he had cause to remember in later days, that he was only preparing a scourge for himself. James would never allow a successor of Somerset to occupy any other position than one of complete dependence upon himself, and he would support him in overreaching the men through whose countenance he had risen to power. Abbot obtains the assistance of the Queen.

In spite of such warnings as these, Abbot persisted in his entreaties for assistance. He knew that the Queen's intervention was indispensable, for it was one of James's peculiarities that he never would admit anyone to stand on an intimate footing with himself unless he had first secured the Queen's recommendation. This was in order that, if the Queen afterwards made any complaint against the person who had been thus advanced, he might turn the tables upon her by answering that it was her fault for making such a recommendation.

The Queen at length withdrew her opposition. It must have been a curious scene, on the evening of the 23rd of April, when the Queen pressed the King to confer upon Villiers the office of Gentleman of the Bedchamber. Outside the door was Somerset on the one hand, and Abbot and his friends on the other, all anxiously watching for the King's decision. Somerset, who felt that his high position was at stake, sent a message in to the King, begging him at least to be content with giving Villiers the inferior place of Groom of the Bedchamber. Abbot met this by sending a counter message to the Queen, pressing her to insist upon the higher post. At last James gave way, and Villiers received the appointment for which the Queen had originally asked. The new Gentleman of the Bedchamber was also knighted and endowed with a pension of £1,000 a-year.* Villiers made Gentleman of the Bedchamber.

* Abbot's narrative in *Rushworth,* i. 456.

CH. XIII. 1615.

Somerset's requests refused by the King.

Somerset's falling fortunes were still more decidedly marked by his failure in obtaining two objects upon which his heart was set. He was anxious to retain in his own hands the Wardenship of the Cinque Ports, which had, upon Northampton's death, been provisionally intrusted to his care, and he was no less anxious to obtain for Bishop Bilson the office of Lord Privy Seal, partly, no doubt, as a reward for his services in the divorce case, but still more from a desire to keep the place out of the hands of any of his rivals.* On the 13th of July, the Cinque Ports were given to Lord Zouch, who had not even asked for them; and about the same time the King, though he gave Bilson to understand that he had no personal objection to himself, wrote a sharp letter to Somerset, refusing even to see Bilson, and advising that the Bishop should return at once to his diocese.† From this letter it appears that Somerset had irritated the King by telling him that though he could no longer feel any affection for him, yet he was ready to serve him as a faithful subject. James knew well enough that, in the position which Somerset held, such a distinction was simply impossible.

Somerset attempts to procure a pardon.

It was at the time when the favourite was thus feeling that the King's support was failing him, chiefly in consequence of his own arrogance and folly, that he took a step which afterwards brought him under grave suspicion. Knowing, as he did, that it was almost impossible for a man through whose hands important State business had passed to be secure against the interpretation which might be put upon his actions by his enemies, he had a pardon drawn out which might cover the greatest number of possible offences. He was, however, unable to obtain the consent of Yelverton,‡ who, as Solicitor, examined it, and refused to allow it to pass the Great Seal. Upon

* Chamberlain to Carleton, July 15, 20, 1615, *Court and Times*, i. 364.

† The King to [Somerset], Halliwell's *Letters of the Kings*, 133. It is strange that the editor was unable to discover to whom the letter was addressed. Its date must be between the 13th and the 19th of July, when the King was at Theobalds.

‡ It is to Yelverton that the refusal is ascribed in Cotton's examinations, Cott. MS., Tit. B., vii. 489, and in the account of the trial, Amos, 156. Other accounts ascribe it to the Chancellor.

this, he directed Sir Robert Cotton to draw up another, which he framed after the model of that which had been granted to Wolsey, in the reign of Henry VIII. Stress was afterwards laid upon the fact that amongst the crimes which were mentioned occurs that of being accessory before the fact to murder.* The answer which he then gave was in all probability true—that he had left these details to the lawyers.† It is hardly likely that, if he had been really guilty of murder, he would have allowed nearly two years to slip by without procuring a pardon on some pretence or another.

CH. XIII. 1615.

James attempts to reconcile him with Villiers.

According to a story which has not come down to us upon any very good authority, but which may probably be true, James made an attempt to put an end to the quarrel between the rival favourites. He directed Villiers to wait upon Somerset, and to request him to take him under his protection. Somerset's reply was what might have been expected from the ill-temper in which he had been for some months. 'I will none of your service,' was his short and hasty answer; 'and you shall none of my favour. I will, if I can, break your neck, and of that be confident.'‡ That James was still hoping to win back Somerset to take his old place by his side is rendered probable by the fact that a few days after this scene is said to have taken place, Bishop Bilson was admitted, avowedly at Somerset's recommendation, to a seat at the Privy Council.§

1614. Consultations at Madrid.

It must have been about this time that Somerset entered into an intrigue with Sarmiento, by which he hoped to recover the influence which he had lost. In the summer of 1614, whilst the negotiations were still on foot for the marriage of Prince Charles to the French Princess, Sarmiento took alarm at the prospect of seeing England and France once more in close alliance. He accordingly wrote to his Government, begging them once more to hold up before the eyes of James the prospect of a Spanish marriage for his son, in order to thwart the

* To poisoning, according to the report of the trial (Amos, 151), but this is certainly an embellishment of the speaker or reporter.

† Amos, 108.

‡ Weldon (*Secret History*, i. 407).

§ *Council Register*, Aug. 30, 1615, *Carew Letters*, 15.

CH. XIII. 1615.

progress of the arrangement which was being made at Paris. Upon the receipt of this despatch Philip laid the matter before the Pope, who at once refused to give his consent to the marriage of the Infanta with a heretic. In spite of this declaration, the fear of losing his hold upon England was so powerful with Philip that he was unable to let the matter drop. Unable to make up his mind either, on the one hand, to expose his daughter to the risk of the contamination of English Protestantism, or, on the other hand, to desist from an alliance which would secure his influence in England, at the same time that it might be used to relieve the sufferings of the English Catholics, he contented himself with asking the advice of every one, without coming to a decision. Theologians and councillors of state were summoned in crowds to help the King in his difficulty, but it was long before he could be prevailed upon to take any step in the matter.*

Lerma's proposal to Digby.

At last, apparently in the course of the summer of 1615, Lerma proposed to Digby to resume the negotiations on the subject of a marriage for Prince Charles with the Infanta Maria. It is not likely that the Court of Spain was in earnest, or that any decision had been come to in face of the opposition of the Pope. Although we, at present, know nothing of the motives of the King of Spain, we shall hardly wrong him by attributing † to him no desire to do anything more than to draw James on, by the prospect of an alliance with the House of Austria, to give up the position which he was occupying among the Protestant States of Europe. As soon as Digby heard the proposal, he replied that he could forward no overtures to his master until he heard what were the particular intentions of the King of Spain. Upon this Lerma presented him with a paper containing the demands which he proposed to make on the point of religion. Digby replied that these demands were altogether inadmissible, and that he durst not send such a paper home to England. Upon this Lerma professed

* Guizot, *Revue des Deux Mondes*, July 15, 1862, xl. 275–278.

† M. Guizot has shown that a few years later he had no intention whatever of assenting to the marriage, although he was then professedly favouring it.

his readiness to give way in some of the conditions, and several conferences were held in which Digby, though always protesting that he had no commission from the King to treat upon the subject, consented to take part. He, however, took care to send a copy of Lerma's paper to England, and to acquaint the King with all that was going on.

Whilst matters were in this condition, Somerset sent Sir Robert Cotton to Sarmiento, who was still acting as the Spanish Ambassador in London, and assured him that the King was inclined to agree to the proposed marriage. He recommended, however, that the negotiations should be taken out of Digby's hands, and that they should be transferred to London, where they might be carried on between Somerset and Sarmiento, through the medium of Sir Robert Cotton. Upon this Sarmiento procured from his Government full powers to treat with Somerset. Cotton frequently repaired to the Ambassador's house, and on one occasion showed him Lerma's paper, which had been sent home by Digby.

Probable intention of Somerset.

Altogether, this secret negotiation forms one of the strangest episodes in Somerset's eventful history. If he really undertook it on his own responsibility, his conduct on this occasion affords a remarkable insight into that overweening self-confidence against which the King had remonstrated so strongly some months before. And yet it is difficult to come to any other conclusion than that this was the case.* The probable explanation is that Suffolk and Somerset found that James was not altogether averse to listening to Lerma's proposal,

* App. III. Nos. 2 and 3. Digby, at least, distinctly states that this negotiation was carried on without the King's privity, and he could not have derived this assurance from any lips but those of James himself. It is of course possible that James, in denying that he knew anything about the matter, may have been false, and this would, no doubt, help to explain his behaviour during Somerset's trial, but his order for Cotton's examination is dated on the 20th of October (*Court and Times*, i. 371), and the denial which must have formed the basis of Digby's assertion of James's ignorance of the intrigue must have been later than this. Even if he could be supposed to invent the story that Somerset had acted on his own responsibility, he would hardly have done so after he knew that the matter was likely to be investigated. Somerset himself, too, hung back from confessing to his dealings with the Ambassador. Bacon's *Works* (ed. Montagu), vi. 226.

CH. XIII. 1615.

which had come at a time when he had failed of success in his scheme of a French alliance, and when the Dutch seemed every day more likely to thwart him in his plan for carrying out the treaty of Xanten. Under such circumstances they may have thought that they had a good opportunity for re-establishing their influence, by bringing the negotiations privately into a state in which they could address themselves to the King as men who had succeeded where their rivals had failed. The appointment of Bilson is enough to show that their policy was not at that time completely rejected by the King.

Information of Overbury's murder brought to Winwood.

It was whilst Somerset was in the midst of this intrigue that the blow fell which dashed to the ground any hopes which he may have entertained of regaining the favour which he had lost. A few days before the conclusion of the progress, when James was at Lord Southampton's house at Beaulieu, Winwood informed him that he had received intelligence to the effect that Sir Thomas Overbury had met his death by other than natural means.* What the precise information was which he had received we do not know, but the most probable account is that the apothecary's boy by whom the murder was actually committed, falling ill at Flushing, contrived to convey the information to Winwood.† As no immediate steps were taken in consequence, it is probable that the confession did not enter into details, and, indeed, it is not likely that the criminal was aware of anything inculpating the higher personages by whom he had been employed.

* *Carew Letters*, 16.

† This is the story given by Wilson (Kennet, ii. 698). Trumbull's name was mixed up with it by Weldon, probably because it was known that he came over to London about this time, but his letters in the Record Office show that he came on another matter. Winwood himself says: 'Not long since there was some notice brought unto me that Sir Thomas Overbury . . . was poisoned in the Tower, whilst he was there a prisoner; with this I acquainted His Majesty, who, though he could not out of the clearness of his judgment but perceive that it might closely touch some that were in nearest place about him, yet such is his love to justice that he gave open way to the searching of this business.' Winwood to Wake, Nov. 15, 1615, *S. P. Savoy*. The idea that Winwood knew of the murder some time before, and only brought it out when Somerset was out of favour, is totally inadmissible. Somerset had been in less favour in the spring than he was now. As early as July, however, there had been whisperings about the murder, which had frightened Mrs. Turner.

It must have been within a few days after the return of the Court from the progress, that is to say early in September, that a circumstance occurred which gave Winwood an opportunity of obtaining further information. The Earl of Shrewsbury, who had long been a patron of Helwys, spoke to Winwood in his favour, as a gentleman whose acquaintance was worth having. Winwood answered that he should be glad to befriend him, but that at present there was a heavy imputation upon him, as Overbury was thought to have come to a violent and untimely death whilst he was under his charge. Helwys, as soon as he heard what Winwood had said, having now no doubt that the whole matter was discovered, acknowledged that he was privy to an attempt which had been made to poison Overbury through Weston, but that he had prevented its being carried into execution. Winwood laid this confession before the King, who directed that Helwys should set down in writing all he knew about the matter.* On the 10th of September, accordingly, Helwys wrote to the King, acknowledging that he had met Weston going up with the poison, and had prevented him from attempting to give it to Overbury. He stated that renewed attempts had frequently been made to convey poison to Overbury in his food, but that he had succeeded in frustrating them, till the apothecary's boy at last eluded his vigilance. Who sent the poison he did not know. The only person whose name he had heard mentioned in connection with it was Mrs. Turner.† It is not improbable that this confession was, in the main, true, though there can be no doubt that he was aware of Lady Somerset's participation in the plot, and that he had allowed her to suppose that he was assisting her in carrying out her intentions.

CH. XIII.
1615.
Confession of Helwys.

As soon as James saw the letter, he charged Coke to examine into the affair.‡ He let it be known that he

* Bacon's charge against the Countess of Somerset, (*Works*, ed. Montagu, vi. 196). His story presupposes that Winwood was already in possession of some information.

† Helwys to the King, Sept. 10, 1615. Amos, 186.

‡ The story in Roger Coke's *Detection* is too full of palpable blunders to be worthy of notice. It is, perhaps, a distorted recollection of a message sent to Coke by the King to examine Helwys.

CH. XIII. 1615.

was determined to search into the crime without fear or favour.

Coke appointed to examine the suspected persons.

Coke was of all men then living the one who would take most delight in conducting an inquiry of this nature, and he was perhaps also the most unfit for the purpose. His natural acuteness and sagacity were overbalanced by his readiness to look only to that side of the evidence by which his foregone conclusions were supported, whilst his violent temper made it impossible for him to scrutinise doubtful points with any degree of calmness, and his ignorance of human nature prevented him from seeing a whole class of facts by which the judgment of a wiser man would have been influenced.

Weston's confession.

It was not till eighteen days after Helwys wrote his letter to the King that Weston could be brought to confess that he knew anything about Overbury's murder at all. As late as the 27th of September, he declared that the prisoner's death was caused by a cold caught in sitting too long at an open window. The next day, however, he acknowledged the truth of the Lieutenant's story of the scene in which he threw away the poison in consequence of Helwys's rebuke. This confession, coupled with the long delay, is no slight corroboration of the general accuracy of Helwys's account of what had happened.* On the following day he was, at his own request, re-examined, and for the first time implicated Lady Somerset in the affair,† and on the 1st of October he stated that Lady Somerset had herself, in Mrs. Turner's presence, directed him to administer to Overbury the poison which would be sent to him.‡ A day or two afterwards, Rawlins, a servant of Somerset, gave information that he had been the means of conveying a powder from his master to Overbury.§ Mrs. Turner steadily denied that she knew anything about the matter, and Sir Thomas Monson, who was suspected as having recommended Weston to his place, was equally steadfast in maintaining his own innocence.

Lord and Lady Somerset implicated.

* Examinations of Weston, Sept. 27 and 28, 1615, Amos, 177.

† Examination of Weston, Sept. 29, 1615, *S. P. Dom.* lxxxi. 118.

‡ Examination of Weston, Oct. 1, 1615, Amos, 178.

§ Relation of Giles Rawlins, Oct. 1615, *S. P. Dom.* lxxxii. 24.

It must have been shortly after Weston's confession of the 29th of September that Coke petitioned the King to allow some who were of higher rank than himself to be joined with him in conducting examinations which threatened to inculpate persons of such standing as the Earl and Countess of Somerset. The King at once consented, and nominated the Chancellor, the Duke of Lennox, and Lord Zouch.* CH. XIII. 1615.

Somerset's dismay.

As soon as Somerset heard that he was suspected, he left the King at Royston, and came up to London to justify himself. He must have felt ill at ease.† Even if, as was probably the case, he was innocent of Overbury's murder, he must have known that the difficulty of proving his innocence was so great as to render it almost a certainty that he would not escape if the King determined to bring him to trial. As he reviewed the circumstances of the case, he must have remembered how many of his actions, which at the time seemed to

* Bacon's charge against the Countess of Somerset. *Works* (ed. Montagu), vi. 199.

† There is a difficulty in making out the chronology here. Weldon (*Secret History*, i. 410) makes Somerset to have accompanied James to Royston, to have returned immediately to London, and there to have been arrested at once. Of course this cannot be the case, as James was at all events at Royston before the 9th of October, and probably at least a week earlier, and Somerset was arrested on the 17th. According to Weldon, the day of Somerset's departure from Royston was a Friday, *i.e.*, the 6th or 13th of October; I incline to think it was on the 6th. This would give some explanation of his story of James's behaviour. The King, he says, parted from Somerset with extraordinary demonstrations of affection, telling him that he would neither eat nor sleep till he saw him again, but after he was gone he said, 'I shall never see him more.' Three or four days before the 6th, news would have reached Royston that there had been suspicions against the Earl, who finding them acquiring strength may have determined to go back to London, 'to still the murmurs vented against him' (Wilson, in *Kennet*, ii. 698). He would, of course, as he left, declare boldly that it was all false, and that he would soon come back with his character cleared. The King's conduct admits of various interpretations. The ordinary explanation is that he pretended hypocritically to part with him as a friend, whilst he knew he was running into destruction. On the other hand, Wilson's account is probably correct, which assumes that Somerset knew perfectly well that he was going to meet an accusation. It is possible that his bold assertions overpowered the King for a time, and that he really dismissed him with the hope of seeing him return in a few days triumphant over his accusers, but that as soon as he was gone the force of the accusations recurred to him, and he may well enough have added, 'I shall never see his face more.' All depends upon the gesture and look with which the words were uttered. Wilson says it 'was with a smile,' but Weldon, who was at Royston at the time, omits this.

CH. XIII. 1615. be trivial enough, would hardly escape the very worst interpretations. His share in Overbury's imprisonment, the double part which he had played towards him, the food and medicines with which he had supplied him, the intrigue into which he had entered with Helwys and Northampton to keep him in ignorance of his real feelings towards him, all formed a network of evidence from which it would be difficult to escape, even if the judges before whom his cause was to be tried had been more impartial than they were likely to be.

There was but one course for him to take. He ought to have sat down at once, and after calling up before his memory every circumstance which had taken place during those months of Overbury's imprisonment, and collecting every scrap of evidence which it was in his power to procure, to have laid before the King a true and full statement of his case.

Unfortunately for himself he did not take this step. No doubt it would have cost him something. He would have had to confess much that was to his discredit, and would, in all probability, have lost all chance of regaining the King's favour, but he might possibly have been able to convince the world that he was not a murderer.

Instead of this, he took the most damaging course which it was possible for him to have selected. Again and again he wrote to James, assuring him that the whole accusation was a mere factious attempt to ruin him. The King, he said, had allowed himself to give way too much to Coke's wilfulness. Ellesmere was not a fit man to investigate the charge, as he had always been his enemy. He reminded the King of the share which the Chancellor had taken, as Solicitor-General, in the proceedings against the Queen of Scots, and begged that the examination might be conducted by the twelve judges, and that no Privy Councillor might be allowed to take part in the proceedings. If he had been contented to urge in a moderate manner that it was unfair that his conduct should be investigated by his political enemies, what he said would have been deserving of attention, but when he thus descended to personalities, he threw away all chance of making an impression. It was still worse when he actually threatened the King that his behaviour on this occasion would lose him the support of the whole family of the Howards.*

James refuses to alter the course of investigation.

To these applications, which were supported by Suffolk, James returned a positive refusal. He told Somerset that his conduct, and that of his father-in-law, was that of men who shrunk from investigation. As to himself, he was determined that the examination should be conducted in the strictest possible manner. None would rejoice more than he would if the charge should prove false; but neither abuse of his ministers, nor threats directed against himself, would hinder him from doing justice.

On the 17th of October the Commissioners, who by this time had accumulated sufficient evidence to satisfy themselves of the guilt of the Earl and Countess of Somerset, wrote to both to direct them to remain in their respective apartments, without seeing any one except their servants.† It was on that evening that Somerset burnt a number of his own letters to Northampton, having previously delivered those which he had received from Northampton and from Overbury to Sir Robert Cotton. His first idea seems to have been to affix false dates to them, in order to make them serve as the basis of a fictitious account of his dealings with Overbury. This was actually done by Cotton, but Somerset changed his mind, and preferred to send them away to a safe place of concealment. This treatment of the letters was afterwards, when it was discovered, very

* The substance of Somerset's letters may be inferred with tolerable accuracy from James's reply (Halliwell, *Letters of the Kings of England*, 134). That reply must have been written about the 15th or 16th of October. It was certainly after the Chancellor and others had been directed to examine into the murder. It could not have been immediately after their appointment, for James speaks of a message sent by Lennox 'long ago' to Somerset on the subject. On the other hand, the desire expressed by the King that Somerset should show his letter to Suffolk, seems to prove that he was still at large, and this view is confirmed by the absence of any reference to Somerset's arrest, and by the possibility suggested that Ellesmere might be directed to take a certain course in the examinations, which appears to imply that they had not yet commenced.

† Amos, 40, 41.

CH. XIII. 1615. damaging to his case; but from the fragments which have come down to us, we can quite understand how he might have feared that, by a very easy process, they might be used to support the charge against him, though they did not in reality prove his guilt.*

The next day the Commissioners, hearing that, two days before, Somerset had abused his authority as a Councillor, to send a pursuivant to get possession of some papers relating to Mrs. Turner, and that he had sent a message to Mrs. Turner herself that very morning, committed him to the custody of Sir Oliver St. John, at the Dean of Westminster's house.†

Trial of Weston.

On the 19th of October, the day after Somerset was thus committed to St. John's custody, Weston was brought to trial at the Guildhall. Those who take an interest in observing the progress which has been made in our judicial institutions since the reign of James I., can hardly find a more characteristic specimen of the injustice which once prevailed universally in criminal courts than is to be found in this trial of Weston. Strange to say, Coke, who had prepared the evidence against the prisoner, held the first place amongst the Commissioners on the Bench. But this, revolting as it is to our feelings, is a very small matter when compared with the method by which the indictment was drawn up. The principal facts, as we know, were these—that Weston received certain poisons to give to Overbury; that Overbury had lived on in a way which is perfectly inexplicable, on the supposition that the poisons had really been administered; and that, finally, a poison was given by an apothecary's boy, by which the object desired by the plotters was accomplished. It is plain that there was no evidence whatever that Weston had murdered Overbury, unless, indeed, the fact that he afterwards accepted a reward from Lady Essex is to be considered as evidence that he had really earned the money. If Coke had lived in our own day he would have thrown up the case at once. But that he should

* Amos, 83, 95; Cotton's examination, Cott. MS., Tit. B. vii. 489.

† Somerset to Poulter, Oct. 16. Declaration by Poulter, Oct. 18, *S. P.* lxxxii. 49, 65, 66. Commissioners to the King, Oct. 18, 1615, Amos, 38.

take such a course as this was not to be expected. Every temptation which could offer itself to him urged him on. His professional reputation was at stake. Such an opportunity of tracking out a great crime through a maze of contradictory evidence does not occur twice in a man's life. Nor is it to be forgotten that a failure to procure Weston's conviction would at once set every one of the criminals at large. Overbury's blood would still be unavenged; Mrs. Turner and the Countess of Somerset would once more be beyond the reach of the law, for there was not one of all the guilty crew whose fate was not bound up with that of Weston. It was a maxim of English law that the accessory could not be punished until the principal had been convicted, and Weston was the only man in the hands of the Government who could on any pretence be called a principal in the murder. The true murderer, indeed, according to all probability, was the apothecary's boy; but it would be enough to constitute Weston a principal if it could be shown that he was present at the time that he was administering the poison, and that he aided him in doing so. The indictment against Weston not only asserted distinctly that he had given his aid on that occasion, but also stated that the other poisons were actually given by Weston to Overbury in his food. Of the truth of these two statements not one shadow of evidence was produced at the trial, nor, as far as we know, was there any such evidence in existence.

Character of the indictment.

At the present day, a lawyer who should have a hand in drawing up such an indictment as this, or in allowing it to be pressed against a prisoner, would undoubtedly be guilty of the most deliberate act of wickedness which it is possible for a man to commit. And yet, strange as it seems, there is no reason to suppose that any one of those who took part in the trial suspected for a moment that there was anything wrong. So inured were the lawyers of that day to the habit of disregarding the simplest principles of evidence, and of seeing the case in hand through their wishes rather than their judgment, that there would be little difficulty in coming to the

CH. XIII. 1615. conclusion that Weston was the real murderer. He was certainly a liar, by his own confession; why therefore should he be believed in anything that he had said? and, if he really had a hand in the murder, were he and all the rest of his confederates to escape because of a mere formality? After all, it was by no means material that indictments should be correct in their assertions.* If a few things were inserted which could not be proved, no harm would be done. The main point was that Weston was a villain, and deserved to be hanged; and hanged he should be, in spite of the rules of the law.

Weston refuses to plead.

An unexpected obstacle was presented to carrying out immediately this foregone conclusion, by the refusal of Weston to put himself on his country. This refusal, which would now be equivalent to a conviction, was at that time a bar to all further proceedings. The only resource was the horrible torture known as the *peine forte et dure.* The prisoner refusing to plead was laid under weights, which were from time to time increased till he could bear them no longer, at the same time that he was exposed to the utmost severity of cold and hunger. On this occasion, after the court had been addressed by Sir Lawrence Hyde (who had once been a leading member of the popular party in the House of Commons, but had now become the Queen's Attorney), and a long string of examinations had been read, the proceedings were adjourned to the 23rd, in order to give Weston time to consider the course which he would take.

He gives way.

There can be little doubt of the truth of the supposition which was generally entertained at the time, that Weston had been tampered with by those who hoped, by his refusal to plead, to escape the punishment of their misdeeds. Every attempt was made to induce him to reconsider his determination, but for some time without effect. Two Bishops, Andrewes and King, exhausted to no purpose the arguments which could be supplied by the different schools of theology to which they respec-

* This was laid down by Coke himself at Somerset's trial. See Amos, 247.

tively belonged. What the Bishops were unable to do, however, was at last effected by the servant of the sheriff, on the morning of the day on which Weston was to have been brought again before the Court. The change which he effected was attributed by Coke to 'the instance of the Holy Ghost;' but the result was probably obtained by a vivid description of the tortures which Weston, if he continued obstinate, would have to undergo, and by the conviction that he was only serving, at his own expense, those who had led him to destruction. When he saw the sheriff, he told him that he was now ready to put himself on his trial; and added that he hoped that there was no intention of making a net to catch the little fishes, whilst the great ones were allowed to escape. CH. XIII. 1615.

He was accordingly brought up for trial. The examinations were read, and Hyde again told his story. As on the former occasion, Lord and Lady Somerset were put forward as the authors of the murder, and it was boldly stated that the poison had actually been administered by Weston. A lawyer would have made short work with the evidence, but in those days the criminal was not allowed the help of counsel. Weston stammered out some words in his own defence, but he was quite incompetent to sift the story which had been brought against him. To make it still more easy for the jury to bring in what he considered to be a proper verdict, Coke declared it to be good law that it was utterly immaterial whether or no Overbury had really been murdered by means of the poisons mentioned in the indictment. It was enough that they could come to the conclusion that he had been poisoned by Weston, without expecting any exact proof of the way in which it had been done. Under such guidance as this, it is no wonder that the jury, without difficulty, brought in a verdict of guilty against the prisoner.*

If ever any man was murdered by a judicial sentence, Weston was that man. Never were the evils of the system under which, at that time, evidence was got up Weston judicially murdered.

* *State Trials*, ii. 911. Amos, 371.

CH. XIII. 1615. against a prisoner by the officers of the Government, and even by the judges themselves, placed in a clearer light. Defective proof was, in this case, eked out by a too ready imagination, until the collectors of the evidence actually allowed themselves to take for granted the only two points which had any direct bearing upon the guilt of the prisoner. Proof that Weston administered the poison, or was present when anyone else was administering it, existed only in the vivid imagination of Coke and of those who worked with him. It has been said that this system was admirably adapted for the discovery of the truth, if the Government could be credited with acting fairly on every occasion. To suppose, however, that they could act fairly, is to ascribe to them superhuman virtue. Even if the trial was not a strictly political one, those who prepared the evidence were, by the very nature of their employment, interested in making out a case; and it must be remembered that, to all intents and purposes, the previous examination was the real trial. Excepting, indeed, where political passions were aroused against the Government, it was not to be expected that twelve men, utterly inexperienced in the difficult task of sifting evidence, could come to a fair conclusion, when all the legal talent of the bench and the bar was arrayed on one side, and on the other was a poor helpless prisoner, charged with the basest crimes, and utterly unprepared, from the circumstances in which he was placed, to stand up, alone and unprotected, against the storm which was sweeping down upon him from every side.

Proceedings in the Star-Chamber. Naturally enough, the Government were exceedingly jealous of any imputations which might be thrown upon the justice of their proceedings. At Weston's execution a number of persons present asked him whether he were really guilty or not. He refused to give any explicit answer, acknowledging that he died worthily, and saying that he had left his mind behind with the Chief Justice. Two of the questioners, Sir John Holles and Sir John Wentworth, were summoned before the Star-Chamber on a charge of having virtually impugned the decision of the Court, and were condemned to fine and imprisonment.

Two other persons were also imprisoned by order of the Council for the same reasons. At the same time Lumsden, a dependent of Somerset's, was also fined and imprisoned for presenting a petition to the King, in which he stated that Weston had declared that the statements which he had made during his examination had been untrue.*

Trials of Mrs. Turner,

On the 7th of November Mrs. Turner was brought up for trial. The story of the apothecary's boy was put as much into the background as possible, and the prosecution rested their case upon the conviction of Weston as a principal in the murder. Assuming, as they did, that the verdict against him had been true, they had little difficulty in showing that Mrs. Turner had been accessory to his proceedings. In the course of the trial a curious scene took place. After some letters of Lady Somerset's, of the most indecent character, had been read, some magic scrolls and images were produced in court, which had been used by Dr. Forman and Mrs. Turner. Whilst they were being examined, a crack was heard in one of the scaffolds, probably caused by the crowding of the spectators to see the exhibition. The impression produced by the noise was, that the devil himself had come into the court, and had chosen this method of testifying his displeasure at the disclosure of his secrets. So great was the confusion in consequence, that a quarter of an hour passed before order was restored.

As a matter of course, the prisoner was found guilty. Though attempts were made, after the trial, to extract additional information from her, no evidence of importance was obtained, and she died with expressions of sorrow on her lips for the crime in which she, at least, had taken a principal part.†

and of Helwys.

Helwys was the next who was called upon for his defence. As far as the evidence went which was brought against him, there was nothing inconsistent with his own

* The King to the Commissioners, Oct. 21, 1615, *S. P. Dom.* lxxxii. 80. *State Trials*, ii. 1021; *Carew Letters*, 17. All excepting Holles and Lumsden were released within little more than two months after the sentence, and Holles was certainly at liberty in the following July.

† *State Trials*, ii. 929; Amos, 219. Castle to Miller, Nov. 28, 1615; *Court and Times*, i. 376.

CH. XIII. 1615. account of the part which he had taken. It was shown that he had entered into an intrigue of some kind or another with Northampton; but that he had been directly guilty of giving culpable aid to Weston was not proved. He might, as far as anything was shown in court, have contented himself with hindering Weston from administering the poison, although, from fear of losing his place, he did not give information of what was going on. Under these circumstances he made a not unsuccessful defence, and it was generally expected by the spectators that he would be acquitted, when Coke produced a confession which had been made by Franklin, the person from whom the poison had been procured, that very morning. In this Franklin declared that he had once been present when Lady Somerset put into his hands a letter which she had received from Helwys, in which he wrote of Overbury that, 'The more he was cursed the better he fared.' It is true that Franklin's character was very bad, and that he showed a tendency to fling his accusations broadcast, in hopes of procuring his own safety; yet, as Helwys never denied the words, it may be taken for granted that he really wrote the letter. This sudden production of new evidence struck him dumb at once, and the jury, seeing the impression made upon him, took it as an evidence of guilt, and brought in a verdict of guilty. Yet, even if we admit that Helwys wrote the words attributed to him, it does not necessarily follow that he had promoted the murder. They only show that he had been careless of Overbury's life, and would have been quite satisfied to see him die, if his disease should happen to carry him off.* The same may be said of the statements which he made previously to his execution.† Even if he was culpably negligent in not at once removing Weston from his post, and if he was satisfied in not having himself a hand in the murder,

* *State Trials*, ii. 935. If Northampton's letter, as printed in the second report of Somerset's trial (Amos, 141), is correct, there can be no farther doubt of Helwys's fullest complicity. But the documentary evidence in this report is not, by any means, to be trusted.

† The worst was his admission that, upon Weston's saying, 'Why they will have me give it him first or last,' he said, 'Let it be done so I know not of it.'—Amos, 215.

it must be remembered that there is no proof whatever that any poison was actually administered, excepting by the apothecary's boy, and that no evidence was ever alleged that of this Helwys had any knowledge at all.

Trial of Franklin.

On the day after Helwys's trial, Franklin was placed at the bar. He could not deny that he had procured the poisons for Mrs. Turner. After a short deliberation the jury brought in a verdict of guilty against him too. Before he was executed he threw out wild hints of the existence of a plot far exceeding in villainy that which was in the course of investigation. He tried to induce all who would listen to him to believe that he knew of a conspiracy in which many great lords were concerned; and that not only the late Prince had been removed by unfair means, but that a plan had been made to get rid of the Electress Palatine and her husband. As, however, all this was evidently only dictated by a hope of escaping the gallows, he was allowed to share with the others the fate which he richly deserved.

Sir T. Monson's trial postponed.

Of the four who had now been executed, Franklin and Mrs. Turner were undoubtedly guilty; of the criminal participation of the other two, doubts may reasonably be entertained. There was still one more of the inferior criminals to be brought to the bar of the Guildhall, and against him not a particle of reasonable evidence was in existence. Sir Thomas Monson had, indeed, assisted in recommending Weston to Helwys, and had had something to do with the correspondence which passed between Overbury and Somerset; but that seems to have been the extent to which he went. On the 4th of December he was arraigned, but he was informed by Coke that he was suspected of worse crimes than that for which he was now called in question, and that the trial would be postponed, in order that the investigation might be completed. It is said also that Coke dropped hints that he had come upon the traces of a plot of no ordinary magnitude, and that he even let it be understood that he had discovered evidence that Prince Henry had met his death by violent means.* There can be no doubt that, although Coke had no intention of sparing Franklin's life, his imagination was

* *State Trials*, ii. 949.

CH. XIII. 1615.

greatly excited by his disclosures. He had imparted to the King his supposed discovery without doing more than darkly indicating its nature.* At the same time we know, from the best authority, that James had looked over the evidence against Monson, and had come to the conclusion that no sufficient proof existed against him.† This feeling on the part of the King, coupled with a desire to know more about Coke's mystery, would be quite enough to account for his giving directions for the postponement of the trial.‡

Coke did his best to follow up the scent, but he did not find that it led to much. All that he was able to discover were such valuable facts as that, on a certain occasion, more than six months before his death, Prince Henry had eaten some dried fruits which had been prepared by a Roman Catholic confectioner, and that the cook who prepared the tarts which were sent to Overbury had once been in the Prince's service.§

Information extracted from Cotton.

There was, however, another quarter in which Coke was more successful. On the 26th of October, the King had written to some of the Privy Councillors, informing them that he had been told that Sir Robert Cotton had communicated information of importance to the Spanish Ambassador, and requiring them to examine him, and, if it were found to be the case, to sequester his papers, and to take proceedings against him.‖ What was the immediate result does not appear, but Digby was written to, in order that he might give any additional

* Coke's letter, printed in Amos, 392, presupposes a former letter to the King to this effect.

† Examination of John Lepton, Feb. 2, 1616, *S. P. Dom.* lxxxvi. 31.

‡ Weldon's story of the King's discovering, the night before the trial, that Monson meant to say something disagreeable, and of his sending, in consequence, to Coke to let him see the evidence, and then returning a message that it was insufficient, refutes itself. The King was at Newmarket, and there was not time for all this in the course of a single night. Besides, Coke's letter, just quoted, contains no reference to messages passing in such desperate haste. If it is still supposed that there may have been some foundation for the story, it must be remembered that Monson had it in his power to make the King very uncomfortable, as he must have known all about the Spanish pensions from his brother Sir W. Monson.

§ Amos, 482. For other charges of a similar description, see Bacon's *Works* (ed. Montagu), vii. 417.

‖ *Court and Times,* i. 371. For the date, see *S. P. Dom.* lxxxii. 111.

information in his power on the subject of the pensions, and especially as to Somerset's connection with Spain. He answered,* that Sir William Monson could give more information on the subject of the pensions than any other man; and that, as to Somerset, he believed that he had been careless, and had shown important State papers to persons who had allowed them to get abroad, but that he had no reason to suppose that he had ever accepted either a pension or a reward of any kind from the Spanish Government. Somerset had, however, been carrying on an intrigue with the Ambassador by means of Cotton. If Cotton were arrested, he would tell what had happened. Accordingly, Cotton was placed in confinement,† and probably confessed to taking papers from Somerset to the Ambassador. Not long afterwards, Sir William Monson was committed, and Digby was sent for to return to England, in order to give further explanations.

Coke on a wrong scent.

When Digby arrived, he found that Coke had, in the course of his investigations, discovered that one of the despatches which he had himself written with an account of the pensions had fallen into Somerset's hands, and that he had come to the conclusion, which was perhaps not unnatural, that Somerset had kept back the paper from the King in order to conceal his own supposed participation in the Spanish bribes. Digby accordingly remonstrated with the King at these proceedings on Coke's part, which could only lead to disagreeable consequences by spreading abroad information respecting the pensions, with which Somerset had nothing whatever to do. A few days afterwards he was called upon to confer with the Chancellor and with Bacon on the questions which were to be put to Cotton. Much to Bacon's dissatisfaction, when the subject of the pensions was again brought up, Digby positively refused to say a word, alleging that he had the King's warrant to be silent.

What followed upon this is not very clear. We have an undated examination of Cotton, in which he acknow-

* Appendix III. 2. † On the 29th of Dec., *Carew Letters*, 21.

CH. XIII. 1616. ledges having taken to the Spanish Ambassador Lerma's paper of demands. Digby was commanded to acquaint Bacon and the Chancellor with the secret of the pensions, and both Cotton and Somerset were again examined.* Coke was apparently compelled to withdraw from his unprofitable investigations,† and Cotton was some little time afterwards set at liberty.

It was not till the beginning of April that Digby assured the examiners of Somerset's innocence of any connection with the pensions. Three months before this, the Earl and Countess had been indicted before the grand jury at Westminster, and a true bill was then found against them.‡ The trial itself, however, was postponed, no doubt in order to wait for Digby's evidence. Lady Somerset had, in her hour of misfortune, been delivered of her only child, a daughter, who lived to be the mother of the Lord Russell whose execution is one of the darkest blots upon the memory of James's grandson. The Countess was allowed to remain with her child till the 27th of March, when she was sent to the Tower, where her husband had been imprisoned for some weeks previously. The only sign of emotion which she showed was in her urgent entreaty that she might not be sent to the lodgings which had once been occupied by Overbury: a request which was at once acceded to.§

In the proceedings at the Guildhall, Bacon had taken

* Cott. MS., Tit. B., vii. 489. Appendix III. 3. Bacon's *Works* (ed. Montagu), vi. 221, 226; vii. 407. This examination, most probably, was taken about this time.

† If it is true that Coke's proceedings with reference to these trials brought him into disfavour with the King, there is quite enough to explain it without adopting the gratuitous hypothesis that James had a hand in the murder. Coke let it be known that he believed that Prince Henry had been murdered, on the exceedingly slender grounds which have been already mentioned. Indeed, it would seem, from the length of time which, according to Coke's theory in this and the Overbury case, poisons might remain in the system without affecting life, anyone might be accused of poisoning who had ever supplied food to any person who died long afterwards under suspicious circumstances. Coke's blunder about the pensions too, though far more excusable, must have been still more provoking to James.

‡ *Carew Letters*, 23.

§ Chamberlain to Carleton, April 6, 1616. *Court and Times*, i. 395. She was at first lodged in the Lieutenant's own room, and then in Raleigh's apartments, which had been just vacated by him.

no part whatever. Either from disinclination to appear upon a stage which Coke had made so peculiarly his own, or from a natural dislike to scenes of this kind, he had allowed the prosecutions to be conducted by others. But the same reasons did not apply to the trials of the Earl and Countess. As peers of the realm, they would be summoned not before the ordinary judges, but before the High Steward's Court, which consisted of a certain number of peers summoned by the Lord High Steward, who was always a peer specially appointed by the King for the occasion. Consequently, though Coke would be present with the other judges, he would not sit in any place of authority.

Part taken by Bacon in the cases of the prisoners.

Nor was the scene itself in which Bacon was called upon to take part one which was unsuited to those powers of manœuvring which he possessed, and on which he looked with too great complacency for his own fame. He knew beforehand that he was not about to engage in the uncongenial operation of hunting to death a suspected person, who might possibly be innocent. He was aware that it was the King's intention to pardon the prisoners, and that it devolved upon him to do his best to procure a condemnation from the peers, at the same time that he took care to leave an excuse to James for exercising his prerogative of mercy.

His knowledge of the King's intention to pardon the Earl and Countess.

The correspondence in which he engaged with the King on the subject of the trials stands in striking contrast with the language which Coke had used on the same subject; a contrast which is by no means in favour of Bacon. Coke's errors were those of a man who rushes headlong into a delicate investigation, and who blindly grasps at everything which suits his purpose, whilst he no less blindly flings aside everything which contradicts the conclusion at which he has arrived. Bacon's errors were those of a man who, after calmly surveying the field before him, deliberately goes astray, and speaks, without passion or excitement of any kind, of treating the solemn provision of the law for the trial of criminals as if it were a mere sham, which would be useful to veil the designs of the King from the eyes of the world. With regard to the prisoners themselves,

Character of his correspondence with the King.

CH. XIII. 1616.

Bacon's opinion on the question of Somerset's guilt.

neither he nor anyone else could have any doubt whatever of the guilt of the lady. Somerset's case was, however, by no means a simple one. There were arguments of very great weight which might be brought on either side. To us, who look calmly on the whole affair, and who are in possession of some evidence which perhaps Bacon had not seen,* it seems to be more than probable that Somerset was an innocent man; but there is no reason to doubt that Bacon might have come to a very different conclusion in perfect good faith. In all probability he frequently talked the matter over with the King, but of those conversations no record has been left. His opinion seems to have been that, although it was exceedingly probable that Somerset was guilty, yet, that the evidence being incomplete, there was no absolute certainty to be attained.†

His efforts to procure a conviction.

The inference which would be drawn from this by an Attorney-General in our own time, would be, that it was unfair as well as inexpedient to prosecute a man of whose guilt he was not himself thoroughly convinced. The inference which was drawn by Bacon was, that it was proper to bring the prisoner before the Court, to produce the evidence, and to do all that was in his power to procure a conviction, because he was aware that the conviction would not be followed by the death of the supposed criminal.

It is, happily, not necessary at the present day to point out the profound immorality of such a conclusion, or to do more than simply to state the fact, in passing, that such a course is as degrading to the lawyer who allows himself to be influenced by such reasons, as it is demoralising to the whole society in the midst of which a solemn investigation is allowed to take place under such circumstances. It is impossible to maintain a due regard for the courts of justice when such a trial as this is treated by the officers of the Government as a scene

* That is to say, of some of the papers printed in Appendix IV. As they are not to be found among the *State Papers*, it is probable that they were not in the possession of the Government. This, however, is by no means a necessary inference.

† In his letter to the King of the 28th of April, Bacon acknowledges that the evidence 'rests chiefly upon presumptions.'

which it is necessary to enact with as much dignity as possible, but which it is totally unnecessary to regard as having any influence whatever on the ultimate fate of the prisoner.

His erroneous ideas.

But it is one thing to be convinced that Bacon allowed himself to take part in a miserable intrigue; it is another thing to assert that he was conscious of doing anything which was wrong. In fact, the point of view from which State trials were regarded at the beginning of the seventeenth century was one which it is now impossible to bring before the mind without considerable effort. That the part taken by the officials in conducting the examination was of far more importance than that taken by the judge and the jury in open court, was a belief which could hardly fail to root itself in the minds of those who went through the toil of conducting those examinations. It was hardly in the course of nature that they should resist the liability to regard the trial itself as a hard necessity which had to be endured, as a form which must be gone through in order to satisfy the people, but which could scarcely be expected to be of any value as a means of eliciting truth. If, therefore, those who had previously investigated the case came to the conclusion that the prisoner was probably guilty, but that the evidence was not perfectly satisfactory, they would without difficulty fall into the miserable error of thinking that it was necessary, for the credit of the Government, that a verdict should be obtained, but that everything would be well done if a pardon were afterwards to be granted. In order to come to such a conclusion as this, however, it was necessary to adopt another theory, which has since been wisely rejected by all English lawyers. That theory was, that it was the duty of the Court to find the prisoner guilty, unless there was some positive reason to suppose that he was innocent. It is this theory which comes out unexpectedly in one of Bacon's letters, which, utterly unintelligible as it is to the present generation, may enable us to understand how he reconciled it with his conscience to act the part which he took in these trials. If Somerset was in all probability guilty, and if it was the duty of

CH. XIII. 1616.

the Court to convict a man against whom no more decisive evidence could be brought, he may have fancied that he was doing no wrong in helping the Court to do its duty, whilst at the same time he was helping the King to do his.*

His views on the question of pardoning the prisoners.

Even if it be admitted that Bacon may very well have pursued the course which he took from other than consciously base motives, the way in which he viewed the question of the pardon which James was prepared to give to both the prisoners, cannot be viewed otherwise than as a symptom of a want of delicate moral perceptions. He ought to have perceived at a glance the truth which lay at the bottom of Weston's hope that the great fishes would not be allowed to escape at the expense of the lesser ones, and to have used all the eloquence of which he was possessed to persuade the King that justice could not be satisfied unless those who were in high places shared the lot of their meaner accomplices. Unfortunately, he did nothing of the sort. His habit of looking upon reasons of State as something sufficient to justify exceptional proceedings; his custom of thinking of the prerogative as a power lifted above the ordinary laws which regulated the proceedings of subjects; and his undue deference for the wishes of the King (who was, by his office, the very foundation-stone upon which the whole political edifice rested), made him blind to the true bearing of the case. He cast about for one reason and another to justify the course which James was determined to take. He allowed himself to adopt such sophisms as that the blood of Overbury had been already sufficiently avenged; that the downfall from their places of dignity would be sufficient punishment for such great persons; and that, if they could be brought to confess their fault, their penitence would be sufficient to call for mercy.

* 'For certainly there may be an evidence so balanced, as it may have sufficient matter for the conscience of the peers to convict him, and yet leave sufficient matter in the conscience of a king upon the same evidence to pardon his life; because the peers are astringed by necessity either to acquit or condemn; but grace is free: and, for my part, I think the evidence in this present case will be of such a nature.'—Bacon to the King, April 28, 1616. *Works* (ed. Montagu), vi. 231.

CH. XIII. 1616.

Reasons why the King desired to pardon the prisoners.

The reasons which moved James to desire to pardon the prisoners were of a very mixed nature. If he did not still retain any great regard for Somerset, it would undoubtedly have been very much against his wishes to send to execution a man with whom he had lived for so many years upon terms of such intimate familiarity.* In the case of Lady Somerset, he had less personal reason for standing in the way of justice; but he could not but feel that it would be hard for him to meet the Lord Treasurer, day after day, if he had consigned his daughter to a murderess's grave. Nor is it impossible that he may have remembered that he had himself been to blame for that too early marriage, which was the root from which all these evils had sprung. No doubt he ought to have set such feelings aside, but it would have been most discreditable to him if he had not entertained them. In addition to these reasons, he must have felt that, as regarded the Earl at least, the evidence was not completely satisfactory. His doubts on this point manifested themselves in an extreme anxiety to induce the accused man to confess that he was guilty. The little tricks to which he condescended, in order to attain the desired end, were innumerable. But it was all in vain. Somerset maintained that he was an innocent man, and that he had no confession to make.

Somerset threatens to accuse the King.

A few days before the trial, Somerset threatened to bring some charge or other against the King himself. James at once wrote to Sir George More, the new Lieutenant of the Tower, telling him that this was merely 'some trick of' his prisoner's 'idle brain;' that it was easy to see that he intended to threaten him by laying an aspersion upon him 'of being in some sort accessory to his crime.' All he could say was that, if he had any message to send about the poisoning, there was no necessity to send it in private; if he wished to communicate with him on any other subject, he must wait till

* It is generally said that he cannot have been influenced by such feelings, as he was already tired of Somerset. The letter, however, which he wrote in the beginning of 1615, proves that, though he was extremely dissatisfied with his conduct, he was by no means indifferent to him: and it has been shown that there is a probability that, in the latter part of the summer, they were on better terms with one another.

CH. XIII. 1616. after the trial, as he could not listen to him then without incurring the suspicion of having in reality been accessory to the crime.

A day or two later Somerset's resistance seems to have taken another turn. He declared that he would not go to his trial, on the plea, as it appears, of sickness.* On the very night before the day for which his trial was fixed, he made, if we are to believe a not very safe authority, another desperate effort to save himself from being brought to the bar. Sir George More came to the King, and as soon as he was awakened, told him what Somerset had been saying. What the words were we do not know; but the King seemed much disturbed, and offered a great reward to More if he would help him out of his difficulty. More accordingly went back to the Tower, and persuaded Somerset to go down quietly to Westminster. As soon as he was there, he took measures against any outbreak by providing two men who were to hurry him off, if he attempted to make any attack upon the King. It is also said that the King was excessively nervous during the whole day of the trial, till he knew that everything had passed off quietly.†

Even if we admit the truth of this last story, there is nothing here which is not easily explicable without resorting to any of those strange hypotheses in which

* The King to Sir George More (Amos, 273, 276). It is not quite clear whether he pretended to be sick or not. The supposition that James had anything to do with the Overbury murder is quite inadmissible. It is not only in contradiction with all that we know of his character, but it is rendered improbable by these letters themselves. If it had been true, would James have refused to receive any private message from Somerset? would he have sent Lord Hay and Sir Robert Carr to see him? Murderers, if they choose anybody to be a confidant of their secrets, would take care not to double the danger of disclosure by employing two persons where one would be sufficient. Again, it is plain that when James wrote that Somerset intended to threaten him, Somerset himself had not actually done so. It is not likely that James would have been the first to put the idea into More's head. But, in fact, the theory above referred to, stands on no basis sufficiently solid to admit of argument. It is impossible to prove a negative in such a case.

† Weldon's story is, that More persuaded Somerset to go, by telling him that he would have merely to appear, but that there would be no trial. But it is impossible to put any credit in the details of Weldon's stories. The fact of the King's nervousness, however, is placed beyond doubt by a letter of Sherburn to Carleton, May 31, 1616, *S. P.* lxxxvii. 40.

modern writers have so often taken refuge. The King, it may easily be supposed, desired to obtain a confession, because, though he believed Somerset to be guilty, he wished for some fuller assurance than was to be obtained from the evidence. Somerset, on the other hand, knowing himself to be innocent, having failed to persuade anyone of the fact, stood at bay, and threatened to accuse the King of anything that came to hand. James, having a distinct recollection of the language which Somerset had employed towards him at the beginning of the previous year, and remembering how little he had allowed himself to be influenced by considerations of his own interest on that occasion, naturally dreaded a repetition in open court of the scenes to which he had submitted in private. Nor was Somerset altogether without information which would, if he had chosen to produce it, have been exceedingly damaging to James. He knew, for instance, that a certain number of the King's Ministers had been at one time in receipt of pensions from Spain, and that James, after he had learned the fact, had not dismissed them from their posts. He knew also that, during the past year, James had been dallying with proposals for an alliance with Spain, and he might easily have erected on these facts a charge which would have been accepted from one end of the kingdom to the other. It is easy to say that James ought to have known that Somerset would not dare to fling away the only chance of life which he possessed, by conduct of this kind. Even if James had been a cooler calculator of probabilities than he was, there was something in Somerset's nature which made it extremely difficult to calculate what he would do in any given circumstances.

The right thing for James to have done would no doubt have been, to bid Somerset to do his worst. But there is a penalty awaiting every Government which envelopes its proceedings in mystery. James was now reaping the fruits of the seed which he had sown when he had caused a prosecution to be set on foot against Whitelocke for questioning the justice of his acts. He had proclaimed abroad on that occasion, that his actions

CH. XIII. 1616.

were to be preserved from the contamination of free discussion. Three years only had passed away, and he was trembling before the empty threats of a prisoner whom all agreed to consider as a murderer. It was because he had never allowed his assertions to be contradicted, that he discovered, when it was too late, that he might speak the truth without obtaining belief in his veracity.

Arrangements for the trial.

Bacon had been for some time engaged in arranging with the King the manner in which it was intended that the trial should be conducted. Bacon's first wish was that the wild stories which Coke had adopted from Franklin should be kept out of sight, and that the evidence should be restricted to that which had a direct bearing on the case.* He had also made arrangements for withdrawing the Countess from the court as soon as possible, lest she should make public declaration of her husband's innocence,† and had proposed that a similar course should be pursued towards Somerset himself, if he allowed himself to use language derogatory of the King's honour.

Trial of the Countess.

On the 24th of May the Countess of Somerset took her place in Westminster Hall, as a prisoner, at the bar of the High Steward's Court. It was to this that the passions and the frivolities of her young life had led her. The Hall was crowded with the faces of men who had come to look upon her misery as upon a spectacle. No wonder that, whilst the indictment was being read, she turned pale and trembled, and that when she heard the name of Weston first mentioned, she hid her face behind her fan. When the indictment had been read, she was asked, according to the usual form, whether she was guilty. The evidence was too plain, and there was nothing for it but to plead guilty. After Bacon had made a statement of her connection with the poisoning,

* This seems to be the meaning of the letter of the 22nd of January (Bacon's *Works*, ed. Montagu, vi. 219). In asking for the choice of a 'Steward of judgment that may be able to moderate the evidence and cut off digressions,' Bacon, probably, was thinking of the way in which Essex's trial had been allowed to lapse into a scene of mutual recrimination.

† Bacon to Villiers, May 10, 1616 (*Works*, ed. Montagu, vii. 422).

she was asked whether she had anything to say why judgment should not be given against her. In a voice which could scarcely be heard, she said that she could not extenuate her fault. She desired mercy, and begged that the Lords would intercede for her with the King. Ellesmere upon this pronounced judgment, and the prisoner was taken back to the Tower, to wait for the King's decision.* CH. XIII. 1616.

Trial of the Earl.

On the following morning, her husband took his place at the bar. All the efforts which had been made to wring a confession from him had been in vain. In spite of threats and promises, he pleaded not guilty. After a few words from Montagu, Bacon opened the case. He spoke of the horrible nature of the crime which had been committed, a crime from which no man could ensure his safety, and which, when it was once committed, it was almost impossible to detect. He then proceeded to lay down the doctrine which, however iniquitous it might be, was generally accepted at the time, that the Peers were bound to consider the verdict in Weston's case as fully proved, so that they might not allow themselves to raise any questions as to the fact of the poison having been administered, as that verdict declared. All that he had to prove was that Somerset was accessory to the murder, the facts of which must be taken for granted. He then gave his account of the connection which had existed between the prisoner and the murdered man. Somerset, he told the Court, had been on terms of the closest intimacy with Overbury, till he found that his dependant did his best to deter him from the marriage upon which he had set his heart. Upon this Somerset grew alarmed, as he had entrusted Overbury with important state secrets, which might be easily used to his ruin. At the same time, Lady Somerset and Northampton agreed in hating the man who was opposing the marriage out of dislike

Bacon's speech.

* *State Trials*, ii. 951. Chamberlain says, 'She won pity by her sober demeanour, which, in my opinion, was more curious and confident than was fit for a lady in such distress, yet she said or made show of some tears divers times.' Chamberlain to Carleton, May 25, 1616, *Court and Times*, i. 406. It is easy to see that there was a difference of feeling on the part of the observers. Chamberlain was evidently in a critical mood.

CH. XIII. 1616.

both to the lady herself and to the whole family of the Howards. It was agreed amongst them that Overbury should be invited to go abroad, whilst Somerset was to induce him to refuse the employment offered to him. An excuse would in this way be found for his committal to the Tower, where it would be easy to get rid of him by poison. Whilst Weston, by Mrs. Turner's direction, was giving him one poison after another, Somerset was doing what he could to prevent his obtaining his enlargement from the King. Bacon then stated that there was evidence in possession of the Government sufficient to prove four points: namely, that Somerset bore malice to Overbury before his imprisonment; that he contrived the scheme by which that imprisonment was effected; that he actually sent poisons to the Tower; and that he did his best to suppress the proofs of his guilt. The first two of these he proposed to deal with himself, the others would be left to Montagu and Crew, who were his assistants in conducting the prosecution.

Evidence produced by him.

There could be little difficulty in proving the two points which Bacon had selected for himself, as they referred to facts of which there could be no reasonable doubt. The letters which Overbury had written, together with Somerset's answers to Northampton, were now available as evidence, having been brought to Coke by the person to whom they had been delivered for the purpose of concealing them. By means of these and of some other evidence which was produced, it was shown beyond a doubt, that Somerset had entrusted Overbury with state secrets, and that Overbury considered that he had been ill-treated by his patron. But when Bacon proceeded to argue that it was the fear of the disclosure of these state secrets which made Somerset desirous of putting Overbury to death, he was simply begging the question at issue.*

* 'That,' he says, 'might rather cause him to fear him than the hindrance of his marriage; if that had been it alone, his going beyond sea would have served the turn.' Not at all, if he was afraid that Overbury might give information to the Court then sitting, which would lead it to reject the suit for the dissolution of marriage. He might do this by letter; which was the very thing he was prevented from doing in the Tower.

With the second point there was as little difficulty. Somerset had himself acknowledged that he had had a hand in procuring Overbury's imprisonment, and it was easy to establish the fact that he had taken part in the appointment of Helwys and Weston. Passages were also produced from Northampton's letters to Somerset, which proved that there had been some plot in which they had both been concerned, and that Helwys had expressed his opinion that Overbury's death would be a satisfactory termination to his imprisonment.* As soon as Bacon had concluded the part which had been assigned to him, Ellesmere pressed Somerset to acknowledge his guilt. 'My lord,' was Somerset's reply, 'I came hither with a resolution to defend myself.'

CH. XIII. 1616.

Montagu's argument.

The evidence by which it was intended to prove that the poison had actually been administered with Somerset's knowledge, was then produced by Montagu. He first showed that Somerset had been in the habit of sending powders to Overbury. Being, however, destitute of even a shadow of evidence to prove that the powders were poisonous, he was obliged to fall back upon the irrelevant assertion that four several juries had declared by their verdicts that they were poison. He then produced a letter of the Countess of Somerset's, written to Helwys, to prove that the tarts and jellies sent had contained poison, and from which, by the interpretation of an expression which had been disavowed by Lady Somerset herself, he attempted to show that Somerset had been the person who had sent them. That there had been any poison in the tarts at all, was supported by a declaration of Lady Somerset; but we have no means of knowing whether it might not have been made after she had discovered that it was impossible to make any satisfactory defence for herself, and

* In the printed trial it is said that the Lieutenant concludes that Overbury 'will recover and do good offices betwixt my Lord of Suffolk and you, which, if he do not, you shall have reason to count him a knave; or else, that he shall not recover at all, which he thinks the most sure and happy change of all.' In the other report, the last sentence stands, 'but the best is not to suffer him to recover.' If Northampton really had written this, it is inconceivable that no more use should have been made of it by the prosecution.

CH. XIII. 1616.

when she was ready to confess anything that her examiners wished. Even if there had been poison in the tarts, it would be necessary to show something more than that the tarts had been originally sent from his kitchen. Accordingly, a deposition of Franklin's was produced, in which he declared that Lady Somerset had shown him a letter written by the Earl whilst Overbury was in prison, in which he said that 'he wondered these things were not yet despatched;' and added, that 'Overbury was like to come out within a few days, if Weston did not ply himself.' Montagu took care not to breathe a syllable of the worthless trash which Franklin had sought to palm off upon the examiners in hopes of obtaining a pardon, which would have been sufficient to prove that no credit whatever ought to be given to the most solemn declarations of so unblushing a liar.

Crew's argument.

The attempt to show that Somerset had had any connection whatever with the administration of poisons to Overbury having thus, according to our notions, thoroughly broken down, and not even an attempt having been made to prove that he had so much as heard of the bribe which had been given to the apothecary's boy, by whom the murder, as far as we can judge, was actually effected, Serjeant Crew rose, and took up the comparatively easy task of drawing inferences from the subsequent proceedings of Somerset. His suppression of the letters which had been written at the time, and his attempt to procure a pardon from the King, were undoubtedly indications that Somerset had done something of which he was ashamed. But that they proved that he had poisoned Overbury, was another matter altogether, which Crew himself could only take for granted.

Close of the case for the prosecution.

Upon this the case for the prosecution was closed. In our own day the counsel who would appear on behalf of the prisoner would have little trouble in overthrowing the evidence which had been produced. He would probably content himself with pointing out, in a few short words, that no sufficient proof had been alleged that Overbury had ever been poisoned at all, and that, if he had been, it had certainly not been shown that Somerset had had anything whatever to do with the crime.

Difficulties of Somerset.

How different was the case when Somerset stood at the bar to reply to the charges which had been brought against him! He knew that there were some amongst his judges who had long been prejudiced against him, and that even if they came with the most honest intentions, they had never been trained to the difficult task of sifting evidence so as to arrive at the truth, and that they were liable to be led away both by their own feelings and by the skill and eloquence of the lawyers who had been previously addressing them. He was allowed no counsel to undertake his defence, and, unpractised as he was, he was called on to point out the defects in a long train of evidence, of much of which he had, on that day, heard for the first time, without the power of summoning any witnesses, or of producing any evidence which it had not suited the purposes of the Crown lawyers to bring forward of their own accord.

All these difficulties Somerset laboured under, in common with every man who, in those days, stood in the position which he was occupying. But there was one obstacle in his way which was peculiar to himself. It was necessary for him not only to show that the evidence against him was insufficient to justify his condemnation, but to make out a story in which the facts were sufficient to account for the suspicious circumstances connected with the imprisonment of Overbury, and with the subsequent destruction of the letters which he had written and received at that time. Unless, however, there is something utterly inexplicable in the whole affair, this story would not bear telling. He could not well tell the Court that he had entered into an adulterous connection with Lady Essex before the dissolution of the marriage, and that he had plotted and intrigued to detain Overbury in prison, through fear lest he should give evidence which might prevent the passing of the sentence of divorce, which his paramour was then desirous to obtain by means of false

CH. XIII. 1616. representations. And if he had told this tale of shame in the face of the world, what hope was there that the Peers would believe him, or, if they did believe him, that they would abstain from pronouncing a verdict against him, which they might easily justify to themselves by the loose views which prevailed in that age? Yet, it is hardly possible that anything less than this can be imagined which will account for the facts which had been proved by the evidence which was before the Court.

Whatever may have been his faults, and even his crimes, it is impossible not to look with some respect upon the man who stood up, exhausted as he was by the long course of the trial, to make his defence in what he must have known to be a hopeless cause, rather than purchase the pardon which was held out to him by confessing himself to be guilty of a murder of which he was innocent. It was late in the evening when he began to plead in defence of his honour rather than of his life. The daylight had died away before the Crown lawyers had done their part, and the torches threw their glaring light over the faces which were all turned in one direction, to hear what defence could possibly be made by the man of whom such a tale could be told as that to which they had just been listening.

His defence.

He began by acknowledging that he had consented to Overbury's imprisonment, in order to put it out of his power to hinder his marriage with Lady Essex. If any means had been used to poison Overbury whilst he was in prison, he had known nothing of it. As to Northampton's letters, they proved nothing against him. He then referred to the letter which, according to Franklin, had been written by him, and which formed one of the strongest parts of the evidence against him. 'If this letter,' he said, 'be to be produced, if Frances ever confessed that I did ever send such a letter unto her, I am then guilty and convicted without excuse; but I call Heaven now to witness I never wrote any such letter, neither can such be produced. Let not you, then, my noble Peers, rely upon the memorative relation of such a villain as Franklin, neither think it a hard request when I humbly desire you to weigh my protestations, my oath upon my honour and conscience, against the lewd information of so bad a miscreant.' He then proceeded to answer the charge of having been concerned in sending poisons to the Tower. The tarts, he said, which he had sent were good; if his wife had sent any in which poison had been mixed, this was nothing to him. As for the powders, he had received them from Sir Robert Killigrew, and sent them on; and Overbury had himself acknowledged, in a letter which was before the Court, that he had not suffered from them. Here he was interrupted by Crew, who told him that the three powders which he had received from Killigrew had been otherwise accounted for. The powder in question was one not sent by Killigrew, and must have been poison. The discrepancy was not material, as it was not likely that Somerset would remember the exact history of the powders which he had sent to Overbury two years before, and that this fourth powder, however acquired, was poison was a mere assertion of the lawyers. But with the general feeling of the Court against him, Somerset's inability to explain the origin of this powder was undoubtedly damaging to his case. Nor were his explanations as to his reason for destroying the papers and obtaining the pardon altogether satisfactory.

The verdict.

When he had concluded his defence, the Lords retired to consider their verdict. On the one hand they had heard an argument which had no inherent improbability in itself, and which was supported by a chain of evidence of which they, at least, were unable to see the deficiencies. On the other hand, the prisoner's defence had been made with courage and ability, but it was not without some reticence on points which it was necessary to clear up. He had failed to prove his innocence to be beyond question, and the Peers unanimously agreed to pronounce him guilty. Somerset, after expressing a hope that the Court would intercede with the King for mercy, was removed from the bar.*

* Amos, 65–111; 122–156. It is difficult to say what is the principle upon which the differences between the reports rest. The two reports of Lady Somerset's letter show that neither reporter had access to the docu-

CH. XIII. 1616. Pardon of the Countess.

It was now left to the King to decide what he would do. The proper course for him to have taken would have been to pardon the Earl, on the ground of insufficiency in the evidence, and to send the Countess to execution. It was in vain for him to flatter himself that justice could be satisfied on any terms short of this. Whatever might be thought of the other actors in the tragedy, if there had been one thing which had been more plainly proved than another, it was that Lady Somerset had been the main instigator and author of the murder. It was cruelly unjust to take away the lives of her tools, whilst she herself was allowed to escape. Yet James never seems to have entertained the thought of allowing the sentence to pass upon her. Her youth and beauty, her powerful friends, her very womanhood, with its impulsive, passionate nature, all concurred to plead hard for her. On the 13th of July her pardon was sealed,* though the imprisonment in the Tower was not remitted. Before it was completed it had been sent back to Bacon, with directions† that he should insert in it the false excuse that she had been drawn into crime 'by the procurement and wicked instigation of certain base persons.' Bacon, without making any objection, inserted the clause at once.

Somerset's life is spared.

We are left to depend upon conjecture for the motives which James allowed to influence him in sparing Somerset's life. We know that he refused to allow his arms to be taken down from amongst those of the other Knights of the Garter at St. George's chapel at Windsor. We also gain glimpses of a negotiation which was going on, by which Somerset might have obtained a pardon if he had chosen to submit to the conditions offered.‡ A

ments read in Court, as do also the mistakes in the nicknames applied to persons in the Overbury correspondence. If this is the case it would not be right to attribute the alterations in the first report to an official hand. Yet some of the discrepancies noticed by Mr. Amos (113–120) are suspicious. It is curious that he does not mention the most important of all, that in the letters from Northampton.

* *State Trials*, ii. 1005. Sherburn to Carleton, July 13, 1616, *S. P.* lxxxviii. 15.

† This is implied in Bacon's letter to Villiers, *Works* (ed. Montagu), vi. 240.

‡ Nethersole to Carleton, Sept. 2, 1624, *S. P.* clxxii. 2.

letter* has also been preserved, written by Somerset to the King, apparently after it had been agreed that his life should be spared, in which he states that he had renounced all claim to pension, place, or office, and, as far as can be made out from the obscure allusions to circumstances which are unknown to us, refuses to accept of the intercession of some person whose name is not given, which he was, as it would seem, to purchase by the sacrifice of some portion of his property. Knowing as we do that there was a proposal to grant to Villiers the

CH. XIII. 1616.

* The letter is printed in *Cabala*, i. 1. It has been used to prove that Somerset was aware of some secret with which he was able to threaten the King, a use which can be made of it only by those who come to the reading of it with a foregone conclusion. The intention of the writer is evidently to ask for the restitution of his property from the King himself, without being obliged to obtain the intercession of anyone. The passage, 'I will say no further, neither in that which your Majesty doubted my aptness to fall into; for my cause, nor my confidence is not in that distress as for to use that means of intercession, nor of anything besides, but to remember your Majesty that I am the workmanship of your hands, &c.,' plainly bears the meaning which I have assigned to it, as does the earlier sentence, 'I am in hope that my condition is not capable of so much more misery, as that I need to make myself a passage to you by such way of intercession.' The whole letter, I think, presupposes that Somerset's life had already been granted him. He is now petitioning for the restoration of the whole of his property. He distinctly declares his innocence. 'I fell,' he says, 'rather for want of well-defending than by the violence or force of any proofs: for I so far forsook myself and my cause, as that it may be a question whether I was more condemned for that, or for the matter itself which was the subject of this day's controversy.' Another passage is very curious; 'Aspersions are taken away by your Majesty's letting me become subject to the utmost power of the law, with the lives of so many of the offenders. . . . Neither ever was there such aspersion (God knows), in any possibility towards your Majesty, but amongst those who would create those pretences to mislead your Majesty, and thereby make me miserable.' Does not this refute the idea that Somerset threatened James that he would accuse him of having part in the murder of Overbury? The idea had first proceeded from the King himself, who wrote to More that he could not hear a private message from the prisoner without making himself accessory to his crime. The aspersions just spoken of evidently refer to James's fear lest he should be supposed to have had part in the crime. Would Somerset have written thus, if he had ever threatened James with accusing him of taking such a part? Still, however, the difficulty remains unsolved as to the real purport of Somerset's messages, which threw James into such consternation. There is a slight hint in the letter which may, perhaps, help us a little. 'Nay, to some concerned in this business, wherein I suffer, you have pardoned more unto than I desire, who (as it is reported), if they had come to the test, had proved copper, and should have drunk of the bitter cup as well as others.' Does not this refer to the Monsons? And if we put this together with whatever fact is at the bottom of Weldon's distorted story about the trial of Sir T. Monson, it makes it not altogether improbable that it was something connected with the Spanish pensions which Somerset threatened to blurt out at the trial.

CH. XIII. 1615.

manor of Sherborne, which had been repurchased by Somerset from the Crown in the preceding summer, it is by no means unlikely that a pardon was offered to Somerset, with full restitution of his property, if he would agree to make use of the intercession of Villiers, and to give up to him the manor of Sherborne. This however was what Somerset steadily refused to do. He declared that he was an innocent man, and as such he would accept favours from no hand but from that of the King himself. It was in all probability in consequence of this firmness that he was kept in prison, with the judgment which had been pronounced against him hanging over his head, till January, 1622, when he and the Countess were permitted to leave the Tower, though they were still confined to certain places of residence which were allotted to them. At last, a few months before the King's death, Somerset received a formal pardon for the offence of which he had been convicted.

He is kept a prisoner for many years.

But receives a pardon at last.

Whatever may have been the exact details of James's negotiations with Somerset after his conviction, enough is known to throw an extremely unfavourable light upon his character. Here, as in so many other instances, he showed that, whilst he professed the utmost regard for justice, and probably imagined that he had done his best to act in conformity with its dictates, he permitted his personal wishes to influence his conduct, till he allowed himself to act in a manner which proved that he had no real idea of what justice was.

Liberation of the Monsons.

The Monsons did not remain long in prison. In July, Sir William was set at liberty.* Sir Thomas was allowed to leave the Tower, on bail, in October, and his case was referred to Bacon and Yelverton, who reported that there was not sufficient evidence to proceed against him. Accordingly, a pardon was granted to him, which he pleaded at the bar of the King's Bench, declaring, at the same time, that he was perfectly innocent of the crime which had been imputed to him.†

* *Carew Letters,* 39.

† *Carew Letters,* 47. Bacon and Yelverton to the King, Dec. 7, 1616. Statement of the case of Sir Thomas Monson, Feb. 12, 1617, *S. P.* lxxxix. 65; xc. 62. *State Trials,* ii.

CHAPTER XIV.

THE DISGRACE OF CHIEF-JUSTICE COKE.

THERE is one subject which presents itself again and again with increased monotony to all who study the history of the Stuart Kings. Whilst everything else was changing around them, the emptiness of the Exchequer continued to perplex the brains of a whole succession of Treasurers. On the 24th of September, just after the Government had come upon the traces of the poisoners, James, who was every now and then seized with a desire to free himself from his embarrassments, assembled the Council at Greenwich, and informed them that he was anxious to pay his debts, and to reduce his expenditure, and that he looked to them to tell him how it was possible to effect the object which he had in view.

CH. XIV.

1615.

James expresses a wish to pay his debts and to reduce his expenditure.

The next day the Council met again, and, after full deliberation, decided that the debt, which was now above £700,000, was far too great to be met in any way excepting by a Parliamentary grant. Three days later, a discussion was opened as to the measures which it was necessary to take in order to induce the House of Commons to treat the King with liberality.

The Council recommend a Parliament.

The first who spoke was Lake. He had no difficulty in putting his finger upon the real points at issue. It was a general impression, he said, that the King was too bountiful, and that he was acting illegally against the liberties and privileges of his subjects. With a view to meeting the first complaint, His Majesty must be moved to stay his hand from gifts until his estate were in a more flourishing condition, and to reduce his expenses in whatever way might appear to be most practicable. As

They discuss the measures to be taken before it is summoned.

Opinion of Lake.

CH. XIV. 1615. to the other matter, let the grievances of 1610 be submitted to the King's Council, and if any of them were selected as being fit to be redressed, let them be dealt with without any further delay. Of all the grievances, that which roused the greatest opposition was the levy of the Impositions, and it would be necessary to deal with them in some way or another. Although, however, he saw where the difficulties lay, he did not propose that the King should relinquish his right to the Impositions altogether; and it is certain that no other step would have given satisfaction to the House of Commons. The two following speakers, Sir Julius Cæsar and Sir Thomas Parry, contented themselves with expressing a general assent to these views.

Of Coke. Coke, who spoke after Parry, advocated still stronger measures. It would be necessary, he said, that, in addition to the contemplated reduction of the expenditure, a stop should be put to the payment of pensions till the King's debts had been liquidated. It would also be well that a statement should be drawn out of the expenses which had been incurred at the commencement of the King's reign, and that it should be presented to Parliament, in order that it might be seen that the difficulties of the Treasury did not arise from prodigality. He then proceeded to advise that no attempt should be made to influence the elections. He had seen in the last Parliament that all efforts of this kind had only recoiled upon their authors. He then recommended (and it is difficult to believe that he was not influenced by a desire to put a check upon the influence of his great rival) that none of the King's learned counsel should have seats in the Lower House, partly because they were needed in the House of Lords, and partly because their presence was disliked by the Commons. He concluded by moving that committees might be formed of members of the Council to consider of the particular concessions which were to be made. On the great point of the Impositions he did not utter a word.

Of Greville. Sir Fulk Greville, the Chancellor of the Exchequer, seemed unwilling to give up the revenue which he derived from that source, but he finally consented to make over the whole subject to the new Parliament, to deal with it as it would.

CH. XIV. 1615.

And of Winwood.

Winwood was the next speaker. He agreed with Coke, as far as he had gone, but he expressed a wish that a special committee might examine the Impositions, to see in what way relief could best be given. He added a suggestion of his own, that assurance should be given to the Parliament that whatever they might give should be employed upon the public service, and in no other way.*

The design of calling Parliament relinquished.

Here our report fails us. It would have been interesting to know how the question under discussion was received by those who sat at the upper end of the table. Of that which has been preserved, the most remarkable point seems to be, that it was possible for six Privy Councillors to speak on such a subject without uttering a syllable which would lead us to suppose that they had the slightest idea that the Commons looked upon the Impositions as a wrong to be resisted as a breach of the law, and not merely as a burden which they desired to diminish.

The next notice which we have of these discussions is from a letter written by the Council two months later, from which it appears that they had not yet come to any determination on the question before them.† From some reason or another, the proposal for assembling a Parliament was allowed to drop. Probably the King could not make up his mind to grant the necessary concessions.

Negotiations for the surrender of the cautionary towns.

It was about this time that he turned his eyes towards a resource which would at all events enable him to tide over the ensuing year. Caron, the Ambassador of the States, had long been pressing him to make some arrangement by which the cautionary towns might be at once surrendered to their rightful owners; but it was not till the end of 1615 that James in any way listened to the proposal. At that time Caron found that his request was supported by some members of the Privy Council. James listened to what they had to say, but

* Details of a consultation in Council, Sept. 28, 1615, *S. P.* lxxxi. 115.

† Council to the King, Nov. 27, 1615, *S. P.* lxxxiii. 68.

CH. XIV. 1616.

refused to give a decision on his own responsibility. At his request the whole subject was thoroughly discussed in the Council, and Commissioners were appointed to treat with Caron on the amount to be received. At last, on the 23rd of April, it was agreed that the towns should be surrendered on condition of the payment of £215,000, of which sum £15,000 was to be made over to the officers of the garrisons, and the rest was to be paid into the Exchequer.*

Objections which have been made to the treaty.

Perhaps no treaty which has ever been concluded has received a greater amount of obloquy than this agreement. Few amongst the contemporaries of the men who signed it spoke of it with any degree of favour, and fewer still, amongst the writers who have referred to it in later times, have described it otherwise than as a hard bargain, to which James was compelled by his necessities to submit. Curiously enough, however, although these two classes of critics have been unanimous in the opinions which they have adopted, they have given very different reasons for coming to the same conclusion. It is not difficult to account for this discrepancy. Those who wrote in the seventeenth century shut their eyes to the principles upon which independent nations ought to deal with one another; those who have written in the nineteenth century shut their eyes to the facts of the case which they were discussing.

Those made by contemporaries.

The objections which were made in the Privy Council are probably well represented by a paper which was drawn up for the use of Sir Fulk Greville.† The writer was afraid lest the King should sacrifice his honour, lest England should be excluded from the Continent, lest there should be no longer any place where Englishmen could be trained for a military life, lest France should become too powerful, and, above all, lest the Dutch, when they were relieved from the fear of the English garrisons, should bring scandal upon Protestantism by the en-

* Reasons by Winwood for giving up the Towns. Undated, 1616. Winwood to Carleton, May 23, 1616, *S. P. Hol.*

† Reasons against the surrender, written by Sir John Cooke for Sir Fulk Greville, April 24, 1616, *S. P. Hol.* Danvers to Carleton, April 22, 1616, *S. P. Dom.* lxxxvi. 147.

couragement which they gave to heresy and schism. We have learned to estimate such objections as these at their real worth. In the whole paper there is only one point which was in any way worthy of consideration. The writer doubted the propriety of abandoning the towns, because Flushing and Brill were the keys of the navigation of the Rhine and the Meuse, and without the possession of them the English merchants might be debarred from trading in the regions which were watered by those rivers. It must, however, be remembered that neither Flushing nor Brill guarded, as Gibraltar does, the communications with an open sea. They were only valuable so far as they afforded means of retaliation upon the Dutch in case they were inclined to make use of their superiority at a greater distance from the sea, to hinder English merchandise from passing into the interior. Under such circumstances, it would certainly be better to retain the friendship of the Dutch by an honourable course of policy than to exasperate them by retaining garrisons in places which they justly regarded as their own.

CH. XIV.

1616.

Those made by later writers.

In modern times it has usually been said,* that though James was quite right in surrendering the towns, yet if he had not been in extreme distress he would have bargained for more money than he actually got. It is no doubt true that he would have made rather a better bargain if he had been able to wait, but it is not true that he was in any way cheated out of what he ought to have received, or that he did not benefit by listening to the overtures of the Dutch. At the time when he agreed to the surrender, the amount owing to him was indeed no less than £600,000, which was to be paid, as long as the truce lasted, in half-yearly instalments of £20,000 each. If, then, the truce were renewed at its expiration in 1621, he might expect to receive the whole sum by the end of 1630. On the other hand, as the expenses of the garrisons amounted to £26,000 annually, his real gain would be reduced to £210,000, coming in slowly in

* Hume has stated the matter with perfect correctness, excepting that he supposed that the King received £250,000.

CH. XIV. 1616.

the course of fifteen years. It will be seen, therefore, that the result of James's bargain was to give him at once rather more than he could ever hope to obtain by slow degrees in the course of a long period. Nor was it at all certain that the advantages which accrued to him by the surrender which he was making would not be greater still. It was always possible that the truce might not be renewed, and that, as eventually proved to be the case, the war might break out again. He would then find that, after having rejected £215,000, he had succeeded before 1621, the year in which the truce was to expire, in obtaining a bare £70,000, and that there was before him an indefinite prospect of an annual expenditure of £26,000 for the support of the garrisons.* Nor was this all. The fortifications of the towns were sadly out of repair, and if James had refused the offers of the Dutch, an immediate outlay would have been necessary, which would have swallowed up some considerable portion of the future payments.

Court appointments.

The manner in which this whole question had been referred by James to the Privy Council is significative of the change which had been effected, by the fall of Somerset, in the King's relations with that body. Its members were no longer to be kept in the background, whilst affairs of State were decided in private consultations between the King and the favourite. James had already shown his approbation of the opposition against Somerset by appointing Pembroke to the office of Lord Chamberlain,† and Worcester to that of Lord Privy Seal.‡ The Mastership of the Horse, which was vacated by Worcester's promotion, was at once given to Villiers.§ It can hardly be doubted that it was not by a merely accidental coincidence that on the same day Sir Thomas Lake was sworn in as Secretary of State. Somerset had, without the title, transacted much of the business which properly belonged to that office. There were now to be two Secretaries to share the duties of the post between

* Winwood to Carleton, and Winwood's Reasons, as before quoted.

† On the 22nd of December, 1615, *Carew Letters*, 21.

‡ On the 2nd of January, 1616, *Carew Letters*, 22.

§ On the 3rd of January, 1616, *Carew Letters*, 22.

them. Villiers was only to deal indirectly with State affairs. He would be, in fact, the King's private secretary, supplying him with information on what was passing, receiving suits and petitions in his name, and acting, on the whole, rather as his familiar companion than as an officer of State.

Position of Villiers.

For us who know what was the history of Villiers' subsequent career, and who are able to see at a glance that it was unreasonable to expect that any man should occupy the position in which he was placed without encroaching upon what was justly regarded by the Privy Councillors as their own peculiar border, it is difficult to realize the satisfaction with which the rise of the new favourite was regarded by those who had looked upon the old one with such thorough detestation. And yet there must have been something extremely fascinating in the young man who had thus risen at a bound to the highest position in the realm. It is agreed by all that he was modest and affable, and that his hands were, at least as yet, free from the bribery with which those of Somerset had been soiled. If his education had been neglected, he was not deficient in quickness of apprehension, and he was ready enough to apply for instruction to those who were able to afford him information on any point. Abbot looked upon him with the fondness of a father, and hoped that his influence would be steadily exerted in favour of the cause which he himself had so much at heart. Bacon must have thought of him, as he had once thought of Essex, as the man who might direct the Government into that nobler path in which he would fain have seen it walking.

1615. Bacon's advice to Sir George Villiers.

It was to Bacon that Villiers applied to be his instructor in political affairs, in order that he might be sufficiently acquainted with such subjects to satisfy the King. Bacon replied to his application by a letter of advice,* which, more than any other of his works, places before us the strength and the weakness of his

* 'Advice to Sir G. Villiers' (*Works*, ed. Montagu, vi. 400). It can hardly have been written before Somerset's fall, nor after Villiers became Master of the Horse. If it had been later, Bacon would have said more than, 'You are not only a courtier, but a bedchamber man.'

CH. XIV. 1615.

statesmanship. After giving him some good counsel as to the best mode of dealing with suits which were brought to him for presentation to the King, he proceeded to give his opinion on the state of the Church. Since he had written his Treatise on the Pacification of the Church twelve years before, times had changed. To all outward appearance at least, the policy adopted at Hampton Court had been successful. The questions about forms and ceremonies had dropped out of sight for the time. Good Protestants no longer saw Popery in a surplice or in a ring. Nonconformity still had its adherents, but they were far less prominent than they had been at the close of Elizabeth's reign. Bacon, therefore, who had formerly stood forward as the advocate of moderate change, now declared himself to be opposed to all innovation. He was the more anxious to avoid all farther change, as he saw the quarter from which danger was to be apprehended. He knew that there was a generation arising amongst the clergy who objected to the existing forms of public worship, not because they were too ceremonious, but because they were not ceremonious enough. He knew, too, that there was a rooted dislike in the minds of his countrymen to anything that was new, especially if it were introduced in the high-handed fashion in which these men were likely to deal with matters with which, as they fancied, none but the clergy should be allowed to meddle. Changes introduced under their superintendence would be sure to startle thousands who would go on contentedly enough if their eyes were not allowed to light upon anything different from that to which they had been accustomed in their childhood. If no unwonted forms were presented to them, they would never trouble their heads with nice inquiries into the extent to which such things fitted into the theological system which they had adopted. But whilst all change was to be avoided, care must be taken to encourage ability and learning, in order that the clergy might be in reality a body of men who were in every way fitted to be the teachers of the people.

His views on Church affairs,

Perhaps no other man in England could, at this early period, have foretold the exact nature of the danger which was threatening the Church of England. Certainly no man could have failed so completely in providing a remedy. Here, as on all other subjects, his orderly mind, though it was ready at all times to modify restrictive laws as circumstances might arise, utterly failed to perceive the value of the spontaneous irregularities by which life manifests its presence. It would have seemed to him monstrous to assert that his scheme of toning down all violent exhibitions of zeal could only result in producing a dull and colourless uniformity, if it did not give rise to an explosion of resistance on the part of those to whom their own one-sided views appeared to be the perfect truth.

on the laws of England,

Bacon then turned to speak of the administration of justice. The laws, he said, were the true arbiters between the King and his people, and between one subject and another, and care must therefore be taken that nothing should be done to bring them into disrepute. He entreated Villiers never to interfere, by word or by letter, in any cause depending in a court of justice, or to help men to the bench who sued for the appointment, far less those who offered to purchase it.*

on Parliament,

Bacon's view of the functions of Parliament was that which had prevailed at the Court of Elizabeth. It was, according to him, a great council occasionally summoned to advise the King in matters of weight and difficulty. It was to prepare laws, which were without force till the King gave life to them by his assent. That it should attempt to overrule the policy of the Government was an idea to which it did not occur to Bacon even to allude.

* One paragraph in this portion of the advice deserves special attention:—'If the King shall be wholly intent upon justice, it may appear with an over-rigid aspect; but if he shall be over-remiss and easy, it draweth upon him contempt. Examples of justice must be made sometimes for terror to some; examples of mercy to others; the one procures fear, and the other love. A king must be both feared and loved, else he is lost.' The perfect good faith in which this really atrocious position, that the prerogative of mercy should be used according to political motives, is evident. That Bacon should have so expressed himself, makes James's treatment of the Somersets less extraordinary, and will also serve as an answer to those who think that Bacon must have been consciously corrupt, because they imagine that he always knew what was right.

CH. XIV. 1615.

On the Privy Council. On the other hand, the Privy Council was a standing body. It should be composed of men of ability, and of varied knowledge, in order that they might be ready to give an opinion upon every kind of business.

Policy of the Government. Bacon then, having said all that he could on constitutional questions, went on to give his advice on the policy which ought to be adopted by the King. If peace were to be preserved, England must be prepared for war; the navy must be kept in good order, the Treasury must be filled, and, above all, the alliance with Holland must be maintained. In order that the country might be well provided, tillage must be encouraged, marshes reclaimed, uncultivated lands brought under the plough, and the navigation of rivers improved. Care must also be taken that the balance of trade be preserved, and that monopolies be not admitted under any specious pretext whatsoever. Nor should the foundation of colonies be neglected, which would be valuable by the outlet which they would afford to the superfluous population, as well as the trade which would spring up with them when once they were thoroughly settled.

Such advice as this shows what were the advantages which Bacon expected to reap from the Government, and which would, as he feared, be unattainable from the clamours of the unorganized popular assembly to which he had been accustomed. He was led astray by his habit of regarding great reforms as things to be done by the courage and wisdom of the few; whilst he was blind to the value of free political life in raising the many to appreciate, and to adopt as their own, the truths which they would never have discovered for themselves.

Coke and the King. It was not, however, with any question connected either with the administration of the Government, or with the relations between the Sovereign and the Parliament, that Bacon's mind was occupied at the time at which he penned this remarkable paper. For some time there had been symptoms of a collision impending between the Crown and the Chief Justice of the King's Bench. The resistance of Coke to the King's claim to impose penalties by proclamation, and to the jurisdiction of the Ecclesiastical Commission, had revealed a spirit of defiance in him which arose partly from personal ruggedness of temper, but partly also from a strong sense of the necessity of maintaining the independence of his office. The treatment which he had received in Peacham's case had tended, not unnaturally, to rouse his indignation against those who had adopted such means, in order, if possible, to elicit from him an opinion which he believed to be untrue.

A collision unavoidable under the circumstances.

The collision which ensued, however, was far more the result of the position of the Government than of the personal character of the Chief Justice. As long as the Sovereign and the House of Commons had worked together, no question had arisen of any importance by which the independence of the judges could be affected. But as soon as the King was at open war with the representatives of the nation, it was inevitable that, in some form or another, the claim of the judges to decide upon constitutional questions would meet with opposition.

Bacon's views.

No man could be better fitted than Bacon to appear as the champion of the King against the judges; for no man could be more thoroughly convinced that the judges had no right to hold a position independent of the Crown. There is abundant evidence in his writings that he looked upon the defence of the prerogative as especially entrusted to the care of the judges. If there were any doubt on this point, it would be sufficient to quote the illustration of the lions under Solomon's throne, of which he so frequently made use. In one of his Essays, for instance, he writes that 'Solomon's throne was supported by lions on both sides. Let' the judges, therefore, 'be lions, but yet lions under the throne, being circumspect that they do not check or oppose any points of sovereignty.' But it is needless to quote individual passages to show that he accepted a political theory which lies at the root of everything which he thought or said upon the subject.

His reason for adopting it.

Bacon's dislike of admitting the judges to be the supreme arbiters on political questions arose originally from his profound conviction that such questions could only be properly treated of by those who were possessed of political knowledge and experience. He felt,

CH. XIV. 1615.

truly enough, that the most intimate acquaintance with statutes and precedents was insufficient to enable a man to decide upon State affairs; and if he had ever been inclined to forget it, the example of Coke was constantly before his eyes as a proof that no amount of legal knowledge will ever constitute a statesman. Nor was this a consideration of small importance. As the relations between James and his Parliament then stood, the judge who decided upon the law which assigned limits to each could not avoid usurping the functions of a statesman. He not only declared how far the existing law applied to the facts of the case, but he fixed the constitution of the country for the future. It was true that, theoretically, the decisions of the judges were liable at any time to be reversed by Act of Parliament; but the day was far distant when it would be possible to obtain the joint assent of the Crown and the Parliament to any Act affecting the powers of either. For the present the judges, if they succeeded in maintaining their independence, would have in their hands the supreme control over the Constitution. They would be able, without rendering an account to anyone, to restrain or to extend the powers of the Crown for an indefinite period. In 1606 they had, by a decision from the bench, assigned to the King the right of levying Impositions, which, in spite of all opposition, he retained for no less than thirty-five years. If it pleased them, they might deprive him, in the same way, of rights which he considered to be essential to the exercise of his government.

How far it was justified by modern experience.

Although Bacon's wish to bring the judges into subjection to the Crown has found no favour in later times, it must be remembered that his doctrine of the necessity of referring elsewhere than to the judges for the final decision on all constitutional questions has stood the test of modern experience.* The victory of the Parliament has,

* The following remarks of De Tocqueville (*Dem. en Amérique*, i. chap. 6) are particularly applicable, 'Si, en France, les tribunaux pouvaient désobéir aux lois sur le fondement qu'ils les trouvent inconstitutionnelles, le pouvoir constituant serait réellement dans leurs mains, puisque seuls ils auraient le droit d'interpréter une constitution dont nul ne pourrait changer les termes. Ils se mettraient donc à la place de la nation, et domineraient

indeed, thrown the supreme political power into other hands than those in which Bacon would have placed it; but it is not one of the least happy results of that victory that it has now become possible to exercise a control over the judges without sacrificing their independence. It is Parliament which decides what the Constitution shall be, and having this power in its hands, it is by no means inclined to interfere with the judges in declaring, in the exercise of the proper duties of their office, what the Constitution is at any given moment. An Act of Parliament at once makes any obnoxious decision of the Courts impossible for the future. There was no longer any necessity to fear a repetition of the judgment on Impositions, or of the judgment on Ship Money, as soon as it was certain that there would be no difficulty in rendering the judgment innocuous, and in providing, at the same time, against a repetition of the offence.

CH. XIV. 1615.

Impossibility of anticipating our solution of his difficulties.

But no solution of this kind was possible for Bacon. As long as the Crown and the Commons were engaged in a conflict with one another, all chance of legislation upon the parts which they were respectively to occupy in the Constitution was at an end. The Crown and the Commons might either of them have just causes of complaint against the judges; but until they could make up their differences, they were both debarred from interfering by a general and prospective law, and in no other way was it possible to interfere with advantage. Having refused to acknowledge the rising claims of the House

la société, autant du moins que la faiblesse inhérente au pouvoir judiciaire leur permettrait de le faire.

'Je sais qu'en refusant aux juges le droit de déclarer les lois inconstitutionnelles, nous donnons indirectement au corps législatif le pouvoir de changer la constitution, puisqu'il ne rencontre plus de barrière légale qui l'arrête. Mais mieux vaut encore accorder le pouvoir de changer la constitution du peuple à des hommes qui représentent imparfaitement les volontés du peuple, qu'à d'autres qui ne représentent qu'eux-mêmes.' The power of appealing to the Common Law to interpret, or even practically to overrule the statute law, gave to the English judges a right in some measure analogous to the right of interpreting a written constitution of which De Tocqueville speaks. Such a right would throw into their hands the final decision on constitutional questions to a far greater extent than would have been possible if they had been fettered by a written text. Bacon's solution of the difficulty was very different from that given after the experience of two centuries and a half by the modern writer; but it is probable that they both felt the same objection to the theory which they were combating.

CH. XIV. 1615.

of Commons, therefore, Bacon had no choice but to go wrong. His feelings of the impropriety of trusting to such men as Coke the final decision on questions which might involve the welfare of the whole community, led him insensibly to choose, of two evils, the one which was infinitely worse than the other. If the Crown could not legislate independently of the Commons, it was to make use of its superior power to tutor the judges to see things as they were looked upon at Court. They must regard themselves as bound to support the prerogative which was in the hands of the King for the benefit of the Commonwealth.

Mischief of Bacon's course.

It is needless to say that such a view of the office of the judges, though it was plausible enough to impose upon the mind of Bacon, was no less ruinous to the prerogative itself than to the independence of the judicial bench. If the King and his Council were to interfere with the opinions of the judges on every question in which the constitutional rights of the Crown were involved, it would speedily be found that the office of a judge would be one which no honest man would deign to accept. Nor would it be long before the decisions of men who were known to be influenced by other arguments than those which were furnished by the law-books would cease to be received as having any authority whatever. Even that object which Bacon was justified in aiming at would not be attained. The only way in which it was possible to restrain the judges from settling constitutional questions was by making legislation once more possible. Till that was done all that could be accomplished would be success in securing that all their decisions on such questions should be on one side. As an attack upon the judges was only the natural result of the quarrel with the Commons, its consequence would be to embitter that quarrel, and to simplify the dispute, by bringing the parties face to face.

Position occupied by Coke.

Bacon was the more easily drawn on in the course which he adopted, as he could hardly avoid regarding the whole affair as a purely personal question. Till within a few years, the judges had been, on the whole, favourable to the prerogative. The great cases of the Postnati and of the Impositions had been decided upon grounds which would have satisfied the most thorough-going champion of the Crown. But not long after Coke's accession to the bench, a different spirit began to prevail. Coke was accustomed upon every occasion to appeal to the law as that which was to decide every question which could possibly arise; but, unfortunately, in the arrogance of his bearing, and in the narrowness of his intellect, there was something which robbed the noblest principles of their attraction. What he meant by the law was neither the collection of written statutes, which would have been utterly insufficient to settle the complicated questions which were continually arising; nor was it, on the other hand, the application of great principles to particular cases. He meant that where the statutes failed him, he was to have recourse to those numerous precedents which he was able to quote with such profusion out of his retentive memory. At the same time he showed a disposition to bring every court in England under the control of the court over which he himself presided. Bacon, in spite of the taunts with which his rival so frequently assailed him, never failed to express his admiration of the extent of his legal knowledge; but it was not strange that he should stand in determined opposition to the man who seemed to be bent on establishing in England a despotism of mere book-learning and antiquarian lore. There can be no doubt, indeed, that in this he did Coke wrong. With all the infirmities of his temper and the errors of his judgment, the great lawyer was in reality fighting for something far more valuable than anything that the highest statesmanship could give. His law may frequently have been quoted in support of injustice; still it was law, and not mere arbitrary power. He believed in his own learning as the one thing needful to maintain the institutions of his country. The sympathies of posterity have always rightly been with Coke, and not with Bacon. No one can read the account of the rivalry between the two men impartially without throwing aside impatiently all that can be said, truly enough, of Coke's many faults, and bowing his head reverently before the man who, in times of difficulty and danger,

CH. XIV. 1615.

stood forward, regardless of all personal consequences, as the champion of the majesty of the law. Yet, bound as we are to feel with Coke, we cannot wish him complete success. It was the rise of the constitutional importance of the House of Commons, by which the difficulty would be solved.

Case of Brownlow v. Michell.

The momentous question in debate between the Crown and the judges was first brought to an issue on a comparatively unimportant case. In 1611 the King had granted to a person named Michell, at the request of John Murray, one of the Grooms of the Bedchamber, the sole right of making certain writs in the Court of Common Pleas. Upon this Brownlow, the prothonotary of that court, finding that his own fees were diminishing, brought an action against Michell in the King's Bench, on the ground that he had been deprived of his rights by the defendant. It so happened that an attempt to create the same office as that which had been assigned to Michell had been made in the reign of Elizabeth, and that, the judges having resisted the attempt, the Queen had, with her usual good sense, at once withdrawn her pretensions. James, if he had ever heard anything about the matter, neglected to profit by her example.*

Bacon produces a writ 'De Rege Inconsulto.'

The matter in dispute was one of no great importance in itself; but it afforded a field on which to try the question, how far the judges could decide, upon merely legal grounds, upon the right of the Crown to make administrative appointments. It happened that there was in existence a writ which was admirably suited to the purpose of a man who wished to deprive the judges of all claim to interfere in such matters. By this writ, 'De non procedendo Rege inconsulto,' the Common Law judges were prohibited from dealing with a case in which the interests of the Crown were concerned, before the question in dispute had been first referred to the Court of Chancery, and its permission had been obtained for the parties to proceed with the suit.† Bacon not only

* Heath's Preface to the Argument on the writ De Rege inconsulto (*Works*, vii. 683).

† The working of this writ, if Bacon had obtained his object, would have been, to some extent, analogous to that iniquitous provision which has been

brought this writ into court, but he demanded that it should be at once received as an authoritative command, which the judges were not entitled to allow the counsel for either party in the case before them to dispute.

Importance of this step.

It was plain that, however cogent the precedents might be by which Bacon could support the step which he had taken, it was a concession of no slight importance which he asked the judges to make. At the best, the writ had been but a clumsy mode of ascertaining that the rights of the Crown would suffer no damage by a suit in which it was not itself a party; but as long as it had only been issued in cases where the tenancy of a few acres of land, or the right to some petty office was at stake, it is not probable that any great harm had been done. In the reign of Elizabeth, Bacon would have been right in saying that it ought to be a matter of indifference to the parties whether the cause were tried before the Chancellor or the Chief Justice. In either case, substantial justice would probably have been done. But now that an opposition had sprung up between the Crown and the courts of law, and that every case such as that which was before the Court was sure to be regarded from different points of view by those who took part on either side, the question had ceased to be one merely concerning the honour and dignity of the Crown. What Bacon really wanted he acknowledged in a letter which he wrote at the time. The Chancellor was a great political officer as well as a jurist. There would be no fear lest he should be led astray, either by respect for legal technicalities, or by jealousy of the Government, to overthrow any arrangement made by the Crown which was not utterly indefensible in itself.

In fact, if Bacon had had his way, all pretensions of the judges to act as arbiters between the King and his subjects would have been at an end for ever. It is no wonder, therefore, that the judges refused to take Bacon's

found in so many French constitutions, according to which no agent of the Government can be summoned before a tribunal, for acts done in the exercise of his office, without a preliminary authorization by the Council of State. The effect of the English writ being confined to cases where the King was himself supposed to be injured, would have been of less universal application, but the principle on which it rested would have been equally bad.

CH. XIV. 1615. view of the case, and directed that the question of the legality of the writ should be argued before them.* The King, too, was not behind them in perceiving the importance of the question at issue. He gave special directions to Coke not to presume to give judgment until he had an interview with himself.†

1616. Bacon's argument. It was some time before the case was brought to a close. It was not till nearly a year after it had first been brought into the court, that Bacon rose, on the 25th of January, 1616, to speak on behalf of the King. His speech was acknowledged, even by Coke himself, to be 'a famous argument.'‡ He prudently dropped all allusion to his real motives for wishing to bring cases of this nature under the Chancellor's jurisdiction, and treated the question simply as one of propriety. He had no difficulty in quoting a goodly array of precedents in support of his view of the case. There is nothing more remarkable than the ease with which he threw off his character as a statesman, and, treating the question as one of purely technical law, dealt with it in a manner which Coke might well have envied.§

The suit compromised. It was perhaps the difficulty of resisting Bacon's precedents, combined with the disinclination of the judges to assent to his conclusion, that led to a compromise of the question. Brownlow gave up his claim to Michell's office, and the King promised that in future he would not give his assent to the creation of any office which would lead to a diminution of the profits of the existing officials.

Failure of Bacon to obtain the assent of the judges to his scheme. So far Bacon had failed. He had been unable to obtain the recognition of the Common Law judges to a doctrine which would involve the abdication of one of their principal functions. But it was not likely that much time would elapse before he would again be brought into collision with the Chief Justice. In fact, very few weeks passed after Bacon's great speech on the writ of 'Rege inconsulto,' when Coke allowed his temper

* Bulstrode, *Rep.* iii. 32.

† Bacon to the King, Jan. 27, 1616 (*Works*, ed. Montagu, xiii. 65).

‡ *Works*, vii. 687.

§ This remark is borrowed from Mr. Heath, Preface to Bacon's 'Argument on the Jurisdiction of the Marches' (*Works*, vii. 581).

to get the better of him in such a way as to afford a golden opportunity to his wary antagonist. CH. XIV. 1616.

A custom had gradually arisen of seeking redress in Chancery, in cases where the Common Law courts had failed to do justice, on account of the strictness of the rules which they had laid down for their guidance. Such a practice was, naturally enough, regarded with dissatisfaction by the Common Law judges, and by none more than by the Chief Justice of the King's Bench, who had long looked upon the Chancellor in the light of a personal opponent, as well as in that of a thorough-going supporter of an obnoxious system. If Coke, before he complained of the interference of the Chancery with his jurisdiction, had set himself steadily to work to remedy the evils which were complained of in the practice of his own court, he would probably have gained the support of all impartial persons; for it is manifestly objectionable that the judgments delivered in one court should be liable to reversal in another, unless that other court has been constituted expressly for the purpose of hearing appeals. But, instead of this, he plunged at once into the contest with that violence of temper which was certain to disgust all who knew that real and substantial justice was frequently afforded by the Chancery to those who had failed in obtaining it at Westminster. Quarrel of Coke with the Chancery.

As he was thinking over the best means of punishing those who had insulted the court over which he presided, it occurred to him that a statute* had been passed in the reign of King Edward III., directed against those who appealed to Rome against sentences obtained in the King's courts, in which were words which, if taken without regard to the context, might possibly mean that no one was to question a judgment of the King's Bench in any other court, under the penalty which was attached to a præmunire.† He accordingly advised‡ two The præmunire.

* 27 Ed. III. St. i. cap. 1.

† The words 'in any other court,' in the statute are translated also 'in the court of another,' apparently correctly, as the French is 'en autri court.' This would overthrow Coke's case at once, as is remarked by the author of the *Jurisdiction of Chancery Vindicated*, appended to vol. i. of *Chancery Reports*, p. 30. But the context is quite enough to settle the question.

‡ Such, at least, was the general belief, though he denied it. Perhaps he

CH. XIV. 1616. scoundrels* named Glanville and Allen, who had met with something less than their just deserts in Chancery, after judgments had been given in their favour in the Common Law courts, to prefer indictments in the King's Bench against all who had had anything to do with the proceedings in Chancery.

Glanville's case. The first to present himself before the Court was Glanville. He had swindled a young man named Courtney out of a large sum of money, by representing the value of a jewel to be £360, which was in reality worth only £30. He sold him this jewel together with others which were worth £100 more, and obtained from him an agreement to pay £600, upon which, when he found that the money was not forthcoming, he surreptitiously procured a judgment in a Common Law court. When Courtney discovered the fraud to which he had been subjected, he attempted to get redress; but was refused, on the ground that the judgment having once been obtained, nothing farther could be done. He then applied to the Chancery, from which he at once obtained the justice which he was seeking. In order to revenge himself for having been forced to disgorge his unlawful gains, Glanville now preferred an indictment of præmunire in the King's Bench against Courtney himself, and also against the counsellor and the clerk who had taken part in the proceedings.

The grand jury return an ignoramus, Coke, however, who was upon the Bench awaiting the success of his scheme, found an unexpected obstacle in his way. The grand jury, who probably knew nothing about the statutes and precedents which were appealed to as determining the relations between the two courts, but who knew perfectly well that they were asked to assist a baffled swindler in taking vengeance on his dupe, were by no means in a hurry to find a true bill in the case. On this Coke sent for them, and refused to grant

contented himself with giving them a strong hint that he would support them.

* There is a full account of these men in Harl. MS., 1767, foll. 37–44. Compare for Glanville's case, *Croke, Jac.* The sums of money are differently stated. I have adopted those from Croke. The cases are frequently quoted as if they had been one, 'Glanville *v.* Allen,' which is, of course, a mistake.

their request for further time to deliberate; as the case was, in his opinion, too plain to need any delay. The jury remonstrated on the ground that they had no evidence that the judgment in question had been duly obtained. Upon this Coke sprang upon his feet, and attempted to browbeat them into submission. They retired for a short time, and, on their returning without having complied with his orders, the Chief Justice told them to go back again. He would not leave the bench till the business was done; if they refused to do as he told them, he would commit them for their conduct.

In spite of all this, the grand jury refused to be bullied into submission. They returned once more into court, and, to Coke's disgust, returned an ignoramus. Angry as he was, Coke did not dare to carry his threats into execution. He told Glanville and Allen to be ready by next term, when he would have a better jury to decide upon the cases.*

Bacon writes to the King.

At the time when this violent scene was taking place, Ellesmere was lying ill, and, though he ultimately recovered, was not expected to live. Bacon, who was of one mind with him on such a subject as this, and who had been visiting him in his sickness, wrote to acquaint the King of what had happened, and promised to send him the particulars as soon as he was able to obtain a trustworthy account.† A few days later, he gave his opinion of what had passed.‡ The defenders of the Common Law courts rested their case partly upon the statute of Edward III., which was, in reality, directed against the Papal Courts, and partly upon another statute of Henry IV.,§ which contained a simple declaration, without any penalty annexed, that, after judgment given in the King's courts, the parties should be at peace. The reason assigned was because many persons whose cases had already been decided, had been made to come,

* Proofs of the proceedings, printed in Lord Campbell's *Chancellors*, ii. 236. The story so often told about the witness kept away, which will be found in the same page, does not fit into the cases of either Glanville or Allen.

† Bacon to the King, Feb. 15, 1616 (*Works*, ed. Montagu, xii. 34).

‡ Bacon to the King, Feb. 21, 1616 (*Works*, ed. Montagu, xii. 36).

§ 4 Hen. IV., cap. 23.

CH. XIV. 1616.

to their great inconvenience, before the King himself, or the Council, or even the Parliament. This statute, as Bacon argued, was only intended to prevent parties from having to argue the same question over again, and not to prevent the institution of suits in Chancery, when the case of one of them had never been properly heard at all, on account of the strictness of the rules observed in the Common Law courts.

Opinion of the law officers.

The whole question was referred by the King to the Attorney and Solicitor-General, the two King's Serjeants, Montagu and Crew, and the Prince's Attorney, John Walter, one of the most rising lawyers of the day. After consideration, they gave it as their unanimous opinion that the Court of Chancery was justified in the exercise of the jurisdiction which had been so violently assailed.*

Case of Commendams.

Before, however, the King had decided upon the course he would take, another question arose which embroiled him still farther with the stubborn and independent Chief Justice. It happened that, during the time that Bishop Neile had held the see of Lichfield, he had received from the King the grant of a living to be held in commendam with his bishopric as long as he occupied the see. Two persons of the name of Colt and Glover brought an action against him. They not only asserted that the presentation was theirs, and not the King's, but they pleaded that, on account of certain legal objections, the grant was invalid in itself. As the case was of great importance, and had never before been argued, it was adjourned into the Exchequer Chamber, in order that all the twelve judges might deliver their opinions. Whilst the case was being argued, information was given to the King that his prerogative was being questioned. He accordingly deputed Bishop Bilson to be present in court in his name, in order to make a report to him of the language which was used. On his return, Bilson told him that he had heard Serjeant Chibborne maintain that the King had no power to translate a bishop, and that, though it was true that in cases of necessity he might

* 'The Jurisdiction of Chancery Vindicated,' in *Chanc. Rep.* i. Cary's *Reports.*

grant a commendam, yet that it was impossible that there ever could be any necessity for such a step. The King was eager to put a stop to this kind of language. About a month or two before, he had ordered Coke not to proceed to judgment till he had communicated with him in person. He now directed Bacon to write to the Chief Justice, repeating his command. CH. XIV. 1616.

Accordingly, on the 25th of April, Bacon wrote to Coke, requiring him to intimate to the other judges that it was expected that they would postpone the delivery of their opinions until they had spoken with the King. On the receipt of this letter, Coke felt that it was necessary to make a stand on behalf of the independence of his office. An anecdote, which has been preserved by Whitelocke, is enough to give an insight into what was passing in his mind. In the autumn of the previous year, whilst he was still smarting under the treatment which he had received in Peacham's affair, Coke was present at the sermon at Windsor. As soon as it was concluded, Whitelocke, who was also among the congregation, accompanied him out of the chapel to his coach. Seeing that he was about to drive away, he asked him why he did not remain to the dinner at the Court. Coke replied that the King was fond of asking him questions which were of such a nature that he preferred being as far off as possible. 'I guess,' was Whitelocke's remark as he noted down this conversation, 'it was concerning matters of prerogative, which the King would take ill if he were not answered in them as he would have it.'*

Bacon writes to Coke, ordering him not to proceed with the case.

Coke's feeling on the point.

Since that time the argument of Bacon on the writ of *rege inconsulto*, and the known determination of the King to check him in his resistance to what he regarded as the interference of the Chancellor with his own peculiar jurisdiction, had exasperated him still more. He may well have seen in Bacon's letter an attempt to carry, by a side wind, a point which he had failed to gain by direct attack. If the Attorney-General had been unable to convince the Court of King's Bench that it was obligatory upon it to refuse to decide upon all cases in which

* Whitelocke, *Liber Famelicus*, 48.

CH. XIV. 1616. the Crown was concerned until it had obtained the Chancellor's permission to investigate the matter, it would serve his purpose equally if he could reduce the Common Law judges to such a state of subservience that they would be unlikely to resist the expressed wishes of the King. No method could be imagined more likely to attain that end than the one which was now proposed. If, whenever a case arose in which the prerogative was concerned, the judges were to be called into the presence of the King to debate the point with him, a habit would speedily grow up of looking to the wishes of the Sovereign rather than to the dictates of the law.

The judges go on with the case.

To Bacon, Coke returned a short answer. He directed the messenger who brought the letter to tell his master that if he wished the judges to receive the information which he had just given him, he had better write to them

April 26.

himself. On the following day, Bacon, who had no intention of allowing any mere question of etiquette to stand in his way,* wrote to the other judges.

Their letter to the King.

To Bacon's surprise, the judges did not even take the trouble of answering his letters. On that very day they proceeded with their arguments as if nothing whatever

April 27.

had happened. The next day† a letter was despatched to the King, written apparently by Coke, but signed by all the twelve judges. They said that they were on all occasions bound to serve His Majesty, but that the case before them depended upon the construction of two Acts of Parliament, on which they were bound to deliver their opinions faithfully and uprightly. The point in dispute, moreover, was one which earnestly called for a speedy decision, as it was one in which two parties were interested in a question of property. The letter which they had received was contrary to law, and they

* 'His answer by word to my man was that it were good the rest of the judges understood so much from myself: whereupon I, that cannot skill of scruples in matter of service, did write on Friday three several letters,' &c. (Bacon to the King, *Works*, ed. Montagu, vii. 308.) The meaning is plainly as I have given it above. Bacon did not say, as he is sometimes charged with saying, that he was unscrupulous in the King's service.

† This is the date of the letter, as given in *S. P.* lxxxvii. 44, ii., which is evidently right.

were bound by their oaths to pay no attention to it. They had therefore proceeded with the case on the appointed day.

CH. XIV. 1616.

Technical nature of Coke's objections.

Considering how very strong Coke's case really was, it must always be a matter of regret that he allowed such a letter as this to go forth as the expression of the opinion of the judges on a question of such importance. It assumed, what was certainly untrue, that the case was one in which merely private interests were concerned, and it entirely ignored all that might be said upon the other side. What reasoning there was in it was of a narrow and technical character, to which James, instigated by Bacon, had no difficulty in replying.

The King's reply.

In his answer, the King told the judges that he had no wish whatever to interfere in any question which merely concerned the interests of parties; but in the present case he himself was, to all intents and purposes, a party to the suit. Was it fitting, therefore, that his rights should be adjudicated upon without his being allowed to say a word in his own defence? As to the judges' oath that they would not delay justice, they were perfectly aware that they were frequently in the habit of postponing the hearing of cases from one term to another, for reasons which at the time appeared sufficient to themselves. All he asked was, that they should do the same when the delay was necessary in order that he might lay before them his own case whenever his rights were involved.

The judges acknowledge their offence.

On the 6th of June, the judges were summoned before the Council, in the presence of the King. After the letters which had passed had been read, James proceeded to state his case. His arguments were those which he had previously set down in his letters. As soon as he had concluded, all the judges threw themselves upon their knees and asked pardon for their error.

Coke still protests.

Coke, however, though he joined the other judges in demanding pardon, did not allow the King's reasoning to remain unanswered. He reiterated his opinion that the postponement required by the King was in fact a real delay of justice, and he declared that the judges, at the time when they refused to obey the letter, knew that

CH. XIV. 1616.

they had no intention of saying anything, in delivering judgment, which would affect the prerogative. He added that if they had not proceeded with the case on the day appointed, the case would have dropped altogether, as it would have been impossible to adjourn it excepting to some certain day, whereas no such day had been named in the letter of the Attorney-General.

The King's reply.

A far less practised disputant than James would hardly have missed the transparent sophistry of this last argument. The King had no difficulty in answering that the judges might easily have fixed any day they pleased, and that, when it arrived, if they had not yet had time to confer with him, they might have adjourned the case again. He then stepped upon more dangerous ground, asserting that they had no right to decide before consulting with him, in order that he might know whether the question concerned his prerogative or not. As to the oath, he wished to know what was the Chancellor's opinion on the point.

Bacon's opinion on the obligation of the judges' oath.

Ellesmere, with a timidity which may easily be accounted for in a man of his age, who had but lately recovered from a dangerous illness, shrunk from being the first to engage, on such a point, in a contest with Coke. He therefore asked that, as the question related to a matter of law, the opinion of the law officers of the Crown might first be taken. Upon this, Bacon reiterated what had been already said by the King, and concluded by an argument which was no less sophistical than that which had been used by Coke. The oath of the judges, he said, bound them to give counsel to the King whenever they were called upon to do so, 'and if they will proceed first in a business whereupon they are called to counsel, and will counsel him when the matter is past, it is more than a simple refusal to give him counsel.' In this opinion he was supported by the other law officers who were present.

It is hardly to be believed that Coke neglected such an opportunity of exposing the blunder which Bacon had made, in confusing counsel given by the judges to the King with counsel which the King wished to give to the judges. But such was his inveterate wrongheadedness, that he preferred treating his adversary with contempt, even to the easy task of exposing the weakness of his argument. It was the place of the Attorney-General, he said, to plead before the judges, not to dispute with them. Bacon replied that he had a right to declare the truth in the King's name against any subject whatever, and appealed for redress for the insult which he had received. James, of course, took his part, and rebuked Coke for the language he had used. Ellesmere then declared that his opinion coincided with that of Bacon.

The judges give way.

After the Chancellor had given his opinion, the judges' oath was read at his request, and the terms in which it was couched were discussed. The question was then put to the judges, one by one, 'whether if, at any time, in a case depending before the judges, His Majesty conceived it to concern him either in power or profit, and thereupon required to consult with them, and that they should stay proceedings in the meantime, they ought not to stay accordingly?' Eleven of the judges gave way, and promised that they would in future act according to the King's wishes. The cause of this dereliction of duty (for, after all that may fairly be said on their behalf, it amounts to nothing less) was no doubt in great measure the fear of offending the King, whom they had been accustomed to treat with reverence, and to whom they owed all their future prospects of professional advancement. But it must not be forgotten that Coke had thrown away every opportunity of supporting his cause by arguments which were in any way worthy of attention. If Bacon had needed any additional evidence to prove that a strictly legal training is not the best preparation for deciding finally upon political questions, he might have found it in the manifest incapability of the man who was confessedly the first lawyer of the day to defend his position in a question where, on all the main points, he was decidedly in the right.

Coke alone holds out.

Coke, however, though he could not refute the arguments which were brought against him, took refuge in that which was better than any argument. Nothing more could be drawn out of him than that, whenever the

CH. XIV. 1616. case should come before him, he would do what was fitting for a judge to do.

It is by his conduct on this day, more than by any other action in his life, that, in spite of his failure in argument, he has deservedly acquired the admiration of posterity. It has rightly been felt that, in politics as well as everywhere else, one act of rugged independence was worth all the statesmanship in the world. If his mind was incapable of discovering why he was right and why his opponent was wrong, he had no doubt about the fact. He was required to prostitute the independence of the judicial bench to the arbitrary interference of the King. In whatever light we view the matter—however much we may be ready to acknowledge that there was a side of the question on which Bacon, too, was in the right—there, and nowhere else, the root of the matter lay; and sooner than give way here, he was ready to sacrifice that high position to which he had risen by his own merits, and which he, no doubt, prized more highly than the possession of any crown in Europe. After making what deductions we will, the fact remains behind, that he sacrificed for conscience sake all that was most valuable in his eyes. At that moment he occupied a nobler position than he had ever done in the day of his power, when he was browbeating unhappy prisoners from the bench, or even than that in which he stood twelve years later, when, amidst the applause of the House of Commons, he stood up to advocate the Petition of Rights.

Interview with the judges. Leaving Coke to assert his independence in his own way, the King then turned to the other judges, and asked them whether in their argument they meant to touch upon his general power of granting commendams. In the conversation which ensued enough was said to justify Coke's repugnance to the meeting which had been proposed. It was anything rather than a consultation in which the King laid before the judges his view of the case as far as it affected himself, or in which he asked their opinion as to the extent to which his prerogative was affected by the law. The judges engaged not to allow any other view to be taken than that which he had adopted, and promised to silence any lawyer who presumed to call the prerogative in question. It is no wonder that James expressed his satisfaction, and that he dismissed them with assurances of protection.* The case was accordingly proceeded with without further delay, and though it was finally decided against the Bishop, it was on grounds which left the general prerogative of the Crown untouched.†

Bacon becomes a Privy Councillor.

Amongst the names which are appended to the Act of Council in which these proceedings are reported occurs for the first time the signature of Bacon, who took his seat upon the 9th of June.‡ When Ellesmere had been ill, in February, Bacon had applied to be appointed his successor in the event of his death, which was at that time hourly expected. In the letter which he wrote he set forth at length the services which he hoped to be able to render in that office.§ It is needless to enter upon the hopeless task of discriminating between the motives by which Bacon was influenced in making the application. No doubt the desire of benefiting his country was mixed up with the longing for a sphere in which to exercise his talents, which few men of his genius are without, and this again may have been mingled with more ordinary motives. It is enough that he believed, with justice, that he was eminently fitted for the place, and that he laid his claims before the King, from whom alone he could obtain the object of his desires, and whose policy, in the main, he approved, though he would gladly have found an opportunity of drawing him on to a bolder and more comprehensive action.

Ellesmere, however, unexpectedly recovered, and Bacon had to wait a few months longer, knowing that

* Bacon, *Works* (ed. Montagu), vii. 307–338.

† Hobart, *Rep.*

‡ *Council Register*, June 9, 1616.

§ Bacon to the King, Feb. 12, 1616, *Works* (ed. Montagu), xii. 31. It is in this letter that the celebrated 'gloria in obsequio' occurs. 'For myself,' Bacon writes, 'I can only present your Majesty with a gloria in obsequio.' Obsequium is simply obedience, not obsequiousness. All Bacon says is, 'If you appoint me, I shall do my best to obey your orders.' His theory of the relation between the King and his officials was undoubtedly faulty, but it was sincerely entertained.

CH. XIV. 1616.

he was sure of the Chancellor's good word whenever his claims to the succession might be discussed. In the meanwhile he applied for a place in the Privy Council, which would open before him a sphere of action which was still more suited to his abilities than any merely legal office whatever. After some delay he was offered the choice between a Councillorship and the reversion of the Chancellor's place. He unhesitatingly chose the latter, which would introduce him at once into the public business of the Government. The Chancellorship would be sure to fall into his hands when the time came.

The King comes into the Star-Chamber.

On the 20th of June, a fortnight after the altercation with Coke, the King came down into the Star-Chamber, in order to give a public exposition of the principles by which his conduct had been governed. It would not be impossible to detect a superficial resemblance between the speech which he delivered and those which afterwards fell from the lips of Cromwell. There is the same tendency to quote texts of Scripture, and the same appeal to God as to the foundation of all civil order. But here the resemblance ceases. With Cromwell the whole of the scene which is passing around him is instinct with a living presence, and he feels that his own work can only be rightly done in proportion as he yields himself to become the instrument of Him who is the only true actor in the events of the world. With James, between heaven and earth there exists merely an external relation. God appoints the King, and the King appoints the judges. It is a hierarchy in which James himself plays the principal part. The chief thing which he remembers is that he has a right to plead the appointment of God against all who dispute his title, and that, as he has appointed the judges, he has himself a claim upon their obedience. With all this there is a kind of easy-going assurance in the infallibility of his own judgment, which is not put prominently forward, simply because it never occurs to him to question it.

His speech.

Adopting this theory of government, all the deductions which he drew from it are legitimate enough. He admired, he said, the Common Law of England, and would never shrink from giving his support to the judges. But they must take care not to encroach upon the jurisdictions of other courts, which were necessary in their several spheres. There were, no doubt, defects in the law, some of which he hoped to see amended in Parliament, and others, which were traceable to the innovations of the judges themselves, he was himself ready to correct. He commanded the judges to do justice boldly between himself and his subjects wherever the merely private interests of the Crown were concerned; but in matters of prerogative he warned them not to proceed until they had consulted either with himself or with his Council. The prerogative rights of the Crown must never be called in question by the lawyers in their pleadings. Every court must keep within its own bounds. Each had its own work to do, and perpetual quarrels between them would end only in the vexation of suitors. Especially the courts of Common Law must avoid making attacks upon Chancery, for claiming to decide questions with which they were themselves incompetent to deal. Under proper limitations, the judges and the justices of the peace were to execute their offices freely, and to be active in maintaining order and in suppressing vice.*

Its character.

The speech was long, and was not deficient in a certain vein of shrewdness running through it. The remarks on the evils consequent upon conflicting jurisdictions must have appealed at once to the good sense of the hearers. The one fault in the whole is that it was untrue that James was, either personally or officially, the proper depositary for the salutary control to which he laid claim.

Coke censured by the Council.

It remained to be seen whether Coke would submit to this Royal exposition of the Constitution. On the 26th he was called before the Council, and after being charged with some pecuniary transactions of doubtful character in which he had been engaged some years previously, he was censured for the words which he had used to the jury in the cases of Glanville and Allen, for his indecent behaviour in refusing to listen to the argument

* King James's *Works*, p. 549.

CH. XIV. 1616. of the Attorney-General in the King's presence, and for his steadfastness when the other judges gave way. A few days afterwards he was again summoned before the Council. He was then suspended from his seat at the Council table, and from taking his part in the ensuing circuit. The harshest part of the sentence was a recommendation that he should employ his leisure in looking over his Reports, and in correcting the extravagant and exorbitant opinions which were said to be inserted in them.* A few days after this personal question was settled, the King gave his final decision on the disputed jurisdiction, which was, as might have been expected, in favour of the Court of Chancery.

His suspension.

Coke's Reports objected to.

The requisition made to Coke was enough to exasperate the meekest of men. He was attacked both as a lawyer and as a judge. He was requested at the same time to surrender what he regarded as the just rights of his office, and, at the instigation of men who were immeasurably his inferiors in legal knowledge, to repudiate the opinions which he had publicly advanced on points of law. It was not till after three months' consideration that he sent in a statement that he had detected five errors in the Reports. They were, however, of such a trivial nature that their selection was looked upon as equivalent to a denial of the existence of any real mistakes whatever. James accordingly directed that five others, which he was alleged by Bacon and Yelverton to have committed, should be laid before

* Proceedings in Council, June 26 and 30, 1616 (*Biographia Britannica*, Art. Coke, Note R). The clause concerning the Reports is as follows: 'Lastly, that during this vacation, while he hath time to live peaceably and dispose himself at home, he take into consideration his books of Reports, wherein (as His Majesty is informed) there be many exorbitant and extravagant opinions set down and published for positive and good law. And if, in the review and reading thereof, he find anything fit to be altered or amended, the correcting thereof is left to his own discretion. Amongst other things His Majesty was not well pleased with the title of that book, wherein he styled himself Chief Justice of England, whereas he could challenge no more than Chief Justice of the King's Bench. And having corrected what in his discretion he found meet in those Reports, His Majesty's pleasure was that he should bring the same privately to himself, that he might consider thereof as in his princely judgment should be found expedient.'

him, and that he should be required to give an answer to these.*

His answers to the objections.

Coke's replies, which have all been preserved, are sufficient to show how frivolous was the nature of the charges brought against him.† In fact, there can be little doubt that what was expected was an acknowledgment of submission to the King's prerogative. As there was no sign of his lowering himself sufficiently, it was at last determined to supersede him altogether in his office, and accordingly on the 15th of November he received notice that he had ceased to be Chief Justice.

He is deprived of his office.

Coke was, at the time, almost universally regarded as a persecuted man. The treatment which he received at the hands of men who were far his inferiors was shameful. It was remarked that, when he was called upon to answer to the questions put to him on the subject of his reports, he was not even asked to sit down, and that Ellesmere's servants went so far as to neglect to take off their hats in his presence. To the men who took pleasure in insulting the fallen judge, Bacon stood in honourable contrast. He disliked his character, and he was desirous of depriving him of the power of doing harm to the King's service. But, in spite of the many insults which he had received, he never ceased to treat him with respect, and was often heard to say that a man of his learning was not to be found every day, and that it was easier to mar him than to make him.‡

* Remembrances of His Majesty's Declaration, Oct. [?] Ellesmere to the King, Oct. 22, 1616, Questions demanded of the Chief Justice, Bacon's *Works* (ed. Montagu), vii. 349, 371, 457.

† Coke's answers, Bacon's *Works* (ed. Montagu), vii. 459, 373. One of Coke's replies is noticeable, as showing the extent to which he was ready to go in order to propitiate the King. In speaking of the case of monopolies he alleged that monopolies were to be condemned, not so much because they were against law or injurious to the subject, as because they prevented the King from exercising his prerogative in granting permission at any time to other persons to import the article in question, although there might be an express statute forbidding the importation. For the other side of the question, respecting the alleged errors in the Reports, see Lord Chancellor Ellesmere's observations on Lord Coke's *Reports*, of which there is a copy in the Museum Library.

‡ Chamberlain to Carleton, Oct. 26, 1616, *Court and Times*, i. 431. I look with strong suspicion on the 'Expostulation to the Lord Chief Justice

CH. XIV.
1616.
Importance of this step.

By the deprivation of Coke, James obtained at a blow all that he had been seeking by more devious courses. There was no longer any necessity of urging the acceptance of the writ *de rege inconsulto* when the Common Law judges themselves held their offices practically, as well as theoretically, at the good pleasure of the Sovereign. From henceforward the prerogative was safe from attack in the courts of law. From henceforth, also, it stood on its own merits, and could no longer expect to obtain that moral support which it had hitherto received from the decisions pronounced from the bench by judges who were, comparatively at least with those who held office subsequently to Coke's disgrace, independent of the favours and the anger of the Crown.

Rumoured negotiations between Villiers and Coke.

At the time when Coke's fate was as yet undecided, it had been rumoured that an offer had been made to him of forgiveness, if he would consent to give his daughter in marriage to the favourite's brother, Sir John Villiers. Coke, it seems, hung back, on the score that the fortune which was asked with his daughter was more than he was inclined to give. It is hardly likely that James would have consented to restore Coke to the bench on

Coke.' (Bacon's *Works*, ed. Montagu, vii. 296.) It seems to me to be neither written in Bacon's style nor to express his thoughts. In Bacon's mind, Coke's disgrace came upon him because he refused to acknowledge the prerogative rights of the Crown. Of this there is not one word in the Expostulation. On the other hand, there are expressions as unlike anything which Bacon was likely to use as it is possible to conceive. For instance, 'Wherefore, we thank you heartily for standing stoutly in the Commonwealth's behalf'— and 'Walk therefore circumspectly, and if at length, by means of our endeavours and yours, you recover the favour that you have lost, give God the glory in action, not in words only; and remember us with sense of your past misfortune; whose estate hath and may hereafter lie in the power of your breath'—can hardly be Bacon's sentences. Still less is Bacon likely to have given advice to regain power by bribery, apparently in order that Coke might be able to carry out a more thorough persecution of the Catholics.

The discourse was, at the time, circulated anonymously. A contemporary writer says of it, 'Some father it upon Mr. Attorney, some upon Joshua Hall, or Doctor Hayward, and some upon one of those you name, but certainty we have none.' Chamberlain to Carleton, Feb. 22, 1617, *S. P. Dom.* xc. 79. In the Cabala (1654) it appears, without any signature, among Bacon's letters. In Stephens' collection (1702) Bacon's name is appended to it. Having once been attributed to him, these steps would be easy. Mr. Spedding will doubtless inform us whether there is any MS. authority for attributing it to Bacon; but until he has pronounced a decision in its favour, I shall continue to regard it as spurious.

such grounds as these; and if he was acquainted with the scheme, he can hardly have failed to ask that Coke's concession to Villiers should be accompanied by some demonstration of his readiness to withdraw from all future attacks upon the prerogative. However this may have been, and whatever may have been the particulars of which we are ignorant, it is certain that the proposal was rejected, and that nothing further was heard of it till it was revived under different circumstances.

Villiers created a Viscount.

Whilst the fortunes of Coke—who, with all his faults, was the representative of the law—were declining, Villiers was every day rising higher in the favour of the King. On the 27th of August he was raised to the peerage, by the title of Viscount Villiers and Baron Whaddon.* No sooner did Bacon hear of his proposed advancement, than he wrote to adjure him to dedicate himself to the public welfare, and to distinguish himself, above all who had served the Crown in a confidential capacity, by his care in recommending none but men of ability to office. At the same time, he took the opportunity of reminding him that there could be no excuse for him if he misused the advantages of his position in order to enrich himself, as the King had taken care that he should have no need to complain of want of means to support the dignity of the peerage.† It had been at first intended that Sherborne, which had again reverted to the Crown by the attainder of Somerset, should pass into the possession of Villiers. Villiers, however, refused to build his fortune upon the ruins of his predecessor in favour,‡ and Sherborne was given to Digby, who had no such scruples. Villiers may, perhaps, have been influenced by an opinion which was current at the time, that the possessors of that estate were doomed to misfortune, in consequence of a curse which had been pronounced by an early Bishop of Salisbury upon all who should presume to possess it in defiance of the rights of the See.§ The manor had certainly, of late years, passed rapidly from hand

Grant of lands to him.

* *Carew Papers*, 43.

† Bacon to Villiers, Aug. 12, 1616. *Works* (ed. Montagu), xii. 60.

‡ Castle to Miller, Oct. 26, 1616. *Court and Times*, i. 429.

§ *Carew Papers*, Appendix, No. II.

CH. XIV. 1616.

to hand. Somerset had resold it to the Crown almost immediately after it came into his possession, and Prince Henry, to whom it was soon afterwards given, died before he could fulfil the intention which he was said to have entertained, of restoring it to Raleigh.* Somerset repurchased it, but only enjoyed it for a few months, a circumstance which contributed to invest it still more, in the popular eye, with the character of being an unlucky possession. Whatever may have been the motives of Villiers's refusal, he was not allowed to be the loser. Lands were given him of more than double the value of the estate which he had declined.†

He is assisted by Bacon.

Bacon took care to put himself at the favourite's disposal in the negotiations relating to these arrangements. In all questions which arose, he adopted his interests, and defended them as warmly as if they had been his own. Nor did he show any less zeal in fighting his battle in a dispute in which he was involved in relation to an office of which he had obtained a grant from the King.

Roper's office in the King's Bench.

The enrolment of the pleas in the Court of King's Bench was attached to an office which had long been held by Sir John Roper. In 1612, the reversion of this office was granted by the King to Somerset, at that time known as Viscount Rochester, and to the son of Lord Harington, who were, after Roper's death, to share between them the profits derived from the fees. As, however, it was not desirable that the names of men of rank should appear on the face of the grant, each of the real holders was to nominate a person, and the patents were to be granted to the two nominees, who were in turn to enter into bonds to pay over the proceeds of the office to the great men. As a reward for allowing their names to be thus made use of, each of the nominees was to receive a twelfth part of the fees. Somerset named

Grant of its reversion to Somerset and Harington.

* So it was believed. Yet Prince Henry had the land in his hands for more than a year.

† Sherborne was exchanged for land valued at £32,000. The total value of the land given to Villiers was £80,000. Chamberlain to Carleton, Oct. 12, *Court and Times*, i. 425. Bacon to Villiers, Nov. 29, 1616, *Works* (ed. Montagu), xii. 237.

Robert Heath, a lawyer, as yet of no great eminence; Harington's choice fell upon Whitelocke. The patents were, therefore, made out in the names of Heath and Whitelocke.* Early in 1614, Harington, who had a few months before succeeded to his father's title, died, without leaving children; and his sister, the Countess of Bedford, disposed of the share in the reversion which had become hers to Somerset. Before the bargain was completed, Somerset, who was unwilling to charge himself with the expense of more than one person to execute the duties of the office, required that Whitelocke should be bought off. Accordingly, Lady Bedford gave to her brother's nominee a sum of £800, in return for which he covenanted to surrender the office whenever Somerset might request him to do so. From that time, therefore, Whitelocke, though his name was still to be found in the grant, had nothing more than a nominal connection with the reversion.†

It comes altogether into Somerset's hands.

Within a few days after Coke took his seat as Chief Justice of the King's Bench, in 1613, he had given his consent to the arrangement which had been made in favour of the two noblemen.‡ It is, however, probable that, at one time or other, he had expressed his disapprobation of such a manner of disposing of the office, and that he was anxious to sequester its profits for the sake of increasing the salaries of the judges of the court. If it was at this time that he attempted to resist the King in his claim to dispose of the place, he found it necessary to give way at once. If, on the other hand, it was not till after the fall of Somerset that he attempted to get possession of the office for the judges, he was not long in learning that his wishes would not be granted. At all events, when, in January, 1616, a false report was brought to him of Roper's death, he immediately declared that he had no intention of prolonging a contest which was certain to prove ineffectual, as it was by this time known that the King intended to

Coke's resistance.

* July 7, 1612, Pat. 10 Jac. I. Part 14.

† Whitelocke, *Lib. Fam.* 29, 46.

‡ On the 4th of November, 1613. Whitelocke, *Lib. Fam.* 59.

CH. XIV. 1616.

bestow upon Villiers the reversion which had fallen into his hands by Somerset's attainder.*

Negotiation between Villiers and Roper.

Villiers was well pleased to receive the reversion, but he would have been better pleased if he could have entered into immediate possession. He was not without hope of being able to gain this point too. He knew that Roper had set his heart upon a peerage, and that, in 1612, he had attempted to bargain with Somerset for a seat in the House of Lords. He had, on that occasion, declared his readiness to relinquish his office at once if his wishes were granted. Somerset had turned a deaf ear to his proposals,† but he might find that the new favourite was not so squeamish as his predecessor had been.

Terms of Roper's surrender.

A bargain was accordingly struck between Roper and Villiers. When, however, it came to the point, a new difficulty arose. James was willing to raise Roper to the peerage, but he was himself in want of money, and required a payment of £10,000 before he would confer the honour. Roper paid the money, and became Lord Teynham, but, naturally enough, refused to relinquish the profits of his office as well. All that he could be induced to do was to engage to put Villiers in possession, upon the understanding that the fees were to be paid over to him during his life. It was true that by this arrangement Villiers would be no richer than he had been before, but he would perhaps be exposed to fewer

* The story, as told in Roger Coke's *Detection* (1719), i. 92, places Coke's resistance in the autumn of 1616, and makes it out to have been the cause of his final dismissal. The narrative is full of blunders, so that an additional mistake more or less is of no great consequence. It is unaccountable, if the date were correct, how Chamberlain can have missed such a story, and how Bacon could have avoided referring to it in his letter to Villiers of Nov. 29. Besides, we know that, in October, Coke's friends expected that he would be allowed to take his place on the bench for the express purpose of receiving Roper's surrender, which would surely have been most unlikely if he were then the main obstacle to the surrender being effected (Chamberlain to Carleton, Oct. 26, 1616, *Court and Times*, i. 431). On the other hand, we know, from Bacon's letter of the 22nd of January, 1616 (*Works*, ed. Montagu, xii. 139), that there had already been resistance on Coke's part, of which we have no particulars. I have, therefore, taken it for granted that it was this resistance of which a distorted image is found in the *Detection*.

† *Egerton Papers*, 455. I suppose there can be no doubt that 'Sir J. Ross' is a misprint for 'Sir J. Roper.'

risks than if he had continued to be a mere expectant. As in Somerset's case, the favourite's name was not to appear on the face of the grant. Two nominees were to be designated, who, after Lord Teynham's death, were to account for the profits to Villiers, reserving only a fixed proportion to themselves. So jealous was he of any interference with his office in his lifetime, that he stipulated that they should have nothing to do with the execution of the duties till after his death.

CH. XIV. 1616.

He wishes to nominate Whitelocke as one of the holders.

Here, however, another difficulty arose. Teynham demanded to have the nomination of one of the holders, and it was known that he intended to propose that Whitelocke's name should again be inserted in the grant.* Villiers, on the other hand, wished to name two dependents of his own. Heath, who had transferred his services from Somerset to himself, might be welcome to remain, but the second place he had destined to Shute, a lawyer, who made up for the indifference of his character by his devotion to the favourite. Teynham, however, pleaded hard for Whitelocke, and most of the officials who had to do with the arrangement were inclined to give way. Bacon, however, took up Villiers' cause, and did all that he could to induce Whitelocke to surrender the original grant. He told him that he hoped better things for him than such a poor office as that which was in question; and finding that Whitelocke paid little attention to his persuasions, he even condescended to threaten him with the consequences of the King's displeasure if he still held out.

Whitelocke withdraws his claim.

Under these circumstances Whitelocke thought it better to withdraw his claim. Bacon probably reconciled his conduct to himself by remembering that no positive wrong was done to Whitelocke, who had sold his interest in the office to Somerset for £800. Still it was a question what might be the legal effect of Somerset's attainder upon a claim so involved as this, and Whitelocke was perfectly justified in refusing to surrender a

* It is not quite clear whether Teynham expected to gain any advantage by the nomination. He probably only wished to do a good turn to Whitelocke.

CH. XIV. 1616.

tittle of his rights without having them previously submitted to a court of law.* It must be confessed that there was something very dubious in the whole affair, and that it did not promise well for the realization of Bacon's prospect of seeing a new era arise under the auspices of Villiers, in which merit alone should decide upon the claims of the competitors for the highest offices of the State.

Coke succeeded by Montagu.

Whitelocke's resistance had postponed the arrangement which Bacon desired till after the decision had been taken to remove Coke from his post. Bacon was not altogether dissatisfied with this delay, as he knew that if Whitelocke continued obstinate, Coke might, if he retained his office, be able to throw obstacles in the way of Villiers and his nominees, and he suspected that he would be likely to use his influence in favour of the original holders, whose tenure of office had been confirmed by himself.† The man who was chosen to be the successor of Coke was Sir Henry Montagu, whose constant agreement with the Court on the various questions which had been at issue since the accession of James had recommended him to favour, and who, if far inferior to Coke as a lawyer, had at least the advantage of being able to make himself popular by the suavity of his manners. Before, however, he was installed in office, Bacon took the precaution of obtaining from him an engagement to admit Heath and Shute to the office which Lord Teynham was ready to vacate. Montagu made no difficulty in giving his consent, especially as it was agreed that the office should be burdened with a pension of £500 a year, to be paid to himself. On the 19th of November, the day upon which he took his seat, Whitelocke and Heath surrendered their grant into his

Lord Teynham's office made over to the nominees of Villiers.

* Whitelocke, *Lib. Fam.* 57. Bacon to Villiers, Nov. 29, 1616 (*Works*, ed. Montagu, xii. 237). I suppose the question was whether the deed of 1614 had constituted the office Somerset's property, so as to be forfeited by his attainder. Whitelocke (p. 46) says that in it he covenanted with Somerset 'to surrender up the office at his request, and not execute it but by warrant under his hand and seal.'

† This seems to be the meaning of the passage referring to Coke in the letter cited above. But the words are rather obscure. Whitelocke's silence is an additional argument against the supposition that Coke had himself opposed Heath and Shute.

hands. Upon this, Heath and Shute were at once admitted, and Teynham was put off with an agreement that in case either of the two should die during his lifetime he should be allowed to fill up the vacancy.* CH. XIV. 1616.

The Chancellor's speech to Montagu.

On the 18th, Montagu had taken the oaths of office in the presence of the Chancellor, who had recently been rewarded by the King for his long and faithful service with the title of Viscount Brackley. In addressing the new Chief Justice, he advised him to follow in the steps of his grandfather, who had occupied the office to which he now succeeded. He was unable to forbear from recommending him to avoid the example of his immediate predecessor, in a tone which showed that his thoughts were occupied more fully with his quarrel with Coke than with the business with which he was engaged.† The lawyers of Westminster Hall, who were almost to a man devoted to Coke, whose integrity and ability they respected, revenged themselves by reminding one another of the saying, 'Many Montagus, but one Markham,' which had once been current, to the disparagement of the new Chief Justice's ancestor. In the same spirit, they amused themselves by translating the Chancellor's title of Brackley into the more intelligible one of Break-law.

The French alliance.

During the months in which James was engaged in the conflict which terminated in this ill-omened victory, he was preparing to make one more attempt to obtain the hand of the French princess for his son. He had given no intimation to the Spanish Government of any intention to accept the offers which had been made to Digby and to Somerset in the preceding year. Digby had, indeed, been received on his return with every honour. To the astonishment of those who were not in the secret of his skilful discovery of the mystery of the pensions, he had been appointed Vice-Chamberlain, and had been made a member of the Privy Council, an honour which was seldom bestowed upon so young a

* Whitelocke, *Lib. Fam.* 58. *Coram Rege Roll,* Mich. Term, 14 Jac. I. Rot. 200, *P. R. O.*; *Grant Book,* p. 189. The last reference is by a misprint given in Mrs. Green's *Calendar* as 195.

† Moore's *Rep.* 826.

CH. XIV. 1616.

man. But he was not allowed to engage in any authorized negotiations with the Spanish Ambassador till a final answer had been obtained from France.

Lord Hay's embassy.

In order to obtain this answer, James determined to send a special ambassador to Paris, ostensibly in order to congratulate the young King on his marriage, but in reality to induce the French to give a definite reply to his own proposals on behalf of his son. For this purpose he selected Lord Hay, who was sure to go through his part with ostentation, and to attract the notice of the people amongst whom he went; but who, though possessed of the equivocal distinction of knowing how to spend money at a more rapid rate than any other man in England, was not without a strong fund of common sense, for which the world has hardly been inclined to give him credit.

Points on which Hay is instructed to insist.

In negotiating with France, James had made up his mind to make a stand on three points; he asked that, in the case of the decease of the Princess without children, he should not be required to reimburse her portion; that the marriage, though solemnized in France, after the forms of the Roman Catholic Church, should be again solemnized in England according to the Protestant ritual; and that the Princess should not be forced to renounce the claims to Navarre and Bearn, which she would have, in the improbable case of the decease, without heirs, of her two brothers and of her elder sister.

Probable intentions of James.

There can be no doubt that the whole negotiation was founded upon a mistake. James ought not to have thought of marrying his son to a Roman Catholic princess at all; but if he was to make the attempt to win a daughter of France, he ought to have been prepared to give way upon such points as these. The fact is that it is difficult to us to realize to ourselves the extent to which such a negotiation resolved itself in James's mind into a mere question of dignity, or the real ignorance of the deeper currents of the age, which beset him in spite of his continual meddling with political questions. If France would grant him terms which would satisfy his vanity, he would readily accept them. If not, he would turn to Spain.

It was in this spirit that Hay was directed to demand that all previous negotiations should be treated as null and void, and to require the French ministers to make new propositions, which were only to be listened to if they conceded the three points upon which the King had set his heart. CH. XIV. 1616.

It is difficult to imagine how James should have conceived it possible that the French Ministers would give way, or that he should not have allowed Edmondes to sound them on the subject before he sent a special ambassador to encounter a certain rebuff. Setting aside the money question, he could not have been ignorant that the Queen Mother would never consent to a repetition of the marriage ceremony, which she considered to be a sacrament; and the idea that any French Government would ever agree to the future dismemberment of the monarchy was so preposterous, that it would have appeared probable that James had only introduced that clause in order to ensure the rejection of the treaty, if he had not pressed it in the preceding year, when he was certainly in earnest in his wish to come to terms.*

State of affairs in France.

Perhaps he saw, in the events which had taken place in France during the past year, some reason for expecting that he would find the Queen Mother more pliable than she had been on former occasions. The Princes of the Blood, headed by the Prince of Condé, who had been too timid to put themselves at the head of the third estate in the Assembly of the States-General, had broken out into rebellion on behalf of a national and liberal policy. They had been unable to prevent the Queen from fetching home the young Spanish Princess, but they had forced her to give way to their demands, and Condé was now, to all appearance, the most powerful man in the kingdom. James may easily have persuaded himself that as there could be no doubt that the party of Condé, in whose ranks was to be found the greater part of the French Protestants, would prefer an English to a Spanish alliance, he might, without difficulty, obtain all that he desired. He forgot, however, that in France successes

* Hay and Edmondes to Winwood, July 31; Winwood to Hay, Aug. 19, 1616, Appendix VII.

CH. XIV. 1616. of this nature were usually short-lived. It was the misfortune of that country that, during the early part of the seventeenth century, liberal principles usually went hand in hand with the extremest aristocratical pretensions, and that one or other of these characteristics of the party which was opposed to the Queen Mother was sure to discredit it in the eyes of those classes from which it might naturally expect to obtain support.

Hay's want of money.

At the outset of his mission, Hay met with an obstacle of which many an ambassador had complained before. If he was to enter Paris with the magnificence which he thought fitting for the occasion, he must have money; and, as usual, the Exchequer had none to spare. The device resorted to was in the highest degree disgraceful. An idea had already been canvassed from time to time, that it might be possible to raise money by the sale of peerages. The precedent of the baronetages was sure, sooner or later, to turn the thoughts of the needy King in that direction; but as yet he had held back from such a desecration of the prerogative. It would be impossible to disguise the transaction under the pretence that the honour was granted for services rendered. It would make the grant of the highest dignity which it was in the power of the Crown to bestow into a mere matter of bargain and sale. Yet to this it was necessary to come. There were plenty who were ready to pay the required sum. One of those who were selected was, as we have seen, Sir John Roper; the other was Sir John Holles. They paid £10,000 apiece, and were, as a recompense, decorated with the titles of Lord Teynham and Lord Houghton. The sum paid by the first of the new barons was handed over to Hay. Half of Lord Houghton's money was taken possession of by the King; the other half went to Winwood, who was promised £5,000 more when the next baron was made. No doubt Winwood had worked hard for many years with little reward; but it speaks volumes for the corrupt atmosphere of James's Court that a man of Winwood's integrity should have condescended to accept payment from such a source.*

Sale of peerages.

* Chamberlain to Carleton, July 20, 1616 (*Court and Times*, i. 408).

Hay's entry into Paris.

As soon as he had thus acquired the money which was necessary to enable him to leave England, Hay started on his journey. His entry into Paris was long talked of by the French as a magnificent exhibition. His train was unusually large, and they were all attired in a sumptuous costume which surpassed all that had ever been seen on such occasions. That his horse was shod with silver shoes, which were intentionally attached so loosely that he dropped them as he passed along the streets, is probably a tale which grew up in the popular imagination; but all accounts agree in speaking of the train with which the Ambassador entered Paris as one which astonished the spectators by the gorgeous spectacle which it presented. It is more important, however, to note the reception which he met with from high and low. The whole populace of Paris cheered him as he passed, and from all ranks of the people he received a greeting which assured him that the English alliance would be welcomed by thousands who were heartily weary of the subservience of the Queen to Spain.

His difficulties.

It is proof of Hay's good sense that he was not intoxicated by his reception. He talked over with Edmondes the instructions which he had received, and sat down to repeat to Winwood the misgivings which he had expressed, before he went away, upon the success of his mission. He felt, he said, that the course which he was directed to take could end in nothing but failure. The negotiations would be broken off, and the fault would be laid upon James.* It is probable that if Winwood had been left to himself he would have coincided with

Sir J. Holles had been condemned to fine and imprisonment only a few months before for his proceedings at Weston's execution.

* 'And we must confess we find ourselves extremely troubled how to disguise His Majesty's intentions, so as they may not here plainly discover he hath a desire quite to break off this match, and take advantage thereby to drive that envy upon us which, if they had not yielded to His Majesty's desires, would have lighted heavily upon them from this people whom we find generally much to desire this alliance might take effect.' (Hay and Edmondes to Winwood, July 31, 1616, Appendix VII. 1). This almost looks as if James had determined to break off the match at all hazards; but Winwood's reply of the 19th (Appendix VII., 2) still directs them to agree to the match, if they can get better terms. Hay, therefore, probably meant only to express his fears lest the French should discover the King's intention in case of not getting his demands granted.

CH. XIV. 1616.

Hay. But he was obliged to write a despatch ordering him to persevere in the course which had been marked out for him.

Imprisonment of Condé. Aug. 21.

Before that despatch arrived in Paris, an event had occurred which made it still more inexpedient to lay James's proposals before the French Government. Condé had felt that, for some time, the position which he had attained gave him little more than a nominal dignity, and he had formed designs against Concini, the Queen's favourite, whose influence was supreme at Court.* In the place of the Queen and her dependents, he would have organised a Council, in which the principal parts would have been played by the Princes of the Blood. The Queen saw the danger, and anticipated the blow. Instigated perhaps by the young Richelieu, then first rising into note, she attempted to surprise the heads of the opposite party. As far as Condé was concerned, she was successful in her attempts. The first Prince of the Blood was thrown into prison. His confederates succeeded in making their escape. No popular commotion ensued upon this sudden blow. In spite of the liberal professions of Condé, it was difficult to persuade the nation that it would be happier by substituting for the Government which had been carried on in the name of the King, a Council principally composed of the Princes of the Blood.

Interview of Hay and Edmondes with the French ministers.

Five days after the seizure of Condé had taken place, the English Ambassadors had an interview with Villeroi and the other principal ministers. Hay, being asked what proposals he had brought from England, gave in a paper which related simply to the grievances of which his master's subjects complained. The Frenchmen were not to be put off the scent in this manner. They asked, at once, what he had to say about the marriage. Hay, according to his instructions, could only answer, that the King of England was dissatisfied with the last reply of the French Government, that he would have broken off the negotiations at once, if he had not been unwilling to do so at a time when France was suffering the

* Such at least is the explanation derived by Ranke from the despatches of the Venetian Ambassador, *Französische Geschichte*, i. 201.

miseries of a civil war, and that he was now waiting for them to make some new propositions which might be more acceptable. The French ministers said that it was necessary to discuss the old proposals before bringing forward any new ones. They were not long in discovering that on the questions of the repetition of the marriage ceremony, and of the renunciation of the right of succession, neither party would give way to the other.* Hay, therefore, had nothing to do but to bring the negotiations to a close, and to return to England, whither he was soon followed by Edmondes, who, in reward for his long diplomatic services, was raised to the dignity of a Privy Councillor. James was now free to listen, if he pleased, to the advances of the Spanish Ambassador.

Sir Dudley Carleton in Holland.

It was unfortunate that, at the very time when James was allowing himself to be tempted by the offer of a Spanish Princess for his son, circumstances were occurring which, to some extent, gave rise to a coolness between himself and the Dutch. He had again been making unsuccessful attempts to carry into effect the treaty of Xanten. Sir Henry Wotton, who had returned from the Hague weary of his twelvemonth's sojourn amongst the imperturbable Dutchmen, had been once more despatched to an elegant retirement in the more congenial atmosphere of Venice. He was replaced at the Hague by Sir Dudley Carleton, who had long been to the full as eager to escape from Italy as Wotton had been to return there.

As a diplomatist, Carleton takes rank as one of the most prominent members of the school of which Winwood was the acknowledged chief. He had, at one time, acted as secretary to the Earl of Northumberland, and had been involved in his patron's disgrace, being for some time causelessly suspected of some connection with the Gunpowder Plot. As soon as his character was cleared, he succeeded in obtaining the goodwill of the all-powerful Salisbury, and was by his influence appointed, in 1610, to the embassy at Venice. A post of this nature could hardly have satisfied him under any

* Hay and Edmondes to Winwood, Aug. 26, 1616, *S. P. Fr.*

CH. XIV. 1616. circumstances. He longed for the free air of a Protestant country, and he was anxious to be less completely cut off from his friends in England, and he took an interest in the opposition to Spain, which made him anxious to find another sphere for the exercise of his talents. It was therefore with no small pleasure that he received the news of his appointment to the post which had just been vacated by Wotton.

The Dutch decline executing the treaty of Xanten.

It was to no purpose that he did his best to obtain the consent of the Dutch to the execution of the treaty of Xanten. Rightly or wrongly, they believed that there was a settled disposition on the part of the Spaniards to make themselves masters of the disputed territories, and that even if the Spanish troops left the country after the withdrawal of their own forces, they would either return under some pretext or another, or the Emperor and the German Catholic League would carry out that which Spinola had been unable to do. Towards the end of the year, Carleton was directed to inform the States* that a declaration had been made by the Spanish Ambassador in London, that, if the treaty of Xanten were not executed before the end of the ensuing February, his master would consider himself justified in retaining as his own the places which he was occupying. Even this threat was without effect upon the Dutch, who persisted in looking with distrust upon every proposition emanating from Madrid.

James has no intention of deserting the Dutch.

Although, however, James was on less cordial terms with Holland and France than had formerly been the case, and although he was on the point of opening negotiations with Spain, it would be a mistake to suppose that he had any intention of turning against his old allies. He was guilty of no such base treachery to the Protestant cause, of which, in words at least, he had constituted himself the Protector. During the very year in which these differences had sprung up, he had been anxiously urging the Duke of Savoy to join the union of the Protestant Princes of Germany in a defensive league which would support him in his resistance

* Winwood to Carleton, Nov. 13, 1616, *Carleton Letters*, 70.

to the encroachments of the King of Spain.* His error was that by which the majority of Englishmen were led astray during the years which preceded the Italian war of 1859. He did not see that the questions at issue between the opposing powers which divided Central Europe between them lay too deep to be settled by the withdrawing of a few garrisons in one quarter, or by the rectification of a frontier in another. He was anxious that peace might be maintained, and he thought he could effect his object if he could obtain influence with all parties alike. He thought no trouble too great if he could discover a form of words which might relieve two or three towns from the pressure of a hostile garrison; but for the crying wrong and the organized injustice under which half a continent was labouring he had no thought whatever. Was it likely that when the crisis came, and when Germany burst out into a flame, he would be ready to take his part in a struggle which he had no heart to understand?

His ignorance of the real points at issue.

James's commercial policy.

Unfortunately it was not merely on political questions that James was, at this time, at variance with the Dutch. In his ignorant but well-meaning endeavours to improve the trade of his subjects James had rushed headlong into a commercial blunder which, coming, as it did, so soon after the disputes on the subject of the East India trade and the whale fishery, bid fair, for a moment, permanently to disturb those amicable relations which had hitherto subsisted between the two nations.

The cloth manufactory.

So long ago as in 1613, if not at an earlier time, the attention of the King had been called to the condition of the English cloth trade. The manufacture of cloth was in the seventeenth century as much the staple trade of England as the manufacture of cotton goods has become in our own days. From time to time statutes had been passed for the encouragement of the trade, the object of which had been to secure that the cloth should be dyed and dressed, as well as woven, before it left the country. With the greater part of the cloth exported this legislation had been successful. But there was one part of

* Wotton to the King, May 22, 1616, *S. P. Ven.*

CH. XIV. 1616.

the Continent which refused to take any cloths excepting those which were undressed. Whether it was that our mode of preparing the cloth was in reality inferior to that which prevailed in the countries bordering on the Rhine, or that from economical causes the later stages of the manufacture could be more profitably carried on abroad, it was certain that, in the whole domain of the great company of the Merchant Adventurers, which extended from Calais to Hamburg, it was impossible to command a market for cloths which had been dressed and dyed in England. So far had this feeling or prejudice reached, that whenever, in obedience to the interference of the Government or of the Legislature, the merchants consented to carry any such cloths abroad, they found they were actually unable to sell them for a price even equal to that which was commanded by those upon which no labour had been expended after the first rough process of the manufacture.*

Cockaine's proposal accepted by the King.

In spite of these reasons for leaving the trade to take its natural course, there were some persons who, with Alderman Cockaine at their head, pressed the King to make another effort to bring the whole process into the hands of English workmen.† Whatever their arguments may have been worth, they succeeded without difficulty in inducing James to issue a proclamation in which he declared his wish to throw work into the hands of the Englishmen, and expressed his dissatisfaction at the injury which was done to the cloth by the unscrupulous treatment which it met with in the hands of the foreign dyers. They were, as he alleged, accustomed to stretch it, in order to make it cover the greatest possible number of yards. The consequence was that the cloth which had been thus maltreated wore badly, and the blame was thrown upon the English manufacturers. In order to protect the foreign consumer, as well as the English workman, he had determined upon withdrawing all

* Merchant Adventurers to the Council, April [?], 1606. A Merchant of the Eastland Company to ——, March [?], 1613, *S. P. Dom.*, xx. 10; lxxii. 70. The King to Coke and others, Dec. 3, 1613, Add. MS. 14,027 fol., 254.

† Reasons of the Merchant Adventurers, with Answers by Cockaine and others, Lansd. MS. 152, fol. 282.

licenses for the exportation of undyed and undressed cloth. The charter of the Merchant Adventurers, in which, apparently, some legal flaw had been discovered, was to be cancelled, and a new company was to be formed, with Alderman Cockaine at its head. The new association was to be open to all who would give in their names, together with a statement of the amount of money which they intended to embark in the trade during the three following years.*

The new company.

After some resistance, the old company delivered up its charter on the 21st of February, 1615, and Cockaine and his followers had the whole trade at once in their hands. They soon began to feel that it was impossible for them to fulfil the magnificent promises which they had made, and they were obliged to ask for leave to export undyed cloths as their predecessors had done, on condition of making some beginning in carrying out the trade upon the new principle.† After considerable haggling they consented to export six thousand dyed cloths within the year, and twelve and eighteen thousand in the second and third years respectively of their corporate existence.‡

They had not been many months at work before the Government expressed its dissatisfaction at the manner in which they were carrying out their contract, and it was even in contemplation to put an end to the agreement which had been made with them. Accordingly the members of the old company received permission to meet and to make proposals for a more effectual method of executing the King's designs.§ As, however, the meeting persisted in declaring that there was no reason to suppose that trade could be carried on on the terms proposed to them, and refused to do more than to offer to export one thousand cloths by way of an experiment,‖

* Proclamation, July 23, 1614. See also the proclamation of Dec. 2, *S. P. Dom.* clxxxvii. 29, 35.

† Chamberlain to Carleton, Feb. 23, 1615, *S. P. Dom.* lxxx. 38.

‡ *Council Register*, June 7 and 19, 1615.

§ Warrant, Feb. 7, 1616, *S. P. Dom.* lxxxvi. 48. Bacon to the King, Feb. 25, 1616, *Works* (ed. Montagu), xii. 144.

‖ Old Company to the Council, May 1616, *S. P. Dom.* lxxx. 110. Endorsed May, 1615, aud so calendared by Mrs. Green; but the warrant just quoted shows this to have been a mistake.

CH. XIV. 1616. the negotiation was broken off, and the new company was allowed to proceed with the undertaking.*

Resistance of the Dutch. It was not long before James met with an unexpected check. The intelligence that the English were endeavouring to get into their own hands the dressing and dyeing of the cloth roused the Dutch to resist the change by every means in their power. They declared that if the English would send them nothing but dressed cloths they would refuse to buy them. They would be able, without difficulty, to establish a manufacture of their own. It was soon seen that these were not mere words. A bounty was offered for every fresh loom which was set up, and, after a few weeks, Carleton reported that, as he went about the country to examine the progress which had been made, his ears were saluted by the busy sound of the shuttle in all directions.† It was in vain that James stormed against the ungrateful Dutchmen who were thwarting him in his beneficent intentions, and that he protested that he would not be the first to give way. The Dutch continued to weave their cloth in spite of all that he could say.

Distress in the clothing districts. Before the English Government had time to take any violent measures against the Dutch, they found themselves involved at home in difficulties of their own creation. It was impossible that the disturbance of the course of trade should fail to produce injurious effects in the English clothing districts. Even before the Dutch had time to carry out their plan of opposing prohibition by prohibition, a petition came up from Gloucestershire, complaining of the number of hands which had been thrown out of employment by the new regulations. The measures taken by the Government in consequence of this petition were characteristic of the ideas prevalent at the time on such subjects. They sent for the governor of the new company, and asked him why the Gloucestershire clothworkers were out of work. He excused himself by saying that they made bad cloth, for which it was impossible to obtain a sale. The excuse was at once rejected, and he was ordered to summon a meeting of

* Chamberlain to Carleton, March 27, 1616, *Court and Times*, i. 392.

the company, and to tell the members that they were expected to buy any amount of Gloucestershire cloth which might be exposed for sale. If, in spite of this, any clothier should discharge his workmen, he would be duly punished by the Council. Either stimulated by the example of the Gloucestershire clothiers, or urged by the increasing distress resulting from diminished exportation, Worcestershire and Wiltshire soon joined in the cry. Bacon, who had taken a great interest in the King's scheme, now advised that a proclamation should be issued, forbidding any Englishman, during the next six months, to wear any silken stuff which did not contain a mixture of wool. This would give employment to the manufacturers, at the same time that it would show the foreigners that the King had no intention of receding from his purpose.*

Bacon's proposals.

Either this last proposal carried interference too far for the cooler heads in the Council, or, as is more probable, the members of the new company themselves were frightened at the difficulties which were before them. They seem to have made demands which the Government refused to concede, and after some months of fruitless negotiation, they surrendered the charter to the Crown.† A few months later the old company was restored to its original privileges.‡ James did not, indeed, resign his intention of attempting to change the course of trade, though he found that it was impossible, at the moment, to carry out his designs. Unhappily, his pretensions, which had been so injurious to the individual interests of his subjects, had also served, in some means, to diminish the good understanding which ought always to have prevailed between England and the States.

Restoration of the old company.

At the close of 1616 the position in which James found himself, both with respect to domestic and to

* Council to the Justices of the Peace in Gloucestershire, Aug. 2; Council with the King to the Council in London, Aug. 6; Council in London to the Council with the King, Aug. 13 (*S. P. Dom.* lxxxviii. 41, 45, 51); Bacon to the King, Sept. 13, 1616, *Works* (ed. Montagu), xii. 234.

† *Council Register*, Jan. 9, 1617.

‡ Proclamation, Aug. 12, 1617, *S. P. Dom.*, clxxxvii. 50*.

CH. XIV. 1616. Affairs in Ireland. foreign policy, was one in which apparent success concealed the causes of future failure. The course which had been taken by his Government in Ireland had been attended with a precisely similar result. There, indeed, the support of the new colonists set the Government above all fear of a fresh rebellion. But the very strength which James had thus acquired was likely to lead him into difficulties. If he did not conciliate, whilst it was yet possible, the more advanced portions of the Irish society in the south, he would find himself reduced to struggle at the head of the colonists against an united opposition, in which the native chiefs, the Lords of the Pale, and the citizens of the port-towns, would be welded together for the first time into a firm and compact body.

1610. Grievances of the Irish. The grievances of which these different classes complained at the time of the plantation of Ulster were various. The port-towns, in addition to their old hardships, had lately been deprived, by legal process, of a privilege which most of them claimed by charter, of refusing to pay any customs into the Exchequer. The lords and gentry were stripped as much as was possible of all political influence, unless they would give their full support to the Government, and would adopt the Protestant religion. At the same time the chiefs and their dependents were in constant fear lest the example which had been set in Ulster might be imitated in other parts of Ireland.

The Recusants. There was, however, one question on which all classes, dissimilar as they were in other respects, could agree together: they all clung to the religion of their fathers. It was not only the faith which they had learned to honour from their infancy, it was the symbol of their independence hung out in the face of the English Government, and every effort which had been made to shake their conviction only tightened its hold upon them. As long as Chichester was at the head of affairs, indeed, the Government was not likely to proceed to extremities. Proclamations were issued for the banishment of priests, orders were given to deprive of their office the magistrates who refused to take the oath of supremacy, and the shilling fine was still held threateningly over the heads of those who refused to attend the Protestant churches; but the Deputy's supreme tact kept him from carrying these threats into execution, excepting in a few scattered instances.* CH. XIV. 1610.

Such a condition of things was pregnant with future disaster. Enough was done to provoke opposition, and not enough to disarm it. It may indeed be conceded that it would be difficult enough for the Government to give up its long-cherished convictions, and to surrender a share in the administration of affairs to men who were regarded as traitors by the very fact of their refusing to take the oath of supremacy, and who were using all their influence to prevent the poorer classes from accepting that religion which, in official eyes, was synonymous with loyalty.† But, however difficult it may have been to recognize the fact, it is certain that the main danger of Ireland was no longer to be looked for from a rebellion of the Catholics against a weak Government, but from a harsh and tyrannical oppression of the Catholics by a Government which was strong because it was supported by the Protestant north as well as by the armies of England.

A Parliament proposed.

But if the Government was blind in refusing to look the question of Irish Catholicism fairly in the face, there is something absolutely astonishing in the infatuation with which James allowed himself to hope that it would be possible to gather together in a Parliament the representatives of hostile races and creeds, without provoking an immediate collision. If, indeed, he had allowed the declaration of his intention to call a Parliament to be preceded by an announcement of his willingness to consent to a repeal of the disqualifications to which the Catholics were subject, he might have been welcomed as a mediator between the two bodies into which the inhabitants of Ireland were now unhappily divided, and

* In his letter of Nov. 1, 1611, he says that the Pope has more heart than the King. The only right way to act is to bring the nobility, lawyers, and the chief men of the corporations to church. But, he adds, this would cause a rebellion.—*S. P. Irel.*

† See, for instance, the Report of the Bishop of Ferns in Mant's *History of the Church of Ireland*, 371.

CH. XIV. 1610. might even yet have laid the foundations of a united Irish nation. Without some such step as this, he was merely opening a battle-field for contending factions.

The new constituencies. The members of the Irish Government were not slow to perceive that if they wished to have a majority they must make it for themselves. Unless they could fill the benches of the House of Commons with new colonists and Government officials, any measures which they were likely to propose would only be thrown in their faces by a hostile majority. They were not without good excuse for attempting to change the character of the House. The old constituencies represented only those parts of Ireland which had been reached by the English civilization of the Middle Ages, and it was at all events necessary to extend the right of voting over the unrepresented districts. In assigning members to every county they could hardly go wrong. Of the sixty-six county members who would be thus elected, it was calculated that thirty-five would be found voting with the Government. On the other hand, it was certain that the great mass of the members returned for the old boroughs would be sturdy recusants, and the only hope of outvoting them lay in an extensive creation of new constituencies.

Charters were accordingly granted to forty-two new boroughs, returning no less than eighty-four members, and as in these cases the right of election was confined to the exclusively Protestant corporations, there could no longer be any doubt on which side the majority would be. In the House of Lords no difficulty was expected. It was true that, of the twenty-one lay Peers who were of age, fifteen were recusants; but the seventeen Bishops were quite enough to turn the scale the other way.*

Feeling of the Catholics. There was one thing which both James and Chichester had forgotten. Valuable as a Parliamentary majority

* There is a list, very imperfect, supposed to be by Davies, among the *State Papers, Irel.*, undated, but probably made up in 1611. A fuller list, almost complete, has been used in the above calculation (April 1, 1613, *S. P. Irel.*). The gaps have been filled up by reference to the list in the *Commons' Journals, Irel.*, i. 5.

is when it is the exponent of the feelings and opinions of a nation, men are not likely to pay much regard to its decisions when it represents nothing more than the unreasoning will of a set of Government nominees. The Irish Catholics saw at once that, in such a Parliament, their cause was hopeless. The tribunal by which they were to be judged was packed against them. It would be in the power of adversaries who would probably refuse even to listen to their case, and who would certainly not give themselves the trouble to understand it, to give the force of law to the most oppressive measures which theological enmity might dictate. Nor had they any prospect of being able to convert, at any future time, the hostile majority into a minority. While the Government was what it was, it would be able to maintain the requisite number of votes on its side as long as there was a hamlet in the north of Ireland which could be dignified by the name of a borough.

They wish to know what Bills are in preparation.

As soon, therefore, as it was known, in the autumn of 1611, that a Parliament was to be summoned, and that new corporations were to be erected, the Catholics were by no means unreasonably anxious to know what Bills were to be laid before the Houses when they met. According to the provisions of Poyning's Act, these Bills were to be sent over to England in order to be submitted to the Council for approbation, before the Irish Parliament was allowed to express an opinion upon them. At least in the course of a few months, therefore, Chichester might have been able to accede to their request; but he was unwilling to admit them into his counsels, and preferred to leave them to imagine the worst. At last they obtained information, in some surreptitious way, that, amongst other unobjectionable proposals, there was one which affected them deeply. The English Council had been asked to give its sanction to a Bill by which every Catholic priest was to be banished from Ireland, under a penalty of being adjudged guilty of treason if he refused to leave the country or afterwards returned to it. Nor was this all: any layman receiving a priest into his house, or affording him any

The proposed Bill against Jesuits and priests.

kind of support, was for the first offence to pay a heavy fine, for the second to undergo the penalties of a præmunire involving imprisonment and confiscation of property, and if he was found guilty of a third offence was to suffer death as a traitor.*

The petition of the Lords of the Pale.

Such provisions as these were new to Ireland. Even if this were all, it would be enough to place every Catholic layman at the mercy of the Government; and it was obvious that the same arrangements which would render it possible to pass such a measure might be counted upon, with equal certainty, to give the force of law to any still more iniquitous scheme which it might please the King and his ministers to propose. Accordingly, on the 23rd of November, 1612, a petition was forwarded to the King by five of the Lords of the Pale.† They complained that the Deputy had not acquainted them with his proposed measures, and expressed their apprehension lest unfair advantage should be taken of the new corporations to give the force of law to extreme measures. Most of these corporations, they said, were erected in places which were mere hamlets. It would be far better to wait till commerce had, in the course of time, turned them into towns, and in the meanwhile to be satisfied with the representation which the county members would give to the newly-settled districts. If the King would call a Parliament in which Ireland was fairly represented, and would give his

* The Bill is printed in a Latin translation by O'Sullivan (*Hist. Cath. Hib.* 240). I believe it to be genuine, not only because it explains the proceedings of the Catholic Lords, but because, excepting that it sets the fine at £400, it agrees with the notes of the proposed Bills in Cott. MS., Tit. B, x. 289: 'An Act that Jesuits and seminary priests shall be adjudged traitors if they shall be found within that kingdom after a certain day to be preferred, and that their receivers and relievers shall for the first offence forfeit £100, for the second be in case of præmunire, and for the third in case of treason.' This is probably the Act which was actually sent over which is described in another copy of heads as 'An Act against Jesuits, seminary priests, and other disobedient persons,' &c. (Feb. 23, 1612, *S. P. Irel.*) Another Act (Cott. MS., Tit. B, x. 295), begins 'All the statutes of religion made in England (especially concerning Jesuits, seminary priests, and recusants) to be enacted here;' but this was never adopted by the Irish Government. The list of proposed Bills in O'Sullivan (240), are mere notes of business, having, for the most part, nothing to do with Parliament at all.

† *Desiderata Curiosa Hibernica*, i. 158. According to the heading it was sent by six lords, but there are only five signatures.

consent to the repeal of the penal laws which were already in existence, he would win the hearts of his subjects for ever.

To this letter, temperate and loyal as it was, no answer was vouchsafed, unless, indeed, an order,* which was forwarded on the 11th of May, to the Deputy to send over Sir Patrick Barnwall to London, may be looked upon as an expression of the determination of the English Government to place itself in communication with one of the leading men amongst the Catholics of the Pale. But, however that may have been, it was too late to stop the course of events. The elections had taken place in April, according to the Government plan, and the session was to open on the 18th of May.

Protest of ten Lords.

On the day before the meeting, ten of the Catholic peers waited on Chichester, and laid before him a written protest against the new boroughs, and against the choice of the Castle as the place in which the Parliament was to be held. Being told that everything had been done by the King's directions, they went out to consult upon the steps which were to be taken to avert the impending evil.†

Opening of Parliament.

The next day the Deputy rode in state to St. Patrick's, before opening the session. As soon as the train reached the door of the cathedral, the Catholic peers drew back, and remained waiting outside till the conclusion of the service, when they again took their places in the procession. Chichester rode straight to the Castle, and took his seat in the room which had been prepared for the House of Lords. After a long speech from the Archbishop of Dublin, who was also Lord Chancellor, the Deputy addressed the House of Commons, telling them that the King had recommended to them Sir John Davies as a man fit to be their Speaker, and that he hoped they would immediately elect him. When he had finished his speech, the Commons returned to their own house.

It was hardly to be expected that the Catholics in the

* *Council Register*, May 11, 1613.

† A brief relation, &c., *Des. Hib. Cur.* i. 421. Chichester and Council to the King, May 1613, *S. P. Irel.*

CH. XIV. 1613. Election of a Speaker.

House of Commons should take this recommendation in good part. As soon as Sir Thomas Ridgway had proposed the election of Davies, Sir James Gough, a staunch Catholic, started up and argued that both the members who represented the new boroughs, and those who, though they had taken their seats for old constituencies, were not residents in the places where they had been elected, were disqualified from sitting as members of the House. It would, therefore, be necessary to decide who had been lawfully chosen before they were entitled to elect a Speaker. As soon as he had said this, several members called out to him to tell them the name of the man whom he proposed instead of Davies. Gough, whose theory required that he should hold his tongue, and refuse to nominate anyone till the elections had been scrutinised, like a true Irishman as he was, blurted out the name of Sir John Everard, a name which was dear to Irish Catholics as that of the man who had, for conscience sake, resigned his dignified position upon the Bench. It was in vain that Sir Christopher Nugent and William Talbot, the legal oracle of the party, tried to bring back the discussion into its old channels. Sir Oliver St. John, with the authority of an old member of the English House of Commons, rose to second Davies' nomination, and insisted on putting the question immediately to the vote. It was at that time customary that those who voted in the affirmative should leave the House, whilst those who voted in the negative should remain in their places. When, therefore, St. John, with those who voted with him, were gone, the Catholics saw that the field was left to themselves. Unable to resist the temptation of gaining a momentary advantage, they threw their arguments to the winds, and seated Everard in the chair before their opponents had time to return.

Struggle in the House.

It was not likely that the leaders of the Government party should be disconcerted by such a manœuvre as this. Having quietly counted the number of Davies' supporters, they announced that as their candidate had obtained one hundred and twenty-seven votes, and as, though their opponents had refused to be counted, it was impossible, from the numbers of those who were known to be present, that they could muster more than ninety-seven, Sir John Davies was duly elected Speaker of the House. Finding that, in spite of all that they could say, Everard showed no signs of any intention to leave the chair, the two tellers, Sir Thomas Ridgway and Sir Richard Wingfield, took Davies in their arms and dropped him in his opponent's lap. Even this somewhat unparliamentary proceeding, however, was insufficient to effect its object, and it was only after an unseemly struggle, in which Everard was nearly pulled to pieces between the Protestants who were trying to drag him from his place by the legs and the Catholics who clutched hold of his collar in the hope of being able to keep him in his place, that the candidate of the minority was finally ejected from his seat. As soon as Everard and his partisans perceived that they had no chance in a conflict of this kind, they left the House in a body. When they reached the outer door they found it locked, and it was some time before they were able to make their way out. To all entreaties to return, they answered that those who remained were no House, and that their Speaker was no Speaker. As justice was not to be obtained, they would appeal to the Deputy and to the King. As soon as the seceding members were gone, those who were left behind adjourned to the 21st, the day which had been fixed for the presentation of the Speaker to the Deputy.*

Petition to the King and Council.

Before they met again, the Catholic Peers had signified their adhesion to the step which had been taken by the members of their party in the Lower House. On the 19th they joined with their friends in the Commons in requesting Chichester to forward to the King and the English Council a request that they might be allowed to send a deputation to plead their cause in London.† On the 20th the recusants of the House of Commons waited again upon the Deputy, and asked to be excused from attendance

* Farmer's Chronicle. The Commissioners' Return; True Declaration; A Brief Relation, &c.—*Des. Cur. Hib.* i. 168, 196, 351, 404, 421. Farmer erroneously places the election on the 19th.

† The Petitions, *Des. Cur. Hib.*, i. 197, 201.

CH. XIV. 1613. upon their duties, on the extraordinary plea that their lives were not safe. They also asked what authority Chichester had received from the King to empower him to erect the new corporations. On the 21st, which was the day on which the Speaker was to be presented, they at first expressed their willingness to take their places on certain conditions, but after further consideration they refused to do so unless the members for the new boroughs were sequestered from their seats until the elections had been examined. In this they were supported by the Lords, who also begged to be excused from attendance, and again asked that the whole matter might be referred to the King.* These conditions were, as a matter of course, rejected, and Chichester went down to the House and formally installed Davies in his office. On his return, he wrote to the English Government, giving full account of what had passed, and recommending that the proposal of sending a deputation to England should be accepted.† The next day eleven of the Catholic Lords formally seceded from the Upper House. It was in vain that a proclamation was issued by the Deputy, in which they were required to return to their places, if it were only to pass the Act of recognition of His Majesty's title. Chichester was told that they were quite ready to recognize the King's authority, but that they would never take their seats till their grievances had been redressed. Accordingly, finding that there was nothing to be done, Chichester adjourned the two Houses, and despatched the Earl of Thomond, Sir John Denham, and Sir Oliver St. John to England, on the 28th, to give an account of his proceedings to the King; and a day or two later gave permission to six of the recusants to follow them. As soon as he had received an answer to his letter of the 21st of May, he gave directions that others of the recusant members should go over to England to join the

Davies installed as Speaker.

The deputation to the King.

* *Des. Cur. Hib.*, i. 355, 424, 425. The account of the last-mentioned petition is introduced, 'The same day, the 24th of May, 1613, they exhibited,' &c. It should be undoubtedly, 'The same day, the 21st of May, 1613, the Lords exhibited.' I have no doubt that it is the petition given in full in Cott. MS., Tit. B, x. 297.

† This letter is referred to in a letter of the Council to Chichester, *Council Register*, May 30, 1613.

original deputation in laying their complaints before the throne.* On the 17th of June, Parliament was prorogued to a more favourable opportunity.†

What chance had they of being heard?

The Irish deputation can hardly have expected that their complaints would be very favourably received. Even if they had had no prejudices to contend with in the mind of James, they must have known that, in its original shape, their theory was utterly irreconcilable with Parliamentary practice, and that in its final form of a claim to ignore the King's prerogative in the creation of boroughs, until it had been confirmed by themselves, they were still more directly flying in the teeth of Parliamentary usage. On the other hand, however, they knew that it was not of very much importance whether they had the letter of the law on their side or not. It was under the cover of strict legal right that the King had attempted to do them a great injustice. By the help of a factitious Parliamentary majority he had intended to give the colour of law to his own iniquitous designs. All that it was necessary for them to do—all, in fact, that they were able to do—was to show him, in the plainest manner possible, that they would not be parties to such a transaction. If the new settlers were to impose laws upon all the older population of the country, it could not be helped; but, at least, their tyranny should be seen in its true colours. The work of a faction should not bear the appearance of proceeding from the representatives of the nation. So far the Irish Catholics had been successful, and they might even hope that their determined attitude might induce the King to reconsider his designs, and to learn that a constitution must be carried out in its spirit, and not merely in its letter.

Petition brought by the agents.

The petition,‡ which was brought over by the agents of the Irish recusants, was drawn up with some ability. It began with a complaint of the numerous false returns which were alleged to have been made by the sheriffs. After the slightest possible reference to the question of

* *Des. Cur. Hib.* i. 206, 207, 216, 426. Chichester and Council to the King, May 1613, *S. P. Irel.*

† *Commons' Journals, Irel.* i. 11.

‡ *Des. Cur. Hib.* i. 211.

CH. XIV. 1613.

Everard's election, it passed on, leaving wholly unmentioned the contested right of creating new constituencies, to the only point upon which its authors were formally in the right. By an Act* which had been passed in the English Parliament in the reign of Henry V., and which consequently, like all the older English statutes, was valid in Ireland, it had been enacted that none should be elected to Parliament who were not resident in their several constituencies. The Act had long ago become obsolete in England, but it might fairly be argued that a time when an attempt was made to carry unpopular measures through the legislature, by means of men of an alien race, was not one in which it was possible for Irishmen to surrender their strict legal rights on such a point.

The Irish heard before the English Council.

On the 8th of July the question came on for a hearing before the King and the Council. An additional number of the members of both Houses had been sent for,† and they, as well as the original deputation, were patiently listened to. On the 17th James concluded the discussion by a speech in which he told the complainants that he knew that the question of religion was at the bottom of the whole dispute, and whether their objections to the elections were justifiable or not, they were certainly in the wrong in seceding from Parliament. He then asked them whether they disputed his power to make new boroughs. They were forced to answer that they could not object to the prerogative which he claimed, but that they thought that the use to which he had put it was decidedly inexpedient.‡ They were then left to wait till James had time to consider their case, and to pronounce a decision upon it.

Talbot questioned.

Unfortunately, the amicable course which these proceedings were taking was interrupted by a wholly uncalled-for dispute between the Government and one of the leading members of the deputation. A book had recently been published by the Jesuit Suarez, in which the

* 1 Hen. V. cap. 1.

† *Des. Cur. Hib.* 230.

‡ Lansd. MS., 156, fol. 241, 242. Amongst other things, these notes contain the heads of an unpublished speech of Bacon's.

right of subjects to depose and murder their Sovereigns, after sentence of deprivation by the Pope, was maintained in all its naked atrocity. In the course of the discussions, Abbot, who had made extracts from this book, laid them before the Irish who were present. One of them, Wiliam Talbot, hesitated to express his abhorrence of the doctrines in question, but, after some delay, signed a paper in which he asserted that the opinions of Suarez concerned matters of faith, of which he was not a competent judge. As for his own loyalty, he was ready to acknowledge King James to be his lawful Sovereign, and to bear him true faith and allegiance during his life.* With this the Council ought, undoubtedly, to have been content; but in those days the inexpediency of attacking speculative error by force was not so well understood as it is at present. Talbot was accordingly committed to the Tower.† A few days afterwards another member of the deputation, Thomas Luttrell, was sent to the Fleet for a similar offence.‡ Luttrell was probably released not long afterwards, but Talbot, having refused to make any further submission, at least until after orders had been given to proceed against him in the Star-Chamber,§ was sentenced by that Court to a fine of £10,000. He was, however, permitted to return to Ireland, and, in all probability, the fine, as was usual in such cases, was remitted.‖

CH. XIV. 1613.

New grievances.

In addition to the original complaints, a paper had been handed in to the King, in which was set down a long list of grievances under which the Irish were suffering.¶ He accordingly made up his mind to send over four Commissioners, who were directed to investigate upon the spot all the charges which had been brought against the Government.** The four Commissioners, Sir

Commissioners sent to investigate them.

* Bacon's charge, *Works* (ed. Montagu), vi. 452; *Des. Cur. Hib.* i. 232.

† *Council Register*, July 17, 1613.

‡ *Council Register*, July 22, 1613.

§ On the 25th of Nov. 1613, *Council Register*.

‖ *Des. Cur. Hib.* i. 321.

¶ Delivered in on the 15th of July, 1613, Lansd. MS., 156, fol. 241, b. A fuller collection was delivered to the Commissioners in October, *Des. Cur. Hib.* i. 237. Compare i. 362.

** Instructions to the Commissioners, *Des. Cur. Hib.*, 327.

CH. XIV. 1613. Humphrey Wynche, Sir Charles Cornwallis, Sir Roger Wilbraham, and George Calvert, arrived in Dublin on the 11th of September.* After a long and patient investigation, they sent over their report on the 12th of November.†

In the first place, they reported that they had investigated fourteen cases in which complaints had been made of undue elections, amongst which they only found two in which the charge was, in their opinion, substantiated. In some cases it appeared that the Irish had not taken the trouble to make themselves acquainted with the English election rules, in others, the license which the prevailing faction had allowed to itself was certainly not greater than that which was often taken by the sheriffs of English counties. After narrating the proceedings at the choice of a Speaker, and lamenting the evident prevalence of recusancy, they proceeded to comment on the general grievances of the kingdom. They acknowledged that much oppression had been exercised by the soldiers, but alleged that few complaints had been made on the subject, and that the Deputy was determined to lose no time in redressing the evils petitioned against. Of the remainder of those complained of, they denied that some were grievances at all; for those the existence of which they admitted, they promised, in the Deputy's name, immediate redress.

1614. As soon as this report was received in England, Chichester was directed to send over a certain number of the members of the two Houses, who had returned to Ireland in the preceding summer, in order that they might be present when the King delivered his judgment.‡ At the time when these orders reached Chichester, the Irish Catholics were in a state of considerable excitement. One of the members of the deputation, Sir James Gough, had given out, on his return, that the King intended to grant liberty of conscience. On examination, it proved that Gough had heard James

* In *Des. Cur. Hib.*, i. 283, this date is given as the 25th. The Commissioners themselves say that it was the 11th, *Ibid.* i. 362.

† The Commissioners' return and certificate, *Des. Cur. Hib.* i. 334.

‡ Council to Chichester, *Council Register*, Jan. 27, 1614.

say, as he had already said so often, that he had no intention of meddling with any man's conscience. He had neglected to report that the ordinary language of the King proved that these words had reference only to the secret belief of his Catholic subjects, and not to the external practice of their religion.* If the Catholics still misunderstood the King's intentions, they must have been undeceived by a proclamation which was shortly afterwards sent over from London, in which James declared himself to have been thoroughly satisfied with the course which Chichester had taken throughout the whole affair.† At the same time, Chichester was himself summoned to England to be present at the final sentence.

The King's decision.

On the 12th of April, 1614, James delivered his judgment. As might be supposed, that judgment was altogether against the Catholics. In almost every step which they had taken they had been formally in the wrong, and of this James was sure to make the most. The only point on which he gave way, was that the members for the few boroughs which had been erected since the writs had been issued should not take their seats during the present Parliament.‡ On the 7th of May, the Irish deputation was directed to sign a form of submission which was presented to them. They did so, under protest that they merely meant thereby to testify their readiness to admit Davies as their Speaker, but that they had no intention of relinquishing their claims to the redress of the grievances of which they had complained.§ A few days afterwards, they were once more before the Council. Their legal objections were listened to, and Coke employed his unrivalled stores of learning to overthrow their assertions, by quoting a succession of English precedents.‖

May 20. Coke disposes of their legal objections.

It was easy for Coke to gain a victory in such a contest as this. But it was far more difficult for James to decide upon a policy which would assure to him the

* *Des. Cur. Hib.*, i. 287.
† *Des. Cur. Hib.*, i. 291.
‡ *Des. Cur. Hib.*, i. 302.
§ Petition, May 8, 1614, *S. P. Irel.*
‖ *Council Register*, May 18, 1614. Lansd. MS., 159, fol. 110 a, 111 b.

CH. XIV. 1614.

Chichester returns to Ireland with instructions to carry out the laws against the recusants.

loyal submission of his Irish subjects. The course which he finally adopted, was one of those half-measures which purchase immediate success at the price of future failure. When Chichester returned to Dublin, he carried with him instructions which authorized him to put in force once more all the worn-out schemes for driving the Irish into the Protestant Church. He was to republish the proclamation for the banishment of Jesuits. He was to exact the shilling fine for recusancy. He was to take the sons of the Catholic Lords from their parents, and to send them over to England for education. If the towns persisted in electing magistrates who refused the oath of supremacy, he was to confiscate their charters. Foreseeing that such orders as these were likely to rouse opposition, James added directions that citadels should be built at Cork and Waterford, that Dublin Castle should be put in a state of repair, and that all suspicious persons should be disarmed. It would also be more than ever necessary to make Ulster into a huge garrison against the Irish population, by forbidding those marriages which had already begun to take place between the Scottish colonists and the natives, which threatened to obliterate the line of distinction which it was so necessary for the Government to preserve, as long as it was carried on upon the principles which seemed so indispensable to the minds of the King and his ministers.* On the other hand, in a letter which was forwarded to the Deputy, not long after his arrival in Ireland, James announced his intention of overlooking the past offences of the recusant members, and of withdrawing the obnoxious Bill against Jesuits and their supporters, which had been originally the real though not the ostensible ground of the dispute. To this concession was added a direction not to allow the members of the eight boroughs which had been created since the issue of the writs to take their places. The same fate was to fall upon the representatives of three places who had not been able to show any right to elect

Withdrawal of the Bill against Jesuits.

* Instructions to Chichester, June 5, 1614, *S. P. Irel.*

members at all, and upon those of two boroughs where the elections had not been duly conducted.*

Universal discontent.

What was likely to be the effect of neglecting the opportunity which had been offered to James to come to terms with his Irish subjects, by throwing overboard the irritating but ineffectual checks upon recusancy which were in existence, might have been learned by the perusal of a paper which was written about this time, apparently with a view to its being laid before the Government.† That by which the author was most struck, was a new feature which had lately arisen on the face of Irish society. In former times rebellions had been partial; some part of the kingdom, or some class of the inhabitants, had remained faithful to the Crown; now, however, nothing of the sort was to be expected. For the first time, the merchants of the cities, the lords of English origin, and the native Irish, were banded together, as one man, against the new colonists, and the alien religion which they brought with them. It was true that, for the present, the King's Government had force on its side, but let anything occur which would offer a chance of success to a rebellion, and there was 'just cause to fear the union of that people whose hearts are prepared to extirpate both the modern English and the Scots, which is not difficult to execute in a moment, by reason they are dispersed, and the natives' swords will be in their throats in every part of the realm (like the Sicilian vespers), before the cloud of mischief shall appear.' It is true that the writer could recommend no better remedy against the evil than that which could be obtained by the building of additional forts, and by similar repressive measures; but his words of warning were none the less ominous, because neither he nor his readers were able to discern the true path of safety.

Prospects of a quiet session.

But if the distant prospects of the country were dark and lowering, all was bright in the immediate future. The concession made by the King in withdrawing the Jesuit Bill seemed likely to be rewarded by a quiet

* The King to Chichester, Aug. 7, 1614, *Des. Cur. Hib.*, i. 323.

† 'A discourse of the present state of Ireland, 1614.' By S. C. *Des. Cur. Hib.* i. 430.

CH. XIV. 1614. session whenever Parliament should again meet in Dublin. The recusants, finding that the intention was relinquished of forcing new laws upon them by means of a factitious Parliamentary majority, and having so far gained their object, saw that, whilst they had everything to lose by further opposition, they might possibly obtain additional concessions by taking part in the debates, and that at all events their presence would act as a check upon the Protestant members.

Meeting of Parliament.

Accordingly, when the session began on the 11th of October, Davies took his place in the chair as quietly as if no disturbance had ever happened. On the following day, indeed, a member proposed that the disputed elections should be examined in the House. After some discussion, however, it was agreed to refer the whole question to a committee, which was chosen from amongst the members of both parties indiscriminately. After some time had elapsed, the committee reported that it would be advisable to let the question drop, at least for the present session; and in this decision the Catholic party, being unwilling to contest what had now become for them a mere point of form, at once acquiesced,* especially as they were assured that the present return should not be used as a precedent.† As to the Government measures for recognition of the King's title, and for the attainder of Tyrone, they were all passed without difficulty.

Postponement of the subsidy.

There was, indeed, one point upon which Chichester foresaw that he would have greater obstacles to contend with. Like all Deputies, he was much in want of money, and the English Privy Council was always more ready to supply him with advice which he did not want, than with the gold of which he stood in need. Under these circumstances, an English Parliament would have been asked at once for a subsidy; but a subsidy had never once been heard of in Ireland, and it seemed a dangerous experiment to introduce a novelty of this kind at a time of such excitement. Accordingly, some weeks before

* *Commons' Journals, Irel.* i. 11, 14, 23. Davies to Somerset, Oct. 31, 1614, *S. P. Irel.*

† St. John to Winwood, Nov. 4, 1614, *S. P. Irel.*

the meeting of Parliament, an attempt was made to raise a Benevolence, in imitation of the contribution which was making such a stir in England.* It was, perhaps, because this measure was coolly received that the Deputy decided upon preparing a Subsidy Bill. As, however, it was necessary to send it over to England for approval, and the prevalence of westerly winds made it unlikely that an answer could be received in time to pass the Act before Christmas, Chichester determined to prorogue Parliament, and to hold another session in the spring of 1615. The prorogation accordingly took place on the 29th of November. Before he had signified his intention, a paper was handed to him, containing a list of grievances, amongst which was found a petition that the recusant lawyers who had been debarred from practising since Chichester's return from England, might be permitted to resume their avocation.†

Prorogation of Parliament.

1615. Opening of another session.

Grant of a subsidy.

It was on the 18th of April that the new session was opened. Chichester replied to the grievances of the Commons, but could grant them no hope of the removal of the restrictions upon the lawyers. In spite of their disappointment, however, which the Catholics must have felt, they gave their full support to the Subsidy Bill, which was carried up to the Upper House within ten days after the commencement of the session.‡ To increase the satisfaction of the Government, the Commons had renewed their order of the last session for allowing the question of the elections to drop for the present,§ and were employing their time upon two Acts which, upon their own request, had been sent over to England at the close of the last session. By one of these all legal distinction was taken away between the different races by which Ireland was inhabited; by the other, a statute was repealed by which the intermarriage of Irish with Scots had been prohibited.|| James, therefore, had consented to relinquish at least one of the

* St. John to Winwood, Sept. 3, 1614, *S. P. Irel.*

† *Commons' Journals, Irel.*, i. 44.

‡ *Commons' Journals, Irel.*, i. 61.

§ *Commons' Journals, Irel.*, i. 52.

|| *Statutes of Irel.*, 11, 12, & 13 Jac. I., cap. 5 and 6. These and the following statutes were passed in this session.

CH. XIV. 1615. measures which he had pressed upon Chichester when he left England in the preceding year.

Grievances. It was impossible that the Catholic members would allow the opportunity to slip of expressing their hope that their conciliatory behaviour would be met in a similar spirit by the Government. It would seem as if Chichester had been desirous of meeting them half-way, for when the question of the recusant lawyers was brought forward, Sir Thomas Ridgway, who would hardly have acted in opposition to the Deputy, himself proposed that a petition should be presented in their favour. Accordingly, when, on the 16th of May,* the petition of grievances was presented, it was found to contain, amongst other recommendations, a wish that the recusant lawyers might be restored, and that the Act of Elizabeth by which the shilling fines were imposed might be repealed.† As there is no trace upon the Journals of any debate on these points, it is to be presumed that the proposals made received the assent of both parties. There must have been moderate men amongst the Protestants, who, after sitting for some time on the same benches with Sir John Everard and others who resembled him, must have discovered that, whatever theorists might say, there was no reason to fear lest the stability of the throne should be shaken by the cessation of a petty persecution which only served to irritate those who were the objects of it.

May 16. Prorogation of Parliament. To the petitions of the Commons were annexed a number of Bills, which they requested the Deputy to send over to England. As soon as he had received them, he prorogued the Parliament to the 24th of October, when it was understood that a third session was to be held, at which it was hoped that the requests of the Catholics would be granted.

Dissolution of Parliament and recall of Chichester. Unfortunately, for many years after the prorogation in the spring of 1615, the trustworthy information upon Irish affairs which has come down to us is exceedingly scanty. All that we know is, that on the 22nd of

* *Commons' Journals, Irel.* i. 68.
† *Commons' Journals, Irel.* i. 92.

August James wrote to appoint Commissioners for the purpose of dissolving the Parliament upon the day which had been fixed for its meeting;* and that, on the 29th of November, he wrote again to Chichester, recalling him from his post, and directing him to hand over his authority to the Chancellor and Sir John Denham, who were to act as Lords Justices till the appointment of a new Deputy.† It is difficult to resist the conclusion that the real cause of Chichester's recall was his unwillingness to turn a deaf ear to the petition of the Commons. We know that, since his return from England, he had done little or nothing to carry out the King's instructions to put in force the laws against the recusants. An abortive conspiracy, which had been discovered in Ulster at the close of 1614, may well have warned a man who was less ready than Chichester to accept the teaching of facts, that it was not a time to provoke additional enmities. The part taken by Ridgway in the last session, too, is enough to render it extremely probable that the petition which he advocated was not disliked by the Deputy.‡ If it be really the case that his recall was owing to his unwillingness to engage in a fresh career of persecution, all that can be said is, that it was a worthy end to the government of such a man. Once

CH. XIV.

1615.

* The letter is mentioned in the Commission, *Commons' Journals*, i. 97.

† The King to Chichester, Nov. 29, 1615, *S. P. Irel.*

‡ Soon after taking possession of his office, Chichester's successor wrote a letter which countenances the idea that the question of the treatment of the recusants was at the bottom of the change. His Majesty's affairs, he wrote, prosper in all things, 'saving in that strong combination of recusancy wherein the well or ill-doing of this state doth much depend. I make no doubt of the strength of His Majesty's laws in force in this kingdom, if it be extended unto them with convenient moderation, but will work alteration in many of the most obstinate. It hath been at sundry times worthily begun heretofore, *but there hath wanted constancy in the pursuit, whereby it hath been esteemed a work of humour, and for particular ends, rather than a prosecution grounded upon solid judgment.* These people must be otherwise dealt withal. They must not find us abandoning the ground we get, for they will sooner [?] invade upon us. It behoves us to be doing somewhat, and to be doing always, and that legally, moderately, and constantly; otherwise we shall but spin and unspin, and never produce any worthy or profitable effect. Particularly the action of the towns, they grow daily in disobedience, refusing in divers of them to elect any chief magistrates, because they that should supply the places are all recusants.' St. John to Winwood, Dec. 31, 1616, *S. P. Irel.*

CH. XIV. 1615. more, when so many were blind to what was passing around them, and when even his own prejudices stood in his way, he saw the only path in which it was possible to walk with safety. This time he was forced to give way to lesser men.

His government of Ireland. However this may have been, his government of Ireland needs no eulogium beyond the plain and simple narration of his actions. Of Chichester it can be said, as it can be said of few, that, if he failed to accomplish more than he did, it was because he was seldom, if ever, allowed to carry out his own designs in his own way. If full powers had been granted to him to deal with Ireland according to the dictates of his own wisdom, the blackest pages in the history of that unfortunate country would never have been written.

1616. He is succeeded by Sir Oliver St. John. The successor who, after some months' deliberation,* was appointed to succeed him was Sir Oliver St. John. At any other time it would have been a choice meriting approval. He had filled many offices, and had filled them all with credit. He was, at the time of his appointment, Vice-President of Connaught, and Master of the Ordnance. Unfortunately, in the late Parliament, he had distinguished himself as a member of the Protestant majority, and his accession to the office for which he had been chosen can only have served as an advertisement to the Irish Catholics that they had no further concessions to expect.

Position of affairs at the close of 1616. In such a mind as that of James, consistency is not to be expected, otherwise it would seem strange that he was sending a new Deputy to carry out a strong anti-Catholic policy in Ireland, almost at the very time when he was giving up the French alliance in favour of a match which would be regarded with detestation by every Protestant in Europe. Such an inconsistency as this did not augur well for the wisdom of his future policy. The decision of what that policy should be was now more than ever in his own hands. When he first arrived in England, he had found himself surrounded by councillors

* St. John landed in Ireland on the 27th of August, 1616, and received the sword on the 30th.

who had been trained up in the school of his predecessor; and he had met a Parliament which pressed him to accept a policy of its own. Gradually, not by force of intellect or character, but from sheer ignorance and self-conceit, he had set at nought both the warnings of his statesmen and the counsel of his Parliament. To all outward appearance his success had been complete. The members of Parliament withdrew silently to their homes without uttering a murmur. Privy Councillors were unanimous in singing the praises of the prerogative. Puritanism itself was hushed, and a decorous uniformity prevailed in the Church of England. Even the last blow which had been struck at the independence of the Law Courts failed to rouse the dissatisfaction of the nation.

No complaints heard in the nation.

The fact is that, excepting at times when political intelligence is widely diffused, it is seldom that the encroachments of arbitrary power awake resistance until the people have some tangible grievances to complain of. As long as the claims of the prerogative were merely regarded as abstract questions, the mass of the people was ready enough to look upon them as matters which lawyers might discuss, but which were possessed of no general interest for ordinary men. At the beginning of the reign of James there had been considerable excitement amongst the Puritans, but that excitement had died out with those men by whom the vestments and ritual of the Church of England had been looked upon with especial dislike. The grievance of the Impositions had indeed pressed upon the material interests of the nation. But they had been considerably diminished since they had been first laid on, and they were rather objected to as being forced upon the nation in violation of principle, than as being themselves an intolerable burden upon commerce.

The events which in reality stand out most prominently amidst the occurrences of the first fourteen years of James's reign, are his dismissal of his Parliament in 1610, and his dismissal of his Chief Justice in 1616. The Government was to be simplified. Instead of taking its place in a complicated machinery of which the parts

CH. XIV. 1616.

had constantly worked together in harmony, the Crown was to assume the direction of the whole. Parliament must be content to express opinions with bated breath, and to give its consent to the proposals of the Government. The judges were to be content with doing justice wherever private interests were concerned, but to take care how they allowed themselves to meddle with the prerogative.

Real dangers.

Whatever may have been the feeling of the mass of the nation at the time, it is certain that there were many who felt that these were not merely questions for lawyers to dispute about. No political truth is so well supported by evidence as this, that the obliquity of mind which leads a monarch to aim at arbitrary power is certain to lead him on to the abuse of it as soon as it is acquired. The man who feels no desire to submit his actions to the approval of the nation is certain, sooner or later, to act so as to incur their disapprobation. It might be foretold with certainty, that even if the scene at Hampton Court were to be condoned by the Protestants of England, the man who played the principal part in it would, before long, be led on to fresh aggressions upon the religious liberty of his subjects; that even if the dissolution of two Parliaments had been received without a murmur, the Sovereign who dissolved them would be sure to commit some gross blunder which would rouse the discontent of the nation; and that even if Coke stood alone in resisting the aggression of the King, it would not be long before the judges would, with some honourable exceptions, be regarded by Englishmen as tools which the King made use of to throw a decent veil over his own oppressive courses.

The disgrace of Coke as an historical landmark.

With the disgrace of Coke, the period of transition between the history of the Tudors and the history of the Stuarts comes to an end. It is a great historical landmark. Up to this time James has been busy in acquiring the powers which were afterwards to be used with such fatal results to himself and to his son. In two or three years James will be the most unpopular man in the three kingdoms. England will be disgusted by the negotiations with Spain. Scotland will be enraged by the Five Articles of Perth. Ireland will be irritated by the seizure of the charter of Waterford.

How far James had kept within the limits of the constitution.

It cannot be denied that, in grasping the powers which enabled him to do these things, James had kept within the letter of the constitution. No lawyer would venture to affirm that the Crown had no right to dismiss Parliament without granting its requests, or to put an end to a judge's tenure of office; and, least of all, would Elizabeth have suffered her prerogative in these points to be questioned for an instant. But, whilst James was only maintaining rights which he had derived from his predecessor, he was blind to the fact that the whole tendency of the age was rendering his profitable exercise of them impossible. The peace which he had brought with him had put an end to the necessity which had so long called for a strong Government. Not only would the abuses which had been tolerated in the rule of Elizabeth, in the midst of the storm, be looked on with a suspicious eye when no danger was at hand; but there were innumerable branches of the prerogative, which had once been beneficial to the nation, which had now become abuses. The nation panted for liberty, for freedom from restraint, for more active participation in the actions of the Government. As yet there was but little commotion. If the tide, which had set in favour of concentration of authority during the whole course of the Middle Ages, had now turned, it had not as yet begun to flow strongly in the other direction. But the change of direction was manifestly there, and it only required a few unpopular actions on the part of the Sovereign to bring it to light.

Creation of the Prince of Wales.

It was not without important results upon the history of the country that it was precisely at this moment that the King's only remaining son reached an age at which he began to be capable of taking an interest in political affairs. On the 4th of November, 1616, when he was within a few days of completing his sixteenth year, Prince Charles, who had long been known as the Duke of York, was created Prince of Wales. Few anecdotes of his boyhood have been preserved. Every now and then some letter-writer mentions him in terms of commen-

CH. XIV. 1616.

dation; but the absence of any notice of such striking acts and sayings as those which had won for his brother an enduring place in the hearts of the nation leaves an impression of the steady but somewhat backward boyhood which must have followed upon the years of weakness from which he had suffered. The lameness with which he was afflicted in his early years had passed away under the judicious treatment of Lady Carey, who refused, in defiance of all the advice which was so liberally offered to her, to attempt to strengthen his limbs by the use of iron supports; but the physical weakness of his childhood seems to have left its impress upon his tenacious and irresolute mind.

End of the Elizabethan age.

Yet, even with all his defects, it is not impossible that, if he had been ten or fifteen years older, he might have learned another lesson from that which carried him to the scaffold. As it was, at the time when his intellect opened to receive the instructions of those who were around him, the fulness of the Elizabethan culture was already gone. In the spring of that very year in which Bacon was bringing his long controversy with Coke to an issue, and was busily engaged in divorcing politics from law, the greatest of the lights of the age which was fading away was laid in his quiet grave at Stratford. The literature, the theology, and the statesmanship which had been known to the heroes of Elizabeth, were gone. The harmony of their many-sided life was at an end. In its place was rising the strife between opposing theories and the opposition between definite systems of thought and action. There has, perhaps, never been a moment in the history of England at which such a youth as Charles could enter upon manhood with less chance of understanding the real nature of the duties which he was called upon to fulfil. Incapable of forming large and comprehensive views for himself, there was little hope of his being led in the right path by those who were around him. Even the greatest and the best of those who took part in his father's counsels were men whose thoughts lay apart from the main current of the life of the nation; and desirable as it is that diversities of opinion should exist in the body of the people, it is never with impunity that such a separation grows up between a nation and its rulers.

Prospects for the future.

For a moment, however, there was a pause. England was waiting to see what James proposed to do with the prerogative which he had vindicated from all assaults. To himself his position may well have appeared unassailable. His authority now stood out clear and distinct in the midst of the other institutions of the realm. There was no longer to be seen that harmony of action between the Sovereign and the Parliament which had, as a rule, prevailed from the days of the Plantagenets. If James could disembarrass his mind from the recollection of the financial difficulties with which he was still surrounded, or if he could hope at any time to set himself free from the entanglements of debt, he might imagine that he had liberated himself from the trammels of that beneficent law of nature which decrees a speedy downfall to every Government which attempts to act an independent part, and which forgets that it is nobler to guide a nation slowly on the path to greatness, than to do great things itself.

APPENDIX.

APPENDIX.

I.

PROCEEDINGS IN THE STAR CHAMBER AGAINST THE EARL OF NORTHUMBERLAND.

[Harl. MS. 589, fol. 111.]

App. I.

THIS day was brought to the bar the Right Honourable Henry, Earl of Northumberland, from the prison of the Tower of London, against whom Sir Edward Coke, Knt., His Majesty's Attorney-General, informed this honourable court, *ore tenus*, for divers very great and high contempts, misprisions, and offences committed by the said earl against His Majesty. In the proofs whereof, although there fell out matter of a higher nature, not fit for this place, which could not be omitted, being so interlaced together, concerning horrible and unnatural treasons discovered since the 5th day of November last; the one an invasion of this realm intended by foreign power, with the aid of English Catholics and Jesuits, in the latter time of the reign of our late sovereign of famous memory, Queen Elizabeth; the other of this latest (already damned) conspiracy and treason, to blow up with gunpowder the House of Parliament at such time as His Majesty, with all the Lords Spiritual and Temporal and Burgesses of this realm, should be there assembled. Yet this Court, at this time, is to deal with the matters of contempt and misdemeanour only, leaving the said other matters of higher nature for some other time and place at His Majesty's good pleasure. And first, His Highness's said Attorney informed that in the end of the reign of our said late sovereign Queen Elizabeth, and in the beginning of His Majesty's happy entrance into this kingdom, the said earl, seeking and taking upon him to be the head of the Catholics of England, and to have that faction to take a dependency on him, did write two several letters to His Majesty, being then in

App. I. Scotland, and sent the same by one Thomas Percy, his kinsman, a notorious recusant and traitor, and one of the principal conspirators in this last powder treason, acquainting the said Percy with the matter of those letters, in which the said earl advised His Majesty to give hopes unto the Catholics of England for toleration of religion, with further instructions thereof to the said Percy, as appeareth by the said earl's own confession . . . . ? (the body of this faction joining with the head), all the Catholics of England were privy and assisting to it, and they disbursed among them the said Percy's charges and expenses in the same journey. And after Percy's return into England he told the said earl that His Majesty's pleasure was that the said earl should wind and work himself into the Catholics, and give them all hopes of toleration of religion, and to be well dealt withal, as the said earl likewise hath confessed. And although the said answer so brought by the said Percy from His Majesty was far from any truth (His Majesty's goodly and religious zeal having been ever opposite to any such toleration), which the said earl could not but understand, having received a letter also from His Majesty by the said Percy, which the said earl this day produced and was read, whereby His Majesty plainly advertised the said earl that he meant no manner of change or alteration either of the Church or State, which His Majesty sithence on the word of a King hath affirmed he sent no such answer by Percy to the said earl. Yet the said earl to wind and work himself into the opinions of the said Catholics, and that they might depend upon him, and so get to be the head of a faction, did, in the end of the said late Queen's time, and sithence also in the beginning of His Majesty's reign, take upon him to father and countenance the said feigned answer and message of this Percy from His Majesty, and did intimate unto the Catholics of England that His Majesty's pleasure and commandment was that they should have toleration of their religion and should be eased of their persecutions, to the great slander of the laws of this realm, as though they were persecuting laws. By which course of the said earl all the Catholics of England depended on the said earl, and he took upon him and did become to be their head. Unto this also His Highness's said Attorney annexed [?] and observed other circumstances of higher consequence, as, first, at the very time when the said earl so wrote the said letters and took upon him to get this faction to depend upon him, at that instant of time, and a little before the late Queen's death, was Thomas Winter, one other of those damned traitors for the powder treason, employed and sent into Spain by the Catholics of England to negotiate an invasion into this realm. And immediately upon

Her Majesty's death, Guy Fawkes, one other of those powder traitors, was by the Catholics sent into Spain to solicit the same invasion; also insomuch as Fawkes gave out that the King of Spain would set foot in England the next spring. In which negotiation there wanting no means but only horses, the Catholics of England offered to prepare 2,000 horse to assist the same invasion; and at that time the said earl increased his stable with so many horses that (as he told His Majesty himself) his revenue was scarce able to maintain the charge thereof. The place for this invasion was first nominated by Sir Walter Raleigh, a condemned traitor, and to be Milford Haven; and at that time the said earl and Sir Walter Raleigh were very inward and secret friends, and the said earl had then the custody and command of Castle Carew, being the only strength of the said haven. Winter, also, hath confessed that at his going into Spain, a greater person should have gone, but it was doubted it would be a cause of discovery. This purpose of invasion, also, was accompanied with two bulls or breves from the Pope, brought over into England by Garnet, superior of the Popish recusants, being another of those condemned powder traitors, by which breves were excluded all successors to the Crown of England, how near of blood soever they were, unless he were a Catholic, and so advance the Catholic religion with all might and main, and to bind them by oath and sacrament thereunto; which breves the said Garnet showed unto the said Thomas Percy, near about the time that the said earl employed the said Percy into Scotland with his letters for the Catholic cause, as aforesaid. And, at the beginning of His Majesty's entrance into this realm, the said earl also, at the head of the said Catholics, did prefer his petition to His Majesty, on the behalf of the Catholics of England, for toleration of religion, as himself now confessed.

His Highness's said Attorney-General secondly informed against the said earl, that whereas the said Thomas Percy, seeing that, after His Majesty's happy and peaceable entrance into this kingdom, he could not prevail for toleration of Popish religion, and that the State was otherwise settled, did, in September in the first year of His Majesty's reign, and within nine months next after His Majesty's coming to the Crown, make the first motion of this late horrible powder treason to Catesby and some other of his fellow-traitors in the said treason, to blow up the King, Prince, Peers, Nobles Spiritual and Temporal, and Burgesses in the Parliament House, saying, 'I will kill the King, for there [is] no help.' And thereupon afterwards, in May following, being in the second year of His Majesty's reign, the said Percy, Catesby, Winter, Fawkes, and others, the

App. I. plotters of the said treason, did, by the chief instigation of the said Percy, take a corporal oath, and received the sacrament thereupon by the hands of the said Garnet, to effect the said horrible treason, and to keep the same secret among themselves; yet the said Percy, being a villain of so damnable disposition, and the said earl, being, out of His Majesty's grace towards him, at that time Captain of His Majesty's Pensioners, and he then knowing the said Percy to be a Jesuitical recusant and Papist, having employed him into Scotland for the Catholic cause as aforesaid, did, notwithstanding, without regard of his place or His Majesty's person, on the 9th of June next after the said May, when the said treason was so by the said Percy plotted and sworn, put the said Percy into the room and place of pensioner, daily to attend His Majesty's person with a halberd in his hand, a thing most dangerous to such a desperate person; and did also so place and make him pensioner without His Majesty's pleasure and knowledge therein first had. And, in further neglect and contempt of that his place of Captain of the Pensioners, and the care he ought to have had of His Majesty's person, he did not cause the said Percy to be sworn at his being made a pensioner, as he should have done, but to blind the world withal, there was a show and colour made to have him sworn by Alan Percy, brother of the said earl, but, indeed, he was not sworn at all, whereby he was the more at liberty to execute any his intended villainies.

Thirdly, and lastly, His Majesty's said Attorney-General informed against the said earl, that whereas the said horrible powder treason was, on the 5th day of November last, by God's great goodness, discovered, and Percy found to be the chief contriver thereof, and was fled for the same, which the said earl well knew, being then a Privy Councillor of State, and present in Council the same morning that the same matter was examined and found out; and whereas the same day, upon vehement and great presumptions, and causes of suspicion, which, upon further examination of the said treason, fell out against the said earl, the said earl was restrained of his liberty, and commanded to keep his house. Yet the said earl that very day, being prisoner and a Privy Councillor, and knowing that the said Percy was fled towards the place where the said earl's revenue lay, he wrote two letters unto his officers in the country into which the said Percy was fled: the one he sent by post, the other by his servant, to put his revenue and treasure in safety, and commanded them to preserve the same from the said Percy's hands, and to bring the said treasure up unto him; and did therein utterly neglect and forbear to take any order, or give any commandment, for apprehending the said Percy, being so dangerous a traitor; which offence and contempt, His Highness' said Attorney divided into three branches, and to be each of them a very high offence: first, that the said earl, being so restrained and a prisoner, would presume so to write and send abroad his letters, which is plainly against the law; secondly, that, being a Privy Councillor, and sworn to preserve the King's Majesty and the State to his uttermost endeavour, yet he had more care of his treasure than respect of the King or State, in not endeavouring to apprehend so dangerous a traitor as Percy was; thirdly, that his writing and sending abroad his letters into those parts wherein Percy was fled (the said earl knowing at the Council-table how the state of things stood against him) was to give him a watchword and intelligence for his further flight.

To these grievous contempts His Highness's said Attorney, for aggravation, further informed, that at the first hatching of this horrible powder treason, the traitors consulted amongst themselves (as they have confessed) to save some of the nobles of this realm which were Catholics from the blow of the said treason. And Percy named the said earl; and they concluded that he should be saved, to the end to have his aid and assistance afterwards; unto which concurreth the saying of Owen, a confederate in the said treason, who said they were sure of the said earl, for he was sure [to] the Catholic cause; and Percy was the man that undertook to give the said earl warning to prevent the danger thereof; and the said treason being intended to be put in execution the Tuesday, the 5th of November, the said Percy came out of the North the Sunday before. At which time, he being informed, by some of his confederates, that they doubted their plot was discovered, and that they determined to fly, the said Percy advised them the contrary, saying he would first go to Sion, being the said earl's house, and speak with the said earl; and, accordingly, on the Monday he went to Sion, and there spake with the said earl; and at his coming back, he told his confederates that all was well; and afterwards, that Monday, at eleven o'clock at night, Percy sent Robert Keyes, another of the said traitors, with a clock or watch unto the said Fawkes (who was the villain that should have done the deed), and with a match for him to give fire. The said traitors have also confessed, that such of the nobility as should be saved should of themselves have chosen a protector. And after the blow given, it was likewise concluded among them, that the said Percy, and some other in his assistance, should have violently taken the now Duke of York into his custody, they being also sure that the princess, the Lady Mary, being nursed by the sister of Wright, one other of the said traitors,

App. I. was by that means at their dispose. And Percy said, within four-and-twenty hours that the said treason should have been effected, that the said earl would curse him if the said project took not effect. The said earl's money, also, and treasure, as standeth proved, was employed in this wicked treason; for the said Percy brought up £4,000 of the earl's money to employ in that action for powder, and other necessary expense about it. And it being questioned among the said traitors what course and what strength they might depend upon when their treason was effected, it was resolved that the regiment of the English soldiers in the Low Countries should be drawn down to be ready to come over and join with the English here, and this charge to be in the power and leading of Charles Percy, brother of the said earl; and to that end suit was made that the said Charles Percy might have the said regiment of English foot, and Catesby to be colonel of the horse; to the end that, by colour of the war in the Low Countries, they might be ready to assist here when time served.

For all which contempts and misdemeanours before recited His Majesty's said Attorney-General prayed, on the behalf of His Majesty, that the said earl might receive condign punishment by order from this place, as in like cases hath [been usual].

Then the said earl, being present at the bar as aforesaid, was demanded particularly what answer he could make to the said offences so informed against him. Whereupon the said earl, labouring at the first to excuse or extenuate his said offences with accusing the said Thomas Percy that he had long time borne a false heart and hard conceit towards the said earl; for that the said earl had formerly found him faulty, and challenged him to be false in his accounts to him; and that, for the same and other matters which he alleged, the said Percy had railed on him the said earl, and given out very disgraceful speeches of him, whereby it might be understood that there was no likelihood that the said earl would so deeply plunge himself as to be partaker with the said Percy in any his traitorous actions; protesting, also, his innocency in all his proceedings as touching any offence pretended to His Majesty or the realm; yet, in the end, being made to understand by the Court, that those his allegations and protestations extended rather to his further accusation than excuse, the said earl, at the end, after full proof made of the several contempts and offences aforesaid, confessing his errors in the same, submitted himself to the censure and judgment of this most honourable court. Whereupon this honourable court, and the whole presence there sitting, taking great deliberation and consideration of the quality of those heinous offences and high contempts before declared, being altogether inexcusable, and sufficiently proved, as well by the said earl's own confession, as other circumstances and proofs; fully concurring and conceiving the same to be far the greater in respect of the quality of the said offender (forbearing, nevertheless, according to His Majesty's pleasure, to enter into the consideration of such special matters as might in any wise extend or reach to charge the said earl in a higher degree), have convicted the said earl of the said several contempts, misprisions, and offences wherewith he standeth charged as aforesaid, and have thought him worthy of very great and severe punishment for the same; and therefore have adjudged and ordered that the said earl shall, for the same offences, pay for a fine to the use of His Majesty the sum of thirty thousand pounds, and shall be displaced and removed from the place of a Privy Councillor, and from being Captain of His Majesty's Pensioners, and from being Lieutenant of any of His Majesty's counties, and from all and every other office, honour, or place which he holdeth by His Majesty's grace and favour, and hereafter be disabled to take upon him or exercise any of the said offices or places. And that he shall be returned prisoner to the said Tower of London from whence he came, there to remain prisoner as before, during [His Majesty's pleasure].

II.

DOCUMENTS RELATING TO SIR WALTER RALEIGH.

1. PROCEEDINGS IN THE EXCHEQUER IN 1608.

[Memoranda of the King's Remembrancer, Mich. T. 6 Jac. I. 545.]

Dors. Compertum est in libro ordinationum sive decretorum de anno regni Domini Regis nunc Jacobi Sexti: viz., inter ordinationes sive decreta de Termino Sancti Michaelis, folio . Ex parte hujus Rememoratoris, dic Jovis 10mo die Novembris.

App. II. Dors. Whereas Sir Henry Hobart, Knt., the King's Majesty's Attorney-General, in Trinity Term last exhibited his bill into this court on his Highness' behalf, against Sir Walter Raleigh, Knt., Walter Raleigh his son, and John Shelbury, Gent., reciting thereby that, whereas the said Sir Walter Raleigh was seised in his demesne as of fee of and in all and singular the castle, lordships, and manors of Sherborne, Newland Castletown, Wootton Whitfield, Yetminster, Canndell Bishop, and Upcerne; and of and in the moiety of the manor of Pynford with the appurtenances; and of and in the moiety of the manor of Primsley, alias Prumsley, with the appurtenances, in the counties of Dorset and Somerset, or in one of them; and of and in the manor of Colyton Raleigh in the county of Devon; and of and in all messuages, cottages, houses, buildings, orchards, gardens, dovehouses, lands, tenements, and hereditaments whatsoever; with all and singular rights, members, incidents, and appurtenances unto the said several castles, lordships, manors, and to any of them belonging or appertaining; or to or with the said castle, lordships, manors, or any of them, as part, parcel or number of them or any of them belonging, or used, occupied, or enjoyed, situate, lying and being, arising, happening or renewing within the manors, towns, fields, parishes, hamlets, hundreds, limits or precincts of Sherborne, Newland Castletown, Wootton Whitfield, Yetminster, Canndell Bishop, Upcerne, Lellington, Stockbridge, and Primsley, alias Prumsley, and Colyton Raleigh, or in or within any one of them; and of and in the wood and lands called Honicombe Wood and Thornylease, containing by estimation sixty acres, or thereabouts, be it more or less; and of and in all and singular wastes, waste lands, royalties, services, privileges, and jurisdictions, and pre-eminences, warrens, parks, liberties of warrens and parks and hereditaments unto the said castle, lordships, manors, and premises, or unto any of them or unto any part or parcel of them in anywise belonging or appertaining, or with or within them or any of them used, occupied, or enjoyed. And that he the said Sir Walter Raleigh being so seised was, in the first year of His Majesty's reign of England, France, and Ireland, attainted of high treason, by means whereof he the said Sir Walter Raleigh forfeited the said castle, lordships, manors, and other the premises to our said Sovereign Lord the King's Majesty: and that by force thereof His Majesty was of the said premises seised in his demesne as of fee in the right of his Crown of England, and that His Majesty so being seised, of his abundant grace and clemency did by his letters patents bearing date the 3rd day of August, in the second year of His Highness's reign of England, give and grant the said premises or the greatest part thereof unto Sir Alexander Brett, Knt., and George Hull, Esq., to have and to hold to them, their executors and assigns, for and during the term of sixty years, if the said Sir Walter Raleigh should so long live, and that the said lease was by His Majesty given, granted, and intended to and for the benefit and maintenance of Elizabeth the wife of the said Sir Walter Raleigh, and of Walter Raleigh son of the said Sir Walter: alleging further by the said bill that, notwithstanding His Majesty's most gracious favour, the said Sir Walter Raleigh, Walter Raleigh his son, and one John Shelbury, Gent., having gotten into their hands and possession divers evidences and writings concerning the premises, not contented with that estate for sixty years of and in the premises which it pleased His Majesty of his exceeding bounty to give and dispose to the interests and uses aforesaid, did further give out and pretend that the inheritance of the premises after the said term expired was not in His Majesty, but in the said Walter Raleigh the son, or some other person or persons; and that they had and did contrive secret estates of and in the same, to the prejudicing of His Majesty and the countenancing of the said pretences. In consideration whereof, and to the end His Majesty's right to the inheritance of the premises after the said lease expired might be made manifest and preserved, and that the same might not be by any practice impeached or obscured, it was desired by His Highness's said Attorney that the said Sir Walter Raleigh, Walter Raleigh his son, and John Shelbury might be called by process of this court to answer the premises,

App. II.

and to abide such further order and direction in the same as to this court should be thought fit, as by the said bill more at large appeareth; unto which said bill the said parties being served, which parties appeared, and in the said term of the Holy Trinity did make their answers as followeth. And first, the said Sir Walter Raleigh for himself did say that it was true that he was seised of the said castle, lands, tenements, liberties, franchises, and other hereditaments in the said bill mentioned, in his demesne as of fee: and so being seised in the time of the late Queen Elizabeth, being desirous to settle his land in his name and blood, by the advice of his counsel learned in the law did cause a book to be drawn for the conveying of his said lands to the use of himself for time of his life, the remainder thereof to Walter Raleigh his son and heir apparent, and the heirs males of his body, with like remainders to his other sons if God should send him any more, the remainder to the heirs males of the body of him the said Sir Walter Raleigh; and for lack of such issue, the remainder over to Sir Carew Raleigh brother of him the said Sir Walter, reserving the reversion or remainder in fee simple to him the said Sir Walter Raleigh and his heirs for ever. And he further said that the said conveyance for the settling of his lands in such manner and form as aforesaid was afterwards engrossed in a writing indented, made between him the said Sir Walter Raleigh on the one part and Sir Arthur Throckmorton, Knt., and others of his friends and allies whom he had made parties to the same conveyance on the other part; and that he did seal and deliver the same writing indented in Durham House in the presence of sufficient witnesses of good credit whose names were endorsed upon the same indenture, as by the same indenture ready to be showed to this honourable court, whereunto he referred himself, more plainly might appear; protesting the same was done, meant, and intended by him *bonâ fide* upon the consideration aforesaid without any fraud or covin; and, according to such estate as he had by virtue of the said deed indented or otherwise by the law (if the same conveyance were insufficient) he alleged that he was seised of the said castle, lands, and tenements at the time of the said attainder; and that the same conveyance, by the same indenture, such as it was after his said attainder, was, by virtue of His Majesty's Commission under the Great Seal of England, found by inquisition by a jury of the said county of Dorset, as by the same commission and inquisition whereunto for the more certainty he referred himself, might also appear. The validity of which indenture of conveyance the said Sir Walter Raleigh humbly submitted to the censure and judgment of this honourable court, further acknowledging His Majesty's mercy and compassion in granting unto the said Sir Alexander Brett, Knt., and George Hull, esquire, mentioned in the said bill, the said castle, manors, lands, tenements, and other the premises, for the term of sixty years to the use of the wife and children of him the said Sir Walter, if he as long should live, denying that he had contrived any estate of and in the premises to countenance the said former conveyance, or that he had made any conveyance of the premises whereby His Majesty's inheritance might be questionable, other than the said indenture above mentioned. And the said Walter Raleigh, the son, by his said father as his guardian, by way of answer, said that he was under fifteen years of age, and had no understanding in those things, but as a child, was merely ignorant of his own estate, if he had any. And lastly, the said John Shelbury, to such matters in the said bill as concerned himself, did say, that he neither had nor claimed any estate, interest, right, or title in or to the premises, or any part thereof; or that he had gotten into his hands any evidences or writings concerning the premises; or that he was privy or acquainted with any estate or estates of or in the same made by the said Sir Walter to the prejudice of His Majesty, other than the said indenture above-mentioned, as by the said defendant's message amongst other things more at large doth and may appear, which said answer being openly read in court, it was desired by His Highness's said Attorney-General that the said indenture of conveyance mentioned in the said defendant's answer, might be brought into the court to be viewed and considered on by His Majesty's counsel learned, and by the Barons of this Court, which, after several days given for that purpose, was done accordingly, and the same being openly read in the presence of the whole court, and of some of the counsel of the said Sir Walter Raleigh, it was alleged on the behalf of His Majesty by His Highness's said Attorney-General that the said indenture was not sufficient in law to carry and convey the said castle, manors, lands, tenements, and other the premises therein mentioned, to the use of the said Walter Raleigh, son of the said Sir Walter, nor to the use of any other person or persons in the said deed named, after the death of him the said Sir Walter Raleigh, as by the said answer of him the said Sir Walter Raleigh was pretended; but that the said Sir Walter Raleigh remained still seised of the said castle, lands, tenements, and other the premises in his demesne as of fee without alteration as before, notwithstanding the said indenture or anything therein contained, because the same being an indenture intended to raise uses thereby, that part of the sentence that

App. II. should have appointed the said Sir Walter Raleigh, his heirs and assigns, or such as had estate in the same premises to stand and be seised thereof to the intended uses was all wanting and utterly omitted. And therefore His Majesty's said Attorney affirmed that the said castle, manors, and other the premises after the death of him the said Sir Walter Raleigh (for that during his natural life the same were granted away by His Majesty as aforesaid) ought to come and be forfeit to the King's Majesty by force of that attainder of the said Sir Walter Raleigh, and therefore desired that a case in law might be drawn and agreed upon touching the validity and invalidity of the same conveyance. Whereupon, on Thursday, the 27th of October, in the sixth year of His Majesty's reign, it was ordered by the Court that Mr. Serjeant Harris, the younger, Mr. Serjeant Nicholls, and Mr. Crock, who were assigned by the court to be of counsel for the said defendants, should resort to His Majesty's said Attorney-General and should agree with him upon a case in law to be made upon the said deed; and should thereupon attend the Barons of this Court to consider of the same, and to have such further directions from them touching the same and the proceedings therein as to them should seem fit, as by the said order more at large appeareth. But the said Serjeant Harris, Serjeant Nicholls, and Mr. Crock being so assigned of counsel with the said Sir Walter Raleigh as aforesaid, having perused and well examined the deed, having also had conference with some of those which had been formerly of counsel with the said Sir Walter Raleigh, came into the court this present day, and then, in open court confessed that the said fault of the said deed and conveyance was so apparent and gross that it could raise no use, nor could be in anywise maintained or defended, and therefore did in all humility leave the said cause to the judgment of the court, and the estate of the said castle, manors, lands, and other the premises after the death of the said Sir Walter Raleigh to His Majesty's mere mercy and good pleasure. It is therefore this day declared, ordered, adjudged, and finally decreed by the Right Honourable Earl of Salisbury, Lord High Treasurer of England, Sir Julius Cæsar, Chancellor and Under-Treasurer of the Exchequer, and the Barons of the same Court, that the said deed before mentioned (whereby the said Sir Walter Raleigh intended as he had alleged in his said answer to have settled the inheritance of the said castle, manors, and other the premises after his death in his said son) is utterly void, insufficient, and of no force to bar the King's Majesty, his heirs and successors of the inheritance thereof after the death of the said Sir Walter Raleigh; and that His

Highness is and ought to have the same by the attainder of him the said Sir Walter Raleigh from and immediately after his death, the said deed or anything therein contained in anywise notwithstanding.

2. PROCEEDINGS IN THE EXCHEQUER IN 1609.

[Memoranda of the King's Remembrancer. Mich. T. 7 Jac. I. 253.]

Compertum est in libro ordinationum, &c., Jovis 23° Novembris.

Whereas, Sir Henry Hobart, Knt., the King's Majesty's Attorney-General, hath heretofore, viz., in the term of St. Hilary, in the sixth year of the King's Majesty's reign that now is, exhibited an information or English bill into this court on the behalf of his Majesty, showing thereby that whereas Sir Walter Raleigh, late of Sherborne, in the county of Dorset, Knt., was in the term of St. Michael in the first year of the King's Majesty's happy reign of England, for high treason by him committed in due form of law attainted, as by the records thereof may appear, by force whereof and of the laws and statutes in that case made and provided, all his castles, manors, lands, tenements, and hereditaments, together with his personal estate, were forfeited to His Majesty and vested in His Royal person, which his personal estate being of very great value, it pleased His Majesty out of his gracious favour and princely compassion to bestow upon Dame Elizabeth Raleigh, wife of the said Sir Walter, and Walter Raleigh their son, for their relief and maintenance. And further, of his more abundant grace to grant also all the said castles, lands, tenements, and hereditaments of him the said Sir Walter Raleigh by His Highness's letters patent under the Great Seal of England to certain of the friends of him the said Sir Walter Raleigh for many years yet enduring, determinable upon the death of the said Sir Walter Raleigh, which His Highness's said gift was to the use and benefit of him the said Sir Walter, his said wife and son, the reversion and inheritance of the premises being both in His Majesty's intention and in deed reserved to His Majesty, his heirs and successors; yet, notwithstanding His Majesty's manifold and gracious favours showed and extended to the said Sir Walter, his said wife and son, the said Sir Walter, with divers others combining with him, as, namely, the said Dame Elizabeth and the said Walter Raleigh the son, Sir Alexander Brett, Knt., George Hull, esquire, John Shelbury, Robert Smith, John Mere, Henry Mere, Henry Starr, Robert Colbery, and John Browne, Gent., had published, divulged, and given out in speeches that the said Sir Walter had made divers leases and estates of all his castles, manors, lands, tenements and hereditaments, and others, by his means and

App. II.

procurement, had made of some part thereof for many years then in being long before the treason committed by him, and for which he stood attainted; and that the same leases and estates were made *bonâ fide*, and upon just and good considerations, where, in truth, there were either no such leases or estates so made at all, or if any such leases and estates were made by him, or by any other by his means, the same were made but in trust to the use of the said Sir Walter, and not *bonâ fide* to the use and benefit of such as the same were made or pretended to be made unto. And to the end it might appear what the same leases and estates were, and to whom and when they were made and upon what considerations, if any such were, and to the end that His Majesty's title might more plainly and clearly appear to the same leases and estates, and to the end the other conveyances, deeds, and evidences touching and concerning the premises remaining with the said Sir Walter Raleigh, the said Dame Elizabeth or some of her friends, should not be embezzled or purloined, but safely kept and preserved for the further manifestation of His Majesty's title, His Majesty's said Attorney-General prayed that all the said pretended conveyances, together with all other evidences and conveyances concerning the premises, might be by the said Sir Walter and the other afore-named set forth and declared upon their oaths, and brought into this honourable court to be there preserved and considered of for His Majesty's behoof, and to be kept for His Majesty, if the same should appear to belong unto him. And to the end that all the matters might be examined in this honourable court, he prayed process of subpœna against the said defendants, who being served with process appeared. And the said Sir Walter Raleigh, Dame Elizabeth and Walter Raleigh their son, and most of the rest of the defendants, put in their several answers to the said bill, and the said Sir Walter Raleigh in his answer for himself said that in the thirty-fourth year of the reign of the late Queen Elizabeth the then Lord Bishop of Sarum, by his deed, indented lawfully and duly executed and confirmed by the Dean and Chapter of Sarum aforesaid, and enrolled accordingly, bearing date the 18th day of January (as he took it) in the year aforesaid, did demise, grant, and to farm let to the said late Queen, all and singular the castles, manors, and lordships of Sherborne, Newland Castletown, Wootton Whitfield, Yetminster, and Caundell Bishop . . . . for and during the term of fourscore and nineteen years . . . . And so being possessed or interested the said late Queen by Her Highness's letters patents of assignment bearing date on or about the 27th day of Jannary in the said thirty-fourth year of her late reign, did grant and assign over unto the said defendant all and singular the said castles, lordships, manors, and other the premises, with the appurtenances for and during all the term of years then to come in the same, together with the said indenture of lease, to which conveyance of assignment for more certainty the said defendant referred himself. By force whereof he the said defendant was of the said castles, lordships, manors, and other the premises possessed accordingly, and being so possessed, he the said defendant sought to establish the said lands and premises in Walter Raleigh, his then only son, to whose use he conveyed the same twice, as he remembered, by certain grants to certain persons and friends in trust, which were revocable by him the said defendant, and which he did revoke afterwards accordingly. For he said that finding his fortune in court towards the end of Her late Majesty's reign to be at a stand, and that he daily attended dangerous employments against her late Majesty's enemies, and had not in the said former grant made any provision for his wife, he the said defendant made the said former grants void, and then afterwards in the said fortieth year of the said late Queen's reign, for the natural love and affection which he bore to the said Walter Raleigh his then only son, and being still desirous as well to settle and establish some estate of and in the castle, lordships, and manors of Sherborne and other the premises in his said son for his better maintenance and advancement, as also for some livelihood and provision for his wife to be had thereout during his natural life, he the said defendant did *bonâ fide* and for the reasons and considerations in the same deed specified, without any intention of deceit unto any, by his deed or writing under his hand and seal grant and assign over among other things the whole estate and interest then residue of the said lease of the said lordships and manors of Sherborne and other the premises absolutely unto his said son without any power of revocation reserved, but with this declaration and provision that his said son should yearly pay out of the premises after the death of him the said defendant unto the said defendant's wife and mother to his said son £200 per annum, which last mentioned deed or writing he said was made not many months before the now Bishop was consecrated, as the said defendant verily believed, to the which deed for the more certainty he referred himself. But he said that by means of his manifold troubles he knew not where the said deed or writing was, nor in whose hands or custody the same remained. And he further said that her late Majesty having afterwards procured from the said now Bishop of Sarum the inheritance of the said castle, lordships, manors, lands, tenements,

App. II. liberties, franchises, and hereditaments to Her Highness, her heirs and successors, it pleased her late Majesty likewise of her then abundant grace and favour to give and grant unto the said defendant and his heirs by good and sufficient conveyance in law the inheritance of the said castles, lordships, manors, and other the premises as by the said letters patents thereof appeareth. And he the said Sir Walter Raleigh by his said answer further said that after he was so seised of the inheritance of the said castles, lordships, manors, and other the premises, he the said defendant did in truth and *bonâ fide* intend likewise to settle the inheritance of the same premises on his said son, and to that end used the advice of a counsellor at law about the last year of Her late Majesty's reign concerning the same, by whose, or at the least his clerk's, negligence and oversight that conveyance after the attainder of the said defendant in the first year of His Majesty's reign hath been conceived to be insufficient, the said deed being of late brought in question in this court by His Majesty's Attorney-General, by reason whereof the inheritance of the said castle, manors, lordships, and other the premises are alleged to be comen to His Majesty by the said attainder said in the information mentioned. But before His Majesty had disposed of the inheritance supposed to be comen unto him for want of some words in the said conveyance last aforementioned, His Majesty of his great grace and goodness was pleased as well by His Highness's letters patents . . . . bearing date the 14th day of February in the first year of His Majesty's reign of England . . . . to grant unto the said John Shelbury and Robert Smith all and singular the goods and chattels . . . . which then late were the said defendant's . . . . As also by His Highness's letters patents . . . . bearing date the 3rd day of August in the second year of His Highness's reign to grant unto Sir Alexander Brett, Knt., now deceased, and George Hull, Esq., one other of the said defendants, all the said castles, lordships, manors, and other the premises for the term of threescore years determinable upon the said defendant's death, as by the said answer of the said Sir Walter Raleigh more at large appeareth.

And the said Walter Raleigh the son being within the age of twenty-one years . . . . did at last choose in open court the Right Honourable the Lord Carew to be his guardian in that behalf . . . . and by him did deliver in court his answer, wherein the said Walter Raleigh the son did refer himself to the said answers of his father, and did avow the same to be true, adding further that he had heard that his said father had purchased certain freehold lands and leases in the name of him the said Walter, and in the name of others, to his use, which he hoped he should lawfully and quietly enjoy, but the certainty thereof he knew not, as by the said answer at large may appear.

And the said John Shelbury in his answer (amongst other things) confessed that he did never know of any such conveyance made by the said Sir Walter Raleigh to his said son. . . .

And the said George Hull likewise in his answer said that sithence the exhibiting of the said information he had heard of such a conveyance . . . . but when or for what cause or considerations the same was made, or where or in whose hands the said conveyance or grant was, he knew not.

And the said John Meres in his answer (among many other things therein contained) affirmed of his own knowledge that after the time of the said conveyance of assignment of the said term of ninety and nine years pretended to be made by the said Sir Walter Raleigh to his said son, he the said Sir Walter did by his deed surrender the same lease and term to the Bishop of Sarum to the end he might obtain a grant of the premises in fee farm, which he did obtain accordingly. And he further said that ever sithence the said pretended conveyance until the time of the attainder of the said Sir Walter Raleigh, all the said castles, lordships, manors, lands, tenements, and other the premises were in the possession of the said Sir Walter Raleigh and not of his said son nor of any to his use to the knowledge of the said defendant. And that the said Sir Walter Raleigh by himself or his bailiffs, servants, or ministers, and not the said Walter Raleigh the son, or any for him, took the profits, rents, and commodities issuing and coming out of and from the same and every part thereof, and kept the courts thereon, as if the interest and estate of all and every part of the premises had been truly, plainly, and *bonâ fide* in him, the said Sir Walter Raleigh, and not in his son or wife, or in any other person, to his or their use for all the remain of the said term of ninety and nine years: and always before the said attainder, as occasion was offered, the said Sir Walter Raleigh made estates of the said lands, and did dispose thereof as if the same had been truly his and not any other's, or his said son's or any other person's to his use, as well before as after the said fee farm to all intents and purposes, and would have taken upon him, after the said fee farm obtained, to take a surrender of him the said John Meres for a term of threescore years on three tenements there, and thereupon to make an estate to one Standen for three lives. And did also grant to divers persons divers terms of and in the farm lands of Sherborne and other lands. And, as the said defendant thought, made one lease for a great number of years of the grounds called The Orchard to Richard and Robert Foster, and did also,

App. II. sithence the said fee farm obtained, make a lease for fourscore years or more, determinable upon the death of three of the children of the said Henry Meres, one of the said defendants, of Tynner's copyhold unto the said Henry Meres. And the said John Meres in his said answer further setteth forth divers other grants, leases, and estates, made of divers parcels of the premises to sundry persons, and namely of Sherborne Park, to the said defendant; and that the said Sir Walter Raleigh did sue and implead, and was sued and impleaded, and did maintain and defend the same suits touching and concerning the premises in his own name, and did grant divers offices belonging to the premises, sithence the time of the making of the said pretended conveyance to his said son, and had always used the same as his own, without making any mention of any estate thereof to be in his said son or wife, or any other but himself . . . .

And the said Henry Meres in his answer said that the said Sir Walter did make divers conveyances of the premises, but always kept the possession thereof himself, and received the rents and profits, and kept courts and granted copyhold estates and other estates on the premises, in his own name and to his own use . . . .

To which answers the said Attorney-General replied, and the said defendants rejoined so as the cause came to a full and perfect issue, and witnesses were examined on the King's Majesty's behalf, and divers days given by several orders of this court to the said defendants to examine such witnesses as they should think fit for the defence of the said cause, but they have willingly forborne and refused to examine any. Whereupon the depositions taken on behalf of His Majesty were published, and the said cause appointed to be heard this day.

Now, upon full and deliberate hearing and debating thereof.... it is confessed by the counsel of the said defendants, ... that the reason why they examined no witnesses was for that they having talked with such as they did purpose to have examined in the said cause, they found that although they could speak for the making of the said pretended conveyance, yet they could not say whether the same was made in trust or not, and therefore thought it to small purpose for them to examine them. And therefore and for that, as well by the said answers of divers of the said defendants . . . . as also by the depositions of divers and sundry witnesses . . . . it fully and plainly appeared unto this court that the said Sir Walter Raleigh from time to time, and always sithence the said lease of ninety and nine years of the premises made and assigned unto him, as well sithence the fortieth year of the said late Queen, being the time of the said conveyance and assignment thereof, supposed to be made to his son as before, and even until the time of his said attainder, had taken . . . . and received the rents, issues, and profits of all and singular the premises to his own use, and had kept the courts of the said manors, and granted copyholds expressly in his own name, and named and appointed officers . . . . by patent under his hand and seal, and made sundry leases . . . . all in his own name, reserving the rents to himself and his heirs, without ever making mention of any estate or interests thereof to be in his said son. And for it likewise appeared that the said Walter Raleigh the son, at the time of the said pretended conveyance and assignment made unto him, was but of the age of six years, and no more; whereby it seemed utterly improbable that the said Sir Walter Raleigh would convey over his said lease and interest in the said castle, &c., and wholly and absolutely vest the same in the said Walter Raleigh his son, being an infant of so tender years, thereby leaving it in the power of his son, at any time when he should come to years of judgment, to put him out of so main a part of his living and estate. And also for that it appeared that the said Sir Walter Raleigh, after the time of the said pretended conveyance, did, by his deed under his hand and seal well known, and now showed and proved in court, surrender, or pretend to surrender, his term and interest in the said lease of ninety and nine years to the said Bishop of Sarum, of intent and purpose to obtain the fee farm of the premises, which was after that granted unto him by the said late Queen, which act can no way stand well. The said pretended conveyance of the lease aforesaid, and also that sithence the grant of the premises made to the said Sir Alexander Brett, Knt., and George Hull, Esq., by the King's Majesty's letters patents, the said patentees have taken and received the profits, and kept courts, and used and disposed of the premises in their own names to the use and benefit of the said Sir Walter Raleigh and the said Dame Elizabeth his wife, and the said Walter Raleigh, according to the intent of the said letters patents. And that the said pretended conveyance and assignment made to the said Walter Raleigh was never published nor spoken of until the said deed mentioned by the said defendant Sir Walter Raleigh in his answer, whereby he intended, as he said, to have settled the inheritance of the premises on his said son, was by this court adjudged insufficient. It is therefore . . . . this day declared, resolved, and adjudged by the Right Honourable Robert, Earl of Salisbury, Lord Treasurer of England, the Chancellor and Barons of this Court, that the said pretended conveyance and assignment of the said lease and term of fourscore and nineteen years of and in the said castle, &c.,

App. II.

and all other leases and estates supposed to have been made by the said Sir Walter Raleigh, or any other of any the premises, to the said Walter Raleigh his son, or to any other to his use, if any such be, which yet was no way proved to this court, was and were made upon secret trust and confidence to the only use and benefit of the said Sir Walter, and to be disposed at his will and pleasure; and that therefore the King's Majesty ought, and is to have the same, by force and reason of the said attainder of the said Sir Walter Raleigh . . . .

3. SIR W. RALEIGH TO THE PRIVY COUNCIL.

[Add. MS. 6177, fol. 297.]

[*Between Feb. 4th and Aug. 3rd,* 1604.]

	£	*s.*	*d.*
The manor of Sherborne, with the hundred and liberties, with the park, farm, and all other demesne grounds, are of a yearly rent of assize of	150	16	4½
The village called Castleton, wherein the old castle standeth, is of rent of assize	3	12	0
A second street or village within Sherborne town, called Newland, is of rent of assize	3	13	4½
A village in the county, three miles from Sherborne, called Caundell Bishop, is of the yearly rent of assize	21	11	2
A village without the park wall, parcel of Sherborne and a member thereof, is of the old rent of assize	7	13	10½
The farm of Whitfield is of the old rent	13	8	0
The manor of Yetminster is of the old rent of assize, but this manor is a kind of fee simple to the tenants, and the lord hath but a small fine at every death or alienation	12	5	11
Sum total of the old rent	*207	8	0½
The farm of Sherhorne is worth by improvement besides all reprises, if it do not decay	250	0	0
There are certain demesne grounds in Whitfield which are let to farm for the yearly rent of	60	0	0
There are other grounds redeemed out of the tenants' hands, in Caundell Bishop or Down, worth by the year	40	0	0
I do also rent some pasture ground of a tenant of mine, called Swetham, and do make profit of them, besides the rent which I pay him by the year	12	0	0
There are other grounds and closes about Sherborne which may be worth about £30 or £40 a year, so as all these demesnes and farms and fields are worth by the year in the total	400	0	0
There is also a rent charge which Sir Robert Miller doth pay unto me out of Upcerne, and other his lands, in consideration of the fee farm of them, which I procured	22	10	3½
I have also half a demesne in Pinford, called Pinford Manor, of the yearly old rent of	5	0	0
I have also the moiety of the manor of Primsley, of the yearly old rent of	7	2	7½
I have also a mill in Sherborne and twenty acres of ground, which I purchased of her late Majesty, which was in lease to Arthur Swayn for three lives, of the old rent of	6	4	10
I have also a close behind the castle, of five acres, and two or three other little closes, which to be let are worth by the year . .	6	5	6

* There is some mistake here, as the true total is £213 0*s.* 8½*d.*

App. II.

	£	s.	d.
The total of the rent charge	22	10	$3\frac{1}{2}$
The total of the old rent of these parcels	*18	7	$0\frac{1}{2}$
The racked rent of the closes is	6	5	0
	[207	8	$0\frac{1}{2}$]
	[400	0	0]
Sum total of the whole together is or near thereabout	†629	8	4
Reprises which go out of this—			
To the Bishop for ever	260	0	0
To one Edmond Lane, for 25 years or 30 years	30	0	0
In fees due to officers and others	44	13	0
Besides payment to the King for the household and other small charges. But whereas in this deduction of fees the bailiff is to have £3 a year, and the receiver some £7 a year, I do not pay the bailiff because he is mine enemy, and hath abused me, and the receiver being my servant doth exact of me; but yet all this be due, and hence ever been paid.			
Total of these deductions	334	13	0
So remaineth clear	‡295	0	0

* * * * *

If there be any more rents than this to my knowledge, but the herbage of the park, which was never in me, but purchased in my child's name ten years since, and a lease of Pinford grounds in Mr. Heriot for fifty-eight years, then I refuse all grace of and from His Majesty, except I may miscast a matter of £4 or £5 in the whole, or leave out some five or six acres of ground in some quillet. But this is the substance of all, upon my allegiance. And therefore, if it please your honours to make further inquiry, I submit myself unto it; and I beseech your lordships that a copy hereof may be delivered to the commissioners. All that grieves me herein is, that so infamous and detested a wretch as Mere is made a commissioner, as he hath vaunted and sent me word, and who dares not otherwise show his face, having so many executions against him, and hath not forty shillings' worth of ground in the world but of my gift, and promiseth to pay all his creditors with the part promised him out of Sherborne; spreading it abroad that some one of your honours hath employed him with purpose to procure this, the remainder of all which I had in the world of His Majesty, and to turn my poor wife, child, and family a-begging. But I trust that God hath not given so cruel a heart to any worthy man, whom the spoils of me and mine cannot enrich; but that all your lordships will in charity stand my good lords herein, having lost already £3,000 a-year; and I shall remain your humble servant,

W. Raleigh.

* Properly, £18 7*s.* $5\frac{1}{2}$*d.*

† Properly, £654 10*s.* $4\frac{1}{2}$*d.* The two sums in brackets have been inserted from the last page, to make the account a little clearer.

‡ Properly, if the total be taken as above, £294 15*s.* 4*d.*

App. II.

4. SIR WALTER RALEIGH TO THE PRIVY COUNCIL.

[Add. MS. 6177, fol. 305.]

Before Aug. 3, 1604.

* * * * * *

The whole rent of these lands, with the park, and a stock of £400 in sheep in the said park, is but 1,000 marks; out of which I pay unto the Bishops of Salisbury for ever, £260 a-year; and in fees and pensions wherewith the land is charged, and towards the provision of the King's house, to maimed soldiers and the poor, upwards of £50 a-year more;* so as the clear value is not £400 with a stock. My charge in this place for diet only is £208 a-year; and if His Majesty do allow the rest of this sum, to make it £300 to me for all other necessaries, there remaineth not above 100 marks a-year for my poor wife and child and their servants, which, God knows, will not give them bread and clothes. My debts are above £3,000; all the goods that I have left in the world, I protest, before the Majesty of God, are not worth 1,000 marks. That which I have already lost by Jersey, the Wine Office, the Stannary, Gillingham and Portland, is at least £3,000 a-year; so as I trust His Majesty will be merciful unto me for the rest, which, after the payment of my debts, will be but a miserable estate, God knows. Herein I humbly beseech your lordships' favours, that I may not be left to utter beggary; . . . . and I shall ever rest your lordships' most humbly,

W. Raleigh.

5. VALUE OF SHERBORNE AND ITS APPENDAGES DURING THE COMMONWEALTH.

[Abbreviated from an Account in the Royalist Composition Papers, Record Office, 1st Series, xcii. 605.]

Survey of the Earl of Bristol's Estate.

Dorset.	£	s.	d.
Pinford Farm	110	0	0
Whitfield Farm	55	0	0
The Feavors	70	0	0
The Wears	100	0	0
Murmead and Serjeant's Mead	18	0	0
Cold Harbour	5	0	0
Three parts of Barton Farm	40	0	0
Painter's Hill and Whiting's Cross	10	0	0
Half of Primsley Farm	25	0	0

* The 1,000 marks is probably the £654 which should have stood for the total receipts. Raleigh has, however, forgotten the £30 a year to Lane, and deducting as above, £310, leaves £344. Either, however, he is speaking broadly in calling this not £400, or he must have tacitly included other sources of income.

App. II.

	£	s.	d.
Long Close	2	16	8
Castle Ditches	2	10	0
The New Park	70	0	0
The New Purchased Grounds	26	0	0
The Prebend	260	0	0
The Manor Rents	214	0	0
Tenements in hand	54	0	0
	1302	6	8
Deduct payment to the receiver of the revenues of the late Bp. of Sarum	260	0	0
	1042	6	8
Other payments	161	0	0
	£881	6	8

III.

DESPATCHES OF SIR JOHN DIGBY RELATING TO THE SPANISH PENSIONS.

[*S. P.* Spanish Correspondence.]

1. SIR JOHN DIGBY TO THE KING.* Sept. 9, 1613.

App. III.

May it please your Most Excellent Majesty.

Did not the content of doing your Majesty faithful and honest service oversway all other respects, I should write this despatch with some grief and sorrow, being therein to set down particulars of prejudice and stain to a person, the opinion of whose worth and integrity may perhaps be of greater weight than any advertisements, and to whom I acknowledge I have had obligation. Further, I must give warning that some others be narrowly looked unto, and thereby cause jealousies and suspicions, which is an unwilling and unpleasing office, did not my duty to Your Majesty make all things pleasing that tend to your service.

There hath been no care or industry omitted for the discovery of the pot of roses. But it hath not pleased God to give so perfect success thereunto as I hoped for, in regard that some of our engines were not well made. Yet so much hath been attained unto, that did not the hope of a perfect work diminish and lessen the esteem of anything that falleth short of expectation, I doubt not but Your Majesty would judge that which is already done to be of more than ordinary consequence.

* The following is the key to the cypher in which the more important parts of this despatch are written:—

a	e	i and j	o	u and v
39	42	45	48	51
40	43	46	49	52
41	44	47	50	53

b	c	d	f	. . . .	w	x	y	z
1	3	5	7	. . . .	31	33	35	37
2	4	6	8	. . . .	32	34	36	38

All figures above 53 are blanks, excepting those which stand for proper names, which will easily be discovered by referring to the decyphered despatches of the same year.

The first part of this despatch will concern a person, who, though he be already giving (I doubt) a fearful account to the Sovereign Judge of all things of his unjust service to Your Majesty, yet because many roots of him may be yet living underground, and that, by revealing of the principal, his remaining instruments may be detected, I durst not so far dispense with my duty towards Your Majesty upon any regard as not to make you exactly acquainted with all the particulars that are come to my knowledge.

I conceive Your Majesty will think it strange that your late High Treasurer and Chief Secretary, the Earl of Salisbury (besides the Ayudas de costa, as they term them, which are gifts extraordinary upon services), should receive 6,000 crowns yearly pension from the King of Spain.

I would not write it unto Your Majesty, did I collect it only by slight circumstances. But the probabilities are so pregnant, as (to me that only see them without knowing how far we may have acquainted Your Majesty and procured your connivance) they convince my belief of his being an unworthy servant to Your Majesty. I shall set down all the particulars that induce me hereunto, leaving it to Your Majesty to make that judgment of him, as by the knowledge of these, and other things (unknown perhaps to me), Your Majesty's wisdom will be able to do with most truth and certainty.

First, I find in a letter of the Conde de Villa Mediana, bearing date the 21st of February, 1605, that, whereas there is assigned to Beltenebras 4,000 crowns per annum, as to divers others, he finds him so useful to the King of Spain's service, for the great hand he hath in the Government, and the power with the King of England, that he holdeth it fit that the pension of Beltenebras be augmented to 6,000 crowns at the least. In conformity whereof he receiveth the King of Spain's answer by his letters, bearing date the 17th of May, 1605.

Zuniga, in his letters of the 8th of June, 1609, writeth that it was intimated unto him from Beltenebras that he would be well pleased that his pension should cease, and that his services might be recompensed by the piece. Which the party upon conference intimated to grow, for there had been some slowness in extraordinary reward. And that he thought Beltenebras conceived it to be, because they in Spain (it should seem) held him sufficiently content with his pension, which he would have little esteem if he had not extraordinaries. To this letter the King of Spain answereth by his of the 2nd of September, 1609, written in Segovia, that in any case he give all contentment to Beltenebras in any fashion and manner that himself shall desire. And that according to what he shall advise to be fit, shall be remitted unto him.

App. III.

So that hereby it appeareth that from the year 1604, in which the peace was concluded, until the year 1609, his pension was continued, and then further order given for his full satisfaction in that sort as should best like him. It now remaineth that it appear that this Beltenebras was the Earl of Salisbury, which may be easily gathered by the following passages :—

First, by the description of his authority in the government of the State, and his power with the King, in the letter above mentioned of the Conde de Villa Mediana for the augmenting of his pension.

Velasco, in his letters of the 20th of February, 1612, writeth that of late from Beltenebras he received no advice of consideration, and that he is at present in great danger of death.

He likewise writeth, in his letters of the 14th of April, 1612, that there is arrived a secretary from Florence, who bringeth a certain offer of the portion to be given, and hath made promises of 100,000 crowns to Beltenebras, in case he procure the effecting of the marriage.

Zuniga writeth, at his last being in England, in his letters of the 2nd of June, that, since the death of Beltenebras, the match for Florence hath grown cold. For he was the only furtherer of it.

Zuniga, at his last being in England, likewise writeth, in his letters of the 10th of July, that there were certain commissioners appointed to see in what state the King of England's treasure was left by Beltenebras.

But that which makes it apparent, and past conjecture, is that my confidant friend assureth me to have seen and had in his custody a letter written by Zuniga in March last (a little before the departure of Don Diego Sarmiento de Acuna) to the Secretary of State, who required him to advertise what he held fitting concerning the payment of the pensions. To which he maketh answer that, at his coming away out of England, he left a perfect note, what was to be done, with Velasco. Wherein he knoweth little to be altered but that the 6,000 crowns pension of the Earl of Salisbury hath by his death ceased. Sending this letter but from his lodging to the Secretary, it seems there was no need of cypher, or disguise, little fearing it should light into the hands where it hath. And hereby Your Majesty seeth it hath pleased God to clear this riddle.

I have hitherto set down what I can allege against my Lord of Salisbury. Your Majesty may also be pleased to give me leave to write what I can collect, that may in any kind make for him.

Before his death, I find that Velasco advertiseth that he cannot attain to that certain knowledge of things as had been formerly done, for that Beltenebras, of late, gave him no advertisements of consideration as to which there might be credit given. App. III.

Further, Velasco (diverse months, as well before my Lord Treasurer's death as since) hath given hither very false and ridiculous advertisements, which Velasco could not have done [if] my Lord of Salisbury had dealt confidently with him.

Besides, I have observed in these later times (whether it were out of cunning or not I am not able to judge) a great adverseness and hatred in my Lord Treasurer to the businesses of Spain, so that it may be probably, or, at the least, charitably conjectured, that my Lord (at the first conclusion of the peace, when only the furthering of the maintenance thereof was expected from him, and since whilst the hope of some match with Spain was kept on foot) did take what he received for the assisting of those good ends of firm peace and nearer alliance; but having, of late, discovered that the King of Spain did not really intend any such alliance, and likewise seeing, by many arguments, the sincerity of his friendship might justly be doubted of, he withdrew his former inclination and affection towards the Spanish King and State; yet it may be he was content to receive their money and to put many tricks and untruths upon them. I write this unto Your Majesty by way of declaration, and not by way of excuse, for no circumstance can make his proceedings excusable or free from the name of falsehood and treachery unless he freely acquainted Your Majesty with all that passed, and that Your Majesty were contented not to be displeased that the Spaniards should be cozened.

I will only add one thing more concerning my Lord of Salisbury, and so come to the other particulars whereof I am to speak. My confidant friend telleth me that he knoweth that some of the letters which myself have written, and copied, of many of them have been sent hither, and that the procuring of them cost great sums of money. Your Majesty may be pleased to call for all my despatches to such as had the keeping of my Lord Treasurer's papers, and that they may be conferred with the particular note, which I send by this bearer, of all such despatches as I have written since my coming into Spain. Thereby it will be seen what originals are wanting, and, it may be, I shall be able to make some good use thereof, for I already know so much of these things, that sometimes a petty circumstance cleareth a great doubt.

Before I begin the second part of this despatch, I must humbly crave Your Majesty's permission to utter some few words by

App. III. way of apology, for that I well understand how ill it befitteth a gentleman or an honest man to put jealousies into the head of princes against their ministers, upon circumstances that have not strong probabilities; but when the present danger or inconvenience will not fittingly admit of the delay which is requisite for the sifting and clearing of those suspicions which are not without cause conceived, I then suppose that the prejudice of particular men is rather to be adventured than Your Majesty's service or safety in the least manner hazarded. And this is now the case: for I see a person employed in Your Majesty's service in a place of so great consequence and trust, and that in times of danger, if he should be disloyal unto Your Majesty, might have so great power to do hurt, being indeed one of the guards of your kingdom, as may well excuse my giving Your Majesty a caveat to have him carefully looked unto, although my suspicions are not yet come to certain and direct proof. The party is Sir William Monson, Admiral of the Narrow Seas, whom by diverse circumstances and collections I gather to be a pensioner to the King of Spain, as I fear (before it be long) I shall plainly make it appear unto Your Majesty.

Further, I find in a note that hath come into my hands (which though it be imperfect, Your Majesty may give credit unto it, and likewise be pleased to hear divers particulars concerning it from this bearer, my secretary), that at the time when the Conde de Villa Mediana came from England, the King of Spain bestowed every year, in pensions in the English Court, the sum of 36,500 crowns, and that four of the said pensions being suspended, which amounted to the sum of 6,000 crowns, there was order left unto Zuniga for the payment of 30,600* crowns yearly amongst the other ten whose pensions were continued. Now, considering that these persons must of necessity be of extraordinary rank and quality, since to my Lord of Salisbury himself there was given only 6,000 crowns per annum of certainty, I could not satisfy mine own conscience in regard of the faith I owe and will ever perform unto Your Majesty, but that I should highly fail in my duty towards you, if in this conjuncture, when Your Majesty is upon the point of making choice of your Secretary and other great officers, I should not give Your Majesty this warning. And if I may presume so far, in a matter of so great consequence, to write anything by way of advice, I should, with all humility, counsel Your Majesty that since you have by God's providence and your own wisdom so long suspended the choice of your officers, you would yet be pleased for a while to forbear it, until some

* Sic.

clearer light be had of these mysteries. Your Majesty hath ever (I hope) found in me that wariness in my advertisements as not to give Your Majesty unnecessary alarm or to cast jealousies on the persons of any men. Neither would I (in a case of this importance, which belongeth not to me to speak of) adventure to write in this manner unto Your Majesty, were I not induced by such reasons and circumstances as, though they are not yet ripe to be presented unto Your Majesty as formal accusations, yet they are such against some that are not of the unlikeliest men to be called to the places vacant, as will not only make my suspicions justifiable, but they put on me an obligation to give Your Majesty this item. The double cyphers Your Majesty may conceive cannot but make things very intricate, yet circumstances will give some light, so that there may be very well afforded unto me causes to suspect, when there shall not be sufficient appearances for me to accuse, wherein it befitteth an honest man to proceed with slowness, and much certainty, if it be not for the preventing of present inconvenience.

* * * * *

2. SIR JOHN DIGBY TO THE KING.* Dec. 16, 1615.

* * * * *

Concerning the second part of Your Majesty's letter, wherein you are pleased to command me freely and without respect of persons to set down my knowledge concerning such 186 [pensions] as shall have been distributed from Spain amongst servants and ministers, for which purpose Your Majesty, it seemeth, is informed that there is yearly returned from hence to the Ambassador in England the sum of £20,000, Your Majesty may be pleased to understand that, unless it be only this last year, I shall be able, by papers which I have obtained, to set down all such pensions, and most of the sums of money that have been given and distributed in 69 [England] ever since the conclusion of the peace. In the first years, 36,500 crowns were yearly assigned from hence for the payment of the settled pensions, according to a note which I have formerly acquainted

* This despatch is written in a cypher which is different from any other used in the collection. Consequently, though I was able without any great difficulty to discover the key to the alphabet, I cannot be quite certain about all the proper names; I have therefore in these cases retained the cypher, adding the names in brackets. Where proper names are given without any figures before them, they are either written in plain writing or in the ordinary cypher. The following is the key to the other words:—

b	c	d		x	y	z	a	e	i and j	o	u and v
31	33	35	. . .	66	65	67	16	19	22	25	28
32	34	36	. . .	34	66	68	17	20	23	26	29
							18	21	24	27	30

App. III. Your Majesty with, and shown unto 80 [the Earl of Somerset] by Your Majesty's appointment. Afterwards divers of Your Majesty's ministers, refusing to receive that in the quality of a yearly pension which before had been bestowed upon them in the nature of presents and gratuities, first, for their assistance in the concluding of the peace, and after, for their good offices in continuing amity and good correspondency betwixt Your Majesties, the said yearly allowance for pensions was brought down to 21,000 crowns. But the extraordinary sums, upon particular occasions, that were then given to my Lord of Salisbury and my Lady of Suffolk, were very great, two of them (of which I have the account) amounting unto 44,000 crowns, which was promised; and every thing was so particularly bargained for by them with the Ambassador, that both themselves and Your Majesty's service were drawn into strange contempt, as will appear by divers letters written from 149 [the Ambassador]* to 109 [the King of Spain], in so much that he writeth that they are to be bought and sold withal as he would do with shopkeepers; and concludeth his letter with this, that as nothing is to be had of them without money, so for money he thinketh they would sell their souls to hell. But I may not omit to let Your Majesty understand that by the same letters it appeareth that 79 [Suffolk] had no hand in any of these practices, for he saith of him, that he is a good and honourable gentleman, whom the other two abused and ruled as they listed.

Since the death of my Lord of Salisbury, the chief pensions that were given were unto my Lord Privy Seal, which was 4,000 crowns a year of certainty, and to my Lady Suffolk, according as she could agree upon occasions of her service; but unto Lord Northampton, I find not any extraordinary gift to be given more than his yearly pension, only, I conceive, a little before his death he had a good round sum paid him by 149 [the Ambassador] in gold: by what I can guess it was for the arrears of his pension.

If it shall prove certain, as Your Majesty is informed, that 149 [the Spanish Ambassador] spendeth £20,000 a year, it must needs be that he hath very lately fastened some great sums upon some of Your Majesty's ministers. For since the death of Lord Northampton, the allowance for ordinary pensions hath been but only 30,000 crowns yearly, in which I know I cannot be deceived, for that I have the copy of 109 [the King of Spain's] warrant under his own hand for the payment of it, and shall likewise declare unto 70 [Your

* 149 is, I believe, a general cypher for the Spanish Ambassador in London at the time referred to, whatever his name may have been.

Majesty] how it is bestowed. But that 80 [Somerset] should have received anything from 149 [the Ambassador], I have never in any kind been able to discover, neither do I think it.

But I have great reason to conjecture that 149 [the Ambassador] hath been busy to draw my Lady Somerset unto his part, and to oblige her. But the particulars hereof Your Majesty will get the best notice of from Sir William Monson, who hath been 149 [the Ambassador's] instrument to negotiate therein, himself being and having been a pensioner to 109 [the King of Spain] ever since the year 1604. The match being made with him by the Constable of Castile at his return, who then allotted him 4,000 crowns a year pension; and, to that effect, gave him letters to the Conde de Villa Mediana, dated at Gravelines the 12th of September, 1604. Which pension was afterwards by the said Conde de Villa Mediana, upon special occasions for the 109 [King of Spain's] service, augmented to 1,500 crowns, and so hath ever since and doth yet continue. I find likewise in the list for the distribution of 149 [the Ambassador's] ordinary allowance 1,500 crowns ordained to be bestowed, upon occasions, in presents and new year's gifts, upon the Lady Jane Drummond. But I am bound in all conscience to tell Your Majesty that, in all the advertisements that have come to my hands, I can not perceive that she ever received anything but only a slight jewel or two and a basin and ewer of some rich stone, given by 149 [the Spanish Ambassador], as, I conceive, at her marriage. Neither in all the letters and despatches of 149 [the Ambassador] which I have can I find any one thing to her prejudice. As for the third part of Your Majesty's letter, whereby it appeareth that Your Majesty hath received information by 77 [Winwood or Coke's ?] means that 80 [Somerset] should have revealed unto the Ambassador Your Majesty's secrets and designs, I shall freely and undisguisedly set down unto Your Majesty such grounds and inducements as I have had to make me inclinable to that opinion. First, I was of late told by the chiefest confidant I have left in this court, that he would hold no more correspondence with me; neither was it possible for any man to serve 70 [Your Majesty]. For whatever I did here was by those nearest about 70 [Your Majesty] revealed unto 149 [the Ambassador]. And therefore that he would now retire himself, for that he had learned lately that the first light against Santander * came from 149 [the Ambassador], and that all the other proceedings with him were but out of the cunning of this State and Council to disguise and trick the true and first means

* The person through whom Digby obtained his information in 1613. He had lately been detected in another intrigue with the Duke of Savoy.

App. III. of his discovery. But hereof I must confess unto Your Majesty I never had any other ground nor cause of jealousy, but only the speech of this party. And that by the examinations of the said Santander, the copy of which I have obtained, I find that he was chiefly still examined upon the rack concerning me. Although in this particular I would not for the world lay the least imputation upon 80 [Somerset] that he should maliciously have betrayed so great a service, yet I can not but lay great blame upon him for want of secrecy and care in a business of so great consequence. For, first, I got certain knowledge that some parties had full notice of all such things as I had by Your Majesty's appointment delivered to 80 [Somerset] against them, and thereof (as far as I then durst) I presumed to give Your Majesty some inkling; and could (if I were present) quickly, by the circumstances, cause the truth to be discovered unto Your Majesty. Further, speaking one day by chance, by way of discourse with a particular friend of mine, and desiring to understand of him how he heard my services in Spain were accepted, he told me, 'Extraordinarily well,' and that he wondered in his heart how it was possible for me to do those things which I did, viz. to get the copy of the King of Spain's letter, and his 149 [the Ambassador's] despatches—'nay, and as I heard,' said he, 'his very private instructions.' Wherewithal, I, being strucken unto a very strange amaze, seemed to make a jest thereat; saying that some one had raised that rumour for some particular end. Whereupon he told me that, to deal plainly with me, he himself had seen and read divers of them. And, upon further conference, he at last confessed unto me that they had been shown unto him by one Rawlins, a follower of 80 [Somerset]. This party, though I should be grieved, for just reasons, to have him produced, yet, if it may be of any use or moment to Your Majesty's service (to which all other respects must be submitted) the bearer hereof, my secretary, will nominate the party unto Your Majesty; and he may [be] produced face to face with the said Rawlins. This being true, Your Majesty will think I had, then, just cause to show an unwillingness to return again unto Spain, when I saw this business that so nearly concerned Your Majesty's service so carelessly handled. Neither is it impossible that this unfortunate event of this business hath been caused, though not through disloyalty, yet through want of care and secrecy. But thereof I can no further accuse my Lord Somerset, than what out of these circumstances may be collected. But the chief motives that have made me think that Somerset used ill both Your Majesty's name and favour were since my last coming out of England, especially in the speech that hath been for the treaty of a match for the Prince with Spain, wherein, although I absolutely disclaimed in any kind so much as to speak thereof in quality of an Ambassador, and disavowed so much as Your Majesty's privity that any such discourse was held, and to that effect (understanding from divers Your Majesty's ministers in the courts of other princes, that some rumour was raised that a treaty for such a match should be on foot), I wrote unto all parts, giving satisfaction and full assurance that Your Majesty had never entered into any such treaty, neither had any proposition to that effect ever been made, either by Your Majesty, or your order; neither had there anything further passed therein than by way of ordinary discourse. And unto the Duke of Lerma, with whom I only dealt in the said business, I ever likewise disavowed Your Majesty's having any knowledge of what passed, absolutely refusing to make any overture therein unto Your Majesty, till I should see betwixt ourselves all difficulties (which in likelihood might arise) fully agreed upon. And, hereupon, when the Duke of Lerma had delivered me his particular demands in point of religion, I told him I durst not adventure to send them unto Your Majesty, unless they might be much altered and qualified. Which the Duke (after some conferences) seemed not unwilling unto. And to that effect several consultations were had amongst those that were formerly by this King deputed to this business. In the mean time (according to my bounden duty), I held it fit secretly to give Your Majesty notice of all that passed, and to send you a copy of those demands which the Duke of Lerma had given me. All which was discovered unto 149 [the Spanish Ambassador]; and the same articles which I had sent, showed unto him, in the manner that I shall set down. First, one Sir Robert Cotton came unto 149 [the Ambassador] as sent unto him from 80 [Somerset], as a man whom he did afterwards desire to have employed betwixt them, especially in the business now on foot concerning the match. This Sir Robert Cotton assured 149 [the Ambassador] both of your Majesty's inclination and of 80 [Somerset's] will and power for the effecting of it. Only, he said it was resolved to have the dealing therein taken wholely out of 141 [my] hands; and, therefore, if he already had not, he should do well speedily to procure sufficient commission from 109 [the King of Spain] to treat and conclude of it there; and that the business should wholely be managed betwixt 80 [Somerset] and 149 [the Ambassador]. To which, when the Ambassador answered that he conceived the business could not but receive some prejudice, if it should now be taken out of 141 [my] hands, who had formerly been the

App. III. only dealer therein, he signified unto him, that that was by 80 [Somerset] fully resolved on. Which shortly after, and all the rest that Sir Robert Cotton had said, was by 80 [Somerset] himself confirmed unto 149 [the Ambassador]. And at that meeting (as 149 [the Ambassador] advertiseth) he first perceived that 80 [Somerset] mortally hated 141 [me], whom he before thought to have been his great friend. For, said he, alleging that if 141 [Digby] should perceive the business to be thus taken out of his hands, he would questionless, out of spleen, endeavour all he could for the overthrowing of it; and by his advertisements and relations unto 70 [Your Majesty] would do all the ill offices he could. To which 80 [Somerset] answered that 141 [Digby], either out of his discontent and hate, would do some such thing as would be his utter ruin; or, at least, would write in such manner of spleen and passion as he might quickly be discredited with 70 [Your Majesty], and no belief given, nor any reckoning made of anything he should advertise. And hereupon, by Somerset's persuasion, the Ambassador dispatched away a post for such a commission as was desired. The which I understand was accordingly sent unto him. Afterwards, Cotton several times repaired unto the Ambassador, as sent by Somerset, intimating the knowledge of 70 [Your Majesty] of all that 141 [I] had done here in Spain. And, for an undoubted testimony whereof, showed him the demands in religion made unto me by 113 [Lerma], which I lately sent unto 70 [Your Majesty], signifying likewise unto him that the matter might be so handled that 70 [Your Majesty] might be drawn to condescend unto them; with many other particulars, which will be best known by the examination of the said Cotton, if 70 [Your Majesty] shall hold it fit to have him apprehended, though I think Your Majesty will judge it fit to have it done upon some other colourable pretext.

As for my future proceeding upon any discourse that may be offered concerning the match for 72 [Prince Charles] with a daughter of the King of Spain, I shall not therein, nor in anything else, by God's assistance, swerve any whit from Your Majesty's pleasure. So, fearing I have with this long letter presumed too much upon Your Majesty's patience, humbly craving Your Majesty's pardon, I recommend you to the protection of the Almighty.

Your Majesty's faithful servant and subject,

John Digby.

Madrid, the 16th of December,
1615. st°. vet.

3. SIR JOHN DIGBY TO THE KING. April 3, 1616. App. III.

[Written in London, after his return.]

. . . . . By the marginal notes of my Lord Chief Justice Coke upon the enclosed letter, which is the same I received from him, Your Majesty will see in what particulars he desired to receive satisfaction, as judging he might make use of them in this business which he had now in hand, though indeed they have no relation to it; neither, as I conceived, can there any inference be drawn from them concerning it, since it now appeareth that my Lord of Somerset acquainted Your Majesty with the dispatch, and concealed not those businesses of consequence from you, as it seemeth my Lord Coke believed, when Your Majesty commanded me to attend him, for (as I remember) he told me Your Majesty had never seen that dispatch.

I must confess unto Your Majesty that I am of opinion that the coming of this letter unto my Lord Coke's hands hath been the cause of his aggravating matters very far, for he having there found mention made of the discovery of Your Majesty's secrets, of great sums of money bestowed upon Your Majesty's principal ministers, of Spanish pensioners, of the selling of my dispatches, &c., either conjectured these things to have been absolutely held back from Your Majesty, or else, lighting upon them in the prosecution of the business concerning my Lord of Somerset, made a wrong application of them to him, whereas, the truth is, they had only a reference to times past, and I had formerly at large made Your Majesty acquainted with them, and so shall again my Lord Chancellor, as far as Your Majesty shall think it fit for your service.

Of all that I am able to say unto Your Majesty concerning my Lord of Somerset, both of his careless manner of keeping those papers and secrets committed unto him by Your Majesty, as likewise his treating with the Spanish Ambassador in the business of the marriage, both without Your Majesty's privity, and clear in a contrary manner to that which Your Majesty had signified unto me was your pleasure should be held, I have in my former dispatches given unto Your Majesty a full account. But hereunto it is likely much may be added by the light that may be gathered from Sir R. Cotton, if he may be examined concerning all the particulars in which he was employed by my Lord of Somerset to the Spanish

App. III. Ambassador; both how far he therein used Your Majesty's name, as likewise, what hopes and promises were given for the effecting of the said match, and especially whether by my Lord of Somerset's directions, he discovered not certain propositions, and demands in point of religion, which in great secrecy I had sent unto Your Majesty; as likewise, what other advertisement of mine he acquainted the Spanish Ambassador withal.

* * * * *

IV.

DOCUMENTS RELATING TO THE IMPRISONMENT OF SIR THOMAS OVERBURY.

[Harl. MS., 7002, fol. 281.]

1. [SIR THOMAS OVERBURY TO VISCOUNT ROCHESTER.*]

App. IV.

THIS after the receipt of your last. First, for that of R. Killigrew, send it as soon as you can by this fellow, but very secretly for me to have in store; but, for to-morrow, it shall be enough for me to show my legs wonderful little, which I will impute since this, though they were so afore, and then my message by Pembroke, and then I will use this vomit two days after, which will be a new occasion for you to be importunate to send me into the country to save my life, for 'tis not the close air, but the apprehension of the place that hurts me; which you must stand upon. I have now sent by the Lieutenant to desire you (Mayerus being absent) to send young Crag hither and Nesmith. If Nesmith be away, send I pray Crag and Allen, two such as when they go back may go unto the King and relate how much my body is wasted with thought of the King's displeasure, and this place; and this is all, for I will take no physic of them; and upon this reason that till my mind be eased, no physic can cure my body, and so, having showed them this, I will desire them to come to you, then you to carry them in to the King, then you to send them in to the King by Patrick Mauld or so; then presently after, go you in yourself.

2. [SIR ROBERT KILLIGREW TO VISCOUNT ROCHESTER.]

My Honourable Lord,

I have here sent you enclosed the vomit you desired of me, but I would not counsel your lordship to take it, unless the physicians do allow of it, at this time; for though this be as

* This is the third letter of the series. The first is missing, the second contains nothing of importance, excepting the explanation of one or two nicknames used in the correspondence. Wherever these names, or those which were explained at Somerset's trial, occur, I have substituted the true name. For the punctuation I am responsible. The headings in brackets are mine, resting only upon internal evidence; the others are copied from the MS., which is only a bad copy of the lost originals.

APP. IV. good as any can be, yet there is no such medicine good for all persons at all times, of which they are the best judges; but if your lordship be resolved to take it, this bearer can give direction for the manner.

Your honour's devoted servant,
ROBERT KILLIGREW.

3. [SIR THOMAS OVERBURY TO VISCOUNT ROCHESTER.]

I seal this with my own seal, mark it well. I pray you seal with the stag's head hereafter, and send me my little seal again. By no means hear of my going out at all beyond sea, though for an hour, but to Berry*, not by command, but stolen thither by discretion. Send me that vomit enclosed, if I stay here two days longer. Let this fellow be warned to be wat[chful], and get to serve somebody within [this] place, though but for a fortnight. For that letter under my own hand concerning you, put all upon that. Still stand upon that. Best urge nothing till that be done; for this must be done only by way of prayer and kindness. After, justify when I am gone. Though you have a grant, yet accept no delay for disputes. If this come safe write me word.

4. [SIR THOMAS OVERBURY TO VISCOUNT ROCHESTER.†]

I sent to-day a message to Northampton, and had only a fair answer in generalities. Look, therefore, you touch nothing but effects, and urge dispatches, for my life lies upon it, and if this way fail, I pray you answer me directly to this, whether you will not use To‡ for a fortnight rather than leave me thus. I know that will carry it directly. If you deny me that, I am satisfied. Another request, that you would convey that wonderful tale to me under unknown names by Mayerus or the Apothecary. Now he is sick is a fit time to urge a commiseration for my sickness, for I was never worse; and, if you leave me here, I shall never see you more, and that, I fear, my enemies understand well enough, and hope so to come by my office, but do not you be accessory to my death, though you could not conceive my body should have overlived thus much. The two Lords should mitigate my fault, and say I was surprised.

5. [SIR THOMAS OVERBURY TO VISCOUNT ROCHESTER.]

Now for Hansuff's§ new instructions, first, you must tell him

* I do not know what place this is.

† In a short letter, omitted, Overbury describes the effect of the emetic which he had taken.

‡ This word occurs two or three times in this correspondence. It is difficult to say what its meaning is, unless it is some sham illness, with which Rochester was accustomed to melt James's heart.

§ One of the uninterpreted names.

that you are so far from speaking of this, as that you must make him swear, and so he Suffolk, that no man shall know this, but only he and Suffolk, not Suffolk's wife nor any child, neither will you have any of your friends know it; but especially not the King, because he must, in appearance, after the offices be settled, be the author of this reconcilement, and must know nothing of this privately done betwixt you three and me when . . . . know it, and therefore Suffolk must take care not to tell his wife, nor no soul living. Now for the first obligation betwixt you, which is my delivery, say you have prepared it so that if Suffolk do but what you will propose, he and I together will carry him out straight, and that is that Suffolk must come to the King one morning at Greenwich and tell him that the Lieutenant *hujus loci* is come to him, and tell him Overbury is every night so sick as he is ready to die, and that these two or three nights, he hath set one to watch him in another room without his knowledge, who thought still he would not live an hour, and that he, being of a haughty nature, and ashamed of this disgrace, conceals it, and will not so much as confess a word of this to the physicians. Now, for his part, he is afraid he will die in his house, except he be dismissed, and that upon the sudden, ere any know. For, to our knowledge, his keeper knows not of this. Hereupon may Suffolk say, 'Sir, I, hearing this, thought myself bound in honesty to tell you, first for fear he die in the night. It might cost my Lord of Rochester his life too, when you see how passionately he loves him. Next, Sir, for my own part I speak, for the world, thinking me his enemy, would lay his blood to my charge, which I would not have imputed to me for all the world. Now, Sir, take no notice, I pray you, of what I inform; but, what you do, do suddenly, before it be too late, and let my Lord of Rochester know nothing but that you do it for his sake, never taking notice that I have said anything, and, indeed, considering his offence, being only a hasty answer, a month of such close imprisonment is punishment enough.' Here is a plot exquisitely laid, the King understanding no correspondence betwixt Suffolk and you. But now, here is the caution of it. For your enemies insulting, be sure they never hoped for such a day of public glory, howsoever my friends conceal it from you. Bullion,* Deputy of Ireland, all Ambassadors hear of it. You writ me nothing whether you have yet forbid Northampton, as he looks for any friendship from you not to mingle his little business with these present, or else that he and you will be strangers, which I know he will not

* Another of the uninterpreted names.

App. IV. have a public demonstration of. And for him 'tis no matter. Only traffic with Suffolk. You writ me nothing what security you have for the second with Nevill.* That is all neglected, for, if it be his man,† except you have some foreknowledge of it, they will count it no act of yours. Be rid of those you keep, and get me restored, and, if ever you and I engage either for faction or public, never trust me. Let everything go as it will, but if you now . . . . with writing letters, and fit these turns, wait, go to church, be necessary about him till I be restored, then you betray me, for that is all he aims at; but when he sees you make use of every opportunity to no other end, but to rid me out of this place, and that, for other business, you will meddle with none, he will dispatch me. Therefore look now to your fashion, for he observes well whether time work anything, and you see how well he quiets you with kind generalities, but in particular gives you not one effect; as the other day he told you, to cure your sickness, that, if you would do but this, you should obtain your ends sooner than you expect. Upon that presently you made an [—t?] recovered, got abroad; what done, notwithstanding so just a pretence for him as my sickness, he could not grant that of which never man for such an offence as mine was restrained of; nay, such an offence as he himself sought, for he knew, afore they came, I would not go such a journey, nay, what is more, presently after, would not believe you about my sickness; nay, in your last conference, begun to slide back and talk to you of showing his favour to you otherwise, so by that means to call the point itself in question which before you took for granted, and with speed, by reason of his words, 'Sooner than you looked for.' Do but mark this proceeding, and thereupon leave off your confidence, and suspect all but effects. Of that you have not had yet one—nay, he hath not told you yet that so I would reform, I should return to Court. Mark how you are handled. Today I hear nothing of having the liberty of this place, and the fellow is now to be put away, and indeed I would be glad he were gone for our security, for now if you cannot get present access for my friends, and upon my sickness too, I never look for it: a Tuesday is a month close prisoner. Sure the reason to keep me close so long is to try all ways upon you alone, whether he can work your consent to a separation, for, after the doors are open, then, he thinks, we will mingle thoughts again, and after that he will not hope for it. Therefore now is the time he will try you all ways, therefore lose no hour to declare your resolution that God forsake you, if ever you forsake me

* Second secretary, I suppose.

† Winwood.

for any hope or fear, and let it be an example to him that you can forsake him, and tell if ever you rest, eat, or sleep quietly till you have me restored, and this boyish shame taken off you; and then show him your resolution. For me, I shall be reformed according to his instructions never to transgress, which he cannot but accept. If that will not, you will quit all business, to take away the subject of this vexation, or if both these fail, it will have a worse end. You desire Hansuff or Pembroke's brother's liberty, or rather to shut yourself up in a park and die, for this you will never overlive. These three, when he sees sure, he will choose the first and presently tend towards it. For loving me better than him, what he touched,* you must never let such a thing slide by unanswered, for that you are a natural man; where your most love is, there your most company is, and he can never say that anything that this world had drew him one hour from you†, nor ever was with me but when by reason of his business, or other company, you could not be with him, and you fear the satiety of your company hath brought him to this little fondness of you. Indeed, Pembroke, Southampton, Chandos, and Nevill, were company too mean. Look upon their companions, More, Butler; and there was no gentleman that applied himself to you, but were of the best quality and houses of England, as Jermyn, Berkeley, Radcliffe, Mansell, Killigrew, Udall, Lidcote, the best houses in England. You are no old man yet, nor can delight in old company continually. That day Nevill is made,‡ be sure you never so much as to take notice of it, or look cheerful. Tell§ you receive no honour till first you be freed from disgrace. 'Tis the manner of benefits pleaseth, not the matter; but you, for preferring a good servant to lose a friend, was an ill recompense. Besides, for the thing itself, if it be well done now, it had been better done some ten months ago. The delay hath spoiled the world, and the ending of it worst, to take away one that hath deserved as well as ever he can deserve; ever so, without any rejoicing, speak. There engage Nevill presently, as soon as the company is gone, about me. Perchance this man will send Abbot to deal about me; if he do, never answer him nor any else, but say you use not to speak to your master by mediators. You may speak with him himself. If you cannot do something presently, you must take that To again, and not recover till I am out, and be so dangerously sick that you much desire to speak with me before you die. Tell him that is your last

* *i.e.* As for loving me better than him, which he touched upon.

† ? Drew you one hour from him.

‡ Made Secretary.

§ Sic: but probably some name is omitted by the copyist.

App. IV. request to him, and so you must continue till you have got me out, and got Patrick Mauld and Mont.* to be with him still. This do rather than let me live here . . . a . . . this fashion, and my mind overthrow my body for ever. Do somewhat like an honest man and a friend; though you never do more, get me from hence. For the opinion of this deed, alas! you bid me have a good heart. You must know that the best hearts can ever worst bear shame and victory; and so, for my part, I wonder to hear that you [are] abroad and are seen in the world, I being here; for God refuse me if I be not so ashamed of staying here so long that now I never dare open the windows to look out; and, for the offence he speaks, bid him gravely beware lest, when all comes to all, it prove my words imported no contempt. Say 'Sir, 'twere well you thought of that, having restrained a subject's liberty, of his quality, thus long and close, to which, contempts never use to have above a week.'

6. [SIR THOMAS OVERBURY TO VISCOUNT ROCHESTER. (?)]

You must give order presently, and send back for wine, jelly, and a tart to be brought to me to-morrow by James, and then for the jelly and the wine will I never have it up to my chamber at all, but have it conveyed from James to the Lieutenant's wife, which is the best way. So too for a cold pasty of venison, I will send it to the Lieutenant's, but that cannot be done to-morrow. He that brings me this letter brings no tart which is ill lost, for to-morrow I would have the wine and jelly delivered, therefore you must send a footman away all night. The conveyance is better by my man than Giles, for Giles† is more suspected. Instruct Nevill, if he can, to fall in talk about me at Windsor, both for never speaking an undertaking word, but modestly and discreetly, and so for not sending messages to him from hence. Lose not to-morrow for sending. I pray you let me know to-morrow before dinner whether that in the scurvy greasy bottle were legible and whether I shall send an unctious message to Northampton by the Lieutenant, which I think would do well.

7. [SIR THOMAS OVERBURY TO VISCOUNT ROCHESTER.]

Take heed you be not cozened in the relation of this business, for he that the King hath appointed to warn the Lieutenant, and relate to him what is found, may say the Lieutenant saith

* Is this Montgomery?

† Giles Rawlins.

this and that which he never spake. Therefore, the day the King comes to this town, let one be sent afore to the Lieutenant to warn him to come to the King as to speak about my Lady Arabella, and then let him ask of himself directly whether there were any such paper afore, whether any since; so you go to the root, else the instrument of conveyance may overthrow all, but this way you deceive him quite. I tell you what makes me think the Lieutenant never said any such thing, but they feign it upon him. Yesterday, he and I talking of news, I told him how ignorant of all things I was since I came in, he said, 'Nay, you have received wine and tarts.' I took it presently upon the lift [?] and a Testament lying upon the table, I swore upon it that none of all those things ever conveyed any thing to me but themselves; and he took up the book straight again, and swore he never suspected that they did, and the same he swore to me again this morning, taking it unkindly that I would suspect his suspicion. Therefore, the man is belied, and the King abused by the instrument. Now, therefore, look to it. This was on Tuesday night, for the fellow here . . . .* being so far engaged . . . . greedy villain, as your . . . . he now and then seems dainty . . . . or a promise from you . . . . under you. About what . . . . and I will entertain his . . . . him faithful enough, but I . . . have spoken that they should . . . . but so that there is but two . . . sure my landlord is set on to [be] jealous, which is no hard work, for yesternight again he wondered at my being here this long, Mansell out, and returned again to Court, whose cause and manner and time of imprisonment was much different from mine, and he had the same enemies I have, and no such friend. This he told me how much cause you had to venture not only your fortune but even your life for me, for 'twas well known all this malice c . . upon me, not for any fortune or titles that I had, but for making a stranger so great an actor in this State; besides, he knew that, out of my truth to you, I had refused two thousand pounds from Ignatius,† and entered into a quarrel against Pembroke. I told him I wondered too, and I knew 'twas without example, such an imprisonment upon a contempt, and for a man first to show an utter inability, and after that, and in that respect to profess unwillingness, I thought it was a contempt without example. Now, I perceive by that you said of the law-speakers that you [have] been made believe that mine was a fault, and, if it were not for you, much would

* These blanks, and those in a later part of the letter, are in this MS. apparently caused by a mutilation of the original from which the copy was taken.

† Salisbury [?]

App. IV. be done. Sir, be not deceived; as my accusations were all false afore, so is my fault no fault, (what said the Duke* about going over?) nor, had it been the uttermost contempt, is this kind of imprisonment due to it. I said I would not . . . . that I must maintain . . . . for to gain that word . . . . them first I thought . . . . then the lawyer said . . . . not leave my country, which . . . . to be granted, and Pembroke . . . . I be not deceived, they . . . . Mansell too out, so to my . . . . compassion both to the world . . . . what will you say if the King, as he told you at first that you would not have me send him post to . . . . or Oxford straight, so now he say that you would not have me take him out any degree; and so with form put you off again, am not I then in a good state, the progress coming on, by trusting upon you; or have not you done well, the people dissolving within four days, to have those in your hands that, if this trick hit not, you are undone, for I warrant few in England but think 'tis your plots and vanity to keep them in your hands though the State be ruined by it? O have you not husbanded these two months well, both for me and Nevill? In what degree we were both the first hour, there are we still, and I fear that course of quick dispatch which I prescribed must be your refuge now when all is done, for I hope you will neither suffer me here longer nor keep those longer in your hands, whatever course you take, for both those I hope you are resolved. Then I wonder to see you so cozened as to think the King keeps me here in respect of my fault, or in respect of Nevill's business. For he knew at . . . . I was as far from that, as here thus close, but the matter was Libells [?] had told him you governed him, and Agrippina† told him he durst do nothing to discipline you. Now he, to let them see 'tis not so, but that he could discipline you, when he pleased, he hath continued this with making objections, and telling of informations, and so won time upon you by hearing answers and the like. I should be glad to hear Will. Udall's business of hides went on, for his sake no less than my own. For the reversion after Fulk Greville for Jack Lidcote's boy, you may keep any other from having it till a fit time to pass it for him. For Badger's stewardship, I would he had it. For Shirley's do somewhat. 'Tis a fine suit. This year hath been lost both for office and parks. Make that sure at the end of it. Upon you, [you] know, my fortunes depend too. If I had brought it to Pembroke's brother or Hansuff, they had passed it sooner, and I would have made my part £5000, for, in all, 'tis twelve. Pembroke can cause Agrippina make the Archbishop cease

* Of Lennox.

† Probably the Queen.

from being any more of the plots with them, and shame him for what is passed. Her nature is, if it be well followed, now others would oppress me, to be as much for me, as afore she was against me. Do you and Nevill set Pembroke upon this. So there is two taken off, the Archbishop and Northampton, and then one push will rid me hence. If he have a design, rather a wish (I think) than a hope to have me go over for two or three months, which I think he will not have, the answer to that is that nothing helps the spleen so much as our native air, and foreign, though better, hurts it; therefore, of late Mr. Burgess, the famous preacher, having the spleen, though otherwise of a strong body, wasfain to leave his charge at the Hague, only to come to London his native air, for the ease of his sickness: and I whilst I was abroad, was never well [an] hour, as Mayerus knows, which made me return so soon. This late example of Mr. Burgess known will prevent that motion; and best, if it be used by way of discourse beforehand. Mr. Burgess, the silenced preacher, had at the Hague a great stipend, and was fain for the spleen to come to his native air and lose all, being forbidden to preach here; mark that. Will the King mark by this particular if all the tricks and tales they put upon me were for my sake, or to reflect his anger toward me upon Nevill's business, which is a good observation, for they made as though they were only angry at me, without any meaning to hinder the King's intent. I am of opinion that villain Andrew gave them notice of your sending tarts; and for your cousin (if you did not send for him up foreknowing my absence) 't were well you sent him home, for either his charge is to no purpose, or else he is very negligent of it, to live here so long, and you know, in the progress, if he have not stable [and] bed as he please, then his murmuring goes by your nation to the King, and so lights on me, for Gid. and he have their offices in possession.

8. [SIR THOMAS OVERBURY TO VISCOUNT ROCHESTER.]

You might do well to write to the catopard * to-night, to will her make her father sure, which, except he think it will be a beginning of a perpetual friendship with you, 'twill not be. You might do well to write to Northampton to-night, as sorrowing both for his sickness, and also for his absence on Sunday; but desire him to show his love in making others sure though himself be away. 'Twere well, either to-night or to-morrow, to make the King not only passive, but to tell you what he will do aforehand. Be sure to be present yourself, that will do much; and, for the Archbishop and Suffolk, not to trust to any

* Lady Essex.

App. IV. mediation, but to speak to them yourself. For my sickness of consumption and *flatus hypocondriacus*, Mayerus may be called on his oath. If he doubt, your presence when 'tis moved will do much both with the King himself, and the rest will not break promise afore you. Urge to the King Ramsey and Mansell, that something may be done for your sake to me as to others. I pray you let the King know the intent of my letter, both before and now, which was to desire his pardon, that my heart was far from offending him. For my words, they were spoken, as being surprised on the sudden, and spoken in regard of my sickness, not of his command. So by foretelling the effect of my letter, prevent that objection that I sought not the King's favour, when you know I desired to write ten weeks ago. So for sueing to the Lords, that cannot be objected; for when the Lords were here, I being then in a fit of my fever, I got the Lieutenant to desire my Lord Northampton to move the Lords in my behalf for their favour and mediation to the King. But my Lord Northampton returned that he would first speak with you about [it]. I pray you remember this offer of mine, for that prevents to that objection that I sent not to them. If you would, by your catopard,* by Northampton, or in any way make sure Suffolk, all were gained in him only. A message from me to Suffolk would have done good, for otherwise he will fear that when I come abroad, however you stand now, I will direct you. But for that you must give him assurance for me to be his. Northampton being sick, if he deal betwixt you, will hurt it much; but when you see him, speak with Suffolk yourself, and that is best of all. From France keep me, I pray you, though I take physic at the progress at my chamber.

9. [SIR THOMAS OVERBURY TO VISCOUNT ROCHESTER.]

This morning (notwithstanding my fasting till yesterday) I find a great heat continue in all my body, and the same desire of drink and loathing of meat, and my water is strangely high, which I keep till Mayerus come. This distemper of heat, contrary to my constitution, makes me fear some fever at the last, and such an one meeting with so weak a body will quickly, I doubt, end it. And, in truth, I never liked myself worse, for I can endure no clothes on, and do nothing but drink, this is the story, now my request to you, and it may be my last, is that you would get me leave to go to my own chamber to-night, and after nine o'clock I may go thither in the Lieutenant's coach, unseen and unknown . . . . possible to get me hence

* Lady Essex.

to-night because of that business to-morrow, then pressing to-night vehemently will make him condescend for to-morrow night, and besides will keep the other from failing to-morrow; and to-morrow night, however I am, though I die for it, I will, if I may, go out of this place, if I cannot to-night. But if he deny you to-night, and to-morrow night too, then this is my last request of you, which if you deny me, you will tempt me far, that after moving it to-morrow and failing, to go to bed and take To, and not stir though he remove, till I be out. You know, the other business being done, you can have no politic pretence to put me off. My head is weak, and I write this much in pain, if you succeed not in the neither of the former, if you deny me the third.

10. [SIR THOMAS OVERBURY TO VISCOUNT ROCHESTER.]

My fever is relapsed, my water as high as ever, therefore this is the time to strike. What if you should take notice of the tale to the King, and so cut it up by the root? 'Tis wonderful to me, that after three months' capitulation, he should offer to deal so with you at last. You wrote to me that he said he would grant you all your suits.

11. [SIR THOMAS OVERBURY TO VISCOUNT ROCHESTER.]

I was let blood Wednesday ten o'clock. To this Friday morning my heat slackens not, my water remains as high, my thirstiness the same, the same loathing of meat, having eat not a bit since Thursday was sennight to this hour. The same scouring and vomiting. For yesternight about eight o'clock after Mr. Mayerus was gone, I fainted and vomited. The very same dryness.

12. [SIR THOMAS OVERBURY TO VISCOUNT ROCHESTER.]

Though you may not take notice directly, yet you may say, 'Sir, after so many promises you will not deal indirectly with me. I should be sorry to see that in your disposition.' Then say, 'Sure you have been abused in some tale; in that, you will find yourself pitifully abused.' So, afar off, you may shame him out. What censure had Ramsey here? What censure had Pierpoint for the key? O this is strange! You must arm the two Lords with these particulars, especially those public partiality of Du:* Max:† Ramsey. If this fail, there is no way left but immediately upon the refusal and breach of promise, To for a week. That is the last refuge, and your reason is honest, for my fever grows so upon me anew that,

* ? The Duke of Lenox. † ? Maxwell.

 by God, if you leave me here a week longer, I think I shall never see you more; for the fever will never leave me while I am here.

13. [SIR JOHN LIDCOTE TO VISCOUNT ROCHESTER.]

Right Honourable and my very good Lord, according to your lordship's command I have safely conveyed the notes which I received from your lordship. Doubt not of the good use will be made thereof. My brother utterly disclaims that he ever had any distrust in Mayerus' physic, Therefore humbly prayeth your lordship, if it be possible, to remove that apprehension of the King. That which I* spoke to Sir Robert Killigrew myself was rather to show the distemper that the violent working of the physic had brought him to it, than any distrust he had of it. I know your lordship had heard that the warrant for our going to him was presently recalled, so that I have no more admittances to him; but, this morning, it pleased my Lord of Northampton to send for me to let me know that he would grant a warrant to Mr. Lieutenant of the Tower to carry in his will to him to see it published. The Lieutenant but yesterday told my brother's man Lawrence that he wondered that his master's friends were so slack in finishing his will, for, he said, he doubted him now more than ever he did. Yet he makes show to us to be more comfortable in himself than he was. He hath taken all your lordship's *aurum potabile*, is entered into another glass, and surely findeth much good of it, and eateth broth every day. Therefore we hope well of him. The greatest comfort I can give him is the assurance of your lordship's favour, of which he hath had so long and so noble trial as now he cannot doubt the continuance thereof. For which how much both himself and all his friends stand charged in duties to your lordship, I cannot express. Only for mine own particular, I humbly beseech your lordship to stand assured, that I will neither have life nor any other ability that shall not really be at your lordship's command. I have received since your lordship went to Farnham three several letters.

Your lordship's humble servant,
JOHN LIDCOTE.

July 26.

14. [SIR THOMAS OVERBURY TO THE EARL OF NORTHAMPTON.]

To say I could have related anything from your lordship but the effects of your utmost displeasure I cannot yet, notwith-

* 'he,' MS.

standing such hath been your lordship's nobleness as, upon my Lord of Rochester's request to forget things past.

Your lordship hath pleased to been [*sic*] an earnest mediator to His Majesty for my liberty, by which intercession I understand [the] state of my liberty is much bettered, which favour received from your lordship, considering things, past make[s] a greater impression of gratitude in me, than if I had proved it from one from whom I could [have] hoped for it.

But now, if it would please your lordship to add again your lordship's hand to perfect this work so successfully begun, and to be a means first for my present liberty, and after for the recovery of His Majesty's favour, I protest before the living God I will ever hereafter be as faithful to you as your lordship's own heart, and when I digress from this protestation let this letter be a testimony to convince [me] of dishonesty to all the world.

I am yet but weak, which will make the benefit of my liberty more precious, and am not able to write much, but so God deal with me both for my liberty and health as I do not this only out of necessity of my present state, but that I am withal desirous to receive favour from your lordship in this business as the person of so much honour and directness as that next my Lord of Rochester I shall [desire*] to cast myself upon your lordship, if your lordship will be pleased but to accept me, and be to me as I shall deserve. So humbly taking my leave I rest——

15. SIR THOMAS OVERBURY TO MY LORD CHAMBERLAIN.†

Right Honourable,

That which your lordship vouchsafed to do in my behalf [before‡] the progress and at Salisbury gives me this hope though it were at the request of my Lord of Rochester, that your lordship's heart is not irreconcilable towards me, but my desire is not to rest there only [not] to have your lordship my enemy; but if all the service I can perform may win your lordship's good opinion and trust, and make me to be received as one of yours, [so] much honour and [directness §] have I ever seen in your lordship both toward friend and enemy as I shall think it happily employed, and with as much zeal I shall perform it as any creature of your lordship's living. And since it hath pleased your lordship to concur so really with my Lord of Rochester to His Majesty in my behalf, I profess upon my faith and salvation that it shall be my endeavour to the uttermost of my credit to continue that friendship between

* MS. dispre. † The Earl of Suffolk. ‡ MS. or for. § MS. direction.

App. IV. your two lordships firm and inviolable, and that without respect to any either that is or [is] to be; and this is the uttermost assurance that a Christian and an honest man can give: and so humbly taking my leave, I rest,

Your lordship's to be commanded,

Thomas Overbury.

Good, my lord, excuse my blotting, by reason of my weakness at this time.

16. THE COPY OF MR. LIEUTENANT'S LETTER TO ME.*

I humbly beseech your lordship that my Lord Chamberlain receiving my letter† sent together with this of Sir Thomas Overbury‡ may understand that I write another man's wares, not my own, and that where the cross is § he made me alter as mine, and not his own, lest my lord might again think his liberal profession was with reservation, for he is feared lest my lord should not be satisfied. His own direction I have also sent for part his own hand to be a deed to the letter. In that which I delivered to your lordship to be sent to Sir Thomas Monson, his phrase falls short of that which he is now brought unto, [which] must be considered according to the difference of time between his resolutions.

Your lordship's, &c.,

G. Helwys.

I sealed my letter to my lord in his sight after he had read it, and if need be, will justify as his act, whatsoever is therein.

17. MR. LIEUTENANT TO MY LORD CHAMBERLAIN, BY OVERBURY'S DIRECTION. ||

Right Honourable,

I returned Sir Thomas Overbury your lordship's answer, which, because it was not so ample as he looked for, he suspected his own straitness toward your lordship. Therefore he hath thought good to enlarge himself, wishing according to his true and plain heart to your lordship to receive a free and noble answer. The first effect of your favours he hopeth will be showed in your lordship's endeavours for his present liberty, and that as one post is dispatched hither for answer of your lordship's acceptance, so another might be dispatched to solicit

* Northampton. † No. 17. ‡ No. 15.

§ The bracket in No. 17.

|| There are two copies of this letter, one without the clause which is given in brackets, and which was added afterwards. They are both miserably copied; some sentences in each being mere nonsense as they stand. The letter, as given above, is founded upon a collation of the two. The following is a note appended by Northampton to the first:—'This is the copy, without the addition of the postscript, as it should have gone, the first indited by Sir Thomas Overbury, written by the lieutenant.'

his enlargement, else might the services which he intendeth melt and not become so profitable as he heartily doth wish; and, so soon as he is free, doth desire he might make his first address in some private place where your lordship shall appoint that he might give further assurance of that he hath heartily professed, [in mean time protesteth that those things past, which gave your lordship offence toward him, have never proceeded of any ill affection towards your lordship, or yours, in any * personal dislike, but upon many provocations and injuries which your lordship never knew, and such as no man but noted to be sensible.]† Thus commending my endeavours, and all as in any to serve your lordship, I will always be proud to serve you, and will always so rest

GERVASE HELWYS.

18. MY LORD CHAMBERLAIN TO SIR THOMAS OVERBURY.

Sir Thomas Overbury,

The free protestation of your desire to give me satisfaction for former wrongs hath taken so good impression in me as I shall be willing to give testimony thereof by my best assistance for your liberty, wherein notwithstanding, not to be mistaken, I must let you know that I dare not be a peremptory undertaker when I consider in how [great] a degree His Majesty was offended with your contempt, so as I conceive your freedom must be a work of some time. But because you so freely offer yourself to me specially in employing your uttermost endeavours to mediate a fast friendship between my Lord of Rochester and myself without respect of any of your new friends, so much am I affected with this, as I desire to contract with you that when your liberty shall be procured I may call again for this your letter written to me with this assurance and which I now return to you as pledge and assurance of your promised good offices between my Lord of Rochester and me. By it you are engaged to do this, and for this I will be

Your loving good friend

T. SUFFOLK.

19. TO THE EARL OF NORTHAMPTON.

Right honourable and my very good lord,

I received an advertisement yesterday from your lordship by Mr. Lieutenant that my Lady of Essex hath been

* MS. many.

† The first bracket is in the MS.; see No. 16. The second bracket ought to be where I have put it, as the last sentence is in both copies. There is a note to the copy with the interpolation, 'From the mark downward he added by a postscript under his own hand to that which was before written.'

App. IV. informed of some speeches of mine wherein I should wrong her in her honour. 'Tis true, my very good lord, that I have heard from many, yea and from my Lord of Rochester himself, with what bitterness her ladyship would often speak of me, and out of the sense of that 'tis possible I may have spoken with less respect of her than was fit, but that ever I touched her in point of her honour far be from me, for I protest 'twas never in my words, nor in my belief: and this I will profess to all the world, and if either my Lady of Suffolk or the lady herself shall rest unsatisfied, I will be ready to tender as much to their ladyships, and to say the same which now I write to your lordship. And for my Lady of Essex, if only I might be freed from her ill will for time to come, there shall be no man readier to respect and honour her than myself; and so, with inexpressible thanks to your worthy lordship for the favour I have received from you, I rest

Your lordship's most obliged servant to command,

THOMAS OVERBURY.*

From the Tower, 24th of August, 1613.

20. THE COPY OF SIR THOMAS OVERBURY'S SECOND LETTER TO MY LORD CHAMBERLAIN, IN MY LORD OF NORTHAMPTON'S HAND.

Right Honourable and my very good lord,

Your lordship's so clear and hearty acceptation of my service, so that now I am bold to account myself as one of yours, hath † and settled my thoughts as I am confident they shall never be again removed; only my grief is that unhappily I have been a stranger thus long unto your lordship.

I have returned here my letter again aforesaid,‡ and for the contents which engage me, let me perish if I be not as faithful servant between your two lordships as to my own soul, and do conceive to foresee that knot so near tying, which I am confident it will not [be] in the power of man to dissolve; and, for my endeavour therein, that it shall not be in the power of any to divert me, my Christianity lives on it.

Now, good my lord, give me leave as your servant to make this only request that whereas your lordship says it will be a work of some time, that your lordship will be pleased, as much as in you lies, to shorten that time, which I crave of your lordship not only for my liberty itself, but principally for my health sake; for though my disease be gone, yet the piercing air and solitariness of the place will not suffer my strength to grow but slowly, which change of air will quickly recover, and as soon as I am out, and may be so happy as to speak with your lordship

* Copyist's note: 'The above was Sir T. Overbury's own hand, all.'

† Blank in MS.

‡ No. 14.

in any private place that your lordship may appoint, I am confident I shall give your lordship a testimony that I intend to do your lordship faithful service.

This request I was bold to impart your lordship, knowing that your noble nature could have some care of a weak man, add to that a prisoner. So withal taking leave, I rest

Yours faithfully till death,

THOMAS OVERBURY.

From the Tower, 25th of August, 1613.

21. MR. LIEUTENANT'S LETTER, AUGUST 25TH, TO MY LORD CHAMBERLAIN, IN MY LORD OF NORTHAMPTON'S HAND.

Your lordship's letter was so welcome as he could not contain himself for joy, and now no remedy but he will send the first wherein he gave that assurance, which he would have you to keep, he hopeth your lordship will be so active in his business as his desires shall have a speedy end, which the rather he desireth that he may that of his part which above any thing in the world,* and doubteth not but presently to give such a beneficial testimony of his affections as your lordship shall not think you have bestowed your favour on one unworthy. So I humbly take my leave.

22. THIS UNDER IS IN SIR JOHN LIDCOTE'S HAND TO VISCOUNT ROCHESTER.

Right Honourable and my very good lord,

I received a letter from your lordship, sent me by my Lord of Northampton. According to your lordship's directions therein, did I immediately send to my brother, who I find to be very well satisfied therewith. The other letter, which you sent by his man, was presently, although with very great difficulty, delivered to him, before the coming of your lordship's last letter. We cannot as yet persuade the keeper to bring an answer from him, by reason of some late falling out between them, whereupon Weston hath vowed to convey no more letters for him. And besides the Lieutenant hath within these four days had him in very strict examination about his delivery of letters, which jealousy of the Lieutenant's the keeper thinketh hath grown out of something that my brother† hath touched upon in discourse with him, which perhaps savoureth of some intelligence, but I doubt but within few days this vow of the keeper will be past over as many before have been. My brother hath been lately very ill but is now well again. I am very sorry to

* Part of this sentence appears to have dropped out.

† i. e. Overbury, his brother-in-law.

App. IV. hear your lordship hath been sick, but I hope the worst is past, and that your sickness will be the cause of better health, for which I shall ever heartily pray and will be always ready at your lordship's command as

Your lordship's humble and most affectionate servant,

JOHN LIDCOTE.

Westminster, 27th August.

23. THE EARL OF NORTHAMPTON TO VISCOUNT ROCHESTER.*

Sweet lord,

I am infinitely glad that my fortune was to break off in this place upon hope of the Lieutenant's morning visitation. For this medicine of my lord-chamberlain's hath purged choler, as the doctors say, to the very dregs: and according to a maxim of astrology, *Mutata hora mutavit fatum*, and the wind blows favourable out of a better angle.

The melancholy doubts upon delay are vanished. My lord, worthy dealing is magnified, and resolute effects of his part are engaged and promised. The Lieutenant is the man whom Sir Thomas Overbury vows to magnify above all the worthy friends of the world for the sound advice he gave, and in comparison of his skill that hath absolutely cured his *flatus hypochondriacus* by true friendship and effectual receipts, all physicians, even Macoran † himself, is an empiric. His course ‡ shall be henceforth to put out his whole strength by the interest he hath in your lordship to fasten this knot of true friendship between your lordship and my lord-chamberlain. Marry, much depends upon his speedy delivery, for he knows this —— ? hath strong opposites. His heart is now at ease, and contrary to my expectation, I confess, knowing the man's violent and rash desires, he commends my nephew's discretion in undertaking and promising no more speed for accomplishment of this worthy work than he knows his credit may obtain, for he doth acknowledge that impressions in Prince's mind that have been long in festering crave time to be cured. One word fell from him that a good while since he was of the mind that such a course as his must only make all well, but he was crossed of his ends by the passions of others that would never look about when they shall see what difficulties are overcome without his industry.

* Copyist's note: 'In Northampton's hand.'

† Mayerne?

‡ 'His course he shall be,' MS.

24. LADY ESSEX TO HELWYS.

[State Papers, Domestic, lxxxvi. 6.]

[1613.]

[*Notes in Coke's handwriting.*]

* Nota. I have but one sent to me, that must be sent by Rochester, for none sent but they two.

† Nota. I was bid to bid you say. That must needs be Rochester, for none could bid and command her but he.

‡ Nota. I was bid, &c.; that is, if he should send. He is interpreted Rochester. For Rochester in truth sent it.

§ This is expounded thus: Give this tart and jelly now sent wherein is poison, and then all shall be well. Lastly, 'If he send them to your wife' is expounded, 'If Overbury send any part of them to your wife, keep them for me because she should eat some of them.'

Sir, I pray you deliver not these things till supper. I would have you change this tart in the place of his that is now come, and at four o'clock I will send you jelly one pot, for I had but one sent to me.* I was bid to bid you say† that one pot was broken after the man had delivered. If he should know there came two pots he must be answered so, if need be, which I think will not, for he cannot tell what is come now. This much more I was bid to tell you, that if he should send‡ this tart and jelly and wine to your wife, then you must take the tart from her, and the jelly, but the wine she may drink it if she will, for in that there are no letters I know, but in the tart and jelly I know there is, as you shall know, and from whom when we get the answer as that we shall too. I know soon after he has gotten these, Sir Thomas Monson will come this day, and then we shall have some other news. Do this at night,§ and all will be well I hope. If he send them to your wife, then keep them for me I pray you.

25. CONFESSION OF LADY SOMERSET.

8° Januarii [1616].

She confesseth that by these words in her letter to the Lieutenant 'I was bid to tell you that if he should send this tart &c.' that by these words 'If he should send &c.' she meant the Earl of Somerset, for he used to send many tarts and jellies to him.

She confesseth that by these words in her letter 'Do this at night, and all shall be right' she meant that the tart and jellies then sent, wherein were poisons, should be given to Overbury that night, and then all should be well.

26. WARRANT OF THE PRIVY COUNCIL TO THE LIEUTENANT OF THE TOWER.

[From the Council Register, July 22, 1613.]

Whereas information was made unto us of late of the weak and sick estate of Sir Thomas Overbury, Knt., now prisoner in

App. IV. the Tower, and the desire he had to speak with some friends, we were thereupon moved upon the earnest pressing of our very good lord the Lord Viscount Rochester to grant a warrant * unto you for the admittance of Sir Robert Killigrew and Sir John Lidcote unto Sir Thomas Overbury. Forasmuch as we are informed that they have accordingly been with you, and conferred of such matters as he had to propound unto them; these shall be to signify unto you that we think it meet, and accordingly require you that the foresaid warrant do now cease, and that you keep Sir Thomas Overbury close prisoner, as we did before warrant.

* On the 20th of July, Council Register.

V.

AN ADVICE [BY SIR HENRY NEVILLE] TOUCHING THE HOLDING OF A PARLIAMENT.

[State Papers, Domestic, lxxiv. 44.]

App. V.

THERE is a question grown and much debated amongst us, whether the King should relieve himself in his great want (whereof the world taketh knowledge both at home and abroad), by a Parliament, or by some projects and devices to raise money, which may be set on foot to that purpose. For my part, I will not examine what these projects may be, although by experience of such as have been put in use since the dissolution of the last Parliament, I am induced to believe that either they will fail or fall short in the practice, howsoever they may appear likely in the theory; or that they will prove like some medicines, which do rather take away sense of pain for the present than cure the grief for which they were applied. But admit there may be other ways devised to relieve the King, yet am I clearly of opinion that there is none so fit, so honourable, and so necessary as by a Parliament. My reason is this; I consider on what terms the King and the last Parliament parted at the dissolution, full of distaste and acrimony on His Majesty's part, and not without some discontentment on theirs, I consider also that from the Parliament, the apprehensions that are taken there are spread and dispersed over the whole realm. And further that the knowledge of these misunderstandings between His Majesty and the Parliament is not confined within this kingdom only but is flown abroad into all foreign parts that have any commerce or dealing with us. Now what disadvantage this opinion may breed us, and what hopes it is like to raise both in our enemies abroad and our discontented persons at home may easily be gathered. For, as there is nothing that more upholds the reputation of any Prince than the opinion of his strength at home, which consisted principally in the love and concord between him and his people from whence there followeth naturally a sequence of all other duties on their part to make him strong and able to help and hurt his neighbours; so there is nothing that emboldeneth more an enemy, either open or secret, to

App. V.

attempt the disturbance of the peace of any State than the imagination that the Prince and people stand not in kind and loving terms. And to this purpose I remember a story of Antigonus, one of the immediate and mightiest successors of Alexander, who, being solemnly set in great state to give audience to some other prince's ambassador; as he was in that solemnity, his son Demetrius came in from hunting, and being arrayed in his hunting attire, with his darts in his hand, presented himself so unto his father, and after a salutation given according to the manner of that people, sat down by him. The audience being ended, and the ambassadors retiring themselves, Antigonus called them again, and willed them to report one thing more to their masters, namely, in what fashion they had seen his son and him converse together, intending that it would be taken for a great argument of his strength and a great assurance of his safety that his son and he lived in that confidence and concord. If this were true in that case between the father and the son, how much more is it verified between the Prince and the people? And hereupon I conclude that the world being possessed with a conceit that the last Parliament ended with some sourness and distaste on the King's part, and not with the best satisfaction on theirs, there is nothing more necessary for the King's Majesty, either in regard of honour or safety, than to deface that opinion, and to make it apparent to the world that as he was received into the kingdom at his first entry, with the greatest demonstrations of the love and joy of his people that ever Prince was, so he is still rooted and established in their hearts; and that whatsoever cloud or mist might seem to have darkened or overshadowed the kind respects between them at that time, it was no other but that which happeneth often by some distemper, between a tender father and dutiful children which quickly vanish when the distemper of either side is removed.

For the effecting of this I can think of no other way but by another Parliament, for there this error grew, and there and no where else it must be repaired. The harsh conclusion of the former Parliament bred that ill-conceit, and the sweet close of another must beget a better. And by this means two notable effects will be wrought together if matters be well handled; the removing of that erroneous and dangerous conceit of a misunderstanding between the King and his people, and the relieving of the King's present necessities in a sure speedy and plentiful manner; whereas that other cause of projects may happily prove slow and fail in the most, and in very few succeed according to the first design. And for rectifying the misconceit between the King and his people there is no hope at all that way. It is rather to be feared it will do hurt, and rather aggravate than cure that malady if there be not great judgment used in the choice of the projects, and much dexterity in the managing of them. Against this opinion there are two objections. The one that the Parliament may still continue adverse and unwilling to relieve the King at all, and so no hope of making up the breach, the other that as long as it is conceived the King cannot help himself without them, they will play upon the advantage of his necessities and extort some unreasonable demands from him before they yield to do anything for him. Both these objections are grounded upon the same false foundation, namely, that whatsoever the last Parliament did in that kind, they did it out of evil affection, which I do know, and do confidently avow to be otherwise, and have before in speech delivered the true reasons of that averseness, as one that lived and conversed inwardly with the chief of them, that were noted to be most backward and know their inwardest thoughts on that business. So I dare undertake for the most of them that the King's Majesty proceeding in a gracious course toward his people, shall find those gentlemen exceeding willing to do him service, and to give him such contentment, as may sweeten all the former distastes, and leave both His Majesty and the world fully satisfied of their good intentions, and of the general affection of his subjects. It is true (as I lately delivered unto His Majesty), that some things will be desired and expected of him by way of grace, which may both give some contentment to them that shall pay what is given, and justify the care and honest regard of them that shall give it. And, without this, I dare promise nothing; for it is most certain that, as in private families and all other societies, where the straitest bonds of nature or election do concur to unite affections, there is almost a continual necessity of mutual offices of kindness to nourish and maintain that love, so in kingdoms, besides that great bond of protection and allegiance between the sovereign and the subject, there is a like necessary use of the frequent interchange of mutual effects of grace and love to cherish and foster that tender affection that daily is to be renewed between them. But what be the things that will be demanded or expected by the Parliament on behalf of the people will be hard for any one man to set down. Yet what I have collected out of the desires of sundry of the principal and most understanding gentlemen that were of the last Parliament, and are like to be of this, I will be bold to deliver in a memorial hereunto adjoined, whereby it shall appear that they aim not at anything unjust or unreasonable, or that may derogate from His Majesty in point of sovereignty further than His Majesty hath already been pleased to

App. V. offer in writing to the last Parliament (which no doubt will be maintained) nor in point of profit to any matter of certain and considerable value, but only at such things as being now of small moment and loss to His Majesty to depart with, because they have been sifted and ransacked to the bottom, may yet be valued to the subjects, both in opinion and truth, at a high rate, because they shall thereby enjoy a great repose and security from vexation which any of them may otherwise be subject unto.

These things being taken into His Majesty's consideration, and receiving His gracious approbation as matter not unfit to be yielded of grace unto his subjects, the next points to be thought of are the time of holding the Parliament, the things preceding to be done by way of preparation, and the manner of proceeding with the House of Commons when the Parliament is assembled. For the first I see no cause why it should be deferred longer than Michaelmas, for after the session there must be a time proportionable for the Commissioners to sit, and for the money to be levied and brought into the Exchequer, which the sooner it is done, the sooner will the King be eased of his debts for which he payeth interest, and the sooner will his reputation be recovered and settled, which is the thing that most deserves to be respected. If the Parliament begin at Michaelmas, the Term may be adjourned to Hollantide;* or if not, yet till that time there is little business done, so as the lawyers may well attend the Parliament, whose absence will otherwise breed delay. And I do not see but in a month or five weeks this point of supplying the King and of his retribution will be easily determined if it be proposed betimes and followed close afterwards. For the second, which concerns matter of preparation, these be the things that I would humbly offer to His Majesty's gracious consideration, to forbear to use any speech that may irritate, and to seem rather confident than diffident of their affections, casting the fault of any former error upon evil offices done on both sides, and want of true understanding rather than want of good affection. To speak graciously and benignly to the people that shall flock to see His Majesty this progress. And especially to take notice of the principal gentlemen, and let them kiss his hand, and do them some other grace. To give order to the Archbishop to prohibit all books and invective sermons against the Parliament, so as notice may be taken of His Majesty's commandment before the meeting. To peruse the grievances exhibited the last Parliament, and if His Majesty would please to be

* i.e. All Hallowtide.

gracious in any of them, to do it of himself before he be pressed. For a small thing in that manner will give more contentment than much more obtained with importunity. And especially to call to mind if His Majesty promised anything to the last Parliament which is not yet performed; for upon the performance of that men will be like to ground their trust and hopes in those things which shall be offered now. For the last point concerning the manner of proceeding, I wish that His Majesty will be pleased to make his propositions by himself or by his ministers and servants that are of their own body, and not by mediation of the Lords. For the Commons will be rather willing to make oblation of their affections themselves unto His Majesty than that any others should do it, and intercept both the merit and thanks from them. I wish also that the King should forbear to nominate any particular men to be sent unto him from the Commons to treat upon any point or occasion, but after His Majesty hath declared his own desires and made likewise known his gracious inclination to gratify his subjects with any favours and graces that with reason and moderation they can desire for them, His Majesty may be pleased to require the House to nominate a competent number of thirty or forty or fewer which may repair unto him with their demands, and be authorized both to ask and answer such questions as the debate about them shall beget without concluding or binding the House in any point, but only to clear things and report all back to the House. This course, I conceive, will much expedite the business, avoid jealousies, and give good satisfaction to the most, when they shall see that the King shall understand their desire immediately from themselves without any interposition, or danger of misinterpretation, and that upon any point of doubt they shall be admitted to clear their own intentions and not to be subject to the construction of other. Matters being thus prepared beforehand, and thus managed at the time, and His Majesty being pleased to be gracious to his people in the points proposed or any other of the like nature which may be thought of by the House, when they meet (for beforehand no man can precisely say these things will be demanded and no other) I have no doubt, but am very confident, that His Majesty shall receive as much contentment of this next Parliament as he received distaste of the former, and that all things will end in that sweet accord that will be both honourable and comfortable for His Majesty and happy for the whole realm. And when His Majesty hath made use of his people's affection to put him out of want, any fit projects that shall be offered may be the boldlier entertained to fill his coffers. For whatsoever shall be done in that kind will

App. V. be the less subject to offence when there is a perfect renewing of affections gone before; whereas otherwise whiles dislikes continue *seu benè, seu malè facta premunt.*

In this advice it may evidently appear that I have proceeded with more zeal to His Majesty than caution or wariness for myself; for I am not ignorant what a hazard I run if things should fall out contrary to my expectation. But love and faith cast no perils. And I hold it a matter of that consequence both to King and people to have these misunderstandings cleared as well in truth as in opinion, that I would think my life of little value in respect of it, and had rather hazard anything that may befall me than leave such an office unattempted. Wherein if I fail, howsoever my discretion may be censured, yet I am sure the honest purpose and sincerity of my heart cannot be reproved.

VI.

PAPERS RELATING TO THE LEVY OF THE BENEVOLENCE.

App. VI.

1. ACCOUNT OF THE BENEVOLENCE MONEY.*

[Receipt Books and Breviates of the Exchequer, Public Record Office.]

		£	s.	d.
July 9th, 1614.	Paid into the Exchequer	16,000	0	0
July 18th, „		7,000	0	0
Aug. 25th, „		500	0	0
Oct. 19th, „		3,000	0	0
Nov. 12th, „		4,000	0	0
Nov. 21st, „		4,243	8	0
Dec. 2nd, „		2,000	0	0
Feb. 18th, 1615		2,000	0	0
Feb. 23rd, „		1,000	0	0
Mar. 15th, „		2,000	0	0
June 14th, „		1,000	0	0
June 27th, „		1,460	16	0
July 20th, „		1,000	0	0
July 26th, „		100	0	0
Nov. 18th, „		300	0	0
Dec. 7th, „		1,000	0	0
Dec. 13th, „		300	0	0
Dec. 23rd, „		128	16	8
Dec. 29th, „		2,645	8	10
Feb. 6th, 1616		150	0	0
Feb. 20th, „		20	0	0
Mar. 11th, „		100	0	0
Mar. 13th, „		1,200	0	0
Mar. 16th, „		100	0	0
Mar. 19th, „		382	8	0
April 25th, „		200	0	0
April 30th, „		630	0	0
May 2nd, „		126	0	0
June 14th, „		2,000	0	0
July 10th, „		1,000	0	0
Mar. 18th, 1617		100	0	0
		£55,686	17	6
1614–15	Money paid by assignation†	635	0	0
1615–16		5,000	0	0
1616–17		4,851	8	8
		£66,173	6	2

* There must have been some amount of plate brought into the Jewel House besides the ready money; but, judging from the returns preserved among the State Papers, and which extend over many months, it does not seem to have been of any great value.

† These sums are taken from notes in the Dormant Privy Seal Books. They were never paid into the Exchequer. The years end at Michaelmas.

App. VI. 2. CIRCULAR LETTER FROM THE COUNCIL TO THE SHERIFFS, JUSTICES OF THE PEACE, AND MAYORS.

[Council Register, July 4, 1614.]

You cannot be ignorant that upon the dissolving of the late begun Parliament there hath not been yielded to His Majesty such supply of his wants as in congruity of state he might have expected from his loving subjects. Whereupon as well the lords spiritual with many of the clergy, as the lords and others of His Majesty's Privy Council with many other lords and gentlemen of worth and quality, taking the same into serious consideration, and of their dutiful love and great affection to his Majesty in contemplation of the many blessings and happiness which we enjoy by his most gracious government, have of their own free motion, every one for himself with great alacrity presented and given to His Majesty plate, or money, or both, which example we are informed the reverend judges for their parts, as also the gentlemen and others of ability in these adjacent shires and some cities and boroughs have lovingly and readily resolved to follow; and therefore we, very well understanding the forwardness of your affections upon all occasions, and in all things tending to His Majesty's service, have thought good to make the same known unto you, wishing you to impart the same to other gentlemen and all such within that * that you shall discern to be persons of good ability, or otherwise fit to further the service, where by the return and success thereof (which will rest much in your industry and discreet handling) may carry with it a worthy demonstration as well of your own zeal and forwardness as of the general love and good affection of that * towards His Majesty. Whatsoever shall be given, be it in money or plate, they whom in your discretions you shall depute to have the collection and custody thereof are to cause it to be sent to His Majesty's Jewel House in Whitehall, with a register in writing of the value of every particular gift and the names of the several givers, that they being presented to His Majesty's view he may be pleased to take notice of their good affection which he will ever retain in his grateful remembrance. And it is resolved that it shall only be employed for the payment of his debts, as namely for Ireland, the Navy, and the Cautionary Towns in the Low Countries; and so leaving the carriage of the business to your discretions and wisdoms we bid, &c.

* Left blank in original.

3. CIRCULAR LETTER FROM THE COUNCIL TO THE SHERIFFS OF ALL THE COUNTIES, EXCEPTING MIDDLESEX.

App. VI.

[Council Register, September 17, 1614.]

We lately have addressed letters unto you wherein we did exhort you after the example of the lords spiritual and other of nobility then residing about this town, out of your own free and voluntary contribution to concur for the present relief of His Majesty's urgent necessities. If the reasons which then we alleged, that is for the supply of Ireland, for provision of the Cautionary Towns in Holland and Zealand, and for the furnishing of the Navy were then important, the importance of them all jointly and severally is now much improved by the troubles which since have happened in our own neighbour countries to the prejudice of His Majesty's nearest friends and allies, in whose welfare and preservation His Majesty's service is deeply interested. For you cannot but understand that the Marquis Spinola hath amassed together a strong and powerful army which [is] sometime under the name of the King of Spain, sometime as best may serve for his advantage under the commaud of the Emperor, whereby we may conclude that they all three are combined together, and hath carried all the towns in the countries of Juliers and Cleves situated upon the tract of the Rhine, whereby not only the Elector [of] Brandenburg is deprived of the possession of these towns which he hath for many years peaceably enjoyed, whose right His Majesty is bound to defend by virtue of the treaties contracted between him and the Princes of the Union in Germany, but the persons and states of the Elector Palatine and the Princess his lady, His Majesty's only and dearest daughter, environed on all sides by divers armies, are at this present endangered. Between whose countries and His Majesty's dominions, by the usurpation Spinola hath made upon the river of the Rhine, all commodity of the passage and intercourse is intercepted and cut off. The designs of these forces cannot but portend an imminent danger to His Majesty's kingdoms, which he in the providence of his princely wisdom doth hold necessary to prevent, which is the cause that hath moved him to command a general muster to be instantly made through his realm of England, his navy speedily to be put in order, and all recusants to be disarmed, who being ill affected in religion, he hath reason to doubt are not well affectioned to his service. Upon these reasons and finding it strange that we have nothing from you we have thought good to second our former letters, and therefore do pray and require you, as you tender the good of the country in whose preservation you, your wives and children do hold so great an interest, to employ your

App. VI. best endeavours for the speedy return of this contribution, the which, the more freely it shall proceed from you, the more acceptable it will be to His Majesty and the more advantageous for the service. And so, &c.

4. THE COUNCIL TO LORD ST. JOHN OF BLETSOE, Oct. 9, 1614.

[State Papers, Domestic, lxxviii. 14.]

We have not yet had any account from the justices of Bedfordshire touching the voluntary contribution to His Majesty expected from thence. Nevertheless we have heard that there hath been a meeting pretended for that purpose, but the proceeding so unworthy and ill-becoming the assembly as we are exceeding sorry to understand that your lordship was there present and assistant, of whose interest, power, and credit in that country no man is ignorant that knoweth your lordship or the county of Bedford. But that we may not hide anything from you, since out of our good will and respect to your lordship we have given you this private notice, we must put you in remembrance that many eyes were upon you as the principal person there, and that your action and carriage especially did not then pass without observation, whose forwardness and good example, as it might have much advanced the service, so your coldness was noted and did harm, yea even your miscarriage on the very entrance of the business we doubt will be rather attributed to defect of zeal than any mistaking of judgement. These circumstances with the scornful offers which followed thereupon (amongst the rest, of some that were near your lordship) when His Majesty, who is a wise and understanding prince, shall compare them together, and withal find you missing here in the list of those free givers who have already testified their love and duty unto him, perhaps may leave another impression than your lordship doth imagine; which because we should be very sorry it should so fall out, we have thought good as your friends that wish you well to give your lordship this private advertisement, presuming now that in your own wisdom you will henceforth be so watchful over yourself and so careful to preserve His Majesty's gracious opinion as that you will with all alacrity resume the care of this business upon you, and that by your example and other good endeavours as well there as in the other county adjacent (where by His Majesty's favour you are his lieutenant) he may receive such proportions from his loving subjects, as shall be fit for them to offer, and honourable for His Majesty to accept. And so, &c.

5. THE COUNCIL TO THE SHERIFF AND JUSTICES OF THE PEACE OF THE COUNTY OF SOMERSET.

[Council Register, November 15, 1614.]

We did of late address two letters unto you, the first bearing date the 4th of July last, signifying upon what occasion the lords spiritual with many of the clergy together with the lords and others of His Majesty's Privy Council and many other lords and gentlemen of quality had out of their own free motion with great alacrity presented and given to His Majesty plate and money or both. Which example the reverend judges for their parts as also the gentlemen and others of ability in these adjacent counties and some cities and boroughs had lovingly and readily resolved to follow, and therefore little doubting of the forwardness of your affections upon all occasions tending to His Majesty's service did think good to make the same known unto you, wishing you to impart the same unto other gentlemen, and all such within that county of Somerset that you should discern to be persons of good ability or otherwise fit to further the service.—The second of the 17th of September following containing many reasons of State to move you for a speedy return of this free and voluntary contribution. To both which we received yours of the 22nd of September last subscribed by most of the justices of that county importing the disability of the inhabitants thereof, the most of them being, (as you say) unacquainted with any such precedent, and taking notice of a positive law against benevolences of this kind, stand as yet unresolved for any contribution in that manner. We for sundry just causes us moving thought it to be very requisite to call some of you before us as well to certify this mistaking and to let you see the error of those that gave you such information, as to justify our proceedings therein to be very warrantable and no way subject to any such exceptions. And, having informed ourselves as well of the carriage of this business as of the doubts and scruples made in this behalf, it was at this board, in the presence of divers principal gentlemen of that county, evidently proved and manifested by ancient consent and continual precedents and records that the like voluntary and free contributions have been from age to age given to His Majesty's most noble progenitors, as by the same precedents and records particularly appeareth. Wherein nothing was uttered in general terms, but *signatis tabulis*, naming both the roll and particular certainty of those records. Which precedents have been made and pursued from time to time notwithstanding the positive law mentioned in your letter which aimeth only at exactions

App. VI. or charges laid upon the subjects against their wills and liberties, and not at any gift or contribution which proceedeth from a free and voluntary motion and good-will without exertion or constraint, as by the Act itself appeareth. All which was well approved upon just ground by all the whole board, whereof as of the rest then delivered the gentlemen then present can give you further and more particular satisfaction, having learned also at that hearing, that since the making of that positive law, both in the time of Henry VII. and Henry VIII. there were free and voluntary contributions of this kind, and the same confirmed afterwards by several Acts of Parliament. In contemplation whereof the said gentlemen then present did acknowledge the error which you and they together had by mistaking committed therein. And therefore forasmuch as the matter is thus far cleared and that there was nothing moved to persons of disability or impoverished by losses, but either to such as are of worth and quality such as you yourselves are, or be otherwise of means and sufficiency in the country, as at first, so now again we wish you to resume the business to your better consideration, and to redeem that which is past with such demonstration of thankfulness and good affection as appertaineth, and as we are persuaded you will effectually perform. Wherein, forasmuch as you signify in your letter that, having imparted the business to the most able and sufficient persons within your several divisions, you found some of them to plead their own disabilities, and others to pretend other excuses, and most of them as yet unresolved for any contribution in that manner, we are to let you know that it is acknowledged before us by some of your number that, speaking only with sundry persons of good ability of the limits wherein they serve as justices of that county, they did find many of them to answer that they were willing of their free good-will to contribute, if they might have any example given them by the justices themselves, and by those of the chiefest rank and worth of the country from whom they were to take their greatest light. Which we will believe, making little doubt of the general willingness and affection of His Majesty's subjects in this behalf. So how far this answer of theirs may serve for your direction, we leave to your better judgment and consideration. And so, &c.

6. THE COUNCIL TO THE SHERIFF AND JUSTICES OF THE PEACE OF THE COUNTY OF DEVON.

[Council Register, November 30, 1614.]

* * * * * * * *

We did of late address our letter unto you signifying upon

what occasion the Lords Spiritual with many of the clergy together with the Lords and others of His Majesty's Privy Council, and many other lords and gentlemen of quality were moved . . . In answer whereof we received yours of the 26th of August subscribed by most of you the justices of that county importing a general scruple of exceeding prejudice that may come to posterity by such a precedent, so as nothing but the fear of the just blame of after ages could have abated your forward dispositions from performing a service in itself so requisite. App. VI.

* * * * * * * *

7. THE COUNCIL TO THE SHERIFF AND JUSTICES OF THE PEACE OF THE COUNTY OF WARWICK.

[Council Register, Dec. 9, 1614.]

We did of late address two letters unto you, ... to both which we received a letter without any date subscribed by some of you the justices of that county, importing the general willingness and readiness of the gentlemen and others of ability there, to supply His Majesty's occasions according to former use and precedent (which as you say) was always in Parliament by the voice and consent of the knights of the shire, and that for yourselves you desire to be holden as well-wishers to the State as may be and do wish His Majesty may be speedily supplied by the rightest course that may be taken. Wherein you are constrained by this answer given by such persons as you call together, and are of ability in that county, and the inseparable tie between you and them being all members together of that shire to be of the same mind and opinion with the rest: which answer was so unexpected from gentlemen of your quality and understanding and otherwise so well deserving in His Majesty's service, as we thought it very expedient both to certify this mistaking, and to justify our proceedings herein to be safe and free from any just exceptions.

* * * * * *

8. THE COUNCIL TO THE SHERIFF AND JUSTICES OF THE PEACE OF THE COUNTY OF LEICESTER.

[Council Register, Feb. 5, 1615.]

By a letter from some of you unto me the Lord Treasurer, we are given to understand that a resolution being taken amongst you (after several meetings and conferences) for the sum of £1,000 to have been presented as a free gift from that county, the same is at length fallen and reduced unto less than £400. The reason whereof you allege to be for that many have since refused to perform what they had formerly promised.

App. VI. But having since called Mr. Stavely unto this board (whom you had appointed collector for that contribution) and examined the particulars of his collections, we find them to be generally so mean and unworthy as we do rather attribute the backwardness of that county unto the ill example given by some of yourselves than to any other cause whatsoever. Besides, whereas we formerly gave you directions to impart the contents of our letters unto all such of that county as you should discern to be of ability for the furthering of this service, we do not understand that you have at any time called before you any freeholders or others more than such as are justices of peace amongst you; nor have you followed our direction for keeping a register of the names of every particular giver, and the value of every several gift; and, forasmuch as His Majesty cannot but understand so base and mean a gift (being fallen from £1,000 to so mean a sum) to be very unworthy his acceptation, especially comparing it with what hath been presented from others his loving subjects, peradventure not so well able as the inhabitants of that county, we have absolutely refused the receipt of what hath been offered by Mr. Stavely your collector, and have rather thought fitting hereby to admonish the resumption of the business to your better care and consideration. And withal to require you that having used your best endeavours (as well by example as by persuasion) for the furtherance of that service, to return unto us a perfect list, not only of the names of such as shall herein make demonstration of their dutiful loves and affections unto His Majesty, together with the particular value of the several gifts; but also of such as being of good ability shall not be moved to contribute anything at all, especially of those who (as you write) do now refuse to perform what they had formerly promised.

* * * * * *

9. THE COUNCIL TO THE BOROUGH OF TAUNTON.

[Council Register, Feb. 26, 1615.]

Having long expected the free and cheerful manifestation of your dutiful affections unto His Majesty by presenting him with your several and voluntary gifts, as by former letters written for this Board we persuaded and invited you unto, we now perceive (by a certificate sent unto an officer of the Jewel-house) how much you have therein frustrated our expectations, the sum which you offer being so mean as we hold it very unworthy His Majesty's acceptance; and have therefore directly refused the receipt thereof; and that the rather because in the said certificate you inform us that many of the wealthiest inhabitants and of the best ability within that town (being merchants trading beyond the seas) have not contributed anything at all, but do allege for their excuse that they pay custom unto His Majesty for their merchandises, as if none of His Majesty's subjects but they did the like. But forasmuch as we conceive you will easily be able to make them understand the absurdness of this their answer, and how ill it suits with the duty they owe unto His Majesty, we have hereby thought fitting once more to require your serious and best endeavours for the advancement of this service, and to return unto us a perfect list as well of those who being of good ability shall still persist in this denial (being now led by the example of the greatest part of this kingdom) as also of those who gladly and willingly take hold of this occasion thereby to make known unto his Majesty their dutiful loves and affections, both unto him and unto his service, and thus assuring ourselves of your uttermost endeavours, we bid you, &c.

10. THE COUNCIL TO THE HIGH SHERIFFS AND JUSTICES OF THE PEACE OF ANGLESEA, BRECKNOCK, CARDIGAN, CARNARVON, DENBIGH, FLINT, GLAMORGAN, MONTGOMERY, MERIONETH, AND RADNOR.

[Council Register, July 21, 1615.]

It is not unknown unto you how cheerfully and affectionately His Majesty's loving subjects of every county within this realm of England have contributed towards the supply of His Majesty's wants, which makes you the more inexcusable whom neither affection nor example can induce to join with the rest in a service so acceptable. For whereas you allege many colourable reasons of the country's poverty and charge, they may be true in the general; and, being so understood, might as well have served for excuse in other parts of the kingdom as in those counties. But you cannot be so ignorant as to imagine that His Majesty's intention in this ever was* to take anything from the poor, either there or elsewhere, but that whatsoever was expected was from yourselves and such others as were of ability within that county, who by your example would easily have been persuaded to have yielded this testimony of their affection and duty as others have done. It remaineth therefore now that you let us know directly and absolutely without further delay whether you resolve to give anything or nothing, and so for the rest of the sufficient inhabitants of that county: for more forcible persuasions than we have already used cannot be given. And less would have served, if your inclination had been as His Majesty expected. So, &c.

* Ever was not, MS.

App. VI.

11. OTHER LETTERS DIRECTED TO THE SHERIFFS AND JUSTICES OF THE PEACE OF THESE FOLLOWING COUNTIES.

[Council Register, July 21, 1615.]

The ability of that county is so well known as you may be assured in this contribution the backwardness of yourselves and of the rest of the inhabitants by your example will be interpreted as the measure of your affections rather than the effect of want or disability, for which we are the more sorry not in respect of the addition it would have given to His Majesty's supply, but for that it shall be observed that amongst so many gentlemen of quality and means whereof the most are either well known to His Majesty or this board, and many other inhabitants of livelihood, there is found only ——— who in a reasonable proportion of gift have expressed their love and duty to His Majesty. Whether this be all that His Majesty must expect from yourselves and the rest of that county, after so many motions and letters from this board we know not. But whatsoever your resolutions be, we require you to let us now know it directly and absolutely without further delay. For more forcible persuasions than we have already used unto you cannot be given, and less would have served if your inclinations had been as His Majesty expected.

Sussex, 3 contributors	Stafford, none
Hereford, 2	Cumberland, none
Salop, 1	Westmoreland, none
	Bp.* of Duresme.

* *i. e.* Bishopric. There is no number appended.

VII.

DESPATCHES RELATING TO LORD HAY'S EMBASSY.

[State Papers. French Series.]

1. LORD HAY AND SIR THOMAS EDMONDES TO SIR RALPH WINWOOD.

July 31, 1616.

* * * * * *

App. VII.

At my next audience which I expect within a day or two, I intend to find or make some occasion in speech with the Queen Mother to clear His Majesty's actions before this King's marriage, and in the time of the war, from all appearance of contrariety with my errand . . . . And afterwards we will endeavour by all the means and instance we can use to draw satisfaction to His Majesty's complaints, although we can hope for no other than dilatory answers till we come to propound the treaty of marriage; and fear the harshness of that we are then commanded to say will undo all we shall have formerly obtained. For I persist, here upon the place, in the same mind I was bold to declare unto you and His Majesty in England when I received those directions, that it will be a very great informality, and we doubt may be esteemed almost a mockery for us after we have showed a large commission to conclude this business and they deputed persons to treat with us, then first immediately to disannul all that hath been heretofore agreed upon, and after put them moreover unnaturally to make this new proposition. My Lord Ambassador resident confirmeth me much herein, by his concurrence with me out of long experience and ripe understanding in affairs of this nature. And we must confess we find ourselves extremely troubled how to disguise his Majesty's intentions, so as they may not here plainly discover he hath a desire quite to break off this match, and take advantage thereby to drive that envy upon us, which if they had not yielded to His Majesty's desires would have lighted heavily upon them from this people, whom we find much to desire this alliance might take effect.

* * * * * *

App. VII.

2. SIR RALPH WINWOOD TO LORD HAY AND SIR THOMAS EDMONDES.

Aug. 19, 1616.

His Majesty hath commanded me to put you, my Lord Hay, in mind that when at Oatlands he first did impart unto you that part of the instruction for the breaking off of the old treaty, you in your judgment did fully approve it, with this declaration, that it was the safest and soundest course and the wisest resolution that could be taken. For whereas to His Majesty's demands, which were just and honourable, so peremptory refusal had been given, ... His Majesty in the clearness of his judgment could take no other course more for the advancement of his service than to make a fair end of that treaty, nor more agreeable to his affectionate and unfeigned desire to make an alliance with that Crown, than to give you power to receive all overtures which on that part should be propounded with assurance that he would be willing to embrace them if they might stand with the honour of his person and the safety of his state. His Majesty doth well remember that you, my Lord Hay, before your departure did make this exception that it was unproper for the French to propound, and that rather it did more congruously appertain to His Majesty to make new and fresh demands, which your doubt His Majesty was pleased to impart to those of his Council deputed for that service, who unanimously did concur in this opinion that when His Majesty in honour could not relent from his former demands grounded upon justice and equity it did of right belong unto the French, if they did desire the entertainment of this treaty and conclusion of the match to propound such conditions which might be less distasteful, and more agreeable to His Majesty's service. Neither is this to be judged a preposterous, or, as you term it, an unnatural error; for His Majesty hath performed that office which appertained to him. Hitherto he hath acted the part of the wooer. He hath reserched the daughter of France with all due and behoveful respect, tendered conditions of honour and equity, which being refused, this only resteth, for His Majesty to show the continuance of his affection for the advancement of this match, to hear if they will propound anything which the good of his service may suffer to be entertained.

And that you may see that His Majesty doth not impose upon the French unusual or heavy conditions, His Majesty hath commanded me to let you know that when Sir John Digby went first into Spain, he had charge to treat first for the eldest, then the second daughter of that King for Prince Henry of famous memory. Answer being made that a daughter of that King could not be married to his son unless he would change his religion, His Majesty presently broke off that treaty without further prosecution. Since, the King of Spain by his ministers day after day hath made divers overtures for the entertainment and advancement of a marriage to which hitherto His Majesty hath not been pleased to give ear, but, as mannerly as he could, hath declined them and put them by; and, if any such treaty shall be commenced, the overture must come from Spain, and therefore, in the like case, ought to come from France. Now, whereas you seem to be in pain in what manner you are to make your retreat without dishonour and disgrace, you know it is not His Majesty's pleasure that you should abruptly break off, much less to deliver as a resolution in him not to conclude an alliance with that Crown, for both his judgment and affection do carry him rather to make the match with France than in any other kingdom, so that the conditions may hold a just proportion with the greatness of his honour, and the service of his Crown. Therefore, if His Majesty's conditions had been accepted the match by this time had been concluded, they being refused, if any other by that party shall be tendered, His Majesty will entertain them with a willing ear; and in His Majesty's name you may boldly protest that as France shall ever have the preference, so, notwithstanding the report of the young French Queen, which is nothing else but an idle fantasy, His Majesty as he now doth stand free, which on his honour he doth protest to be true, as he told you, my Lord Hay, and so doth require you in his name to aver, so will he keep himself free from embracing any overtures, which almost daily are presented unto him, until the French shall declare, either in plain language, or by real effects, that they have no purpose to match with him, unless it be to the dishonour and disadvantage of his service.

His Majesty hath commanded me to conclude in these few words, that it is now in your power not to suffer him to be entrapped in the former treaty, and to draw from the French fairer conditions of honour and advantage if they have a purpose to proceed in this match. What answer soever you shall receive from them; His Majesty's pleasure is not that you should presently break off, but that with all diligence by post you advertise and freely withal deliver your own opinion which His Majesty will vouchsafe in very gracious part.

* * * * * *

App. VIII.

VIII.

FINANCIAL TABLES.

1. A COMPARATIVE VIEW OF THE ISSUES OF THE EXCHEQUER DURING THE LAST FIVE YEARS OF ELIZABETH AND THE FIRST FIVE YEARS OF JAMES I.

[Abbreviated from *S.P.*, xxxv. 39.]

	Last five years of Elizabeth	First five years of James I.	Increase	Decrease
Queen Anne	...	36,569	36,569	
Prince Henry	...	2,140	2,140	
Ladies Elizabeth and Mary	...	17,366	17,366	
Prince Charles	...	550	550	
Privy purse	5,100	25,810	20,710	
Wardrobe and robes	21,320	84,108	62,788	
Cofferer of the Household	30,815	164,966	134,151	
Treasurer of the Chamber	48,100	72,097	23,997	
Gentlemen Pensioners	20,854	22,054	1,200	
Livery of the Guard	3,617	9,118	5,501	
Master of the Horse	...	6,897	6,897	
Works	26,807	53,924	27,117	
Posts	15,016	15,252	236	
Ambassadors	27,287	60,806	33,519	
Tower and prisons	15,025	16,596	1,571	
Castles and forts	25,313	20,475		4,838
Berwick and the Border	26,120	11,861		14,259
Ordnance and armoury	103,474	44,574		58,900
Low Countries	153,300	121,336		31,964
Ireland	1,398,221	281,589		1,116,632
Navy	418,554	193,504		225,050
Rewards to Officers	10,186	15,641	5,455	
Liberates of Exchequer	5,593	7,255	1,662	
Messengers	2,452	10,332	7,880	
Fees and annuities	138,940	248,758	109,818	
Revels and Garter Herald	433	1,009	576	
Goldsmith and jewels	13,810	106,033	92,223	
Survey of woods	...	1,010	1,010	
Parks and Lodges	...	6,669	6,669	
Diets of Lords Cobham and Grey	...	1,811	1,811	
Tents and toils	...	1,800	1,800	
Diets of Star Chamber and Assize	14,510	15,712	1,202	
Total ordinary expenditure	2,524,847	1,677,622		
Extraordinary expenditure	67,563	327,354		
	2,592,410	2,004,976		
Repayment of Loans	30,327	97,181		
Total expenditure	2,622,737	2,102,157		

2. TOTAL EXPENDITURE OF THE YEAR ENDING MICHAELMAS, 1616.

		£
Ordinary expenditure		457,385
Excess		36,542
		493,927
Extraordinary expenditure :—	£	
King's Privy Purse	3,419	
The Queen	839	
Horses for the Prince	400	
The Lady Elizabeth	130	
Ambassadors	3,769	
Present sent to Spain	1,091	
Foreign Ambassadors	318	
Coat and Conduct Money into Ireland	20	
Ordnance	1,370	
Timber for Navy	700	
Restitution to pirates pardoned	1,226	
Repairs of castles	835	
St. Mary's at York	1,000	
Bridge at St Neots	500	
——— Royston	10	
——— Hackney	20	
——— Berwick	1,500	
New River	915	
Alum Works	1,466	
Draining meadows	100	
Enlarging parks and fencing coppices	350	
Lady Arabella's funeral	406	
Bowey, for wines and fruit	769	
Painting Queen of Scots' tomb	265	
Organs	300	
Books	109	
Sending packets to Ireland	100	
Fowl	80	
Fuel	27	
Masque	400	
Gray to build his house	113	
Jewels	6,970	
Interest	6,544	
Gifts	6,116	
Restitution to patentees	1,898	
		44,075

Total expenditure	538,002
Ordinary receipts	451,096
Excess of total expenditure	£86,906
Actual ordinary expenditure	493,927
Ordinary receipts	451,096
Excess of actual ordinary expenditure	£42,831

3. COMPARATIVE VIEW OF THE ORDINARY REVENUE OF THE CROWN.

[*Lansd. MS. No.* 164, *fols.* 435, 505; *No.* 169, *fols.* 135, 138.]

	June 13th, 1607	Estimated June 20th, 1610	Estimated July 11th, 1614	Ordinary Receipts for the Year ending at Michaelmas 1616
Great Customs	120,000	120,000	136,000	140,000
Silks	8,977	8,977	8,977	15,977
Sea Coals	5,800	6,300	6,300	6,300
Sweet Wines	6,000	6,000	9,000	9,000
French and Rhenish Wines	14,500	17,200	20,300	27,000
Farms and Fee-farms	7,000	8,000	. . .	10,242
Receivers General	55,000	84,000	79,000	80,000
Sheriffs	[9,500]	13,800	8,000	
Chief Butlerage	. .	500	500	500
Exchequer Seal	. .	60	60	
Duchy of Lancaster	[11,500]	11,500	10,500	10,500
Court of Wards	[21,000]	21,000	19,120	25,000
First Fruits	5,000	5,000	5,000	4,812
Annual Tenths of Clergy	1,000	11,000	11,000	12,000
Alnage	500	1,326	1,000	820
Hanaper and Alienation Office	8,500	8,200	8,000	8,283
Dover Castle Rents	[130]	82	82	112
Fines for Leases	[7,000]	2,000		
Seizures	4,000	4,000	2,000	3,447
Debts installed and other debts	8,000	12,000	4,000	2,081
Recusants	6,000	9,000	6,000	6,546
New Year's Gifts	. .	1,100	1,100	1,100
New Impositions	. .	70,000	44,000	51,882
Currants	5,322	5,322	2,800	2,800
Tobacco	1,500	400	400	200*
New Drapery	73	. . .	. . .	98
Cottons and Baize	[200]	2,000	200	200
White Starch	. .	2,833		
Alum	. .	5,000		

Post Fines	. .	2,272	2,272	2,272
Logwood	[1,700]	1,700		
Beer	[600]	600		
Sugars	. .	. . .	4,000	4,000
Venice Gold and Silver	200	200	200	200
Glasses	. .	92	1,000	1,000
Sheeps' Pelts	. .	30	30	30
Steel	. .	10	10	10
Wool	. .	. . .	20	20
Lead	. .	. . .	5	5
Smalt	. .	20	20	20
Deal Wines	. .	13	13	13
Arithmetical Instruments	. .	. . .	. . .	3
Alehouses	. .	4,000		
Mint	3,000	. . .	3,000	2,998
Preemption of Tin	. .	8,000	11,000	12,000†
Unwrought Cloths	1,000	1,000	1,000	1,000
Copyholders' Fines	. .	2,000		
Exchange of Moneys	1,000*	1,000	1,000	
Farthing Tokens	. .	. . .	66	66
Respite of Homage	. .	500	500	615
Fines and Forfeitures reserved for the King's bounty	. .	. . .	3,000	3,000
Fines de Banco	. .	. . .	133	
Original Seals	. .	75	75	75
Issues of Jurors	1,500	1,000	1,000	1,000
Clerk of Faculties	100	200	200	200
Sundries	. .	4,000		
Star-chamber Fines	. .	. . .	1,000	806
Threepence upon Strangers' Customs	. .	. . .	3,000	2,850
Custom of Ireland	. .	. . .	6,000	
Custom of Carlisle	. .	13	13	13
	[315,600,2]‡	461,525	421,896§	451,096

* For half a year. † The Duchy of Cornwall with Tin is the heading to this entry; it should have been the same to the entry in 1614. ‡ The figures within brackets are conjectural, the original document being imperfect. § 461,906 in MS.
I have omitted £40,000 for the Low Country debt, as not being properly placed amongst the ordinary revenue.

4. COMPARATIVE VIEW OF THE ORDINARY EXPENDITURE OF THE CROWN.

[*Lansd. MS. No.* 164, *fols.* 436, 507; *No.* 169, *fols.* 135, 138.]

	Estimated June 13th, 1607	Estimated June 20th, 1610	Estimated July 11th, 1614	Estimate for the year ending at Michaelmas 1616	Excess of actual above estimated ordinary expenditure
Privy Purse	6,000	4,100	6,100	6,100	
Jewel-house	10,000	10,000	12,000	4,230	
Wardrobe and robes	6,515	24,616	30,000	26,000	
Cofferer of Household	86,000	87,000*	81,440	75,060	11,635
Treasurer of Chamber	20,000	21,000	25,000	25,000	1,000
Gentlemen Pensioners	4,200	4,800	5,200	5,772	
Coats of the Guard	[1,100]	1,200	1,200	1,144	
Works	6,100	24,000	12,000	8,000	2,697
Navy	52,000	40,000	50,000	30,476	16,355
Ordnance	} 16,000 (Ordnance, Master of the Armoury, Gunpowder)	6,000	6,000	6,000	
Master of the Armoury		400	400	400	
Gunpowder	. . .	3,200	3,200	3,200	
Posts	3,973	3,600	3,000	2,974	
Berwick	[2,000]	6,073†	. . .	3,761	
Castles and forts	3,831	5,360	5,360	4,917	
Diets of Justices of Assize	} 3,328 (Diets of Justices of Assize, Diets in the Star-chamber)	2,010	} 15,744 (all Diets)		
Diets in the Star-chamber		2,000			
Diets of the President of Wales, and wages and diets of the Council of the North	. . .	4,360		6,989	
Diets of the Earls of Northampton and Dunbar	. . .	1,254			
Diets of the Lords Grey and Cobham	. . .	1,032			
Tower and Prisoners	2,964	4,400	4,400	4,300	931
Surveyor of the Stables	100	100	100	100	17
Ambassadors	9,160	7,200	12,000	10,000	2,425
Fees and Annuities	[70,000]	94,192	104,860	114,409	
Portage of Treasure	. . .	815	800	500	
Liberates of Exchequer and Receipts	1,400	1,400	1,400	1,550	
Rewards for Officers	4,500	5,000	1,000	800	1,133

Repair of Lodges, Parks, &c.	. . .	5,880	4,000	967	
Messengers	2,500				
Gardening	. . .	180	200	348	14
Treasurer of Ireland	32,025	52,584	46,000	24,300	
Low Countries	25,016	25,015	25,016		
The Queen	10,000	14,223	24,500	24,500	
Prince Henry	4,666*	24,600*			
Prince Charles	. . .	650	24,000	46,000	
The Lady Elizabeth's Pension	. . .	. . .	2,000	2,000	
The Lady Elizabeth's Diets and Apparel	4,009	7,000			
The Lady Mary	1,440				
Wares imported custom free	. . .	10,795			
Bowey & Jacob for purchase of Wine	. . .	1,680			
Earls of Suffolk and Northampton	. . .	5,022			
Alms paid by Receivers	. . .	294	814	294	
Rewards for Sheriffs	. . .	519			
Tonnage for Ships	. . .	. . .	. . .	1,500‡	
Master of the Horse	4,000	1,600	1,600	997	
Secret affairs	1,200	1,400	1,400	1,400	
Revels, Tents, and Toils	200	500	500	500	28
Hay for Deer	. . .	100	200	140	
Christmas Presents for Grooms and Pages	. . .	206	206	206	
Defalcations **	. . .	. . .	7,300	9,498	
Fines and Forfeitures reserved for the King's bounty	. . .	. . .	3,000	3,000	
Sundries	. . .	187	1,000	553	307
	394,227§	517,547‖	522,940¶	457,385	36,542

* The two cofferers' accounts are placed together in the MS. I have set the Princes down in 1607 for £4,000, and in 1610 for £19,200, which was the sum paid in 1611. † Berwick and Commissioners of the North. ‡ Probably omitted in preceding years. § The figures in brackets are conjectural. £12,000 for gifts, and £500 for mines in Scotland, have been omitted as not strictly ordinary expenditure. ‖ 517,600 in MS. ¶ 523,556 MS. ** This is different from the payments annually called by the name, and includes payments out of recovered fines, imposts returned, &c.

5. COMPARATIVE VIEW OF
(With the exception of the defalcations), from the year ending

	1601–2	1602–3	1603–4	1604–5	1605–6	1606–7
	£	£	£	£	£	£
Receivers-General	56,712	60,244	50,460	56,158	57,514	58,129
Farms and fee-farms	4,869	12,718	11,071	10,033	9,507	8,656
Sheriffs and Bailiffs	13,676	11,359	11,767	18,016	20,238	14,264
Fines for alienation	4,000	2,394	...	1,390	2,949	2,130
Hanaper	4,422	3,167	5,910	4,247	5,751	4,858
Post fines	...	...	...	...	...	...
Fines for leases	4,980	7,461	3,488	4,868	13,338	7,777
Remembrancer of Treasurer	567	510	528	525	528	544
Defective titles and assarts	3,719	4,777	770	4,003	2,574	3,632
Rents for Dover Castle and Harbour	827	655	333	201	135	114
Court of Wards	18,000	25,300	15,750	15,900	15,000	22,575
Duchy of Lancaster	11,500	23,300	11,500	11,500	13,500	11,500
Faculties	200	200	200	300	100	200
Courts Leet, View of Frank-pledge, and Free-warren	...	...	...	...	...	...
Buildings contrary to proclamation	...	...	...	...	...	...
Customs	78,352	97,182	70,896	112,064	93,340	148,368
New impositions and three pence on strangers' goods	...	...	...	...	...	...
French and Rhenish wines	14,896	21,196	15,447	7,399	19,499	23,148
Sweet wines	6,892	3,743	7,762	3,000	5,409	5,676
Levant Company	4,000					
Currants	...	...	...	2,661	5,471	5,322
Tobacco	...	...	...	...	...	750
Silks	...	9,976	9,976	4,488	9,976	8,976
Sea coals	3,100	1,600	5,800	5,800	5,800	5,800
Alum	...	...	...	...	...	...
Unwrought cloths	1,000	...	...	...	500	1,000
Alnage	568	754	685	697	791	805
Pre-emption of tin	...	...	...	...	...	...
Alehouses	...	...	...	...	...	...
Small farms	...	...	...	...	...	...
Chief Butlerage	289	658	1,000	...	300	200
Low Country exchange	...	...	...	...	...	...
Irish customs	...	...	...	...	...	...
Mint	...	...	...	...	2,000	11,323
Recusants	8,543	7,251	1,414	5,437	10,258	8,544
Tenths and first-fruits of clergy	17,098	14,874	18,156	12,066	14,395	13,909
Installed debts and Accountants' arrears	26,481	33,239	12,536	13,052	10,435	9,431
Casualties and sundries	1,718	281	1,081	4,859	8,913	2,147
Total ordinary receipts	286,409	342,839	256,530	298,664	328,221	379,778
Extraordinary receipts	11,881	12,379	9,386	3,000	6,561	18,000
Fifteenths and subsidies of laity	169,825	88,629	125,493	70,695	29,539	99,005
Subsidies of clergy	19,058	14,543	20,269	9,873	12,786	8,753
Sale of crown property	103,938	19,265	30,699	16,270	4,549	7,789
Total exclusive of loan	591,111	477,655	442,377	398,502	381,656	513,325
Loan	...	...	39,060	70,384	14,413	40,076
Total receipts	591,111	477,655	481,437	468,886	396,069	553,401

THE RECEIPTS OF THE CROWN
at Michaelmas, 1602, to the year ending at Michaelmas, 1616.

1607–8	1608–9	1609–10	1610–11	1611–12	1612–13	1613–14	1614–15	1615–16
£	£	£	£	£	£	£	£	£
69,442	66,623	62,526	56,177	40,321	57,707	55,186	42,789	40,849
8,726	13,596	8,616	7,687	6,397	8,102	7,422	5,867	4,095
18,007	20,044	12,861	9,379	8,489	10,848	8,609	9,324	8,748
2,412	4,063	3,617	3,741	4,192	4,053	3,792	3,375	3,858
4,628	4,388	4,591	4,331	4,204	2,144	4,244	4,150	4,268
2,406	3,084	5,706	3,065	3,264	5,458	4,422	5,568	5,840
1,580	14,688	2,307	463	656	3,422	1,634	259	642
564	559	303	64	601	611	582	581	582
5,912	9,760	12,789	3,192	4,792	2,513	4,647	2,653	4,035
158	104	80	86	92	96	111	104	112
20,544	13,110	14,928	19,795	18,429	22,298	21,775	25,078	21,589
11,500	11,500	11,500	11,500	11,500	11,500	11,500	11,500	11,500
203	150	100	746	100	...	200	250	700
...	...	...	...	...	...	32	55	91
...	361	70	...	...	...	...	1,000	3,000
100,082	123,271	92,639	108,556	103,593	194,018	98,438	227,789	53,815
...	38,642	61,125	56,956	49,993	42,429	47,160	51,048	55,642
10,886	11,733	19,624	16,157	20,658	20,000	17,701	21,304	32,108
3,000	4,716	6,147	6,000	7,500	7,906	5,500	10,000	3,900
5,322	5,356	4,061	2,800	1,800	4,000	240	2,897	3,000
1,503	400	400	400	400	400	400	400	400
14,365	4,488	10,476	9,456	6,956	7,276	8,977	17,455	8,476
5,800	9,400	7,300	6,300	6,300	6,300	6,300	5,299	6,299
...	3,000	1,665						
1,000	1,000	1,000	1,000	1,000	1,000	1,000	1,000	1,500
786	749	309	391	251	380	326	248	247
...	12,000	7,406	4,793	...	10,000	6,772	5,725	2,273
1,219	1,955	2,908	613	175	66	5		
2,139	1,141	1,531	490	1,226	538	1,191	1,914	2,207
233	...	222	222	...	222	444	235	222
...	...	500	1,000	1,000	...	1,500		
...	...	...	...	...	...	3,200	597	858
2,196	1,607	2,000	...	2,575	3,547	3,011	3,169	5,387
8,950	13,965	10,164	8,608	8,690	8,259	8,301	7,728	6,527
17,886	12,535	18,075	22,272	20,216	17,495	16,759	20,633	18,034
18,481	11,301	4,997	...	6,074	5,722	3,798	9,120	6,798
5,463	15,868	7,963	4,786	1,682	11,169	5,058	3,039	2,305
345,393	435,157	400,506	371,026	343,126	469,479	360,237	502,153	319,907
3,078	22,867	8,416	59,511	118,522	169,901	84,711	101,494	220,837
126,560	81,763	76,899	97,497	2,901	1,264	2,447	341	671
13,655	15,863	16,384	23,329	22,522	7,997	150	2	
21,148	272,534	69,685	111,606	43,986	19,555	168,061	12,450	11,476
509,834	828,184	571,890	662,969	531,057	668,196	615,606	616,440	552,891
202,799	4,860	149,000	2,000	95,890	47,675	6,451	8,300	24,692
712,633	833,044	720,890	664,969	626,947	715,871	622,057	624,740	577,583

6. COMPARATIVE VIEW OF THE
(With the exception of the defalcations), from the year ending

	1601–2	1602–3	1603–4	1604–5	1605–6	1606–7
	£	£	£	£	£	£
Queen	...	300	3,634	12,783	10,775	11,449
Prince Henry	...	1,000	7,180	1,900	9,590	5,531
Prince Charles	...	...	...	...	...	150
The Lady Elizabeth	...	2,417	2,417	2,736	2,237	8,595
The Lady Mary	...	...	...	...	...	2,553
Privy Purse	1,500	2,000	6,200	12,800	6,500	4,000
Wardrobe and Robes	13,123	15,117	20,272	30,673	14,173	32,596
Cofferer of the Household and diets of officials.	52,388	56,875	76,105	74,385	67,715	82,620
Wine for household	...	...	4,934	4,157	3,170	1,952
Treasurer of the Chamber	12,300	16,500	16,750	16,000	18,400	29,500
Gentlemen Pensioners	4,164	4,389	5,046	4,543	3,477	5,840
Livery of the Guard	721	2,381	3,032	1,222	863	1,353
Master of the Horse	...	100	1,165	2,080	1,198	1,867
Revels, tents and toils	166	800	...	466	375	192
Masques	...	...	...	...	400	...
Plate and jewels	5,213	...	43,408	30,204	14,248	27,411
Angel gold for the King's evil	...	...	...	...	...	...
Buildings, repairs, and parks	7,290	9,212	11,850	11,614	8,643	15,856
Diets of Star Chamber and Judges	4,013	4,623	3,179	2,933	4,134	4,003
Tower and prisons	2,744	1,394	2,693	3,027	5,056	3,636
Castles and forts	4,307	3,603	3,986	3,871	4,724	2,885
Berwick and the Border	5,315	7,363	643	1,081	6,728	606
Ordnance, armoury, and gunpowder	20,922	12,309	6,686	6,686	9,574	14,491
Low Countries	25,665	25,157	23,556	26,632	23,997	26,677
Ireland	312,380	185,947	65,821	49,705	31,346	42,399
Restoration of Irish coinage	...	...	44,596	15,000	36,408	
Navy	79,958	84,496	42,403	46,484	23,552	40,068
Bounty on ship-building	597	859	1,139	1,755	1,790	1,083
Posts	3,420	3,549	3,372	3,151	863	3,965
Ambassadors	2,805	9,412	7,355	12,086	12,870	10,951
Reception of Foreign Ambassadors	...	1,500	...	5,301	300	72
Secret service	800	900	1,200	1,200	900	1,200
Percentages, &c., on the recovery of debts, &c.	1,775	2,009	224	1,065	...	639
Impost of coals returned	489	...	...	486	1,609	1,093
Fees and annuities	27,760	24,436	34,706	43,213	45,951	63,801
Pension and gift for the King of Scots	7,500	2,500				
Payments to officers, and sundries	7,841	7,429	9,794	11,842	10,588	7,845
Total ordinary charge	605,156	498,577	453,346	441,081	382,154	456,879
Extraordinary charge	10,776	96,426	39,196	70,829	23,195	54,223
Total exclusive of repayment of loan	615,932	595,003	492,542	511,910	405,349	511,102
Repayment of loan	10,300	...	2,540	17,107	...	9,775
Total	626,232	595,003	495,082	529,017	405,349	520,877

CHARGES UPON THE REVENUE
at Michaelmas, 1602, to the year ending at Michaelmas, 1616.

1607–8	1608–9	1609–10	1610–11	1611–12	1612–13	1613–14	1614–15	1615–16
£	£	£	£	£	£	£	£	£
10,513	11,831	21,144	14,500	15,416	17,107	3,250	1,500	305
13,366	16,750	22,459	33,290	45,778	12,399			
725	792	1,195	5,448	7,464	14,166	27,641	20,138	14,098
2,800	6,024	6,265	7,565	7,291	9,156			
1,247								
1,900	3,000	4,600	3,000	4,000	4,000	7,000	4,000	6,000
19,965	31,601	43,641	27,349	27,946	46,566	33,735	21,500	24,154
66,825	81,122	89,003	75,160	79,198	79,092	82,477	74,098	81,317
7,184	4,216	6,784	6,935	4,778	5,054	9,447	15,958	1,984
21,050	26,211	24,800	23,024	24,042	24,240	26,728	30,204	26,800
4,643	4,719	4,954	5,005	5,086	5,474	6,603	5,364	5,773
1,178	1,173	374	1,093	1,178	1,159	1,134	1,142	1,144
1,216	1,954	1,476	980	1,280	1,593	1,639	844	1,017
661	684	428	1,120	2,879	637	564	910	98
915	...	3,765	3,195	368	...	600	...	400
20,840	10,532	19,878	14,346	12,672	13,998	12,041	12,030	5,720
...	...	...	170	300	...	...	400	200
20,734	23,952	40,575	25,712	33,676	14,061	17,941	16,961	13,695
3,108	3,122	3,254	3,462	3,008	2,304	1,639	2,485	1,910
4,514	4,990	5,232	4,092	4,739	3,885	4,989	4,958	4,898
3,364	8,439	2,725	2,812	2,789	2,381	3,972	2,033	4,639
1,644	1,517	6,061	5,460	4,093	3,360	4,600	3,588	4,370
13,999	14,000	12,098	10,402	9,596	13,953	9,068	5,872	23,271
25,332	24,847	23,593	26,542	26,476	29,711	21,410	26,270	16,346
90,309	71,011	71,733	56,286	53,322	53,916	48,286	36,371	27,661
56,847	47,293	34,435	47,510	54,413	59,996	61,011	54,500	46,433
921	614	1,869	676	971	1,078	1,626	979	2,077
3,308	3,603	3,616	3,338	1,507	3,106	3,713	2,974	3,074
14,255	13,833	11,237	12,732	15,894	11,664	23,609	10,433	22,185
...	...	...	1,005	5,999	4,804	1,600	755	318
1,200	1,560	1,400	1,400	900	...	1,050	1,400	1,400
5,561	7,218	10,010	2,499	4,133	4,866	5,275	5,096	6,868
987	1,054	1,167	1,280	2,149	1,890	1,807	1,956	1,953
67,787	62,330	63,606	67,125	70,357	67,953	87,467	89,288	75,498
13,647	13,356	20,385	8,536	8,929	7,164	7,553	8,807	5,132
502,545	503,348	563,762	503,049	542,627	520,733	519,475	462,814	430,738
72,584	94,426	126,869	121,954	93,378	209,056	91,045	140,919	41,445
575,129	597,774	690,631	625,003	636,005	729,789	610,520	603,733	472,183
75,778	83,341	28,649	61,911	9,516	105,295	27,947	2,016	11,991
650,907	681,115	719,280	686,914	645,521	835,084	638,467	605,749	484,174

7. DETAILED ACCOUNT OF THE EXTRAORDINARY RECEIPTS IN TABLE 5.

1601–2.	£
Fines on Essex's followers	2,400
Money for soldiers' equipments	9,481
	£11,881

1602–3.	
Fines on Essex's followers	3,000
King of France's debt	2,483
Money for Irish arms	4,596
Sale of Spanish prize goods	2,300
	£12,379

1603–4.	
Sale of Spanish prize goods	£9,386

1604–5.	
Sale of Spanish prize goods	£3,000

1605–6.	
Sale of Spanish prize goods	£6,561

1606–7.	
Sale of tin	£18,000

1607–8.	
Fines for depopulation	820
Sale of tin	2,258
	£3,078

1608–9.	
Benevolence for Prince Charles	281
Fines for depopulation	130
Copyholds	6,144
Silver mine in Scotland	1,000
Aid for the Prince's creation	15,312
	£22,867

1609–10.	
Benevolence for Prince Charles	155
Copyholds	2,354
Aid for the Prince's creation	5,907
	£8,416

1610–11.	
Benevolence by Lord Wotton	1,000
Copyholds	1,012
Aid for the Prince's creation	529
Baronets	28,470
Fine on lease of sweet wine	28,500
	£59,511

1611–12.	£
Refusal to take the oath of allegiance	1,310
Copyholds	2,502
Aid for the Prince's creation	60
Baronets	29,650
French King's debt	45,000
Low Country debt	40,000
	£118,522

1612–13.	
Refusal to take the oath of allegiance	250
Copyholds	811
Aid for the Prince	7
Aid for the Lady Elizabeth's marriage	18,942
Baronets	28,105
French King's debt	15,000
Low Country debt	58,786
Earl of Northumberland's fine	11,000
Lord Montagu's fine	4,000
Fine on lease of Customs	20,000
Instalment of fine on lease of French and Rhenish wines	3,000
Sutton's executors for Berwick Bridge	10,000
	£169,901

1613–14.	
Copyholds	700
Aid for the Prince	116
Aid for the Lady Elizabeth	1,666
Baronets	7,035
Low Country debt	31,213
Benevolence	23,500
Second instalment of fines on lease of French and Rhenish wines	13,000
Goods sold from "The Pearl"	7,481
	£84,711

1614–15.	
Aid for the Lady Elizabeth	145
Baronets	1,825
Low Country debt	71,549
Benevolence	22,439
Fine on lease of sweet wine	5,536
	£101,494

1615–16.	
Aid for the Lady Elizabeth	113
Baronets	365
Low Country debt	38,449
Benevolence	15,282
Cautionary Towns	166,628
	£220,837

8. DETAILED ACCOUNT OF THE EXTRAORDINARY CHARGES IN TABLE 6.

1601–2.	£
Grant out of the fines of Essex's followers	500
Reimbursements	1,849
Spanish prize money paid to foreign merchants	5,200
Special service	3,000
Interest	227
	£10,776

1602–3.	£
Grant out of the fines of Essex's followers	400
Reimbursements	700
Special service	3,500
Engraving seals	498
Redemption of chief butlerage	1,000
Prize money	2,700
Money sent to the King	6,046
Letters sent to the King	66
Persons sent to the King	350
Queen Elizabeth's funeral	17,301
Coronation	19,724
King's entry into London	10,492
Fireworks	39
Queen and Prince's journey	3,148
Bullion for mint	17,800
Redemption of lands	5,200
Grants out of recusants' fines	130
Gifts and rewards	7,332
	£96,426

1603–4.	£
Journey of Prince Charles and the Lady Elizabeth	1,969
Reimbursements	600
Search for mines in Scotland	200
Purchase of tin	23,550
Grants redeemed	400
Engraving seals	224
Conveyance of prisoners to Winchester	483
Gifts and rewards	9,770
Special service	2,000
	£39,196

1604–5.	£
Expenses of the Queen's childbed	5,420
Visit of the Duke of Holstein	5,795
Gift to the Duke of Holstein	4,000
Queen's debts	1,060
Special services	1,600
Search for mines in Scotland	900
Grants redeemed	6,601
Recusant fines restored	1,700
Purchase of tin	15,000
Clerks of Parliament	130
Reimbursements	600
Purchase of lands	415
Sending prisoners from Germany	120
Grant out of recusants' fines	3,185
Gifts and rewards	24,063
Interest	250
	£70,839

1605–6.	£
Queen's debts	1,775
King of Denmark's visit	5,791
Queen Elizabeth's tomb	765
Queen of Scots' tomb	768
Special service	1,300
Banishment of Jesuits	60
Purchase of land	510
Reimbursements	727
Grants from recusants' fines	1,624
Gifts and rewards	9,625
Interest	250
	£23,195

1606–7.	£
Queen's debts	3,497
Duke of Courland's visit	219
Search for mines in Scotland	500
Present to the Grand Seignor	5,322
Furniture for Theobalds	1,200
Reimbursements	600
Repayment to Customs' farmers for money overpaid	25,608
Purchase of land	4,584
Grant from recusants' fines	1,328
Gifts and rewards	10,131
Interest	1,234
	£54,223

1607–8.	£
Expenses of Queen's childbed	1,347
Queen's debts	20,588
Special service	1,261
Funeral of Lady Mary	131
Funeral of Lady Sophia	53
Reimbursements	1,378
Purchase of Holmby House for Prince Charles	10,708
Purchase of land	7,768
Unpaid Customs	3,021
Grant from recusants' fines	2,089
Gifts and rewards	22,454
Interest	1,786
	£72,584

1608–9.	£
Queen's debts	11,619
Petticoats given by the King to the Queen	100
Special service	1,650
Embroidery for the Prince	422
Carriage for the King	60
Grants redeemed	32,400
Purchase of land	9,397
Reimbursements	1,805
Search for mines in Scotland	140
Berwick Bridge	519
Alum works	40
Lending Irish soldiers to Sweden	950
Reimbursement to currant farmers	1,000
Grants out of recusants' fines	2,047
Gifts and rewards	20,785
Interest	11,492
	£94,426

1609–10.	£
Jewels for the Queen	10,865
Wardrobe debts	13,345
Special service	10,798
Payment to the Court of Wards	670
Redemption of grants	2,000
Paid to Keymis for Sherborne	8,000
Purchase of Sherborne from Carr	20,000
Purchase of land	400
Purchase of tin	875
Starch business	3,206
Lending soldiers to Sweden	5,775
Berwick Bridge	1,997
Creation of Prince	2,820
Duke of Brunswick's visit	2,800
War of Cleves	17,695
Wines custom free	315
Reimbursement to currant farmers	2,000
Reimbursements	522
Grants from recusants' fines	685
Gifts and rewards	18,980
Interest	3,121
	£126,869

1610–11.	£
War of Cleves	1,847
Sending Irish soldiers to Sweden	192
Jewels bought by the Queen	2,800
Imprisonment of Arabella Seymour	1,776
Ulster Commissioners	420
Berwick Bridge	2,000
Fetching Baldwin	120
Wardrobe debts	12,310
Silkworms	258
Barges	378
Scent	629
Tapestry	254
Redemption of grants and leases	15,578
Lord Knollys for loss on post fines	1,438
Special service	1,240
Repayment to tin farmers	2,454
Reimbursements	1,304
Grant from recusants' fines	50
Gifts and rewards	56,875
Interest	21,031
	£121,954

1611–12.	£
Queen's debts	229
Reimbursements	284
Ulster Commissioners	1,109
Berwick Bridge	1,000
New River	570
Alum works	1,000
Ships purchased from pardoned pirates	2,649
Money spent by the Earl of Dunbar in the North	10,000
Instalment of Prince Charles as K.G.	131
Purchase of land	10,181
Gift to Prince of Wales	4,150
Repayment to the tin farmers	3,396
Grant from recusants' fines	596
Gifts and rewards	46,225
Interest	11,858
	£93,378

1612–13.	£
Transfer of the Queen of Scots' body	178
New River	3,242
Alum works	13,653
Berwick Bridge	500
Ulster Commissioners	137
Compensation to the Earl of Northampton for arrears of pension	6,000
Repaid to tin farmers	434
Barges	308
Queen's debts	5,500
Prince of Wales' debts	43,774
Prince of Wales' funeral	16,322
Purchase of land	16,850
Elector Palatine's visit	15,992
The Lady Elizabeth's trousseau	5,655
Marriage festivities	8,355
Diets of the Elector and Electress Palatine	12,382
Journey of the Elector and Electress	21,429
First instalment of the Electress' portion	10,000
Special service	1,000
Gifts and rewards	9,095
Interest	18,245
	£209,051

1613–14.	£
Queen's debts	10,232
Second and third instalment of the Electress' portion	20,000
Present to the Electress	1,297
Sending present to Heidelberg	696
Sending midwife to Heidelberg	484
Embroidered footcloth for Parliament	500
Relief for poor tinners	150
Berwick Bridge	1,000
New River	2,534
Barges	411
Alum works	4,400
Ships purchased from pardoned pirates	700
Redemption of the Earl of Suffolk's grant of the currant duties	10,000
Redemption of the Earl of Nottingham's wine licenses	11,072
Purchase of land	1,826
Expenses of levying fine for refusal of the oath of allegiance	2,000
Grant from recusants' and allegiance fines	7,216
Gifts and rewards	9,565
Interest	6,962
	£91,045

1614–15.	£
Queen's debts	15,720
Last instalment of the Electress' portion	10,000
Present to the King of Spain	380
New River	1,500
Berwick Bridge	500
Alum works	30,100
Ships purchased from pardoned pirates	3,400
Paid for goods from 'The Pearl'	3,250
Redemption of Lord Sheffield's annuity	6,370
Redemption of lease	4,433
Repaid to Customs' farmers for money overpaid	18,000
Reimbursements	1,726
Purchase of land	1,540
Sent to the Duke of Savoy	15,000
Special service	4,550
Grants from recusants' fines	1,533
Gifts and rewards	13,215
Interest	9,702
	£140,919

1615–16.	
Queen's debts	171
Present for the King of Spain	1,122
Lady Arabella's funeral	406
Grant to the garrisons of the Cautionary Towns	5,100
Alum works	1,466
New River	915
Berwick Bridge	1,500
Purchase of land	250
Ships purchased from pardoned pirates	1,226
Painting Queen of Scots' tomb	265
Organ for Holyrood Chapel	300
Reimbursement to Prince Charles from the tin farm	3,000
Reimbursements	624
Redemption of grants	1,300
Grant from recusants' fines	590
Gifts and rewards	12,671
Interest	10,539
	£41,445

EXPLANATORY NOTE TO THE TABLES.

Enormous as is the mass of financial documents in existence relating to the reign of James I., yet, strangely enough, it never seems to have occurred to the officials who drew them up that it would be worth while to keep a balance sheet in which the whole of the revenue of the year should be set down on one side, and the whole of the charges upon the revenue on the other. Hence the impossibility of obtaining an accurate knowledge of the exact condition of the finances at any given moment. All I have been able to do has been to collect a few tables, the defects in which may serve to counterbalance one another.

In order to make them intelligible to those who have not given any study to this class of documents, it will be necessary

App. VIII. to premise, that the revenue and expenditure of the Crown may be divided into six heads.

1. The ordinary payments into and out of the Exchequer forming the bulk of the incomings and outgoings. For this the great authorities are the Receipt and Issue Books, the Pells Declarations, the Breviates of the Receipt and the Dormant Privy Seals Books. None of these series are perfect, but they usually help one another. Where all fail, recourse must be had to the Receipt and Issue Rolls, and the Auditors' Receipt Books.

2. The Assignations, or payments made into the Exchequer with special assignment, to be paid out only to some particular person. The best reference for these is to the Breviates of the Receipt, where they exist. They will be also found specially marked in the Receipt Books themselves.

3. The Assignments of the Court of Wards and Liveries. These will be found in the Accounts of the Receivers-General of the court.

4. The Assignments of the Duchy of Lancaster. Of these it appears, from the Treasurer of the Chamber's accounts, that £4,000 was regularly paid to him every year. The accounts of the Comptroller of the Household are very imperfect, but it seems that the assignment of £7,500 to the Cofferer was not quite so regularly paid. Sometimes the payments were £200 or £300 short, a deficiency which was probably made up in the following year. I have, therefore, allowed myself to assume that the regular assignment was kept to on the average. No other sums were paid by the Duchy excepting into the Exchequer, in which case they appear on the Receipt Books.

5. Crown lands granted for life to members of the Royal Family. Of these no account is kept, excepting in occasional estimates and other stray papers.

6. Defalcations. This is the most unsatisfactory part of the accounts. They consist either in payments remitted, or in money actually paid away by accountants before it reached the Exchequer. No account of them has been preserved, though there are documents in existence which would enable us to regain them for one or two years. They may be divided into four classes:—

I. Payments remitted to farmers of customs, &c., on account of wares admitted customs free. Such sums may fairly be omitted from both sides of the account.

II. Expenses of collection, which may be omitted without any great harm.

III. Payments made directly by the accountants. The loss of these does not alter the balance of the year, but it affects the proportion between particular heads of revenue and expenditure. At one time pensions to the amount of about £30,000 were paid in this manner. They were chiefly taken from the Receivers-General and the customs farmers.

IV. Payments made in the same way for the liquidation of debt. The want of any account of these renders it impossible to make a balance between the revenue and the expenditure. I do not, however, imagine that ordinary revenue was frequently taken for this purpose, though this may have happened sometimes. With the extraordinary revenue it frequently happened. A great part of the debt liquidated by Salisbury in 1608 and 1609 was got rid of in this way, leaving no account excepting in Salisbury's own loose papers.

The arrangement of the tables will now be intelligible.

No. 1 is a comparison between the expenses of the five years of Elizabeth and the first five years of James. Neither the Court of Wards, the Duchy of Lancaster, the Queen's crown lands, nor the Defalcations are taken note of, so that some of the sums, especially the Annuities, and the accounts of the Cofferer, the Treasurer of the Chamber and the Wardrobe, are less than they were in reality. The loss is certainly greater in James's reign than in that of Elizabeth, so that the growth of the expenditure upon those heads must be looked upon as rather greater than it is represented.

No. 2 is an account of the extraordinary expenditure of 1616, of which I shall have to speak presently.

Nos. 3 and 4 give estimates formed at various times of the ordinary revenue and expenditure. These are most important, as they contain everything, even the defalcations. Still they do not cover every year, nor do they include generally either extraordinary receipts and expenditure, or actual excess of ordinary expenditure above the estimate. Nor do they take any account of the variations in the revenue caused by anticipations. The only exception is in the estimate for the expenditure of 1616, which contains the excess of expenditure.

Nos. 5, 6, 7 and 8 are tables which I have drawn up from the sources indicated above. Nos. 5 and 7 present a view of the actual receipts from all sources in any given year, with the exception of the crown lands in the hands of the Queen and the Princes, and still more unfortunately of the defalcations, of which I have been unable to procure any account. The want of these has made me doubt whether the tables are worth printing. But I have thought that, even as they are, they might be worth having. No. 6 is not a table of the actual expenditure of the year, which might have been compiled easily enough on the same plan as No. 5. Such a

App. VIII. table, however, would have been comparatively useless. As James's difficulties became more pressing, the payments on the great heads of expenditure fell more and more into arrear. Thus it frequently happens that out of large payments not more than a small portion is for expenses incurred within the year, the rest is for arrears of the last five or six years. I have, therefore, done my best to transfer these sums to the years to which they really belonged. By the help of the Dormant Privy Seal Books, it has been found possible to do this in the case of the expenditure of the Court and Household, of the buildings, the prisons, the navy, Ireland, and of one or two more. It has not been practicable to carry out the charge in every case, as accounts often run over the year, and it is impossible to assign the different portions of them to the month for which they were due. This difficulty arises particularly with the ambassadors, whose bills for several months intelligences can only be set down at the date at which the last entry is made. In the same way it can seldom be ascertained when jewels were actually bought, but it will be nearer the truth to set them down when the Privy Seal was granted for payment, than to spread the amount over the several following years during which the money was actually paid by instalments, especially as the Privy Seal seems generally to have been granted not very long after the bill was sent in. The difficulty of separating the few pounds and shillings of the fees and annuities from one another, would make the attempt to classify them almost an interminable work. I have, therefore, left them as they stand. It will easily be seen where they have been allowed to fall into arrears. No. 8 is a table of the extraordinary expenditure. Wherever a single payment runs on into several years, the instalments have been transferred to the earlier date. Whether these mere approximations to a real account of the charges arising in the years are worth printing, I must leave it to my readers to judge.

An opportunity occurs of testing their worth by comparing the expenditures of 1615-16, as stated in tables 6 and 8, with that stated in tables 2 and 4.

Even after deducting the Queen and Princes' lands and the defalcations, the differences are considerable. The official paper is, I believe, not intended to show what was the expenditure of the year in question, but to base upon that expenditure an estimate for the following year: thus, the sums which were paid to the garrisons of the Cautionary Towns are altogether omitted, and other differences may be accounted for in the same way. On the other hand, the Cofferer's account is much higher than I give it, probably including an average of the expenditure on wine. The estimate in table 3 is, no doubt, merely a general calculation of the probable expense of next year. Where the payments have been in excess, and there is a chance of that excess being repeated, they are set down; where it is not so, they are omitted. The statement of the extraordinary expenditure in table 5 presents similar discrepancies. Some of the payments have been placed by me amongst ordinaries, it being impossible to draw the line between, for instance, ordinary and extraordinary expenditure of the Ordnance without further knowledge than we possess. Others were not actually made till the following year, and when made contain no indication that they arose from circumstances occurring before Michaelmas, 1616. In the case of interest, account is, I suppose, only taken of interest falling due for the twelvemonth itself. In that of gifts, perhaps, the sums promised, or partially paid, in former years are omitted. I have not attempted to rectify the account of this year, as any nearer agreement with tables 3 and 4 would only give a delusive appearance of correctness to the accounts of former years.

It may be worth saying, that the defalcations upon the ordinary revenue do not appear to have ever amounted to much above £40,000. The apparent diminution of the Queen's income after 1613 is a curious instance of the effect of a change of the mode of levying it. Where the money came from is plain from a glance at the payments of the Receivers-General in table 3.

The only defalcations which I have added in have been the few thousand pounds from the Benevolence, of which a correct account can be obtained from notes in the Dormant Privy Seal Books.

INDEX.

INDEX.

THE END.

CPSIA information can be obtained
at www.ICGtesting.com
Printed in the USA
LVHW100427110522
718424LV00003B/88

9 783375 007195